# THE COMPLETE INNOCENCE SERIES

S.E. Green

S. E. Green

Copyright © 2022 S. E. Green

All Right Reserved

No part of this publication may be reproduced, distributed, or transmitted in any form or by any means, electronic or mechanical, including photocopying, recording, any electronic or mechanical methods, or by any information storage and retrieval system without written permission of the author, except for the use of brief quotations in a book review.

This is a work of fiction. Persons, names, characters, businesses, places, brands, media, events, and incidents are either the products of the author's imagination or used in a fictitious manner. The author acknowledges the trademark status and trademark owners of various products referenced in this work of fiction, which have been used without permission. The publication/use of these trademarks is not authorized, associated with, or sponsored by the trademark owners.

Cover Design – S. E. Green through Canva
Editor – Faith Cavalier
Proofreading – Jessica Fritz & Faith Cavalier

# THE COMPLETE INNOCENCE BOXSET

*Am I allowed to dedicate a book to me? Because I kind of want to dedicate this book to me.*

*I'll dedicate to my brain for providing me with enough fucked up and fucking awesome dreams, including sex dreams… and day dreams… that I was able to write about them.*

*Brain, you know what you did – I appreciate you…*

*Also, my LOL kittys at home (Lila, Ollie, LuLu) – Thanks for not eating my power cord to my computer… you made a valiant effort.*

*Also Also, my family that hasn't read any of these – thank you for not reading any of these… I REALLY didn't want a 'talkin' to.*

S. E. Green

THE COMPLETE INNOCENCE BOXSET

# Table of Contents

| | |
|---|---|
| Dedication | 3 |
| **NORA TITLE PAGE** | **9** |
| From the Author | 11 |
| Trigger Warnings | 13 |
| Chapter 1 – William | 15 |
| Chapter 2 – William | 29 |
| Chapter 3 – Nora | 42 |
| Chapter 4 – William | 57 |
| Chapter 5 – Nora | 71 |
| Chapter 6 – William | 85 |
| Chapter 7 – Nora | 99 |
| Chapter 8 – Nora | 110 |
| Chapter 9 – William | 123 |
| Chapter 10 – Nora | 135 |
| Bonus Epilogue – Nora | 140 |
| **FAITH TITLE PAGE** | **149** |
| From the Author | 151 |
| Trigger Warnings | 153 |
| **DISCLAIMER** | **154** |
| Chapter 1 – Faith | 157 |
| Chapter 2 – Arrow | 167 |

| | |
|---|---|
| Chapter 3 – Faith | 170 |
| Chapter 4 – Arrow | 178 |
| Chapter 5 – Faith | 183 |
| Chapter 6 – Arrow | 192 |
| Chapter 7 – Faith | 197 |
| Chapter 8 – Arrow | 206 |
| Chapter 9 – Faith | 218 |
| Chapter 10 – Faith | 225 |
| Chapter 11 – Arrow | 234 |
| Chapter 12 – Faith | 243 |
| Chapter 13 – Arrow | 255 |
| Chapter 14 – Faith | 265 |
| Bonus Epilogue – Arrow | 270 |
| | |
| **EDEN TITLE PAGE** | **281** |
| From the Author | 283 |
| Trigger Warnings | 285 |
| Chapter 1 – Marcus | 287 |
| Chapter 2 – Eden | 295 |
| Chapter 3 – Marcus | 305 |
| Chapter 4 – Eden | 314 |
| Chapter 5 – Marcus | 322 |
| Chapter 6 – Eden | 328 |
| Chapter 7 – Marcus | 336 |
| Chapter 8 – Eden | 345 |

# THE COMPLETE INNOCENCE BOXSET

| | |
|---|---|
| Chapter 9 – Marcus | 355 |
| Chapter 10 – Eden | 363 |
| Chapter 11 – Marcus | 374 |
| Chapter 12 – Eden | 381 |
| Chapter 13 – Marcus | 392 |
| Bonus Epilogue – Marcus | 395 |
| Glossary of Italian Terms/Phrases | 403 |
| | |
| **LILY TITLE PAGE** | **407** |
| From the Author | 409 |
| Trigger Warnings | 411 |
| Chapter 1 – Fallon | 413 |
| Chapter 2 – Rhett | 424 |
| Chapter 3 – Lily | 434 |
| Chapter 4 – Fallon | 444 |
| Chapter 5 – Lily | 453 |
| Chapter 6 – Rhett | 463 |
| Chapter 7 – Fallon | 474 |
| Chapter 8 – Lily | 485 |
| Chapter 9 – Rhett | 495 |
| Chapter 10 – Lily | 504 |
| Chapter 11 – Fallon | 512 |
| Bonus Epilogue – Lily | 519 |
| A Note from the Author | 531 |
| About the Author | 533 |

S. E. Green

# NORA

**S.E. Green**

S. E. Green

## From the Author

I live for music, so I often get inspired by many contemporary songs and artists when I write. While some books that I write are inspired by multiple songs, this one was a one song repeater for me. It just sort of sucked me in a put me in a particular mood - one that I hope you feel when you listen. It's called **Identity** by *Helen Jane Long*.

Also, as a side note, this story came to me from a dream. My dream was basically the female version of chapter one, my imagination went much further after I woke up.

S. E. Green

## **Trigger Warnings**

Please know that there could be some triggering topics addressed that include **bullying, trauma, and physical abuse (both as an adult and child)**. The childhood abuse is only mentioned without any detailed events.

Having experienced abuse in my past (one sexual assault and one physically abusive relationship), I sometimes draw from how I felt and recovered from it. Everyone reacts differently to trauma, so if you doubt that my character(s) reacted in a believable way, please keep in mind we are all wonderfully different. My therapist told me that our bodies tend to subconsciously protect itself the best way it thinks will keep us the safest. Please seek help if you are being hurt or have been hurt in the past. We all want you safe and feeling loved!

S. E. Green

# Chapter 1

## *William*

"Good morning, Will." I smile at Bernice, the charge nurse for the shift today. She's been here for close to twenty-five years, much longer than I have. The emergency room always seems to run a bit smoother when she's overseeing it.

"Morning, Bernie." I take the charts she's handing out to me and lean against the reception counter. I flip through them to get the rundown on the status of our current patients. "What do you have for me today?"

"I've got a trainee this morning, so I'm going to let her handle the shift report, if that's okay with you?"

I nod my head to the young woman standing next to her to let her know I'm ready. I'm not worried that she's new or that I won't get all the information I need; Bernie will fill in anything she misses.

"Good morning, Dr. Blackwell," she purrs at me in an exaggerated, sultry voice, batting her eyelashes. I glance at Bernie just in time to watch her eyes roll.

Tammy isn't *un*attractive, but I'm not here to meet women. Aside from the fact that it's not allowed, considering I'm so much higher than her in the chain of command, I don't shit where I eat. Or get my honey where I get my money. I love that version too and I internally chuckle to myself.

"*Tammy*," Bernie snaps, causing her to jolt and glare at the older woman before schooling her face and focusing back on me.

"So, umm… In room one, there's a 2-year-old boy with a high fever, vomiting, and rash. He's been given acetaminophen to reduce the fever and is currently getting an IV put in for dehydration."

"Enterovirus?" I ask and she looks at me confused, clearly not understanding that I want to know which one.

"Hand, foot, and mouth most likely." Bernie helps her out, and I thank her before indicating to Tammy she can continue.

Clearing her throat, Tammy shifts her charts to read the next one. "Room two has a 43-year-old female with acute appendicitis and we are just waiting for out-patient surgery to come down to get her. She's been given a low-dose of morphine to control her pain until they can get her into surgery." There's nothing I need to do, so I'll just poke my head in and see how the patient is doing when I get a moment.

"Room three has an 18-year-old female with vomiting, severe headache and soreness in her upper torso. She was just brought back about twenty minutes ago, so only her vitals have been taken. Temp is normal, slightly elevated blood pressure and heart rate, pain level is around a three or four according to her dad. She's been non-communicative with the nurses since she got here."

I furrow my eyebrows the more she describes what's going on. It seems like an odd array of symptoms. I'll need to head to her room first. "Bernie, when we're done here, order a CT for her. The vomiting with possible injury worries me. I want to make sure we aren't looking at something more serious. For now, let's follow concussion protocol."

Writing my instructions down, she nods her head and tells Tammy, "Finish up quickly so we can get started."

"Room five and seven are empty, room six has a 76-year-old male in the late stages of dementia from Royal Oaks Senior Center who suffered a fall. Possible hip fracture. He's on a low-dose morphine to control the pain."

"Get an x-ray for him if it hasn't been ordered yet-" I start to give out my orders when Tammy interrupts me. I bite my cheek to stop from snapping at her. Bernie will let her know on the side for me that it's unprofessional to interrupt the doctor on the floor when they're talking. We've worked together long enough that she knows my ticks.

"Already ordered, Will." She bites her lip at me. I raise my eyebrow, narrowing my eyes at her, and say nothing until she gets the hint that I'm not going to respond to her attempts of seduction. "S-sorry Dr. Blackwell."

I'm 37 years old and I've been here at North Valley Regional Medical Center for over 15 years, including my residency. I'm aware of the women's interest in me around this place. Likewise, I learned early on that I needed to discourage this kind of behavior from the get go to establish the hierarchy and ensure the interested females don't get the wrong impression. Hopefully, Tammy here will figure it out more quickly than some others did.

Grabbing the chart for room one and three, I prioritize the level of emergent need, and decide to visit them first. Unless it's a true emergency, I always stop into the rooms with children first. Parents require that reassurance that they haven't been forgotten, and that their children are a priority. I spend a few minutes chatting with the little boy's mom and alleviate any concerns or fears she has. She's young and this is her first child, so she really needed to hear that he'll be all right.

Shutting the door behind me and heading to room three with the young woman who has the headache and upper body injuries, Bernie steps up next to me. "The hip-injury has been taken to x-ray and surgery has picked up our appendicitis patient."

I sign off on the transfer form she hands me when she jokes, "I also distracted Tammy, so she shouldn't bother you for a while. She's fresh and will figure out quickly that the hospital isn't a dating service. She's smart and has potential to be good once she refocuses on what's important."

"Seriously, thank you. It's Friday, and I'd really love to end my week without any drama. What do you have her doing?" I really do appreciate Bernie's gate keeping methods.

"She's charting and then will help ortho for a bit doing bed pans for their immobile patients. I'll call her back if we get overwhelmed in here."

Laughing at Bernie's retribution, I look back down to check out room three's notes. "Tell me more about three."

Bernie sobers up quickly. "Aside from the brief, I have other concerns. I just popped my head in there to let them know there's new staff here and you'll be around shortly. She's somewhat awake, still vomiting, so I ordered some Ondansetron to help with her nausea. Throwing up that often isn't helping the pain in her head."

"Good… good." Stopping outside her room, I finish reviewing the girl's chart and tuck it under my arm. I reach out to sanitize my hands again before going in and ask, "Anything else?"

"Medically, I don't think so."

"But?" She's clearly got something else to say.

"*But* there almost seems to be something *off* with the family dynamic."

"Explain." I'm anxious to get in there.

Lowering her voice so the occupants inside can't overhear us, she explains under her breath. "She's in there with her father and uncle. Neither were helping her when I walked in while she was vomiting, barely able to hold the wastebasket in front of her. There's a noticeable lack of concern. Uncle seems pissed about being there, father too, but also more nervous or jittery."

"What are you saying, Bernie?"

"I'm simply saying that there is something off. I don't know *what*, but you'll see what I mean. Want me to come in with you?"

I glance at the frosted glass window on the door to room three and see some shadows of movement behind it. "Yeah, why don't you."

She nods her agreement. I open the door to step inside and hold it for her to follow. I don't even get a chance to take in the scene before Bernie shoves past me to the side of the bed, grabbing the small wastebasket from the floor on her way. All I see is long, chocolate brown hair bent over the basket while Bernie helps her, trying to pull her hair out of the way.

The smell in the room is slightly pungent, but not just from her vomit. There are the underlying sterilization scents that you'll find in any area of a hospital. The plastic and metal of the equipment in the room, along with the starched and stiff bedding that isn't supposed to have a fragrance, but does. None of this is what's making me want to wrinkle my nose.

The two men sitting in the waiting chairs against the wall smell of unwashed sweaty bodies, stale cigarettes, and body odor. There's also a faint smell of something floral, lilac or lavender, but the other scents overwhelm it. Grabbing an emesis bag from the container on the wall, I hand it to Bernie to swap out with the trash can.

"Told you those were barf bags on the wall, Denny." One of the men nudges the other, before pinching his nose and mimes gagging, before laughing quietly.

I immediately understand what Bernie was saying about the lack of concern. It instantly pisses me off, putting me on edge. "Hand me the can, Bernie. I'll set it outside."

She does without looking at me, concentrating on our patient, and I set it outside the door. I wave down a nurse before ducking back inside the room. I crack my neck to relieve the tension that wasn't there five minutes ago before I address the people in the room.

Walking to the sink to wash my hands, I introduce myself. "Good morning, gentlemen. I'm Dr. Blackwell, the on-call physician for the day. While my nurse helps out the young lady, why don't you tell me why you brought her in? Aside from the obvious."

Denny sits up a little, scratching his head before answering. "My kid started crying 'cuz her head was hurtin'. I figured it was one of those migraines or somethin', but she started puking all over herself and passed out and sh-… stuff." He stops himself from saying shit and continues. "Rich said it was prolly bad, so we ought to bring her in."

I look at Rich, the man who was making fun of the girl in the bed, her violent retching sounds still behind me. He's smiles at Denny before making eye contact with me. Clearing his throat, he glares at me. "Can you just give her somethin' to stop the pukin'? I'm sure she don't wanna to be here all day."

"No," I tell him simply before directing my attention back to the girl's father. "The intake nurse said her symptoms were nausea, vomiting, severe headache and possibly injury to her upper body. When did this start? How did she get injured?"

"Yeah, so, she slipped down the front steps of our house this mornin' and whacked her head on the concrete." He shoots his brother a nervous look, almost like he wants him to back up the story. "I don't know when her head started hurtin' real bad like this, but she kept pukin' all over herself."

"What time was the fall?"

"I dunno, prolly around 5 this morning."

I don't rule out a concussion causing her vomiting. It would have started shortly after she got it. It could be from the pain as well. Some people can get sick when their pain gets severe enough. My gut tells me a concussion isn't her only issue, though. The meds Bernie ordered should help her out significantly. I'm relieved we already had plans to order the CT.

"Anything else you can think of that may have happened?"

"No man, noth-" Denny starts to say.

Rich finishes up for him. "Nothin', *Doctor*. She just started whinin' that it hurt after bumpin' it on the sidewalk." It doesn't escape me that he tries to belittle me with the way he says 'doctor' before continuing with his obvious lie. I'm done trying to get anything from them.

"Would you gentlemen please step out of the room while I take a look at…" I look back to the chart to read her name. "Lenora? I will call you back in when I'm done."

Shaking his head, Rich crosses his arms and leans back in the chair. "She's scared of hospitals, and I'm sure she wants us to stay with her. You know how girls can be, the whole daddy's girl thing."

Exhaling loudly, I try to not make it *too* obvious I'm irritated. "Then you can stay; your brother cannot." I look at Rich. "Please, step out for her privacy. Your brother can let you know when we're done." Holding the door open for him, he pauses for a moment like he wants to argue with me, before slowly standing up. He's a big dude, out of shape and hefty, but still a good size. Close to my height, he most likely outweighs me by at least 30 or 40 pounds.

"Come get me when you're done here, Den." He leaves the room. Bernie gives me a look, and I nod slightly to indicate I'm aware this is an abnormal situation. Time to look at the girl, now that it seems she's stopped vomiting for the moment.

Bernie takes the bag to dispose, softly encouraging her to lie back. I step up to the bed as I introduce myself.

"Good morning, Lenora. You may not have heard me before, but I'm Dr. Black-" I halt my words when my eyes land on her. Not a girl, she's all woman. I haven't even seen her eyes yet, but it's obvious she's stunningly beautiful.

Her eyes are closed and her brow is furrowed like she's still in a lot of pain.

Quickly, I cover my pause with a cough. "Excuse me. I'm Dr. Blackwell. Can I look at you for a few minutes, see if we can get you feeling better?"

A raspy, soft whisper comes from her. "Sure…" She doesn't say anything else, like the task is too difficult.

"Bernie, would you dim the lights a little? I'm sure it's not helping with her headache." I ask with a lower volume to not aggravate her. I snap on my gloves and roll on the stool over to the side of her bed. I'm tall enough, and the bed low enough, that I'm still a little higher than her. "I'm going to feel around your head to make sure there is no swelling or contusions. The outgoing nurse said you had an injury to your upper body as well?"

I hear her father grunt behind me, but I don't look back at him. I watch as she tenses a little at the sound of his voice before answering, still with a voice so quiet that I must lean in to hear her. She's the source of the flowers I smelled when I first came in. "Umm…"

She's hesitant with her answer. I can't tell if it's because of her father's presence, or just the difficulty to navigate around her throbbing head. She's only able to take deep breaths like she's trying to catch it, wincing each time she breathes in.

"Well, let's take a look anyway. Yes?" I reach up to her head and place my hands over her temples when I feel the tiniest nod of agreement. She's so petite that my fingers stretch all the way to the back of her head and can touch each other.

I palpitate all around her skull, starting at her upper hair line and then move to the back, down to the base of her head and upper neck. I watch her fight to keep back a groan when I find a sensitive area with some decent swelling at the back of her head. I verbalize my findings for Bernie to note in Lenora's file as I continue prodding her head.

Whispering a little lower so her father won't be able to hear anything more than my murmuring, I slide my hands back to the injured spot after finding no other areas of concern. "I'm so sorry, sweetheart. I'll be quick and make this as painless for you as possible."

My heart breaks a little as I watch tears slide from her eyes when I press on her bump again to feel if there are any fractures underneath. She stays silent, alternating between biting her cheek and clenching her teeth.

"I'm going to lift the sides of your gown, left then right, to keep you mostly covered. I need to check out the rest of you." I lay the bed flat and stand up to reach over and move the gown out of my way.

"Hey man! Why you pullin' her shirt up? I don't wanna see her tits!" her father yells at me, not controlling the volume of his voice, and I hear a slight whimper escape from her.

I want to growl at this motherfucker. Instead, I reign it in before turning to look at him, keeping *my* voice quiet for her. "Which is why I asked you *both* to step out of the room, for *her* privacy."

He slouches back against the wall and puts his hands up. "Whatever. I'll just close my eyes."

"Bernie, would you…?" She's always been intuitive and knows what I'm asking her to do.

"Sure." Stepping behind me and putting herself between me and the father, she blocks his view, asking questions to get a detailed family history from him. She's speaking just loud enough to drown out my voice, but not enough to cause more pain for this girl. I take advantage of the window of time she's given me.

Leaning over Lenora again, I pull up one side of her gown, and the first thing I notice is that she's clearly underweight. I also spot a couple of very faint, yellowish-brown bruises, almost fully disappeared. I run my hand over her ribs, feeling areas I can reach without shifting her too much. I feel along her skin toward her back, up to under her breasts, then back down to press on her stomach. After finding no noticeable issues or concerns, I cover her up and move over to her right side.

I grind my teeth when I expose dark bruising along the lower portion of her ribs. I don't need to press on it, it's obvious she suffered some sort of injury here, and not one consistent with a fall down a few stairs. "Lenora, can you tell me how you got the bruising on your right side?" I ask her as I check the surrounding area to feel for swelling or anything that may indicate a fracture or a potential internal issue.

"I don't remember," she chokes out.

"It's okay that you don't, sweet girl. I'm going to help you sit up and lean forward so I can look at your back." I don't wait for her to agree. I move her as quickly as I can to get this part over for her. The bruising reaches all the way around her side and spreads on to her back. There looks to be some reddened areas covering the majority of her upper back as well.

Leaning forward, I get a closer look and see some faint scratching mixed in with the irritated skin. *Jesus Christ, these are fucking rug burns.* I gently lay her back and tuck the sheet back around her while I formulate a plan. The father and uncle need to be gone from here - *now.*

"I'll be as quick as I can, but I *have* to check your pupils. Then, I promise you can rest. It's going to be uncomfortable, but it's necessary."

She mumbles her agreement and then holds herself rigid as I move the beam of light from the outside of her eye inward. I try not to focus on the unique moss green color of her irises and direct my thoughts away from wishing I could see them in a natural light. Her pupils constrict just fine and don't look to be dilated, but the response time is slightly slower than normal. Clicking the light off and pocketing it, I rub her arm in a soothing gesture.

"All done for now. Bernice is going to start an IV for you and we'll get something to help you with the pain as well as some anti-nausea medication. Hang tight and I'll be back in a bit."

I'm pissed. I've also decided that I'm taking control of her care and will be this girl's advocate. My gut is also telling me there is more than just one reason it's important.

## Chapter 2

### *William*

Snapping my gloves off and tossing them in the trash, I turn to face this piece of shit who thinks he's a parent. Clearly this is a domestic situation, and I need to separate her from her family. I've been in enough situations that I'm able to reign in my temper; however, it seems a lot harder than normal this time.

"Alright, Mister…?" I look at him to tell me his last name. I didn't catch it when I read Lenora's chart.

"Fowler. Denny Fowler. Whatcha mean an IV? Why's Lenny need one of those?" He's irritated. I don't know if it's because my ordering an IV is indicative that they'll be here longer, or he thinks it's unnecessary. Or he *could* be worried her injuries are more severe than they originally thought, but I highly doubt that. Whether he's upset because he's worried or upset that he did more damage than anticipated, I'm not certain. Either way, she's legally an adult so he doesn't get to say no.

"Lenny!" he snaps loudly. "Tell 'em you don't need that and to just get you some meds for your headache so we can go."

Mr. Dickhead Fowler is being an ass. Lenora doesn't answer him, most likely she's fallen asleep after exhausting herself vomiting and then all my prodding and moving her around. Plus, I'm uncertain if she's totally aware of everything that's going on.

"*Stop*," I hiss at him. I don't need to raise my voice to get my point across. "We are going to put in an IV line for four reasons." I hold up my fingers, raising one finger for each point I explain to him. "First, it's the easiest and fastest way to administer any drugs she needs now and may need in the future."

He's not really paying attention, but he will shortly. "Second, it's protocol when we perform a CT scan for any patient in this hospital."

"Why the fuck she need a scan for?" Now he's starting to pay attention. I ignore his question and continue.

"Third, she's been vomiting all morning and is most likely dehydrated. This is how we rehydrate her quickly and safely."

"Why can't she just drink some damn Gatorade?" he mutters, glaring at me. "We need to go home!" Again, I ignore him.

"And *fourth*… she's being admitted. We always put in a line for any patient admitted to this hospital, for any length of time, as a precaution. It allows us to have quick access to provide medication in the event of an emergency. This way, we don't have to waste time."

Bernie rests her hand on my back for a moment to calm me before stepping in to deescalate the situation. "Mr. Fowler. Since your daughter is asleep, why don't you follow me outside to one of the offices so we can finish documenting her medical history and get some authorization forms signed for the scan and admittance."

"I'm not going any-fucking-where. You can't admit her if I don't sign." I swear to God, he sounds like a child right now. Looks like one too, with his arms crossed across his chest like he's going to refuse to move.

"Actually, I can. It'll just be extra paperwork. She's 18 and allowed to make her own medical decisions. Either way, she's staying here for the foreseeable future." I gather the chart and the notes that Bernie made for me. I'm fucking done with this guy. "You can't stay in here. She's being moved to radiology for her scan, then into a room upstairs. We will need *this* room for others, which means you must leave."

I turn my back on him to grab the stuff for her IV. A subtle signal that I don't find him a threat. "Bernie, I'll do the IV while you take Mr. Fowler and his brother to an office or the waiting room, I don't care which. Then grab Tammy, and take Miss Fowler to radiology. Put the order in if it hasn't been done and give them a call to let them know you're coming now."

"Will do, Dr. Blackwell." She rarely uses my title, but she does now in front of him to indicate that I'm in charge here. She holds her arm out to guide him to the door. "Why don't you follow me and we'll grab your brother on the way? Did you happen to bring Lenora's wallet with her ID?"

"I'll be back soon, Lenny," he yells over his shoulder, and I wince at the volume of his voice. He once again is not considerate of the sensitivity to sound she has with her headache.

I finally take a deep breath and roll my neck and shoulders as the door clicks shut. It's like he took all that negative shit energy with him right out of the room. I turn back to the tray with the IV kits, smiling to myself when I hear raised voices outside. I can only assume that dickhead's brother was just informed of the change in plans.

Sitting back on my rolling chair, I move over to the side of Lenora's bed, pulling the tray with me.

"Your father is a real piece of work..." I grumble to her.

"I'm sorry," she murmurs. I jerk my head up to look at her. Her eyes are still closed, but I know I didn't mishear her. Fuck... I *really* shouldn't say something like that to a patient, especially about one of their family members.

"No, don't apologize. I'm the one who's sorry. I shouldn't have said that. I'm about to do an IV so you'll feel a pinch and sting. I'm good at it, so at least it'll be quick. How are you feeling?" I take her hand and stretch her skin around to find the best vein. Fuck... I know I said the dehydration thing as an excuse, but she is more dehydrated than she should be. I can't find a place to insert the needle.

"Hmm..." is all she gives me, along with a gentle clasp to my hand that's holding hers. My heart rate picks up at that and I don't stop myself from giving her a little squeeze back.

"I'm going to assume you're following along with what's happening, so I'm going to ask you a few questions. If it hurts your head too much to answer, just give me one squeeze for yes and two for no." She squeezes my hand once. I relax.

"You're awfully dehydrated for the length of time you've been sick. Did this start today? It's Friday morning, in case you don't know."

Two squeezes.

"Yesterday?"

One squeeze.

"Did it start last night?" Two squeezes. Shit... twelve plus hours of no fluids is incredibly dangerous.

"Yesterday morning?" One squeeze.

"Good girl, Nora. Thank you. It's crucial to know how long this has been going on. I'm grabbing a butterfly needle to try to get this going. If it doesn't work, we may have to go to a bigger vein higher up in your arm." I work on getting the needle in a good position, feeling terrible as I watch her face scrunch up in pain. "I know it hurts honey, I'm so sorry."

I'm so pissed at the condition she's in. It's taking everything in me not to charge out there and lay both her father and uncle out. This is the first lie from dear ol' dad that I've confirmed. No wonder they brought her in today. She's probably been blacking out for a while now.

I give up quickly on her hand. I feel rushed to get fluids in her. Bernie and Tammy walk in as I grab a bigger IV kit to get the vein on the inside of her forearm. Her skin is so pale that it's easy to see the blue lines running under her skin. Thank God. This will work, at least for now.

"Bernie, you need to change her file to indicate that she has been vomiting since *yesterday* morning, and not *this* morning. The veins in her hand keep collapsing on me so I'm going for the antecubital fossa. Grab a few more bags of saline, and a warm one if you can. I'm going to push one in quickly before we leave."

"Poor girl," Bernie says, then directs Tammy with a soft '*go on*' to grab what I've asked for. "Her father and uncle are upstairs in one of the waiting rooms. I told them it'll be awhile, and they'll be able to see her once she's settled in a room. Has she really been sick since yesterday? What the hell were those men thinking?" She's as concerned as I am.

"Is there anyone else that needs immediate attention in the ER right now?" I ask, ignoring her question. It doesn't need to be answered.

"Nothing that can't wait. You want me to call someone down to cover you for a bit?" She goes to the other side of Lenora to hold her hand, shushing her when she whimpers as I slide the needle into her arm. I find a good spot and tape it down quickly after that.

Nodding my head yes, I keep my eyes trained on the girl instead of Bernie. "If you can find someone. I want to go with her." I grab her hand again to try to communicate the way we were, before Bernie came back in.

"Lenora, do you feel any pain where the IV is? It may be slightly uncomfortable, but there shouldn't be any pain." I wait for her to squeeze 'yes' or 'no', but I get nothing. Just a limp hand that feels cold and fragile within my much larger, warmer ones.

Looking up to my nurse as she gets all the tubes and hoses organized, I tell her what I discovered while she was entertaining 'dad.' "Come here and look at this." I pull the right side of her gown back to show her the bruising. She sucks in a breath and mutters what sounds like '*good heavens.*'

Now that her father is out of the room, I'm able to take a closer look. I see a slight imprint of a shoe along one side of the darkening bruise. It's partially hidden from all the discoloration, but it's there, nonetheless. Bernie sees it too. "Is that a shoe mark?"

"Yes. She's got a large contusion on the back of her head, and what, I *think*, are floor or carpet burns on her back. I highly doubt this was an accident."

"Want me to make the ca-" She stops talking when Tammy walks back in.

"I couldn't find any warm IV bags," Tammy tells us. I'm thankful that the flirting seems to be a second thought for now.

"We'll have to make do. Go grab several warm blankets. She's going to feel cold when I push this in." She runs out to grab them.

With the IV bag of saline attached to the line in her arm, I squeeze it gently to increase the flow. I watch for any bubbling that could mean I ruptured her vein. It takes about five minutes, but I finally get it emptied. Bernie hooks up the second bag to a steady drip. It's still quick, but at least not as fast as the one I just forced in.

Lenora is trembling now, cold from the inside. I'm sure it feels awful, but in the long run it's for the best. Tammy and Bernie wrap the blankets from the warmer around her and unlock the bed wheels to move her out of the room.

Walking into radiology a few minutes later, Bernie helps another nurse get Lenora set up while I talk to the radiology tech. I'm thankful Mat is the radiologist that'll read her CT scan today. He's been one of my best friends since we met early on in college.

"I want you to do a full body on her. She's got a small head contusion that I'm not overly worried about, but I want to make sure I didn't miss anything. She's also got bruising around her ribs that I want to make sure aren't broken. I'm not sure if there's anything else going on, but I want you to take a good look. Even if it's something old."

Mat gets the machine set up. "It'll take about 30-40 minutes. I have a few other scans to read this morning, but if you need me to read this one first, I will."

"Would you?" I stare at Lenora as she sleeps on the bed as the staff works around her. Mat doesn't say anything until I look over to him.

He studies me for a moment before answering. "She's a patient man. You can't get attached." Clearly, I'm being obvious.

I can't stop the sigh that I release. Running my hands through my hair, I drag them down my face to wipe the concern and sick feeling off. "I know. I see this shit all the time. I'll get over it." I force myself to turn away. I'm not needed here right now. "Have Bernie give me a call when you're done. I'm heading back down."

I spend the next hour and a half visiting new walk-ins and getting them either sent home or to whichever department they need to go to. My thoughts aren't far from the girl upstairs. Each time my mind drifts to her, I force it to the back of my mind. One of the first things they teach us in residency is how to turn it off, to learn that attachment makes for poor decision-making.

Finally... *FINALLY*, I have an excuse to focus back on her without feeling guilty. I answer the call at the front desk from Bernie. "Can you step away for a few? We've got Miss Fowler's results and should go over them before we take her up to her room."

"I'll be there in a few." I'm appreciative that Bernie was able to find a relief for me so I can leave. I let the other doctor know I'll be away for a while and to page if he needs me. Jogging back to radiology, I slip into Mat's office where he and Bernie are waiting for me.

"Is she awake yet?" I ask before we go over anything else.

"She woke up for a short time after the scan. I gave her another dose of meds because she was feeling nauseous again. We've gotten two more bags of fluids into her and a catheter put in for now. She should be to her room. Jeanette from intake took her to get checked in."

Good. She's in a safe spot for now. "Alright, what do we have?"

Mat pulls up multiple screens displaying her scan. "Overall, there's nothing life-threatening that I'm seeing. No internal bleeding or hemorrhaging. Her head is clear, so the contusion is simply that, a minor contusion. Most likely she has a concussion, but again, I'm not seeing anything that would indicate it's severe."

"Okay... this is good so far. What else?" He changes the screen to a new view showing the upper portion of the right side of her body. I see it right away and lean in for a closer look. I beat him to the obvious issue. "Ribs are fractured."

Pointing it out, he confirms it. "Yeah, here and here. They're small and not misaligned." I'm happy that I had already decided to admit her. With fractures like that, I don't want to risk sending her home and developing pneumonia if she doesn't take proper precautions.

"What else?" I'm looking over all the screens he's got up, but nothing is jumping out at me.

"Well, Bernie told me there was a concern that this wasn't an accident, and you mentioned looking for old wounds as well. I looked for any sign that this has happened before..." he trails off. I look at him, saying nothing. Waiting.

"I think you're right, and I think she's been abused for a long time." As he details each injury from her past, he points every one of them out. They're fucking everywhere. "She's had cracked ribs before, some much older than others. Nothing healed incorrectly, thank God. She has signs of hair line fractures in most of her fingers. There's one in her femur that was more severe and must have been treated because it healed up nicely. None of this would mean a lot, looking at each injury individually, but combined with the ribs and her arms, it's obvious."

"Her arms?" I ask. I need the details. I need to focus on the facts because every time he points out another injury, my fury ticks up a notch at her father and makes me want to take care of her that much more.

"She has multiple healed spiral fractures in both arms, and one that's still fresh. She's not wearing a brace or cast, so either it was just removed, or she was never treated for it. Again, it seems to have healed nicely, so she's lucky."

Spiral fractures are one of the most common fractures you see in children that are in abusive homes. It's a sign that someone much stronger than them grabbed their arm and twisted it too hard.

"There are also a few breaks where they didn't go through the whole bone. They're on the sides of her forearms." I'm beyond being able to process all the injuries. They're everywhere. I know what wounds like that in her arms mean, but I really hope he thinks it's from something different.

"Which means?"

"Defensive breaks." He holds his arms up in front of him, pretending to fend off an attack. "She was protecting herself and her arms took most of it."

"*Mother FUCKER!*" I shout, slamming my hand on Mat's desk. I give Bernie an apologetic look when my outburst causes her to jump. "Jesus *Christ*, Mat."

"I know, man. I'm sorry to give you shitty news, but I think you knew it was coming."

"You have everything written up?" I have to pull myself together before I leave. The rest of the staff doesn't need to see me like this. I'm not worried about Mat and Bernie. They both know me well enough to know that I'm not going to act rashly.

"Yup. It's in the computer, all attached to her file."

"Good. Bernie, let's get a call to the police and social services to report this and see what steps we can take. She's not awake to make her own decisions right now, so we get to make that call."

I can see the confusion on her face. "She was just awake a moment ago. I'm sure I could wake her up."

"Nope." I smile at her, a smirk playing across my lips. "She's out cold, probably from the pain meds. They sure do make people drowsy. You should probably make those calls now while you have the time, yeah?"

Her eyes light up with understanding. "Ahh... yes. I think I will. If you don't need me downstairs, I'll go do that now."

"I don't. Thank you, Bernie." Nodding her head in acknowledgment, she slips out of the room, leaving me alone with Mat. He's trying not to laugh at me. "I know man. You don't need to say anything."

He grins at me. "I won't. But Will, friend to friend? Let me know what I can do to help."

I slap him on the shoulder and walk out of the room. "Will do. Thanks, man."

Picking up my pace as I get in the hallway, I make my way to the in-patient wing. I've got a girl to go visit and her dad to get rid of.

# Chapter 3

## *Nora*

Something's not right.

"*Lenora… can you… bruising… side…*"

I bite my tongue when I feel someone poking around at the back of my head. I won't make a sound. I try to never make a sound. That doesn't stop my body from physically reacting to the sharp pains radiating from the back of my head. Why does it hurt? What happened? "I don't remember," I cry out.

They won't stop touching where it hurts.

His voice. It sounds so warm. Gentle. I don't understand what he's saying to me. He's speaking too softly, his voice so low that the rumbling of it overshadows the clarity of his words. His hands are tender as he runs them over my body, soothing the aches plaguing me.

"*… quick as I can…*" I don't hear the rest and try to ask what he's saying.

The pain starts to draw me back down under when he doesn't answer until I feel his gentle fingers on my face, pulling me away from sleep. Is he caressing my forehead? I have no time for more thoughts when I feel his fingers covering my eyes and a blinding light so torturous that it knifes its way through my brain. It's excruciating, and I want to scream, but I *can't*.

Finally, he stops. Then the agony rises in me again when he inflicts the same cruelness to my other eye. It ends faster this time, and I take shuttered breaths, ignoring the other aches in my chest I feel when I breathe like that. I hear him a little more clearly now, but I still don't understand what he's saying.

"*All done… going to… for you… I'll be back.*" I understood that. I want to beg him not to go. I don't know why, but he's safe. I know it. I can feel it in my bones.

I try my best to focus on the sounds and voices around me. I hear a woman and my father… oh God. He sounds so mad. Did I mess up again?

"*LENNY!*" he barks at me, and I flinch. He sounds a lot closer than he was a moment before. Was it only a moment? The movement my body makes, an automatic response when he yells, makes me dizzy. It takes me a moment to regain my focus. He said something else, but I missed it. He *hates* when I don't pay attention.

I try to crack my eyelids open and fail. That small sliver of light is too much for me to handle. My stomach turns over, and I swallow the bile down. I cannot throw up anymore. I'd rather keep it in than suffer through the added pain that will inevitably shoot through my head.

Gradually, my stomach settles. I feel someone moving around me, their hands adjusting my shirt. The hands are different. Not bad, still kind, but colder. They aren't *his* hands. The ones belonging to the gentle rumble, like rocks rolling around in a tumbler being polished.

I hear him now. Is he lecturing my dad? That's not good... *really* not good. He's going to blame me. I start to panic and force myself to steady my breath when I start to feel like I'm suffocating. It hurts so bad to take those much needed deep breaths in.

Not hearing his words, I center myself around the rumble of them to calm myself down while I piece together what happened. Dad woke me up early. He was screaming at me for something and pulled me out of bed. I don't remember what time, but it was still dark out.

Dishes. Shoot. I forgot to clean up the mess in the kitchen from the night before. I swear I was going to. I just wanted to finish up the last few chapters of the book I was reading and must have fallen asleep.

Uncle Rich was mocking me, laughing at the trouble I was in with dad. I briefly looked at his face before dad grabbed a hold of my hair, wrenching my head back. His eyes were bloodshot and glassy. The two of them must have been up all night drinking again.

I remember dad pulling my hair so hard that I tripped. Him dragging me across the floor on my back. I couldn't get my feet under me at that angle, and the scratchy carpet from the living room pulled the back of my tank top down. That must be why my skin feels sensitive back there.

He dropped me in the kitchen when we reached it. The tiles on the floor were so cold. They always keep the AC so low that the floor sometimes feels like ice in the mornings.

*"I'm so sorry dad. I must have fallen asleep. I'll clean it u-"* I started to explain as I stood up. He didn't give me a chance to look up before his foot flew out and slammed into my chest, connecting with my body just below my right breast.

The force of his booted foot hitting me before I even had my feet firmly planted under me caused me to fly back. His kick was so hard that all I remember after that is an explosion of pain in the back of my head when it hit those cold tiles.

I briefly remember rolling over to vomit and Uncle Rich yelling at dad for fucking me up. I don't know which, but one of them pulled me back to my room and set a trash can next to me. I spent the next however many hours vomiting from all the pain and dizziness in my chest and head.

I'm almost certain he cracked my ribs again. I remember feeling the outside air on my face, and now I'm here. They must have brought me to the hospital. The room I'm in smells clinical, and I don't know where else I could be if not at home.

Focusing back on the present, I hear *him* still arguing with dad. I can hear the anger in his voice even though he's not yelling. Does he get mad like dad does? I don't think he does. That thought doesn't stop the shiver, caused by their escalating voices, running through my body, re-lighting the pain in my side.

I've had bruised and broken ribs before. I don't know if they're broken this time, but I know it's going to be a long recovery either way.

A snick of the door and then silence. Blessed silence. Who left? The strangers or dad?

There's a metal sound and someone shifting around me again. Nothing to indicate who's here with me. I try to crack my lids again. I fail... again.

The air moves around me, and I scent something delicious. Sandalwood and freshly laundered warmth. Is there a smell for that? There must be, because I smell it. Like the warm smell from clothes when you've just pulled them from the dryer. This person smells clean, minty even.

Dad and Uncle Rich never smell this good. Alcohol sweats will do that to you. Or that funky 'morning body' when you don't shower the night before and the dirty oils secrete from your body all night long.

I want to gag when I think about that. After living with two grown men who are slobs with poor hygiene habits, I can't help but be particular about my own hygiene, showering twice a day and changing the sheets on my bed regularly. I can't afford those nice perfumes other girls wear, but the cheap lilac scented body wash is fragrant enough to make me feel like I don't need the perfume.

"Your father is a real piece of work." It *is* him, and he's talking to me. He has to be because I'm certain there isn't anyone else in here aside from him. The guilty feeling that he had to deal with my dad while I simply laid here starts to eat at me. I hope he knows I would have intervened for him if I was able to.

I try swallowing to wet my dry throat, but I'm unsuccessful. I force the sound through my sore throat anyway. "I'm sorry." God, just talking is almost impossible. I want to say more, but I just can't. My throat is so sore and dry from all the purging I've done over the last god knows how many hours.

He apologizes to me and grabs my hand. There's the warm again. Warm skin, warm feelings, warm comfort. Warm air, puffed from his mouth, hits my cheek as he leans toward me to speak. Warm mint…

He directs me to squeeze his hand to answer his questions. That makes me happy because it means he'll keep holding it. I swear my hand is the only part of my body that doesn't hurt right now.

No wonder I feel so awful. I learn from him that it's the next day and I've been like this for over 24 hours. The *'good girl'* he gives me makes my heart flutter in a good way. I'm *never* a good girl, no matter how hard I try to be.

Next, he starts to work on putting an IV in my hand. If the dryness in my mouth is any indication, I'm probably extremely dehydrated.

I can't help chewing on my cheek when he moves the needle around in my hand. He eases up as he apologizes for hurting me. Calls me by another sweet name. I'm sure he's nice like this with all his patients because, clearly, it works to make you feel better. It makes me feel special, cared for even.

I feel the pinch higher up in my arm this time. Even though it's a sharper pinch than the one in my hand, it's over more quickly. The warm fluid runs through my body, and almost immediately the pounding in my head is eased. That feeling wraps around me like his hand wrapped around my own.

Slowly seeping back into the nothing, I embrace the release. The pain is forgotten, but now, my veins pulse with ice.

I stay in the cold. I wish he could bring back his warm.

~ ~ ~ ~ ~

There's a gentle beeping that wakes me this time. I become aware more quickly and easily than when I woke earlier. I know what's going on and where I am. Whatever they've given me has reduced the ice picks pounding into my head to a gentler knocking. Steady, but bearable.

I peek my eye open and this time I'm able to manage it. With the lessened pain and the dim lights, I focus on what's surrounding me. I stiffen when I see Uncle Rich in the chair across the room. He's staring at his phone and doesn't notice that I'm awake yet.

I can hear my father outside the room, and I look to the door. He's arguing with a woman, most likely one of the nurses. Poor nurse. No one should have to deal with him and his temper.

A wave of embarrassment flows through my gut. Good lord, what must she think of all of us? I'm sure the staff here can't wait to get rid of me so that the trash leaves with me. Although, I suppose I'd be considered the trash as well. They don't know me, but they certainly know where I come from. What else should they expect from me?

"*Finally*, you're fucking awake. It's about time." I look at Uncle Rich and see he's glaring at me like I should have known I was sleeping too long. "I'm gonna get Denny. You tell them you're fine now and want to go home. You're not puking up your guts anymore, so you know you're fine… right?"

He growls that last word at me. There's an underlying threat there to not argue and do as I'm told. I don't want to, but what choice do I have?

Nodding my head at him, I agree. "I will Uncle Rich. I'm sure they just needed me to wake up, and I feel much better already." I do, but only because drugs are running through my veins. Once they wear off, I guarantee I'll feel miserable again.

The bed is tilted up slightly, so I haven't had to move my body yet to talk to him or to look around. I want to avoid moving, I'm comfortable like this. I'm not warm, not like I was before. I struggle to remember what happened when I got here even though I know *why* I'm here.

Uncle Rich stands up and moves closer to my bed. Standing over me is one of his favorite intimidation tactics. He and dad are so much taller than me, dad being shorter than his brother by only an inch or so. Dad is about 6 feet, so Uncle Rich has got to be a solid 6'1. I don't even have to be sitting for him to tower. I only come to a measly 5'3, and that's pushing it.

Lowering his voice and glancing at the door quickly, he leans over to me and makes his threat a little more obvious this time. "You listen here you little bitch, don't fucking say a word about how you got hurt. We told them you tripped on the front steps and cracked your head on the sidewalk this morning."

Oops. A flashback of a deep, baritone voice asking when I got hurt pops into my memory. I'm certain I told him it was yesterday. I'm not going to tell my uncle that, though.

I remain silent, but still give him my full attention. "You better tell them the same thing. I swear to fuck, if you get your dad in trouble, I'll… Well, you'll still be going home with me. Won't you, niece?"

Swallowing, I just nod my head, slowly so I don't make it hurt worse. He's not wrong. He didn't do this to me. Not this time at least. They can't arrest him just because my dad kicked me.

He glares at me a little longer, still leaning over the bed. Nothing else gets said when the door swings open, followed by a set of feet moving swiftly into the room.

"What's going on in here?" I don't look over, my uncle has me in his stare and I'm afraid what he'll do if I look away. I try to communicate to him that I promise I won't say anything. I can't. What would I do when I go home if I did?

There's a flash of irritation that crosses his face at the interruption, before he straightens with a fake smile and turns to the newcomer. "Lenny just woke up. I was checking in to see how she was feeling. She's doing good, Doc, so I'm sure we can get out of here now."

I *really* don't want to go home yet, and I close my eyes briefly to throw up a prayer that the doctor isn't here to say that I'm being discharged. "Not happening. Not yet at least."

It didn't register when he first spoke that it's the same voice from earlier this morning. I shoot my eyes past my uncle and my jaw drops. No freaking way… my doctor has got to be one of the hottest men I've ever seen in real life. Like, I can't form any words because I'm speechless, hot.

Uncle Rich looks back at me, sneering, "Shut your fucking mouth and wipe the drool, Lenny. Don't embarrass yourself."

The flush to my cheeks is freaking immediate. I snap my mouth shut, sending a strong wave of pain back through my head momentarily. He's right. God, how *embarrassing*.

I can tell that the doctor is looking at me, and I can't stand to see what he must think. I choose to close my eyes instead and try to stave off the blood rushing to my face. Forcing it is only making it worse and I can feel my cheeks heating even more at a rapid rate. My throat starts to close as I feel those stupid tears building. I hate crying, but I especially hate crying in front of people. I'm so freaking embarrassed that I just want to cover myself up with a pillow and hide. It's a childish thought. If I can't see them, then they can't see me.

"Lenny, you're awake!" My dad must have followed the doctor into the room along with another nurse. I hear her mutter a hello to him as she walks over to me. I still refuse to look at him, but I do open my eyes to at least acknowledge my dad.

"Ye-" I have to clear my throat. It's still clogged after choking up and fighting to fend off the tears. I look for a cup of water and come up empty-handed. "Yeah... I'm feeling much better, too." May as well start now.

Uncle Rich's shoulders relax. "Told ya, doc. Denny, tell 'em we can take care of her at home."

Quick to agree, my dad bobs his head up and down. "We definitely can. I'm off work, so I'll be able to watch her all weekend. Won't leave her alone." I can only shut my eyes at that image. It's inevitable that they'll discharge me now, why wouldn't they? I just told them I'm feeling better, didn't I?

"Like I said. Not. Happening." I hear the anger he's trying to temper. Even though I'm mortified that he saw me gawking at him like a stupid teenage girl, the vehemence in his voice forces me to look at him again.

My second look at the doctor is just as shocking as my first, and my body reacts powerfully. That voice absolutely fits his build. My dad and uncle are tall, but this man? He makes them look just... average. He steps up to my dad, towering over him the way Uncle Rich towers over me. Not only that, but he has at least four inches on him, maybe five even.

I glance at the nurse and can't stop myself from asking, "How tall is he?" Immediately I bite my lip when her lip quirks up at my question. Please don't tell me he heard that idiotic question. My filter is already weak normally, but apparently a head injury makes it non-existent.

"Now wait a sec. She don't have to stay if she don't want to. If she says she's better, then she is." My dad argues with him - I still don't know his name - and tries to stand tall. It's obvious he's trying not to cower. It's a weird thing, watching someone intimidate my dad. It's a role reversal I've rarely had an opportunity to see.

"Tell 'em Lenny. Tell 'em you'll be fine," Uncle Rich orders me under his breath.

The doctor must have heard him because now his glare is immediately directed at my uncle. "She can tell me she's fine until she's blue in the face, but it won't change anything. Neither of you are supposed to be up here right now anyway. You both need to step out so I can take a look at *my* patient."

"The fuck you mean I can't be in here? That's my fuckin' daughter!" Dad is yelling now, his face turning red.

The doctor just shakes his head and crosses his arms across his chest. There's something so wrong with me. I don't even care that, at this point, I'm screwed when I get home. I can't stop gawking at him. Uncle Rich is still glaring at me, seething under his breath, warning me to say something. "*Lenny*." I ignore him, focused solely on the doctor. His muscles are *huge*! How he's even able to cross them is beyond me. He's wearing one of those white coats and has a collared, light blue dress shirt underneath it, neither of which are hiding the definition of his biceps.

I watch the two of them like I'm watching a ping-pong match. I know who the winner will be, this time at least. The doctor, *my* doctor - because I'm *his* patient - refuses to back down.

"I mean exactly that, Mr. Fowler. The nurses out front, did they or did they not, tell you explicitly that you're not allowed into this room until I got up here?"

Sputtering, dad is outraged and tries to defend himself. "Well, yeah, but Lenny is my fuc-"

A hand. A simple hand, raised in the air in front of my dad's face, shuts him right up. My eyes widen as big as saucers. I hear the nurse chuckle under her breath next to me as she messes with all the bags hanging from my IV hooks. I want to look at her to see if she's laughing at me or my dad. I would, but I can't tear my eyes away from *him*.

"Mr. Fowler," he looks at Uncle Rich, "and brother. I ask again, please step out. If you find you're unable to, I'll be forced to have my nurse here call security to escort you out."

The stare-down goes on for a full minute, dad chewing on his cheek, trying to decide if he's serious about the security thing.

Finally, Uncle Rich steps next to dad. "Come on Denny, he said it's only 'til he checks her over. We'll just wait 'til he's done and then we can come back." He leans in and says something else in dad's ear. I don't hear him, but my doctor narrows his eyes at them.

"Fine. Lenny, I'll be back. Let them know if you want me sooner."

"This is Dr. Blackwell, Lenora. My name is Bernice, and we were on call when you came in this morning with your… family." I don't respond to her pause. I'm still watching the doctor as he watches my dad and uncle leave the room. His wavy almost-black hair tumbles across his forehead, into his eyes, but it doesn't seem to bother him.

The last thing I hear is one of them mumbling *'fucking bullshit'* in the hallway, and the door clicking shut.

Those eyes turn and focus right on me. Light, vivid cerulean blue eyes, framed with thick lashes that every woman wishes they had, grace his face. The tanned, golden skin crinkles next to them as he smiles, flashing straight white teeth at me. He walks closer to me and my breath hitches. His presence is something else.

"Hi, Lenora. To answer your question, I'm exactly 6'4 and three-eighths. Let's take a look at you, sweetheart."

# Chapter 4

## *William*

"...Let's take a look at you, sweetheart."

I can't help but bite the inside of my cheek to hold back my smile. I know I shouldn't say that to her, but *fuck* if her blush a few minutes ago didn't get to me. I barely got a chance to admire it, study it when it spread across her cheeks. Not when I was dealing with her piece of shit father and equally shitty uncle. I want to see it again.

Ahh... there she goes. It's so fucking inappropriate to get joy out of this while also being her doctor. Add in the fact that she's probably in a lot of pain, and it makes me even worse. All those thoughts still don't stop my eyes from tracking where that blush is emerging from. It starts somewhere below the neckline of the sea foam green patient gown that everyone who's been admitted gets stuffed into.

I follow the trail of blazing red up to the underside of her chin, where it finally settles across both of her cheeks. My smile grows the longer I watch. Thank God for Bernie for snapping me out of it.

She clears her throat, reminding me that we aren't alone in here. "Dr. Blackwell…"

"Will," I cut in.

I see Bernie roll her eyes from the corner of mine. I still haven't taken my gaze from Lenora's gorgeous face. I'm studying her just as thoroughly as she's analyzing me. I want to know what she's thinking. Her face is expressive, a multitude of emotions and reactions cross her face rapidly, one right after the other. Unfortunately, I can't tell what they're saying to me.

"Dr. *Will* Blackwell…" She exaggerates my name. *I know Bernie, I know. I'll knock it off.*

Sighing, I finally look away and glance at my friend. The moment my eyes leave her, I hear her breath whoosh out. She must have been holding it. That thought brings me back to task, particularly that holding her breath is the last thing she should be doing.

Grabbing the stool and sitting down at her bedside, I reach behind me to grab her chart from the small nurse's station and set it on the blanket next to her hip. This is already a habit of mine with most of my patients, so Bernie can't say anything about it. I like to come down to their level, get comfortable, and try to talk to them like I'm a normal person. Besides that, my height can also be a lot to take in.

She still hasn't taken her eyes off my face. I'm not certain, but I sense that she's almost as affected by me as I am her. I don't want to stop looking. Eyes open and alert, I can see her intelligence within them. That makes me happy because I would rather not have to sugarcoat anything.

Looking at her a moment longer, I delve in. "Look, Lenora. Can I call you that? Your dad and uncle called you Lenny. If you'd prefer that-"

"No. I like Lenora. Or Nora. Lenny sounds like a boy's name. They call me that to tease me." She says it like it's innocent fun, but I can tell it's important to her that I *don't* call her Lenny.

"Got it, Nora it is. I like that much better as well." I'm such an ass, finding pleasure in keeping that blush active and alive.

"Thanks…" she whispers. Her voice is raspy, most likely sore from the violence of her vomiting, but I can hear the lightness of it. The sound is lovely, delicately sweet and shy, obviously young.

Young.

I need to remind myself of that. She's very young, only eighteen. Nineteen soon, but still. Eighteen is eighteen. 19 years is a large difference. I did the math shortly after seeing her downstairs. I couldn't stop the thought from crossing my mind.

It humbles me and brings me down to earth. "I'm going to be frank with you Nora. You have some severe injuries that worry me. I know you told us a moment ago that you're feeling better. I won't dismiss that, but it's the pain medication and anti-nausea medication you've received over the past ten or so hours."

She glances at the clock when I say that. "I've been here for ten hours? I thought it'd only been a couple, maybe three at the most."

"No, it's just about dinnertime. Our shift ends at seven, so you'll have someone new with you tonight." I watch the disappointment flicker across her face at my news. "You'll be in good hands, I promise." I don't think that's what she was worried about.

Fuck. Me. She looks really sad. I don't know how to make her feel better about having to leave, it's out of my hands. I look to Bernie for some help.

She shrugs at me, not sure what to do or say. God damnit, her misery is radiating from her in waves, punching me in the gut and making my heart ache. I say her name softly, "Nora…"

Her eyes are glassy when they meet mine and my heart cracks, that last bit of wall remaining is knocked down. I shouldn't be thinking of her in any other way than professionally as her doctor. But as a man? I want take her sad away. I *need* to take it away.

"Nora, are you okay?" She's clearly not, but I'm not sure what else I can say.

Wiping her hand across her eyes, she gives me a stilted smile. "Sorry, I think the headache and meds are just making me overly emotional. It's fine. Would you fill me in on what's going on? When will the hospital send me home?"

Cocking my head at her, I give her a questioning look. I'll give her the credit she deserves; she's trying to pull herself together. "Do you *want* to go home, Nora?"

That's the million-dollar question.

I don't get an answer, she simply bites her lip and gazes at the window.

"Nora, honey," Bernie chimes in. "You're not going to be going home tonight, more than likely won't go home tomorrow either. I hope that's okay with you, keeping you here for a bit longer. We really must insist."

She seems a little relieved with what Bernie is telling her. "If you think I need to, I can't argue, right?"

"Right," I say. There is at least some relief there. It's obvious she doesn't want to go home. "Let's talk about why I want to keep you here. Your family brought you in this morning just before 7 this morning. You were suffering from nausea and vomiting that had been going on for quite a while." She covers her mouth, like she just remembered and is worried about her breath.

Smiling at her, I reassure her. "You're fine, I promise. You may not remember, but after your tests were done, one of the CNAs helped you get cleaned up, brush your teeth, wiped you down a bit. You were a bit of a mess when you showed up here." I wink at her so she knows I'm only teasing.

"Thank you," she says to me, then looks to Bernie. "Both of you. I remember your voice from this morning."

I'm surprised. I thought she was so out of it that she wouldn't remember. "That's good you're able to remember. I was worried about that with the head contusion you have, plus you were extremely dehydrated and seemed to come in and out of awareness."

"I was. I only remember parts." She glances at my hand before looking away quickly. She remembers me holding her hand. My arm is reaching out before I can stop myself. If I pull back now, it'll be more than obvious that I shouldn't be doing it.

Threading my fingers through hers, there's a feeling of rightness that washes over me and settles in my chest. She looks at our joined hands and gives me a little squeeze. Like she can't stop herself, it's an automatic response.

"Nora, would you mind if I step out a moment and grab you some dinner?" Bernie says. Thankful for the time she's offering me, I smile at Bernie, and Nora lets her know it's fine.

I watch as she leaves before turning back and staring at this exquisite woman in front of me. My gaze bounces back and forth between her eyes a moment before I continue. "I'm going to go over this quick because we have a few other things to discuss."

She seems a bit nervous being alone with me now, but licks her lips and says, "Okay, Dr. Blackwell. Should my dad be in here as well?"

"NO!" I'm firm when I tell her and cringe when she jolts at my sudden outburst and then flinches in pain, reaching to soothe her head with her other hand. I wish she would have used my first name, but I'm not going to push her right now.

I reach my hand up and place it over hers while she holds her head. "Sorry about that, but no. He's already been informed of your injuries and what the plan is for now. You came in to us severely dehydrated, possibly concussed, dizzy, nauseous, bruising all along your right side. You were in a significant amount of pain, Nora." She doesn't deny any of this, but also doesn't add anything.

Staying silent, she waits me out. She probably learned early on not to offer extra information if not directly asked. That's not going to work with me. I intend to ask her questions, a lot of them.

"Denny told us you fell down the front steps of your home, hit the concrete walkway." Her eyes squint a bit confused before widening at me. Clearly, this is news to her. I'm thankful she doesn't seem to want. She's a good girl. "That didn't happen, did it?"

A direct question requires a direct answer. "No..." she whispers.

"He also told us that you had your fall this morning. Again, not true. I already knew this for a couple of reasons."

"I told you this morning when we did the hand squeeze answer thingy." I feel another gentle squeeze from her. I also feel her trembling slightly the more I talk about this with her.

Leaning forward, I pull our joined hands closer to my chest and ask her my next question. Her pulse is racing under my thumb that's resting along her wrist. I can also see her artery pulsating under the delicate skin of her neck.

"You have two cracked ribs in the lower portion of your rib cage. When I was examining you, the only bruising I found was directly over those cracked ribs, and the swelling at the back of your head. You obviously did hit the ground, but I don't think it was outside, was it?"

Another whispered, "No..." and the trembling intensifies. She's fucking terrified she'll be in trouble for not lying to me.

"If you had fallen hard enough to break bones and knock your head so hard that you're vomiting from the pain of it, there would have been more widespread injuries across your body." I can't help the anger seeping into my voice as I go over the details of her injuries. "A simple fall like that wouldn't leave a boot imprint covering half of your lower chest."

I watch a tear slip down her cheek. She bites her lip harder to stop it from shaking. She can barely look at me. I don't want that. I need her eyes on me, and I need her not to be afraid of this conversation.

I'm still gripping her hand within mine when I reach with the other to pull her lip from her teeth. "Someone kicked you. Someone kicked you so hard that your ribs broke. Someone, or *someones*, have hurt you for a long enough time that a simple CT allowed me to read your history like a detailed map."

Nora tries to slip her hand out of mine. I don't let her. I need this contact too, and I hope to show her that I'm not going to hurt her.

She needs to feel grounded, and I know that at least for now, I can give her that safety.

She's not fighting me, but she won't look at me either. I move from my seat to settle on the side of her bed. She's so small in it that I have no problem finding room. I grip her hand a little harder, careful not to hurt her, and pull it the rest of the way to my chest, settling it over my heart so she can feel it beat.

My other arm reaches over her body when I place it right next to her ear and lean in, moving my face just a few inches from hers. Hovering over her, I watch as her shame, embarrassment, and fear shine from deep inside her.

I'm so close to her that I don't scare her with my quick movement to catch her next tear with my thumb. I taste the saltiness of it when I bring my thumb to my mouth. At least she's rehydrated. That's a good sign.

I wait, but she's frozen. I need to know for sure, and I need her to hurry before Bernie gets back. Bernie knows I wanted to talk to her about this alone, but she also doesn't need to see me hovering, leaning this close into my patient.

"I don't need to ask who hurt you. I just need you to tell me which one of them did it." She releases a choked sob before sucking it back in almost immediately. It's got to be painful. I mentally note to give her a little extra something to sleep tonight.

"Was it your uncle?" He seems like more of a loose cannon out of the two of them. I don't hope for either one to have been hurting her, but it makes it just that much worse when it's the parent. It's the ultimate betrayal one can inflict on their child.

My thoughts are halted when I feel two slow squeezes in my hand. She's telling me without having to tell me. I'm so relieved.

No, it wasn't her uncle. That leaves her father.

"Was it your dad?"

One squeeze.

That cocksucking motherfucker. I'm going to tear into him the next time an opportunity is presented to me.

She's looking directly at me, not afraid to meet my eye, desperately begging me to read what she's trying to tell me without words.

"Your father kicked you." Not a question, but she gives me another single squeeze anyway.

"Has he hurt you before?" Seriously, someone needs to change the Hippocratic Oath for us doctors because I very much want to pick this little darling up and hold her, then take her father out back for some well-earned justice. The whole 'do no harm' should be based on circumstance. I've never wanted to hold someone more than when she gives me another 'yes' squeeze.

"You said your uncle didn't do this to you. Has he hurt you before?" I know the answer before she gives it to me. Not with a squeeze this time either.

"...Yes." She rasps out. Such a brave girl. I wouldn't be surprised if that's the first time she's ever been asked. If she has, it's most likely the first time she's ever been able to answer honestly.

I release her hand, lifting both of mine to cup her cheeks and keep her attention on me. The moment I released her hand, she fought to grab it back to her. Instead, she grips both of my wrists, hanging on while I continue talking to her.

"Good girl, sweet Nora," I whisper to her. Her eyes flutter shut a moment before opening up to me. "I know this is scary, but you're not alone. We're here to help you."

I know she doesn't believe me when I tell her she's not alone, not yet. I need to make sure she hears me, though. "*I'M* here to help you. I won't leave you alone to be left with them, sweetheart. Do you believe me?"

"Yes..." She might not fully believe me, but she's trying to. I'm sure no one has ever been there for her before, so this is hard for her. She's probably been continuously let down by those around her. Family, friends, school faculty, doctors, coaches, fuck... anyone on the street could have seen something and ignored it.

"I'm not going to let them back in here, either. We've already contacted the police to report that we suspect abuse, along with child protective services. I know you're an adult, but they were our only resource at the moment. If anything, they can help guide us through the upcoming steps we should take."

God, I can tell she's so scared right now. I've already made up my mind about what I'll do this weekend. I'm not scheduled to work, but that doesn't mean I don't have paperwork and charting to sign off on. Probably a couple of reports to work on as well. I'm not leaving her here this alone with a rotating staff, each one new and unfamiliar.

"What happens to me? I mean, after this, after I leave here?" I don't have an answer for her yet, but I will soon.

"I'm not sure yet, but you and I will figure it out over the next few days. Agreed?" I smile at her when she agrees. That blush is back, lighting up her face when I promise I won't be handing her off to someone else.

"I'm going to step out now. The nurses will get you fed and settled in for the night. With those broken ribs, we need to keep an eye on your breathing so you don't run the risk of developing pneumonia. You're going to be stuck with us for at least a week."

"What if they try to come back in here tonight? Or tomorrow?" Nerves rattle through her. God, to be so young and have your life completely tipped upside-down like this must be horrifying. I can't imagine how it would feel to be in that kind of position.

"They *won't*. I'm going to speak to the police, get something at least temporary to keep them away from you. We'll also alert the hospital security and pass along to the nurses and physicians that they are not to be allowed to see you, and *definitely* not left alone with you."

"Thank you, Dr. Blackwell. Truly, thank you." My teeth ache, she's so sweet.

"Will… or William. Whichever you prefer. When I come back tomorrow, I'm not your doctor. I'll be here as your friend." The light goes out a tiny bit, like she doesn't like me labeling myself as simply her friend.

She's still holding my wrists, and I haven't let go of her face. Licking those pink, full lips again to wet them, I can't keep my gaze from being drawn there. "Thank you, William… so much."

Instinctually, I start to lean forward. Thank God for the door opening and Bernie coming back in, because that would have been so, *so* bad. I didn't mean to do that, at least not right now. It felt almost out of my control.

I release her and pull her hands from my wrists. She really doesn't want to let go, and I feel terrible for pulling her off me. That sadness is back again, making me want to go break something to get some control back.

"Get some rest tonight. I'll see you tomorrow, alright?"

"Alright, William." Bernie only raises an eyebrow at Nora's use of my name. I like that she's used my full name.

"Alright." I slap my hands on my legs as I stand up to tell Bernie what I want to happen overnight with Nora and the breathing exercises she needs to do regularly.

I head out the door and give her one last look before turning away. She gives me the tiniest bit of a wave goodbye. I don't want to leave her.

Her sadness about the separation is contagious, I feel it too.

# Chapter 5

## *Nora*

I hear them. My dad and my uncle. Raised voices arguing with the nurses outside my room. Wide-eyed, I stare at the door, afraid either one will burst in here any moment.

I keep waiting.

They keep yelling.

True to Dr. Blackwell's word, they aren't allowed in. There's quite a commotion out there, with all of their yelling and cursing.

I look at Bernie setting up my dinner and give her a small smile. "I'm so sorry for them. God, this is embarrassing." It really is. I don't understand how people aren't ashamed of themselves when they act like that in public. There's no way my family has that little self-awareness of how they're perceived and what's appropriate in this kind of setting. They just don't care.

"Don't you worry about it, honey. The staff knows how to handle them and deescalate the situation. You just need to focus on you right now." She places my dinner tray of broth, pudding, some toast, and jelly in front of me. There are a couple of choices of juices along with some hot tea. My stomach grumbles.

"I'll try not to, thank you." I sip the grape juice she shoved a straw into and handed to me. She also sets down a plastic tube-shaped device with a short hose coming off the side of it.

"You're welcome. So, this here is a spirometer. Your lungs are clear right now, but this is a preventative measure to ensure you don't develop any lung issues. You slowly breathe in here through this tube and keep the indicator between these two arrows." She's points at a couple of lines marked on the plastic. "Do it about a dozen times every hour you're awake. The deep breaths will be uncomfortable on your ribs, but believe me, you'd rather have this discomfort now rather than the painful coughing from sick lungs."

"I will. Thank you again, Bernice." Coughing sounds horrifying to me right now.

"Of course. I'm heading off shift in about an hour, but the night nurses are excellent. Tell them if the pain gets worse. Dr. Blackwell left dosing instructions for them if you need the extra kick to get to sleep. Will you be okay? Do you need anything?"

I don't want her to leave, either. Or at least to be left alone. I can't help basking in all this kindness and goodness. It's making me greedy for more. Unfortunately, I can't think of an excuse to keep her any longer aside from drawing her into conversation.

"Umm... nothing I can think of. Is he really going to come back tomorrow?" I need to know.

Chuckling, she tucks the blanket around me before answering. "Will that make you happy? If he comes back?"

I should feel embarrassed, but Bernie is sweet. She isn't trying to make me feel ashamed. "Yeah... but I don't want him to waste his weekend if he doesn't have to work. It's not his responsibility, you know? To keep me company, I mean." It seems a little above and beyond for just a patient.

She snorts. "Just a patient my ass." Oops, I didn't mean to speak that last bit out loud. Just me throwing myself a little solo pity party.

My eyes widen at her swearing. "I didn't me-"

She shakes her head like it's okay to have asked. "I can tell you right now, that man wouldn't come back in for just a patient. Not one that simply needs some help."

"Umm..." The grumbles of hunger in my stomach change to flutters and dips like you feel on a roller coaster or flying over a steep hill in a car. I really don't want to be just a patient. Nor do I want to only be someone who needs help figuring out her life. He said he's coming as a friend. I should accept that and reign in my quickly developing crush. I need to remember that he's simply trying to be nice and wants to help a girl out in a crappy situation.

Looking at my reaction, she sighs and stops fussing with everything around me. "That sounded bad. He has an incredible amount of compassion for every person he treats here. He's kind, caring, and advocates for anyone whose voice isn't being heard." She studies me before continuing. "That being said, he also knows how to separate his feelings from professional and personal ones. When he leaves here, as most physicians do, he leaves the day at the door. You, my dear, are under his skin."

I want to ask her to keep talking because she obviously knows him well. The feelings of not being good enough battle with my desire for approval from him. I don't want it to stop, I don't want *him* to stop. I can still feel the tingles on my face where his hands were resting, forcing me to keep my eyes on him. But I don't want it to be because he feels sorry for me, either.

"Is it bad? Him coming back to visit me?" Getting in trouble would be bad as well. Will the hospital personnel look at him negatively for it?

"Nooo… not *bad* per se…" She's thoughtful and seems to be working through what she should say and what she should keep to herself. Her underlying tone tells me she's not being completely forthcoming.

Disappointment lands like a lead weight in my stomach, driving away the hunger previously there. Guilt fills me at what seems like disapproval from her, or disappointment. Either one of them makes me feel awful. "You should catch him before he leaves and tell him he shouldn't come back. I don't want anyone to think badly of him."

Her eyes soften. I hope she knows I'm not trying to be selfish. Honestly, he shouldn't want to be friends with someone like me. Someone related to monsters. Someone who barely knows how to be an adult.

"You're incredibly sweet, you know that?" I blush at her compliment. "Do you really want me to tell him that?"

"You should... I think." It hurts to say that, but it's the right thing to do.

Bernie doesn't say anything for a moment. She just clicks away on the keyboard, typing notes into the computer. The steady beeping from the pulse oximeter gripping my index finger along with the clicks on the keys are the only sounds filling the room.

"I'll tell him for you... eat up your dinner. It's not a lot, but every bit will help you gain strength, strength needed to heal so you don't have to stay stuck in here forever." She flips the computer off and heads to the door while my insecurities rage a war inside of me.

"Have a nice evening, Nora. If you're still here on Monday, I'll be sure to pop in and say hi." Thank God she's far enough away that she can't see my eyes filling, again. This is pathetic, crying so much over strangers having to leave because their workday is done.

"I hope so. Night Bernie." That came out soft, but without tears leaking through in my voice. I'm not a baby. I don't need to guilt more people into feeling bad for me.

"Night." She shuts the door behind her as she leaves. I'm alone in here. The incessant beeping still filling the silence, but not enough to drown out my thoughts.

Picking apart the toast on my plate, I run through the last 48 hours of my life, wishing I could go back and change it. All I needed to do were those stupid dishes.

Thoughts continue to eat at me for the next hour or two. Someone came in to remove the tray from my room, leaving the tea for me to sip at. I try not to think about William. I'm sure that Bernie told him by now that he shouldn't come in tomorrow and that I wasn't expecting him. Looking at the clock, I see it's close to eight pm. He's probably home by now.

My regret battles with relief for saying he shouldn't come. I want to see him, but I also know that he's most likely already been told by Bernice that he doesn't have to feel bad for me.

The muted chatter outside my room comes and goes, gradually getting less and less as they get everyone settled in for the night. I haven't heard dad or Uncle Rich for a while. I don't know if that means they've just gone home and will come back tomorrow, or if the police took them because of William and Bernice reporting my injuries.

Staring out the window, I can't see the sunset, but the fading colors are lovely as they change from yellow to pink, red to purple, then blue. My eyes are trained on the sky when the door opens.

"Nora." Holy shit. I jerk my head sideways and see William walking towards me in his regular clothes. His hair is wet like he's recently showered, and he's wearing gym clothes. The t-shirt is stretched tightly across his chest, highlighting the lines of his muscles, more visible now that he's no longer in a coat.

I try to sit up as he comes near, but can't because of the pain in my side. Dizziness flows through my head at the fast movement.

"Why are you... what are you doing here? Did you forget to tell me something?" I can't think of any reason he'd be here right now unless he forgot to give me some instruction he didn't want passed through the nurses.

He reaches out for me and helps me sit up. "You good?"

Nodding, I catch my breath. "Yeah, thanks. Why-"

"Bernie caught me when I was coming out of the locker room. Said you wanted her to tell me I didn't need to come back. That you didn't think I should for *just a patient*." He studies me, gauging my reaction.

The heat flares up again with him putting me on the spot. "Well, I... I just didn't want you to feel like you had to or that I was making you. You don't need to feel bad for me, Dr. Blackwell."

His grin grows the longer I talk. God, I feel so stupid. Stupid and childish. "William... and I don't, Nora."

"Don't?" Confused because I'm distracted by how good he smells, freshly showered and damp. Distracted by his entire presence, really. He fills the surrounding space, pushing everyone else's energies away and wrapping me up in his. It feels like a hug without having to touch me.

"I don't want to come back just because you're a patient and I feel bad for you. If you really don't want me to come back, I won't... but if you're telling me not to come to spare me, don't waste your breath. Save it for this." I smile at his joke when he holds up the thing Bernice wanted me to breathe into.

"But... I can't imagine why you'd want to interrupt your weekend coming back into work. That's *your* time." He's got to be tired after working all those hours. I know he's been here for over twelve just today.

"I'm done with my shift and no longer have to be responsible here, doctoring anyone. Can I be honest with you and probably a lot unprofessional?" His stare is so commanding. Confidence seeps out of him, and his nearness is making my heart race. This crush will be the death of me, and I don't see it going away when he's talking to me like this.

I just nod my head yes, afraid if I speak that I'll spill out a plethora of words that would probably scare him away.

Leaning forward again into the same position he was earlier when he was sitting on my bed, but standing this time, he places his hands on either side of my head again and brings his face close. "I want to come here tomorrow for un-doctorly reasons, Nora." His eyes flicker across my face, looking for my reaction. He must see something he likes because he keeps going. "I want to come here tomorrow to be here for you. I feel a large sense of responsibility for you."

"You don't have-"

"Not responsible because I was the one who treated you. I feel it here..." He pushes his fist into the center of his chest. "I don't understand why yet, but I feel it... and I think you do too. Am I wrong?"

Whispering, the nerves from his closeness don't allow me to even consider being dishonest. "No… you're not wrong."

Putting his hand back, surrounding me again, he keeps himself between me and the rest of the world. I surrender to the feelings. I'll deal with the disappointment that's inevitable later. I have little to no experience with boys, only what I've seen at school. I certainly have zero experience with men. Is he interested in me beyond just friends? I can't imagine why he would be. He's so far out of my league… older, smarter, established. He's a doctor, for goodness' sake. There's nothing I could offer him, nothing that makes me stand out from other women.

I'm too short, too thin, boobs that aren't much to write home about. Although those would probably fill out if I was able to eat more regularly. I've never been asked out by any of the boys at school, leading me to assume that I'm just average, nothing special. Not the ideal woman that most men are looking for. William brings my focus back to him, thankfully drawing me out of my sinking thoughts.

"I want to come tomorrow to get some clarity on *why* I'm feeling this sense of responsibility… an urge to protect and shelter you."

"What happens when you figure it out? Do you stay my friend after I leave here?" I don't want to know the answer, but I know I need to know. I have to be ready for when I'm on my own and he disappears after I've been settled into my new normal.

He gives himself a self-deprecating laugh, shaking his head like he has no control over how he feels versus how he wants to feel. "Friends... do you just want to be friends, Nora? If that's what you want, I'd very much like to be your friend. But I'll be honest, I think there's more here than that."

"... I'm sort of out of my element here. I don't know how I should answer," I tell him. It's a normal reaction, wanting to protect your feelings, your heart from being hurt. What if I tell him and it's not what he's meant? He's also not being entirely clear for me here, and considering I've been on narcotics for half the day, I think I'm excused for being unsure.

His nostrils flare a bit when I say I'm out of my element. "How out of your element are we talking? Have you ever had a boyfriend, sweetheart?"

"N-no... never. No one's ever wanted to be." God, I need to stop talking. How embarrassing to tell this man that no one has ever been interested in me beyond a friendly hello and some polite conversation.

I watch as his full lips curl up, seemingly happy with my answer. I would assume that someone his age would think inexperience with the opposite sex is pathetic.

"You're a *very* good girl, aren't you, babydoll?" Oh, God... I close my eyes at his praise. Receiving it when it's been absent from my life is addictive. "Don't. Don't be embarrassed. I asked, and I want you to be truthful with me. I wanted to give you tonight to get yourself situated, comfortable with what has happened over the past couple of days. It's important to process and accept. I wanted to have this conversation tomorrow, but with the message from Bernie, I just *knew* I had to come up here tonight."

"I don't know what you're trying to tell me. I'm so sorry... I want to be truthful, but it's going to be really embarrassing if I'm misreading you." I don't mind swearing, but I hate doing it myself. It's a sure sign that I'm distressed when I do. So, when I whisper to him, "I'm so fucking confused," he helps me out.

"It's late, it's been a very long day for you. I would rather not leave you stressed and unaware of my intentions... I want you, Nora. I feel this *need* to have you. There's something here. I don't know why I felt it, but I did the moment I walked in to your room in the ER. Watching you suffer broke my heart, and I wanted nothing more than to wrap you up and keep you away from all that's hurt you."

My mouth drops open like it did the first time I saw him, but he doesn't let up and keeps slamming me with his truths.

"You're so incredibly beautiful and brave and kind and sweet. I'm looking forward to getting to know you more. Christ... please tell me you feel the same. Tell me I'm not alone in this, alone with this aching need to be near you. I want you with me when you leave here, but I can't take you until you know for sure. I think coming here tomorrow will help you decide."

He wipes away my tears as they fall, moved and overwhelmed by his words. I believe he's being truthful, but I'm scared he's going to change his mind when he gets to know me. There's also a niggling thought poking at me, asking 'but what if he doesn't?'

"Baby... tell me you want me to come back in the morning." I scream *YES* in my head. Thankfully, I'm not that out of it that I can't control myself.

"Yes. I would very much love if you came back in the morning, Dr. Blackwell."

"Say my name, Nora..."

"William." I blush and look down at my hands.

"Good girl." He grabs the sides of my face again, running his thumbs across my brows, over my lips, down to my chin. Pulling my lip down on the way, his eyes following. "Sweet girl..." He's whispering like he's talking to himself and no longer me. "*My girl...*"

A shudder runs through me. I know he feels it when his grip tightens slightly, responding to it. His name is forced from me and I can't keep it in. "William, I-"

His lips cut me off. They're gentle, warm... *delicious*. Touching mine so lightly, I think he's afraid of hurting me. The slight tickle across my upper and then lower lip as he grazes his across them is intoxicating. I've never been kissed before. Thank God too because I'm seriously worried about having a heart attack right now. My heart is pounding wildly as he shares my air, breathing his warm into me.

I can't hold back the small groan that escapes from deep inside. His hands tighten more, not letting me go or move from where he's holding me. He doesn't move his lips away when he asks, "Nora... is this okay?"

I moan out a '*yes*,' hoping to encourage him to increase the pressure on my mouth. The tip of his tongue licks its way across my bottom lip, forcing me to part my lips to allow his tongue entry to caress my own.

This time, *he* groans as he delves into my mouth. I want to sink my body into his, feel his arms wrap around me and pull me closer, but he doesn't. Probably so he doesn't hurt me. I wish he would, though. I don't care about any of my pain right now. My only concern is feeling him take over all of my senses.

His kiss becomes quicker, more desperate and notching up in intensity for a moment before he pulls away abruptly... both of us gasping for air while staring at each other. My God, I'll never be the same. He's irrevocably changed my DNA to require him for survival. He looks as surprised and shocked by that kiss as I am.

"I won't apologize," he tells me, firm in his convictions.

"Don't..." I agree, staring at his mouth, wishing he'd keep going.

"I want to come here tomorrow."

"Please..." My please is begging for more than just his company here. I'm begging for more of him, more of his contact, more of his warmth. I'm begging for his affection and time. The idea of begging for his love crosses my mind, but I shut it down. I'm already so far gone for this man that it'll break me if I beg for that and don't get it.

Another soft kiss, less intense but no less impactful, is delivered to my mouth before he backs away further than he was when he first came to me.

I'm startled as a laugh bursts out of me when he gives me the biggest smile and an exaggerated wink.

"I'm coming back for you, Nora. Sleep well."

My tongue is too busy remembering his flavor to respond as I watch him walk out the door.

# Chapter 6

## *William*

I spent the rest of my night obsessing over that kiss. It changed me. She tasted like my future, and I can't wait to do it again.

By this morning, I've realized that I may have acted too quickly last night. She's so innocent, never even had a boyfriend before. There's no doubt that she's a virgin. I shouldn't have been so forward, even with how driven I felt.

Scrubbing the stubble on my cheek as I drive back to North Valley, I can't help but kick myself in the ass. She's injured, drugged up. Did I take advantage of her? I hope to God she doesn't feel like I did.

I'm still nervous about her reaction to me when I walk into her room. I shouldn't have worried, though. Her smile at seeing me is enough to convince me that she's still on board. She still feels this. Whatever *this* is.

I debated on whether I should hold myself back from her this morning, back off a bit and let her decide how fast she wants to proceed. Seeing her laying there, looking more alert and a million times better, my desire for her wins out.

"Hi…" I don't slow down when she greets me and lean over to plant another kiss on her lips. She softens immediately for me, and I feel her smile against my lips.

"Hi, babydoll." Pulling back, I roam my eyes over her face to check in on how she's doing. "You're feeling better, aren't you?"

"I really am. I'm still extremely sore and tired, but I slept well last night." Her blush lights up her face, making it obvious that she's remembering our kiss last night.

"Oh yeah?" Smiling wide at her, I can't help but tease her. "Why's that?"

She bites her lip, shy to answer me. "Well… umm…" Twisting her fingers together, she blows out her breath and focuses on a spot over my shoulder. "You know why…"

"I'll give you a pass this time, but there's no need to be shy." I chuckle at her bashful smile, like she's worried that she shouldn't have enjoyed it and is reluctant to talk about it.

Pulling the chair we keep in these rooms for visiting family members over to the side of her bed, I sit down and really look at her. "Tell me how you're really feeling today. Who's been in to see you so far?"

"I promise, I'm feeling all right. My chest is really sore, but it's been easier to breathe this morning. My headache is almost completely gone too, and I'm not dizzy anymore when I try to sit up.

The bump on my head is still tender, but I don't notice it unless I accidentally press on it."

Nodding my head, I'm happy with everything she's saying. "That's so good. Has the doctor come in yet?"

Nora gives me a sly smile. "Aside from you? Not yet."

I frown at that. It's almost nine in the morning. "You've eaten, right?"

"I had some oatmeal about an hour ago." At least she's eaten. It's rare that I've been on this side of things, and I have to try not to be critical of the care she's received so far today.

Jumping up, I look at the computer to see who's on the floor for the day. Reading her notes and vitals throughout the night, I roll my eyes when I see that it's Baker as the on-call physician. He's not terrible, but he's never done more than he has to.

"Dr. Bla-... uh, I mean William. It's fine. I'm sure they'll be in shortly. I promise I'm okay." She assures me, probably seeing the frustration on my face.

"They haven't given you any meds since just after midnight." Clicking through her pages, I keep reading as I ask her questions. "Are you sure you're feeling alright? Where are you at on the pain scale? Have you been using your spirometer?"

My attention is pulled away from the screen when I hear a giggle come from her. "What are you laughing at?" I can't stop from smiling back at her, her giggle is fucking adorable.

"You... it's like you can't help yourself. Honestly, I'm okay. The pain meds are just barely starting to wear off. I'll be okay until they come back in with some more. You really don't need to work today." She sounds positive, reassuring me that she's not just feeding me a line of bullshit.

Throwing my hands up, she laughs when I say, "Fine, *fine*! I'll chill out."

Settling back into my chair and scooting as close to her as I can without hovering, I study her. The light-heartedness we were just feeling disappears quickly as the seriousness of our positions sinks in. What she's been through sinks in. I lean forward, choking my words out. "Baby... they hurt you so bad."

Her eyes fill with those damn tears again, and I want to kick myself for pulling her out of her happy mood. I cradle her hand in mine while she pulls herself together. "I know. I just... I didn't know what else I could do, you know? It's my *home* and he's my dad."

"It's been going on a long time." It's not a question.

"Yeah... not always so bad, but there have been moments that were scary like this." She swallows her fear down as she talks about it.

"How long is a long time?"

"Umm... as long as I can remember." She looks away from me, like she's ashamed to tell me.

I shake her hand to get her attention. "Nora, you know it wasn't your fault, right? Neither of them ever had any right to hurt you like that." I refuse to let her feel humiliated by it, especially around me.

"I know... but if I had just done wh-" I have to stop her there.

"NO! Absolutely not. No matter what you did or didn't do, it wouldn't have changed what happened. If it wasn't whatever set him off this time, it would have been something else. Take my word when I tell you that plenty of people who get pulled out of the same type of situation you've been in feel the same way. Blaming themselves. Like if they were quieter, nicer, acted the way they were told, it wouldn't have happened." I won't let her spend a moment longer thinking otherwise. "It would have changed *nothing*."

She's full on crying now, so I slide up onto her bed and stroke the side of her head, tucking her silky curls behind her ear. "You understand me? You're a good person. A good girl..." Her lips tremble, absorbing everything I'm telling her.

I can't stop myself from pushing further. I feel almost obsessed with this desire to make her understand that this is something big between us. "You're *my* girl, aren't you, Nora?"

Whispering, she pleads with me, her breath shaky on the exhale. "Can I be? I really want to be..."

I kiss her again and speak against her lips. "You can... I want you to be mine."

Jesus Christ, this girl is melting my heart. It's like she's soaking in every moment of affection from me like she's been starved all her life. I won't let her go back to that house with her sperm donor. He isn't her family anymore. My home is her home now. *Our* home. I'm really looking forward to bringing her there.

"I know we were going to discuss options you have, what plans you need to make and where you can go, but we don't need to. Let's just agree that I'll bring you home with me when you're discharged. I want to take care of you." *Please agree babydoll.*

"Are you sure? I feel like it's such an imposition. I don't have anything to bring to the table. It won't be equal." That pisses me off. Most likely she's been taught that she must earn her way, earn affection from others. That nothing is given to her without her paying it back in some way.

"You're bringing yourself to the table. I don't care that you aren't bringing anything with you. That shit is just stuff. I don't need your stuff; I have plenty for both of us." I want her to know I'm not concerned about her money, or lack of it. I make plenty and have for a long time. I've been single most of my life and never really had a good reason to spend it. She gets to be my reason.

"I can really have you? Truly?" God damnit... her questions are so innocent sounding. I should feel bad, like I'm going to taint her, but I'm just selfish and twisted enough to be turned on by it, and that I get to keep her for myself.

"Yes baby. Be prepared because when you're all healed up, things will move fast. Take this time to wrap your head around that." She looks unsure of what I mean, so I clarify. "I'm going to take you..." I kiss her. "Love you..." I kiss her again. "Make you mine in every possible way a man can possess a woman." One more kiss. "I won't ask if it's all right. This, you and me, it's inevitable."

She's trembling. Whether it's from nerves, excitement, or arousal - none of it is bad. I take pride in the goosebumps that pop like a wave down her arms, her nipples hardening through her thin hospital gown, making themselves known for the first time to me. I continue to run my fingers through her hair, down the sides of her neck, arms and then weave my fingers together with hers.

"Will you crawl in here with me?" She's accepting me. *Us.* Her voice shakes when she asks. I feel good knowing that I affect her as much as she affects me.

"Yeah, I will. Let me go get Baker and have them get you checked and then I'll hold you for a while." I hop off the bed releasing her, and I'm surprised at how much harder it was to do than I anticipated.

I get Baker to come in while the nurses give her another round of meds to make her more comfortable. Her lungs are still clear and the bruising along her ribs has stopped spreading. It's darker than it was yesterday, but that's to be expected. They always look the worst a few days after receiving them.

Sometime during the night her catheter was removed. I wanted to help her to the bathroom, but she insisted the nurse help her instead. I get it, she's shy and this is new for her. Combine that with the fact that we only met yesterday – even though it feels like my soul has known her my whole life – it's a lot for a girl who's done nothing more than receive a few kisses.

Everyone's left, so I quietly ask the charge nurse to leave us be unless we call her. I've gotten a few curious glances, but no one has voiced the actual question to me. Technically, I'm doing nothing wrong. Nothing happened until after I was off shift, and Nora isn't my patient any longer.

I dim the lights. Her headache is coming back a bit because they took too fucking long to administer her next set of pain meds. I reign in my irritation and just do what I can for her. I don't need to be her doctor right now, and should really let her sleep. I can settle in the chair and do some paperwork quietly, give her time to nap.

Peeking her eyes open at me, it's obvious she's fighting sleep. "Will you lay with me for a little while?" How do I tell her no? The charts can wait.

"Sure thing babydoll. Let me help you shift over a bit." Together, we manage to slide her over so there's enough room for me to lay next to her. I rearrange the tubing from her IV, kick off my shoes and crawl in next to her.

"I remember when you were with me yesterday in the ER. I didn't get to see you, and I barely remember everything that went on. What I do remember is your warmth. I recognized it immediately as something good, and you were so comforting and peaceful." She giggles sleepily after finishing that.

"What's so funny?" I want to know what's got her laughing.

"I remember thinking you smelled like warm. Like I could taste it radiating from you. It's silly, tasting a feeling." Her eyes are closed now and she's smiling to herself.

You couldn't pay me enough to move away from her, holding her like this. She can't curl into me because of her ribs, but she's leaning her head into my chest, my arm tucked under her neck while fingers run through her hair to soothe her. "It's not silly." I kiss the top of her head and lay my cheek against it, smelling her hair. "You can taste my warm anytime you want, sweetheart."

I grin against her hair while I wait for her to process that. It takes a moment, probably because her mind is running a little slower. I know the moment she catches my double meaning when her shoulders start to shake and she snorts out a laugh. "So dirty..." she whispers.

"Can't help it," I chuckle with her as I continue to stroke her. I hope it's not bothering her, my constant touching. "Go to sleep, I'll be here when you wake up." She's relaxing further into me the longer I lay next to her.

"Tell me a story?" Nora murmurs her request, halfway asleep already. "...your voice rumbles... a story about giants..."

"Giants, huh?" I close my eyes as well, thinking about how to start.

"Mmhmm... 'Cuz you're my giant..." My heart skips when she claims me. I give her what she wants and tell her a story about her giant.

~ ~ ~ ~ ~

I must have dozed off with her because I'm jolted awake when I hear yelling directly outside of Nora's room. The door is open because a nurse is sliding inside which let the commotion outside rattle through the room.

"The fuck is going on?" I ask, blinking my eyes a few times to clear the sleep from them. I look down and see Nora is awake, eyes wide and fearful, staring at the door. "Sweetheart, what's wrong?"

She looks at me briefly and then back to the door. "It's Uncle Rich. Do you think they'll let him in? He sounds so mad!" I can hear him shouting and demanding that he be allowed to talk to his niece, that it's his right.

"I'll be right back." I kiss her head and get out of the bed, sliding my shoes on quickly to go out there and get rid of him. Thank God I'm used to having to wake up alert and ready at a moment's notice because the adrenaline is already racing through my body.

I don't even make it halfway to the door when it's shoved open and her uncle plows his way in, followed by a few nurses yelling and demanding he leave. I hear Nora squeak in fear behind me.

"*YOU FUCKING BITCH!*" he screams at her, not caring that anyone else is in the room, and completely focused on her. "You fucking *trash*, turning my brother in for no good fucking reason. You owe him *everything!*" His spit is flying as he continues to scream, stalking closer as he continues to insult her and spew out his hatred.

"Go! Call security," I tell the nurse whose name I don't know, but recognize, nonetheless. She runs out of the room and I'm quick to put myself between Nora and her uncle.

"Think about what you're doing here." I place my hand on his chest, but he just shoves it off and keeps pushing toward my girl.

"Get the fuck away from me. I can do whatever the fuck I want. And *you*!" He jabs his finger in her direction. A brief look at her has me seeing red. She's hunched down in her sheets, shoulders forward and shaking, struggling to breathe through her quick gasping breaths. He needs to leave *NOW*.

I plant my hands against his chest and shove him away from her. "Last chance. Back the fuck off and leave. You're already in enough trouble as it is." I pull myself to my full height and do my best to fill the space between Nora and the threat.

"Fuck. OFF!" he yells into my face. He tries to take a swing at me, but I'm ready for him. I step out of the way, throwing him off balance, which causes him to stumble when he doesn't make contact.

"Wrong fucking choice," I snap my hand out to grab his throat and slam him onto his back, holding him to the ground.

"*William!*" I hear Nora sob out and it kills me to ignore her right now. I watch as Rich gasps for the air that was knocked out of him when his body slammed to the floor, and I take the advantage.

Leaning over his body and gripping his neck tighter, I deliver a warning that I *really* hope he takes to heart. "You will back the fuck off and walk out of this room when I let you up. Forget you even know that girl over there… she's nothing to you anymore. You are *nothing*. Tell your piece of shit brother the same."

His eyes are furious, shooting daggers at me even while his eyes are bulging from the lack of oxygen. I hiss through my teeth so only he can hear me now. "If I see you or your brother again, I'll fucking end you. I know a few hundred ways to kill you without leaving a trace and I'll use the most painful one I can imagine. No. Contact. You both will fucking disappear from her life. Understood?"

I watch as the realization that I'm not bluffing starts to sink in, and that loathing turns into fear. He opens his mouth to answer me, but my hand is cutting off all sound. I let up slightly to allow him an answer.

Gasping, he coughs to catch his breath and wheezes out, "Ye-Yes… fuck, man. Let *go*! I got it!" He's trying to pull my hand away. I give him another tight squeeze until I see the worry that I won't let go pass through his eyes, and then I release him.

"Get the fuck out of here. I'm sure security is waiting to escort you. She doesn't see you again. Don't forget." I can still hear Nora sobbing behind me. I need to get him out of here so I can go to her.

Rich struggles to his feet and backs away from me. "Fuck both of you!" he yells and then storms out of the room. I lock the door behind him and hurry over to my sweet girl.

I'm really hoping that she's not scared of how I handled him because I force my way back on to her bed and pull her up into my lap, careful to not jostle her too much. She's still sobbing and I'm not sure if she can see me through all those tears. My stomach clenches as I watch her. I can see the pain her crying is causing her across her face.

"Shh... shh... Love..." I kiss her cheeks, her forehead, the crown of her head, all while gently rocking her and speaking calming words. "He's gone baby... I got you... You're all right now..."

She's finally able to catch her breath, but the tears are still flowing. She hasn't said anything to me yet and I'm worried. I tilt her chin up to look at me, wiping those damn tears away, over and over as they fall.

With another kiss to her salty lips, I feel my own emotions threatening to choke me as I watch the agony she's in sweep across her face. Whispering, I lean my forehead against hers and plead with her, "Please, baby... you're breaking my heart here. Tell me how to make this better for you. You're going to hurt yourself if you keep on like this."

I wait for her to come back to me and allow my words to pull her out of this. She grips the front of my shirt, holding tight, and sniffles back the remaining tears she's working hard to get under control.

"They hate me so much, William…" Sighing, I just kiss her and tell her the only thing I can.

"I'll love you twice as hard to make you forget."

# Chapter 7

## *Nora*

*"I'll love you twice as hard to make you forget..."*

William is certainly sticking to his word. I've been here for another six days, and he's spent every moment he could right here with me. He had to work for most of those days, though. He did stop in to say good morning when he got in, and ate lunch in my room except one of the days when a trauma in the ER kept him from me. The evenings he stayed until I fell asleep.

We've talked for hours, getting to know one another. I learned that he's from the East Coast and grew up in Maryland near DC. His family is still there, both of his parents and two brothers, one older and one younger. The brothers are both newly married, so no nieces or nephews yet. He went to school in Boston and then transferred here to North Valley Medical Center where he began his residency.

He's a perfectionist. It coincides well with my minor quirks, which he thinks is adorable. He's extremely health conscious and works out every day after work. I won't ever begrudge him that because those muscles of his make me drool. He's an avid reader, Stephen King and Gillian Flynn are two of his regular go to authors. I've never read any of Flynn's work, so he's going to let me read his favorite when we get to his home.

He enjoys cooking, logic puzzles, which I also enjoy, and he prefers to be active outside rather than inside. He doesn't like going out to party on the weekends. He said he did that enough when he was in his twenties and that he's over it. That's fine with me. I've seen enough drunkenness in my lifetime that if I never go to a bar, I won't be disappointed.

William is also extremely romantic, but I think that's only as side he's shown to me. He was whispering something sweet in my ear when Bernice had stopped by to say hello, and the look that crossed her face when she watched him was hilarious. She looked at him like she'd never seen him before. She did let me know on the side when he stepped out to take a call that she's never seen him like this before. Having known him for over a decade, I trust her when she tells me that.

I've shared a lot of my passions and goals with him as well. A lot of them I didn't think were attainable because of the home situation I was in with my dad and Uncle Rich – both of whom I haven't heard a peep from.

William told me that dad was arrested after he kicked both dad and my uncle out of my room. The report he and Bernie made ended up being critical for my protection because it gave the cops an excuse to arrest him. Dad was released the next day when, oddly enough, Uncle Rich was taken in for his stunt in here. William helped me with the paperwork to file a temporary restraining order against both of them. So far so good, they've both left me alone.

He knows that I've always dreamed to go to college and that I didn't think I ever would be able to go because of the money. He's going to help me apply while I take some time to research loans and funding. He offered to pay for it, but I told him I didn't want that. William was *not* happy that I told him no until I explained that it would mean more to me to do it on my own. It's a way to prove to myself that I don't have to stay dependent to survive.

We've talked about what I would like to study. He joked that I should make perfumes for a living since I loved clean and fresh scents. All joking aside, his suggestion really resonated with me and I very much would love to do exactly that. I'm planning to start with Chemistry and get a feel for what type of degree in that field I'd like to go for.

I'm excited to spend the next few seasons with him since it's only mid-fall right now, and I don't plan to start until *next* fall. Furthermore, I've found that I absolutely *love* making him laugh. Personally, I think I'm hilarious, and I won't let him convince me otherwise.

I'm in love with him.

It's fast and probably too early, which is why I haven't told him. I'm also afraid that if I tell him and he doesn't say it back, it'll mean that he's not as ready for me as I am for him. What if he sees it as me being too needy? When our conversations start to get deep and we start talking about us, I try to subtly change the subject. I can't bear to risk him telling me he's not in the same place I am emotionally.

My anxiety is getting the best of me right now. William is outside pulling together the discharge paperwork for me so we can get out of here. He's taking the next week off and plans to stay home so he's able to help me when we get there. I'm feeling stronger, but still so sore that the smallest tasks are difficult for me.

I'm ignoring the fact that when we get to his home, he'll be the one to help me shower. He hasn't seen me naked yet. The most he's seen of my body was when he examined me the day I was brought to the ER, and when the doctors stop in to see how my ribs are doing.

I know I'm thin, but what happens if when he sees, he finds my body unattractive? What if he's expecting to see someone who looks like those models who have spreads in magazines, dressed in bikinis and underwear with all those curves and big boobs. I have some curves, but they're slight. Just enough to make me seem like I've got a waist, but no hips round enough to swing when I walk. He's told me I'm pretty and beautiful, but will he find me sexy?

"What's got you thinking so hard, babydoll? You're going to give yourself wrinkles if you keep frowning like that." When he kisses me, it pounds so hard that my ribs ache. But it's nothing compared to when he praises me and smiles at me and-

"Seriously Nora, are you okay? You look like you're a million miles away." He squats in front of me where I'm sitting on the bed to look up at me.

"You know, it's insane that you're almost equal height with me sitting up like this and you're squatting on the ground. You really are a giant." I can't stop the smile and blush when I think about how massive he is.

I don't care who you are, but the idea of being completely surrounded by another person, and small enough to be carried around, is exciting.

"Well, I want to avoid giving you a neck ache by making you look up at me all the time. Besides, being this tall has its advantages that you'll soon discover." He winks and stands up, going to gather my bag of the few possessions I've acquired while here for the past week. "Are you ready to go? I've freed you, but we need to make our escape now before we're intercepted. You've made every damn nurse in here fall in love with you."

Grinning at him, I grab the hand he's holding out to me and slowly pull myself up. Walking has gotten easier each day. It's the aches and stiffness I feel after laying down for a long time that are slowing me down now.

I bite my lip and look around the room to make sure I'm not forgetting anything. "I'm ready... I think." Is it awful that I'm scared to leave? What if he gets me to his house and realizes it was a mistake? Where will I go?

I jump when I hear my bag hit the floor and find my chin being tilted up to look at him. God, his eyes are so incredible. "Tell me what you're worried about. Your stress and anxiety are written all over your face, sweetheart."

Chewing on my cheek, I debate on telling him, then quickly dismiss it. I have to know. "Are you sure you want me to go home with you?"

His eyes widen and he looks surprised at my question. "What the fuck? Of course I do... Do *you* not want to come?" Shoot. Now I've got him questioning me.

"Definitely YES!" He smiles and comes in to kiss me, but stops when I keep talking. "But... umm... what if after I get there you don't want me to stay anymore? I don't want you to feel like you're obligated because this is the arrangement we've decided on without giving you any options or outs."

I take a deep breath after spewing all that out and then hold it until he answers me.

"Has this been eating at you all morning, sweetheart?" He's only concerned and not mad, thankfully.

I hold up two fingers with about an inch of space between them. "Maybe just a lot..." He chuckles at my joke and then pets my hair. He's forever doing that, stroking my hair and running his fingers through it. I've already promised not to cut it for a long while.

"Hear me out for a second. How old am I?"

I scrunch my nose over his question. "You're 37."

"37... Would you say I'm smart?" The petting hasn't stopped and it's a little distracting.

I nod my head and smile. "Yes, I think you're brilliant!"

William places a kiss on the tip of my nose. "Ditto. So, being the age I am, having quite a few life experiences under my belt, and as intelligent as Einstein... don't laugh at that!" He playfully scolds me when I snicker.

"Sorry, sorry..." I bite my tongue and let him continue.

"As I was saying. Life experiences... I've had a lot. I've dated, some more serious than others. I know what works for me and what doesn't, and I know when I've found something unique and special. Something that will only come around once in my life. There's no doubt in my mind that this is the right decision for us."

"...Promise?" I ask, leaning my head in to his chest and let him rub my back.

"I swear, Nora. I told you... I have to have you. Even if you decide you want to leave, I'll just follow. I hate to see you worry." His lips are pressed to my head, and I feel his hot breath warming my scalp as he breathes me in.

"Can I tell you something? But I need you to not freak if you don't like it, all right?"

His chest rumbles as he laughs at me. "Promise. I won't be upset by whatever you tell me, unless it's to say that you're not letting me bring you home. If you did, I'd have to fi-"

"I love you."

He pauses his hand for a second before continuing his stroking. I don't let him say anything because I couldn't bear to hear him tell me he doesn't, even knowing it's unlikely he does because again, it's only been a week. I talk into his chest; not brave enough to see what his reaction is.

"I love you, William… like a lot. I know it's only been a week and I'm only eighteen. I'm sure I seem silly-"

"Stop baby." I bite my lip. Damnit… Why did I say it? It wouldn't have hurt anyone if I had waited… oh I don't know… a few hundred years to say it!

My heart sinks when I feel him pull away from me. "William, I'm so-"

"I said stop. Hold on a second." He's looking around the room before he grabs my hand to pull me over to the chair he's had his butt planted in for a week. Leaning down, he reaches one arm under me and the other around my back and before I know it, he's lifted me up to stand on the chair.

"I need you to be up here for a minute." His eyes look like they're glassy, and I still can't tell if he's happy or unhappy that I said it. Staring at me for what feels like an eternity, he finally brushes his lips across mine before pulling back again. "Okay. Say it again, this time so I can watch your face when you do."

Lord, this is embarrassing. "I uhh…" I cough and force the words out. "I'm in love with you. Pretty sure I have been since I smelled you in the ER."

William's head tilts back when he barks out a laugh at the ceiling, planting his hands on his hips. He's still looking up when he stops laughing and he mutters *"Jesus Christ"* under his breath, before grabbing on to me and pulling me closer.

"First, so you don't panic any longer, I'm so fucking in love with you that I wouldn't be able to breathe if you weren't with me." I don't get a chance to respond before he slams his lips to mine and claims my mouth way more aggressively than he's ever kissed me before. Holy crap. My arousal is rising so quickly that I have to squeeze my legs together to ease the ache.

Ending the kiss as abruptly as he started it, he keeps going. "Second, you sort of ruined the plans I had to tell you when we got home. I had planned it all out. I was going to tell you that I'm obsessed with you, and in love with you, and how honored and eager I am to spend a lifetime with you."

I wipe the tears away as he keeps talking. At least they're falling for a perfect reason this time.

"And third, I'm really fucking pissed at your dad right now because I want nothing more than to take you home, lay you down in my bed and show you exactly how I feel about you."

"Well, if you think about it, we should thank him for kicking me." Oh man, William is not happy with me saying that.

"Are you kidding me? In what universe are you living in where he deserves thanks for being the piece of shit that doesn't deserve to breathe the same air as you?"

"You're not wrong. I just mean that had he not done it, I wouldn't have been brought in and we wouldn't have met."

Shaking his head, he disagrees. "Nope. This town is not that big. We would have eventually run in to each other. I have no doubt about that. We were inevitable."

Giggling, I don't argue with him. "Fine. I take it back..." Turning more serious, I need him to know how much this means to me. "William, it's stupid, but thank you for loving me back." I press a kiss to the side of his neck and feel a shiver run up his spine, thrilled for getting a physical reaction out of him as well.

"Don't thank me. It's an honor," he answers huskily, then he lifts me back down to the ground and grabs my hand. "Enough of this now, let's go home."

Walking to the door, he stops me. "Shit, wait here a moment. I need to grab a wheelchair." He sticks his head out the door and looks around, then quickly jogs down the hallway to grab one.

Looking at it, I can't help but cringe. "Can't we just walk to the car?" I feel silly sitting in there when I'm perfectly capable of using my legs. They aren't what's injured.

"No. Sit." I raise my eyebrow at him to hide the little shiver that runs down my spine at his command. We stare at each other for a moment while he considers me, then a wicked grin spreads across his face, and he flashes his teeth at me. Leaning forward, bringing himself down to make sure I'm listening, he speaks under his breath so others won't hear. "If you be a good girl and let me push you out of here, I promise to help you sleep *real* good tonight."

Clearly there's innuendo there, but my lack of experience is leaving me completely blank on what he means. Shoot, I can feel the heat rising in my face when I think of all the things that I know of. I can't help the quieter tone of my voice when I ask him to clarify. "So, umm… I know I should know what you mean, but I don't… uhhh… I'm not sure wh-what…" I trail off, stuttering and unsure how to ask about things I don't know.

Coming closer, he picks me up again, careful not to put any pressure on my sore ribs, and sets me gently on the seat of the chair. He squats down to unlock the wheels so it can move, and then looks around quickly to see if anyone is nearby. Grabbing hold of the arms, his lips touch my ear, and he whispers just as softly back to me, "Your innocence is intoxicating…"

Then he nips the lobe. *Oh God…* The feel of his scruff that's grown over the past twenty-four hours rubbing along my neck makes my nipples harden immediately. Standing back up, he sets my bag on my lap and says nothing more.

I peek over my shoulder to look up at him. He looks down at me and runs his hand along the hair that's flowing down my back, giving me a wink. Yeah, I'm definitely way out of my element.

## Chapter 8

## *Nora*

My mouth falls open the moment I realize what house we are pulling up to. It's a beautiful two-story craftsman house set back in the woods near the end of his property. It's a dark brown wood and looks like it was built specifically for William, masculine to its core.

"I didn't even know there were houses like this around here." I can't keep the awe out of my voice.

Smiling at me, he pulls into the garage. Looking out my window, I see he's got another smaller, sporty looking car and a motorcycle. I've seen the car on television, but I couldn't tell you what kind it is. All I know is it looks fast.

"That's a Bentley Continental GT."

"I don't even know what that means." Leaning forward a little more, my nose comes close to the window as I look at it. "Is looks extremely fast." Now he's chuckling at me.

"It *is* extremely fast. Stay there a moment. I'm going to run your bag inside and then help you out." He reaches behind him to grab my bag, slipping out of the car. He's only gone about a minute before he's back at my side, opening the door for me. "Come on, sweet girl. Let's get you upstairs and settled in."

I barely have a chance to look around at all his stuff and all the rooms we pass through before I'm standing in a large bedroom with a massive king-size bed, raised on a platform. Spying some items on the dressers and pictures on the wall, along with a pair of his slacks thrown over the foot of the bed, I realize he's brought me to his bedroom.

My voice squeaks when I ask, "This is your room?" I'm feeling a sliver of nervousness creep back into my stomach as my new reality and situation sinks in. I'm not uncomfortable, but I've never been inside a man's room before...

Eyeing me, he speaks gently as he gauges my reaction. "Is this okay with you? It was probably presumptive to assume you'll sleep in here with me, but I swear it's not just because I want you in here, which I very much do by the way. There is also the benefit that I can help you out at night if you need it. Plus, this bed is by far the most comfortable one in the house."

It makes sense, and I appreciate his honesty. I nod my head slowly as I continue to look around the room. "I'm fine with that," I softly croak out and then clear my throat. "Umm... would it be alright if I took a shower before I laid down? I feel like I need to wash the hospital smell from me."

"Absolutely." Grabbing my hand, he pulls me in to the bathroom. He reaches into a decent sized walk-in shower with two shower heads and some jets built into the wall, and turns on the water. "I'll let you do your thing. Get undressed, brush your teeth, whatever you need to do. Do you want me to grab you a change of clothes out of your bag, or would you rather wear one of my larger shirts? Mine would probably feel less constrictive on your ribs."

"Yours please." I smile at him in thanks when he dips his head and brushes his lips along mine before stepping back. I barely had a chance to register he was there, and I can't stop the disappointment from crossing my face.

William reaches up and strokes my cheek, then slides his thumb a short way into my mouth, then swipes it across my bottom lip. "Plenty of time, babydoll. I'll check on you in a few to see if you need a hand with anything."

Speechless.

He leaves the bathroom and pulls the door closed behind him. The room is already starting to steam up, so I remove my clothes as quickly as I can, which is still significantly slower than normal. The drive and walk through the house were enough to distract me from noticing the aches along my side. I took some over the counter pain medication an hour or two ago, so it's still feeling dulled. Not the sharp, stabbing pain I feel when unmedicated.

After using the bathroom, I wash my hands and then search through a few drawers to find a spare toothbrush along with his toothpaste. It was a successful search, so I clean my teeth aggressively and then walk into the shower.

I can't stop the groan that releases from the back of my throat when I feel the almost too hot water hit my skin. Add in the luxurious water pressure that makes me feel like I'm getting massaged, and I'm in heaven. I can only stand there, under the stream, soaking in the comfort getting clean gives me. I try not to let my thoughts run away from me, back to where I was *before* I met William.

I'm not certain how long I just stand here, but I'm startled when I hear him, almost directly behind me, whisper into my ear. "Baby girl… are you alright?" I feel his warmth all along my back and I can't stop my shiver at his proximity, nor can I stop the red creeping along my chest. He had a direct view of my ass when he came in here, and it's the first time I've been fully naked in front of him.

"Y-Yes… Sorry, I shouldn't have wasted so much water."

"Hush. You're alright." He stops my ramble that was quickly swirling down the rabbit hole into nervous chatter to fill the silence. He steps even closer, bringing his chest to connect with my back. He reaches around me and grabs one of the bottles off the wall. "Do you have a problem with me coming in to help you?" He's speaking to me in a low, husky voice. Either to soothe me or because of the arousal from the intimate predicament he's put us in.

"Uhh... n-" my voice squeaks. Nerves mixed with excitement are closing my throat up so no sound can escape. I just shake my head so he knows I'm fine with him in here.

His breath fans across the side of my neck. I'm not sure if it's the very tip of his tongue, or his nose that runs along a path from the space between the bottom of my neck and shoulder, to just behind my ear. The shudder that runs through me and the goosebumps that explode from my arms, along with the tightening of my nipples, is overwhelming. I'm responding strongly to the sensitive spot he's giving attention to.

"I'm going to wash your hair for you, so you don't have to try to lift your arms up to do it yourself." I hear the pop of a cap as he opens the bottle he snagged a moment before. Moving back a few inches from me, but not so far that I can't feel his warmth still engulfing me, he takes his time to massage the shampoo into my hair.

Again, the groan that escapes from me is unconsciously released as his fingers dig in, tugging slightly on the roots. It doesn't hurt. It's a good, dominating pull that I can feel all the way to between my legs, like the nerves are connected from one to the other. Thank God I'm in the shower because there's no way that the wetness trickling from me wouldn't have made itself apparent in my clothes.

He continues to massage and lather the shampoo for another few minutes, much longer than it takes me to do, but I'm not complaining. "Turn around so I can rinse your hair."

Turning, I keep my arms up against my breasts, an involuntary need to cover myself. My eyes have been closed through the entire hair washing. I crack them open to see an incredibly well-defined chest with some sort of tribal design tattooed on the left pec. Quickly glancing down, I see that he's is not totally naked, but he's close to it. Instead, he's kept his boxer briefs on, which do not fully hide the enlarged bulge it's barely holding within.

I squeak out another noise, this one slightly higher than the last, and I turn my gaze upwards to look at the ceiling tiles. With a smirk, he captures each side of my head and tilts it back under the water. It only takes a moment to rinse all the shampoo out thanks to his fingers running through the length.

I can't take my eyes from his face, watching as he concentrates on what he's doing. Pulling his hands from my hair, he strokes my face before running his hands down to settle them on each shoulder. His eyes followed the path they took until they stilled, then they shot back to mine, all the heat and desire unhidden from me.

Without releasing the hold on me, he grabs hold of my hands and pulls my arms from my chest, slow enough that I'm confident if I stopped him, he would have allowed me to stay covered. With my arms down at my sides, his gaze holds me for a moment longer before letting it drop to my chest. His nostrils imperceptibly flare at his first sight of me, and he releases a shuttered breath.

Trembling, I wait for him to say something as he examines me. The longer he goes without speaking, the more my excitement turns to concern, then worry over whether he finds my body attractive or not.

I inhale sharply when William reaches up to palm the side of my left breast, his hand so large that I can feel his fingers grazing the edge of my shoulder blade. He pinches his lip between two fingers while he inspects me, running his thumb lazily back and forth across the tip of my nipple. Every swipe of his thumb makes my stomach tumble and my body jolt at the foreign feeling of someone else touching me.

Eventually, he slides the hand on my breast to lay flat against my back and he pulls me to him until our chests connect. "You are beyond gorgeous. I can't find the words to fully explain how fucking lucky I feel to be standing here with your body pressed to mine like this."

I feel like my brain is short-circuiting. I'm so stunned by his compliment, that I awkwardly blurt out, "You're really big…" *Oh God! What is wrong with me?* I want to crawl into a hole and hide. If he wasn't thinking about the difference in our age before, I don't know how he wouldn't be now!

"It's wonderfully adorable watching that blush run across your cheeks and chest. I had wondered how far down it went when you were clothed, so I'm glad to finally have that answer now." He's smiling at me, but the desire hasn't left his face.

"I'm so-sorry for being so awkward… I just never…" I trail off when I feel his cock pulse against my stomach once when I say that.

He knows I'm a virgin but telling him I have literally zero experience in the world of sex has a manic look flaring in his eyes.

Gathering me close to him, he reaches down with both his hands to cup my ass and lift me up, making it easier for our mouths to touch. Having a hand on each plump cheek, he squeezes, making me hiss.

His fingers stretch to touch the creases between the back of my thigh and underside of my cheeks, dipping into the overheated crevice between my legs. The fingers walking along my skin have me hyper aware of every single touch, causing my pussy to get wetter and wetter the longer it goes on.

Running his tongue along my bottom lip, I feel both of us breathing heavier. Nipping where his tongue just was, he quickly soothes the sharp pinch, then dives his tongue into my mouth. The gasp from his bite forced my mouth open and gave him access to stroke mine in tempo with the dipping and sliding of his fingers between my legs.

We kiss for a long while, his kisses growing more aggressive the longer it goes on. I'm doing my best not to pass out from all the new stimulation I'm experiencing, as tingles and a warm, numb feeling starts at my feet and runs up my legs.

He tears his mouth away from me, panting as he slides me down his body, forcing me to feel every bump and ridge of muscle, pounding with his heartbeat. I can feel his cock now standing fully erect. "I know I can't have you entirely until you're better, but right now, I have to taste you."

I quickly nod my head. "Please William. I need… something. I don't kn-"

"I know what you need, princess." Shutting the water off, he grabs a towel and, without drying either of us off, picks me up and carries me in to his bedroom. Tossing the towel on the bed, he sets me down gently so as not to rattle my ribs. I watch as he spreads the towel out on the bed and lifts me once more to settle me on top of it.

I give him a confused look as he arranges me into the position he wants, and with a wink, he answers my unasked question. "Your hair is dripping wet." Then, looking down between my legs, he adds with a wicked smirk, *"You're* dripping wet."

"Oh God, I'm sorry!" I make to move off the bed, horrified by how slick I am. The heat of my arousal is pulsing heavily within my pussy lips.

"Stop." I freeze at his command. "I'm just going to assume that everything will be new for you, so trust me when I say that I *want* you dripping for me." He lays me back again on the towel with a soft kiss before starting his trail down. William works his way from the underside of my chin, licks and sucks all along my collar bone, before finally reaching my nipples that are so hard, it's almost painful.

Circling his tongue around my nipple while cupping and squeezing the other, William teases me until I'm panting and arching my back in hopes that he'll take my nipple into his mouth. He stops to look up at me. "You need to lay still so you don't hurt yourself. If you can't, then we'll have to stop... Do you want me to stop?" He's asking me this as he's running his fingers up and down my side, each time getting closer to my core.

"I will, I will," I quickly promise, even nodding at the same time to show him I'm being earnest. He chuckles at my eagerness and then finally, *finally*, he pulls the rosy tip of my nipple into his mouth and sucks. There's no controlling the moan at the incredibly sweet relief he gives me.

Biting the tip gently, he draws my nipple in further and flicks his tongue across it before sucking harder and then releasing it with a pop. Giving the same attention to the other side, he's still working his hand lower along my stomach, dipping his finger into my belly button which forces me to suck in a breath at the tickling feeling, my stomach caving in. I had no idea I was ticklish there; no one's ever tickled me before.

Alternating, he gives each bud one more gentle kiss, then removes his hands from me and places them on either side of my shoulders to come back even with my face. "I'm going to taste you now, Nora. Do you know what that means?"

I know he means something more than what he's already done, but I'm unsure what he's getting at since he's already *been* licking me. "Umm... like you were just doing?" There's a tremor in my voice when I ask, but not from fear. Just from all the emotions and new sensations he's plying me with.

"No babydoll. It means I'm going to spread your legs as wide as you can go, and then I'm going to put my mouth on this sweet, sweet pussy that is incredibly needy right now. Your scent is so heady, it's making me ravenous to eat you… you understand now?" He doesn't move as he waits for my answer.

Good Lord, this man will shatter every illusion I've ever had of what happens between a man and a woman. I'm also loving that he's talking to me to ease some of my nervous energy. I can only answer one way because I *do* understand now. I lick my lips to wet them and whisper, "Yes, I understand now."

He doesn't kiss me on the lips again before heading back down my body, taking a quicker path this time. Between the valley of my breasts, the swell of my stomach and then, finally, he rests his lips at the top of my pubic bone.

Nuzzling me a moment there when he feels my muscles clenching and relaxing, he stays there until I relax all the way and get used to having him so close to my heat. He continues to rub his mouth there before laying open mouthed kisses as he drops to his knees at the edge of the bed. He kisses me down each thigh as he moves the left to lay open for him, flat against the bed. Keeping one hand there to hold my knee down, he moves his mouth and tongue back to my center, skipping over my pussy, and then heads down the other leg.

"I'm not going to spread you as far as I'd like to this time, but I'll hold your leg so you don't have to strain to stay open for me. Just relax, sweet girl." He may be talking to me, but he's staring at my pussy as he moves my other knee up and to the side a bit without irritating my injuries.

William leans down and inhales me. I want to hide from him, it feels so invasive and embarrassing, but the grunt he releases tells me that he's enjoying this.

"God baby, you're fucking beautiful here," he tells me, running a finger up my pussy, splitting my lips and opening me to him.

I'm trying to watch him when he gives himself permission to lick me. My head falls back to the bed as I feel him feast, running his tongue through my folds up to my clit, licking a circle around it before sucking it into his mouth. The pleasure he's giving me is heavenly, almost unearthly.

The things he's doing with his tongue make me want to worship him. He's sliding it inside me to taste me as deeply as he can reach, then flicking the tip of my clit and then nibbling along my lips. "God Will... That's... oh God, I'm going..."

My babbling trails off when I feel the orgasm build from deep within my core, deeper than I've ever felt it when I've tried to play with myself a few times growing up. "That's it, baby... Come for me, I want to taste all of you." He works his mouth on my pussy more urgently, sensing the orgasm building within me, my breaths coming heavier and heavier, telling him that I'm almost there.

William grips my thighs harder, digging his fingers in and forcing my left knee deeper into the mattress as he attacks my pussy. He sucks my clit entirely into his mouth again and this time bites down while flicking it with his tongue.

I *explode* in his mouth.

Screaming out his name, I feel each wave of pleasure William draws from me pass through my entire body, clenching and releasing at the same time. My pussy flutters at the emptiness I have there, knowing instinctually he's supposed to be there. He continues to lick at me until the calm takes over the violence of my muscles during the frenzy of my peak.

Groaning into the crease of my thigh and pussy, he continues to lick and suck and clean me up, praising me for being so good for him and giving me what he asked for. His attentions slow as my legs collapse. All tension has left my body.

I fall asleep to the sound of William's quiet laughter and a whispered, "*I love you, baby girl.*"

# Chapter 9

## *William*

Six weeks. Six agonizingly long, torturous, blissful weeks with this girl who I fall in love with more and more every day.

Nora is a wonder. She has worked so hard, following every instruction her new primary doctor has given her. She slept a lot those first two weeks, her body needing it after finally feeling like she can relax in a safe space.

I set her up with the best female physician we have, Dr. Diana Schaffer. No way am I letting any of my male coworkers touch my girl. Nora thinks I'm being ridiculous. I'm not… I've heard them talk when they're away from ears, their so called 'locker-room' talk. *Definitely* not sending her to one of them.

She had an appointment yesterday afternoon and I just now got off the phone with Diana. Nora's scan came back showing that her ribs are looking good. Her fractures are healed, but she'll still have minor sensitivity for a little while longer. Her mobility is good, and she only requires over the counter pain meds now and then if she's feeling sore. The ribs are still weak, so she has to be careful for a while, but she can go back to normal activities.

There's one *particular* activity that is in the forefront of my mind.

From the first day I brought her into my home and ate her pussy until she passed out, we've begun exploring each other. Last night, she stroked my cock until I shot my cum across her stomach. She's yet to take me in her mouth. Not because she hasn't wanted to, though. I've been holding her off because I wanted to avoid overwhelming her or hurt her while she was still healing.

Diana called early while I was moving some things around in the garage. Nora doesn't know it yet, but I have intentions to surprise her with a vehicle now that she's able to drive again. Grabbing a couple of bags I was filling with shit to toss, I throw them in the trash and then take the steps two at a time to my bedroom to hop in the shower.

Silently slipping in to my room, I see that she's still asleep naked in the center of the bed. That girl is so tiny that regardless of where she curls up, I still have a ton of space to stretch out. More often than not, the place she chooses to curl up is tucked into my side, leg wrapped over mine and face pressed into my chest.

I never thought myself to be a big into cuddling, but with Nora, I can't keep myself away from her. She's an addiction, an obsession I must keep near me, under me, on me, and any other way I can surround her. She tells me she loves to feel my 'warm,' that it's the first thing that's made her feel truly comfortable, protected, and loved.

Showering quickly and toweling off, I crawl onto the bed behind her and slowly pull the blanket down from her shoulders. Her body doesn't move, and I watch as the goosebumps rise along her skin as I expose inch by inch to the cooler air.

The blanket is down to her waist by the time she starts to shift, seeking the warmth she was just wrapped up in. Not to worry though, I'll have her warmed up soon enough. I plan on devouring her, heating her skin as I slide mine along hers. Fuck, I need to be inside of her.

I run my hand up her back and Nora moans my name, curling in on herself like a kitten stretching to be scratched. I feel a tiny bit bad for making her feel cold when she shivers, her nipples pointing more from the chill than arousal, but I'll change that.

I finish crawling up and spoon her, tucking her back into my chest and pulling her closer. Nipping her ear, I give her a few kisses along the side of her face and hairline, trying to ease her into the land of the living. "Morning, my sweet girl…"

I continue to pepper gentle kisses on her as she attempts to wake up and I chuckle when I realize that she's really struggling to do it. I plan out how to help her along without it being abrupt and decide that she will open those gorgeous eyes when she's on the brink of orgasm.

Tucking my arm under her head, I reach the other one down to her hip and tilt it backwards toward me, pushing her full, round ass further against my cock. Six weeks of eating better added with larger quantities of food have done some wonders on her petite frame. Her ass and breasts have filled out a bit, and her hips and stomach have softened. She's healthy and I love every inch of her.

I slide my leg between hers from behind, forcing them to spread open for me enough that it's easier to reach and pull back over my leg to hold her open. My arm that's cradling her head still has enough mobility to graze my fingers along the swells of her breasts, those nipples popping further away from her body. Pebbled so hard that I'm sure they'd scrap along my chest if they were pressed up against me.

Reaching between her thighs, I start to stroke her pussy until I feel her grow wet and hear her breathing pick up. She's reacting to my touches and with the way her breathing has changed, I expect her to come to any moment. I need her awake now, so I take drastic measurements.

Making sure that she's wet enough for me, I quickly slide two thick fingers directly into her, pressing my palm on her clit and fuck her with them slowly, but deeply. "William..." she groans out in that low, throaty morning voice that reminds me of raw, dirty sex that I'm *very* much hoping we have in the next fifteen or so odd minutes.

Pressing her ass against my cock, my length slips between her cheeks. As I fuck her with my hand, I suck and kiss at her neck before gritting out the news she needs to know. With my cock cradled in her ass, the head of it pressing against her tight entrance, I give her the update from her doctor.

"I just got off the phone with Dr. Schaffer." I kiss on her neck again before moving away to roll her on to her back, my hand never leaving her pussy. "Your scan looked good; the fractures are all healed up." I bend down and kiss her lazily, swallowing her moans as I slide a third finger inside her.

"I'm... I'm... She said I'm good? God, William, please don't stop..." I continue to rock my palm against her clit, loving the sounds of her pants and whines of pleasure she's breathing into my neck, hiding her face as she starts to rock against my fingers.

"Yes, babydoll. Do you know what that means?" Watching as her eyes roll back, I know she's not going to be able to answer me. My hips unconsciously thrust against her hip, the pre-cum running from the tip of my cock dripping on her and getting rubbed into her skin. Marking her as mine.

"It means that I'm going to fuck you, Nora. I'm going to slide my cock inside your untouched, unfucked pussy and make you mine." Rolling over on top of her, I remove my hand and slide her wetness up her stomach and coat her nipples with the taste of her.

Nora spreads her legs for me to settle between and I dip my head down to suck her flavor off her nipples. Jesus Christ, she tastes incredible.

I feel her thread her fingers into my hair, gripping the roots as I suck harder and slide myself along her wet slit, coating my cock in her juices to get it ready to slide into her more easily. "I'm ready... please... I-I'm ready." Her words are choppy, she can only get a few words out at a time. "Will... God, that... that feels..."

Surging up from her chest, I press myself more firmly against her. Sliding my hand under her, I move it up until I've got a grip on the back of her delicate neck. My fingers wrap all the way around either side of it, tucked under both sides of her jaw. I force her to keep her eyes on mine as I line myself up to her entrance.

"Are you ready for me, baby girl?" She nods her head yes, mouth slightly parted as she feels the pressure on her core. "Try to stay relaxed, and I'll go as carefully as I can. You tell me if you need a moment."

Her eyes are already filling, I think more from the moment rather than fear. Clenching my muscles to stop myself from shoving inside of her too quickly, I push the head of my cock just inside of her and pause, letting her adjust. The feelings she's experiencing are completely unbidden to me. I can see everything she's thinking, and she's never looked more beautiful to me.

Leaning down, I press my cheek to hers, feeling it damp from a few tears that escaped, and whisper, "Wrap your arms around me, sweetheart. I've got you." She does as she's told, and I continue to grip her neck as I attack her mouth, showing her with my tongue what we are about to do.

Letting my weight settle on her a little more, I tuck my other arm around her and grip the hair at the top of her head and begin to press myself forward again. She sucks in a breath as we both feel the head of my cock press up against her innocence. I pull back slightly and just dip in and out of her for a moment with the tip of my cock, keeping the slight friction while waiting for her.

Moaning out at my movement, she relaxes her pussy for me. Thank God because just this little bit inside her pussy is incredibly tight. I don't want to keep going until she's ready. The hope is to cause as little pain as possible, but I know I can't protect her from all of it.

"Baby girl, look at me." I wait until she opens her eyes and obeys me. "There you are sweet girl. Keep your eyes on me. It'll only hurt for a moment; I promise you."

I can't wait any longer. She's as relaxed as she's going to get, and I want to avoid giving her a chance to clench down on me. This time when I push forward, I don't pull back. I tear through her quickly and settle myself deep. I feel my heart grow heavy as her eyes quickly fill with tears and she cries out, squeezing her knees to my sides a little tighter.

"Shh... baby girl, I got you." Wiping away her tears with my thumbs, I continue to praise her and tell her how beautiful she is. I can see her discomfort as she feels me stretching her. It must be uncomfortable, pinned down by a man twice her size, being split open. I'm much larger than the average guy, so it makes me extra proud of her to have made it this far.

Kissing her, I distract her from the pain until she forgets what my cock just did to her and begins moving her hips, reaching for that friction she needs to feel. Sliding out and then back in slowly, she tightens again and cries out, but it seems to be a little less shocking this time. I do it again and it's easier. Again. Even easier.

Keeping my pace steady, I stroke my cock into her until her gasps and winces turn into moans for more. "Good girl, taking all of me like this." She's completely relaxed, so I lift up from holding on to her and reach down to slide my arm under her knee, pulling it back and opening her up wide for me.

My hips speed up and Nora cries out every time my body slams into hers, grinding the base of my cock into her, rubbing her clit with every swirl. "Please, William… please, harder. God, that feels so good…" My adrenaline is racing, pleasure rippling through me with the knowledge that I'm giving the same to her.

Sliding in to her a few more times, I pull out and roll over on to my back, pulling her with me. "Wait… what are you-" She doesn't get anything else out when I sink back into her, pulling her down to settle on to my lap.

"I want to watch you. Lean over me, I'll move *you*." She's quick to listen and lays her chest down on mine, tucking her head under my chin. Gripping her hip and wrapping an arm around her back to pin her to me, I begin to slide her back and forth across my cock.

Slowly, letting her adjust to this position, since it puts me deeper inside of her.

Moaning, she's breathing so heavily on my neck, it's tickling the skin there. I lift my hips higher up and continue to hold on to her, slamming inside of her harder when I feel her tongue run along the underside of my jaw. She keeps biting and latching on to my skin as I drive into her, like she needs to do something with her mouth.

The feel of her tight pussy is pushing me over the edge, and I can feel the beginnings of my orgasm start to bubble up from the base of my spine. Holding back from releasing inside of her, I circle my hips up and into her, grinding harder on her clit.

"I'm so close, baby. I want you to come on my cock as it fucks into you." I feel her pussy flutter around me when I say that and she grinds back down on to my cock, searching for her release. "That's right… just like that. Fall apart for me, baby girl."

"I'm almost there Will… I… please, I just… I don't know how to…" My poor sweet girl doesn't know how to let herself go, so I help her along. Reaching down, I slide two fingers to slip on either side of her clit and squeeze until she sits up abruptly and screams as she continues to grind herself on me, an orgasm almost immediately tearing through her small frame.

God damn, watching her come like this is fucking incredible to watch and I can't hold back for another moment. Wrapping my arms around her waist before she's fully through the throes of her release, I flip her again and fuck into her wildly, roaring out my release as I pour myself inside of her. My cock releases pulse after pulse of cum inside of her, leaking out because of the amount I had stored up.

Coming down, I lazily stroke my softening cock in and out until I slip fully out of her and shift to her side to wrap my arms around her. I can feel her pulse racing with my arm resting across her chest, still overcome with what just happened to her.

"Wow..." She says, and then covers her face with her hands, laughing and groaning at the same time. "God, sorry... That was so stupid. It's just, that was... I didn't expect it to be like that." She's still covering her face and now that we're done, her shyness takes hold of her again as that blush makes its presence known once more.

I chuckle and pull her hands away from her face. "You're not stupid, Nora. That was entirely new for me too." It's true, I've never felt this way with someone, let alone the intensity of it.

"What do you mean? That wasn't the first time you've ever done... that." She pauses like she can't say the word. I lace my fingers with hers and pull up to kiss the back of her hand before gently biting the tip of her index finger. I still feel a strong desire to have her, even after coming as hard as I did inside of her.

"No, that wasn't the first time I've done *that*. You don't have to be scared to use the words sex, fucking, making love... whichever you choose. But no, it's never felt like that for me either. Do you know why, love?"

"Because it was you and me," she answers sweetly.

I urge her to continue. "That's right, and what else?"

"Because we love each other, you've never d-" she catches herself, still beat red. "You've never made love with anyone before, not with someone you love."

I kiss her so she knows she's right, both of us smiling while we sip at each other, in no hurry to stop. We just enjoy the satisfaction of laying here and the comfort in the presence of one another.

"Let me get something to clean you up. Stay here a moment. Even though you've been cleared, I still want you to take it easy… especially after all that." I laugh as I walk to the bathroom as she sputters out an argument, but knows she has none.

Wetting a cloth, I come back into the room and see her sitting up, looking mortified. I frown down at her, worried that she's upset. "Hey, hey, what's wrong sweetheart?"

"Shoot…" Looking away from me, she bites her lip when she tells me what has her upset. "I bled a lot and there's a mess on your sheets. I feel terrible…"

Understanding unfurls my brows and I try to alleviate her embarrassment. "That's to be expected, Nora. You were a virgin. Plus, I'm large and I took you harder than I should have. That's why I went to get this. Lie back for me." I hold up the wet cloth to show her.

"I can do that," she protests, but I just shake my head.

"Nope, I want to do it. Lay back for me." She lays back without another argument. My sweet girl listens so well. I quickly clean her up and then haul her out of bed to bring her to the tub. "I want you to soak for a bit. You're going to be sore, so this should help."

"Oh God..." she groans out when I put her on her feet, but this time it wasn't a moan of ecstasy, it was one of discomfort.

Quickly turning on the bath and adjusting the temperature, I pick her up again and hold her against my chest while we wait for it to fill up. She closes her eyes and sighs into me, exhausted from the last hour, even having just woken up from a full night's sleep.

I set her down in the tub and encourage her to lay back. "Relax. Soak. Rest." Turning off the water, I stand and watch her for a few moments, enthralled by her movements as she gently swirls her hands through the water. She looks peaceful. Happy even. I'm glad I've been able to provide that for her.

Kissing her forehead, I whisper, "I love you, baby girl. Take your time in here. I'll be waiting for you downstairs."

Muttering under her breath sleepily, she's drifting off when she answers, "Love you too, William..."

I smile as I slip out of the bathroom, leaving her to rest.

# Chapter 10

**6 months later**

## *Nora*

Slamming the door on the Jeep that William bought me almost half a year ago, I hold the stack of mail I grabbed from the mailbox to my chest as I rush inside. I toss the keys in the basket sitting on top of a table in the entryway, kicking off my shoes as I barely slow down, and start yelling for him.

"William!" Heading into the kitchen, I don't see him. I know he's home because his SUV is in the garage. He just got off a twelve-hour nightshift at the ER and I wanted to try and catch him before he heads to bed. "WILLIAM!!"

A door slams to my left and I redirect over to the office space he has on the other side of the family room. I halt and watch as he walks toward me and my breath catches. He's still wearing his scrubs and that doctor coat from the hospital. It gets me every time I see him in it, and he knows it.

I can barely contain my excitement as I wait for him to get closer. He can tell something is up and drags his feet to tease, smirking at me. "Hey there, my sweet girl." I don't wait and I remove the remaining space between us, throwing myself in to his arms. Laughing, he hugs me. "What's going on? You were yelling for me."

"I got the letter," I tell him excitedly.

"What letter?" I can't believe he doesn't know what I'm talking about.

"I got *the* letter! From Wyndham University. I got the letter, William!" Flashing the large envelope at him, his indulgent smile quickly morphs into one of excitement. He's been completely supportive with my wishes to go to school in the fall.

After the stuff with my dad and uncle, and then having to heal, then get used to a new relationship with William, I needed the break. We also decided that we could both use the time to plan things out, and to really get to know each other.

Things have gone smoothly for me. My dad and uncle both were arrested within those few days that dad put me in the hospital. Dad was only held a night or two, but Uncle Rich was there for a few weeks until dad could come up with the bail for him. They've both stuck to the guidelines of the restraining order that William helped me file.

I had expected at least one of them to try and reach out to me, but I haven't heard from either one of them. A small part of me is hurt that my dad could be completely okay with my absence, but the larger part is relieved that I can let that part of my life go. It's a strange feeling, not feeling some sort of pain all the time.

Although, I do feel a little bit every now and then, but that's when William and I are exploring new... things. I've found that I *really* enjoy being spanked and the rougher sex when he loses his control. We've been working me up to try anal as well. I'm so scared that it's going to be excruciating, considering William has the thickness of a coke can. He assures me I'll enjoy it. We'll see.

"Did you open it yet?" he asks me as he picks me up with a quick kiss hello and carries me back into the kitchen, setting me on the counter. He does that a lot, picks me up and sets me higher to bring me to eye level.

Spreading my legs and pushing his body between them, he plants his hands on either side of me and looks down at the envelope. I've still got it tightly clutched in my hand. "Not yet. I wanted you to do it." I hand it over, too nervous to do it myself.

Grabbing it from me, he tears it open. "I should try to convince you to open it, but I don't want to wait to find out." Pulling the packet out of the envelope, he still stands between my legs as he reads the top letter.

Chewing on my thumb anxiously, I wait for him to let me know if I got into the Science program. I settled on a Bachelor's in Science for now, with a focus in chemistry. "Well? What does it say?"

Still reading, he gives me the news I've been waiting for. "It looks like we will be celebrating tonight, baby girl. You've been accepted to start in the fall." Swooping down, he gives me a fast, hard kiss before handing me the paper so I can read.

"Oh my God." I can't think of anything else to say as I read except to repeat myself. "Oh my God oh my God oh my G-"

"Sweetheart." I don't look up until he calls my name. "Nora!"

Looking up at him, I can't stop the tears from welling, nor the massive smile spreading across my face. "Oh my God William! *I got in!*"

He takes the paper from my hands and sets them down next to us. Grabbing my face, he kisses my forehead, my eyelids, cheeks, down to my chin, then ending on my mouth. Telling me how proud he is of me between each kiss.

"I really wish you would let me cover the tuition for you," he sighs out. This is an argument we've been having since I started applying to surrounding schools.

"I can't, though. It makes me feel like I can really do this on my own, like I'm capable of surviving on my own." I also want to make sure that he knows I'm with him because I wish to be, not out of necessity.

"I know, and I'll stop arguing for now. *BUT*... no way are you going to spend ten years paying off loans, I'm drawing the line there." He's firm with me, like he's expecting me to argue and wants to put his foot down early.

"We'll see. So… William… How should we celebrate?" I still blush every time I try to instigate sex or if we do something that pushes me out of my comfort zone, but I'm trying to be more vocal about what I want.

"Hmm…" he hums out loud, acting like he really needs to think about it. I can't stop the giggle that bubbles up from my throat. "How about I take you upstairs, spread you wide open and eat that delicious pussy until you come all over my face a few times. I think that's a wonderful way to celebrate."

My heart rate picks up at the excitement turning in my belly. His mouth is incredibly talented. "I'm good with that, as long as you'll let me return the favor?"

We've discovered that I love going down on him, and he loves having me do it. I squeal in laughter as he picks me up and throws me over his shoulder.

Slapping my ass on the way upstairs, he rubs away the sting. "I can agree to your terms, but always you first baby girl."

Smiling to myself, hanging upside down with a delicious view of his tight ass, I stay relaxed in the knowledge that I'm safe, happy, and in love.

And that he'll always keep me warm.

# Bonus Epilogue

## *Nora*

William is standing on the balcony of the beach house we've rented for the next two weeks on Marco Island in Florida. He's waiting for me to finish getting ready for the dinner we have reservations for. I can't help but watch him, unaware of me, and enjoy the fluttering in my stomach I get every time I'm around him.

Three years together and I *still* get overwhelmed by my feelings for him. Before I first started school, William took me on a getaway weekend to Las Vegas where he proposed and then married me on the first night we had arrived. We spent that entire weekend in bed and never got out to see the sites. I chuckle to myself when I remember that the only gambling we did was at a slot machine in the airport when we flew back home.

We decided to take some time to ourselves before he dives in fully to opening his new practice. He decided that even though he loved working in the Emergency Room as a trauma doctor, the schedule wasn't ideal. He figured that even though it would be more hours in the beginning to open his own practice, once it's running smoothly, he'll be able to have a normal 9 to 5 with weekends off.

I spend the time that he's gone working in my own space. He built it for me off of the garage so the scents I use to make perfumes, soaps, lotions, and candles don't overwhelm us in the house. After spending two years in college and then doing the perfume thing on the side, I was struggling to make school my priority. Since I've been able to focus all my time on my products, I've made some decent money. There are local stores within a 100-mile radius that sell my products for commission. I've also been in discussions with a spa chain that's interested in working out a deal with me so my products will be sent all across the United States in their stores.

It was difficult to make the decision to drop out of school, but William has been so supportive and encourages me to do what I want in life as long as it keeps me happy.

Fortunately, he's the only thing that's essential to my happiness. Everything else is just a bonus.

Leaning against the wall holding my phone while I watch him, he doesn't see me until I text him.

***Me**: Mr. Blackwell... you're looking awfully sexy standing there in the breeze. I wouldn't mind if we cancelled our plans and stayed in for the night. ;-)*

He reads the text, and then whips his head up to zero in on where I'm standing in the shadows. A sly smirk spreads across his face when he leans back against the railing and texts me back.

*My Doctor: You're a naughty girl Mrs. Blackwell. Spying on me when I've been waiting so long for you. How should I punish you for it?*

Biting my lip, I decide to play along. Slipping back into the bedroom, I see him watching me out of the corner of my eye but doesn't move from his spot outside.

*Me: I'm never naughty Mr. Blackwell. I'm a good girl...*
*My Doctor: You're MY good girl, Nora. But sometimes even good girls, no matter how sweet they are, get in trouble. So, you have two options and the one that makes you blush is the one that you must pick. Deal?*
*Me: ...what are my options?*

I hear him slide the glass door shut to come inside, then to the front door where he slides the deadbolt into place. My heart picks up when I sit on the end of the bed, my dress sliding up my thighs as I cross my legs to start removing my heals.

I'm certain we aren't going anywhere tonight.

***My Doctor***: *Option 1 - You bend over the end of the bed, lift your dress for me so I can spank that ass until your pussy is dripping for me, ready to be fucked…*
***Me***: *…or?*

He doesn't answer me right away, so I stand up with my shoes in my hand and walk over to the closet to set them inside when I feel his warmth along my back.

I shudder at his nearness, his scent washing over me and enveloping me in this small space where there's not much room for both of us along with all our things.

He presses his chest against my back and when I move to turn around, he grips my arms to keep me facing away from him. Leaning down, he growls option two in my ear, "*OR*, I put you on your knees where you'll choke on my cock until I cum down your throat."

I feel his arm band around me and his other hand reaches up to cup my throat, pushing my head back so he can look into my eyes. "I'll cum down your throat baby doll, and then eat that greedy pussy I can smell from here until I'm ready to fuck you."

My breath hitches and I watch his smirk grow at the redness that's spreading across my face. Three years and he's still able to make me blush. He's had to work up from simple compliments and blatant comments about sex, to saying things so filthy that I doubt I'll ever get used to it.

"Hmm…" His thumb runs over my chin. "Option two it is. I'm not sure I can fuck your mouth first though. I think you need my tongue to tide you over."

"William…" I moan. Pushing my ass back into him, I can feel his hardness pressing up against me through his dress pants. He grinds on me, his eyes heated as he continues to stare down at me.

In a quiet voice, he hisses, "Bend over." At his order, he releases my throat and pushes at the center of my back until I've got my hands planted on the floor in front of me. William lifts the back of my dress over my back, exposing me to his gaze.

Clicking his tongue, I feel his heated hand run down the naked skin of my ass. "Nora, you *are* a naughty girl, aren't you? Where are your panties?"

I bite my cheek to keep from giggling. He always asks me to forgo them when I get dressed, so he knew I wouldn't be wearing any. "Umm… I'm not sure. I must have forgot them back ho-"

I grunt and move to catch myself when he slaps my right cheek. It wasn't necessary because he gripped my waist to prevent me from falling. Always protecting me, even in our games.

"Shame, Mrs. Blackwell… I'm not sure you deserve to cum tonight."

I move to stand up at that and twist around to look at him. "*What?* That's not fa-" He's laughing at me and my indignation at his threat. I scowl at him. "Har-har. See how you'd like it if I threatened you with withholding an orgasm!"

Throwing his head back, he laughs as he picks me up and throws me over his shoulder. Walking back into the room, I gasp when instead of setting me back down, he turns us and presses me against the wall.

"Do you remember back when we met and you were in the hospital?" His voice sounds lighthearted, but I know that he hates thinking about what happened to put me there.

Brushing his hair across his forehead, I let my feet dangle and I give him a soft smile. "I do. Why?"

"Well, I know I'm super old and all..." I snicker at that. He knows I love to tease him about his age and the fact that he's almost 20 years older than me. Kissing my nose, he growls, "brat. Anyways, I remember telling you something along the lines of there being a benefit to being with someone as tall as I am. Do you remember that?"

I furrow my brows, not sure what he's getting at. "Yes..." I drawl out. "I vaguely remember some-" My words are cut off when I screech out, "WILLIAM!"

He's got a huge grin on his face as he lifts me further up along the wall, and throws my legs over his shoulders, one of each side of his head. I'm so high up that I'm nervous I'm going to fall without having anything to hold on to. "What are you doing!? I'm going to fall!"

His hands are wrapped around my waist and pinning me to the wall so all I have to grab onto is his hair to steady myself. "Hush sweet girl, I would never drop you. Now, lift your dress for me. Show me your pretty little pussy."

With a shaking hand, I only let one go from his hair as I lift the front of my dress, putting my center directly in front of his face. Then I groan loudly, my head falling back against the wall when I feel his tongue firmly run up the length of my opening then settle directly over my clit. "*God* William… please don't stop…"

Looking down at him, he meets my eyes and smiles into my pussy before fully diving in and devouring me. One of his favorite things to do is go down on me and he's so good at it now that it only takes a minute or two before he's got me screaming and begging for him to let me cum.

Pulling his mouth away right before I explode, I growl at him, "*Nooo!* Please William!"

"Hang on to me a second." With barely enough time to follow his directions, he quickly lowers my body down even though my legs are still over his shoulders and moves us to the bed that's only a few feet away. I scream out again when he drops me to the bed and I bounce once before he falls on top of me, diving back in where he left off. Only this time, he shoves two fingers into me, relentlessly fucking me with them until I'm writhing on the sheets.

"I need you inside me, please William. *PLEASE.*" I try to pull him up and thank God, he gives in to me.

Standing up from me, he yanks his belt off and barely has his zipper down before he's pulled his cock out, stroking it. "Roll over onto your knees for me."

Flipping over, I scramble up to my knees and cry out when he slams all the way inside of me without easing me into it. Slapping my ass a few more times, he pounds into me at a fast pace, both of us so close to the edge already.

I bite my fist when he yells out, "FUCK. *Fuck*, I'm going to cum already. I want you to come with me baby girl. Play with your clit for me."

Moaning, I reach between my legs and rub furiously at my overly sensitive bundle of nerves, and he hisses when it makes me clamp down on him harder. "There you go, my good girl. Just like that. Come for me baby."

His grip is bruising on my hips and our bodies slam together forcing my orgasm to explode out of me. I scream into the room as I shatter around him and he's just as lost in his own release, filling me with pulse after pulse of cum.

Both of us are breathing hard when he falls onto my back, and then rolls us in the bed so he can wrap his body around me. We take a few minutes to catch our breaths, his cock still buried inside of me.

Finally, I can breathe again, my heart rate slowing back down, coming down from the high he took us both to. I sigh and look over my shoulder at him with a smile. "Well Mr. Blackwell, I think we've missed our reservation."

"Worth it, love. I'll just order something to be brought up tonight and we can try again tomorrow." He gives me a soft kiss on my lips and then leans his forehead against mine.

"This will be the fourth try," I giggle at him.

Pulling out of me, he rolls me to my back to look down at me for a moment before kissing me deeply once more. "I don't care. I'd rather stay up here every night and not have to share you with anyone else."

"I love you," I whisper against his lips.

"I love you too. Always *my* girl."

The End

THE COMPLETE INNOCENCE BOXSET

# FAITH

## S.E. Green

S. E. Green

## From the Author

I live for music, so I often get inspired by many contemporary songs and artists when I write. While some books that I write are inspired by multiple songs, this one was a one song repeater for me. It just sort of sucked me in a put me in a particular mood - one that I hope you feel when you listen. It's called **Greyish Tapering Ash** by *Balmorhea*.

Also, as a side note, this story came to me while driving and listing to Balmorhea on my way to work. The trains in the beginning of the song sent my mind whirling into a picture of two strangers meeting in a train car. She's running away, and he's running to her. The religious aspect was thrown in when a good friend of mine referred to her childhood as having suffered through some Catholic trauma. I ran with it.

# Trigger Warnings

Please know that there could be some triggering topics addressed that include **verbal and physical abuse (both as an adult and child), grooming (not in a sexual way– see disclaimer)**. The childhood abuse is only discussed.

Having experienced abuse in my past (one sexual assault and one physically abusive relationship), I sometimes draw from how I felt and recovered from it. Everyone reacts differently to trauma, so if you doubt that my character(s) reacted in a believable way, please keep in mind we are all wonderfully different. My therapist told me that our bodies tend to subconsciously protect itself the best way it thinks will keep us the safest. Please seek help if you are being hurt or have been hurt in the past. We all want you safe and feeling loved!

S. E. Green

## **Disclaimer – PLEASE READ**

I need to make something ***SUPER*** clear. This book is **NOT AT ALL** a true representation of the Catholic faith. This is an example of how misinformation can be twisted and used as a weapon. It can cause an incredible amount of damage; sometimes beyond repair.

So, I leave you with our Lord's message which can be read in *Christopher Moore's* book, **Lamb: The Gospel According to Biff, Christ's Childhood Pal**. Biff shares with us the gist of almost every sermon he ever heard Christ (aka Joshua, pronounced *Jah-shoe-ah*) give in regards to one's salvation:

*"You should be nice to people, even creeps. And if you:*
- a) *Believed that Joshua was the Son of God (and)*
- b) *He had come to save you from sin (and)*
- c) *Acknowledged the Holy Spirit within you (became as a little child, he would say) (and)*
- d) *Didn't blaspheme the Holy Ghost (see c)*

Then *you would:*
- e) *Live forever*
- f) *Someplace nice*
- g) *Probably heaven*

However, *if you:*

*h) Sinned (and/or)*

*i) Were a hypocrite (and/or)*

*j) Valued things over people (and)*

*k) Didn't do a, b, c, and d,*

*Then you were:*

*l) Fucked."*

# Chapter 1

## *Faith*

Showers are about the closest I've ever come to experiencing what I imagine heaven would be like. Peace. Love. Community—not one you're forced into, but those who share the same beliefs as you. Worshipful. But most importantly? Pain free.

I've read the Bible so many times. Many verses Father Michael teaches us are of utmost importance, but none of those come close to my absolute favorite one.

Revelation 21, verse 4. *'And God shall wipe all tears from their eyes; and there shall be no more death, neither sorrow, nor crying, neither shall there be any more pain: for the former things are passed away.'*

I should feel guilty about that. Looking forward to leaving this place to one of safety and comfort. *Should* being the operative word, but I don't. Every time I'm told to fall to my knees for my penance, I zone out from what my father, or Father Michael, is preaching and repeat my verse in my head until my penance is done.

I know that I'll have to confess this sin, along with others that I've committed over the past 7 days since my last confession. Breaking one of the Lord's commandments is going to cost me. *'Honour thy father and thy mother: that thy days may be long upon the land which the Lord thy God giveth thee.'* I already know that breaking this commandment is going to hurt.

For not honoring my father, he will be the one to dole out my punishment. *His* favorite verse is Proverbs 13, verse 24. *'He that spareth his rod hateth his son: but he that loveth him chasteneth him betimes.'*

And my father? He *really* loves me.

I can't prolong my shower any longer. I've been in here for over twenty minutes, and I know my mother is going to be knocking at any moment to hurry me out.

Shutting off the water, I quickly step out and grab a towel to wrap around my body before heading back to my bedroom to dress. I'm to head to morning confession by 9 a.m. Father and mother believe that doing this first thing in the morning is a way to start the day off right, to be freed from our sins.

After drying off and putting lotion on my skin, I stare at the dress and undergarments lying on my twin sized bed and scowl at the source of the constant pain that my shower gives me temporary relief from.

That blasted knotted cord. My emblem of purity. Our *'faith's'* symbol of chastity. The evil thing is worn tightly around my waist.

The rope I received was cut a bit longer than the circumference of my waist and then tied with three knots. Three because of the three sins I committed and commandments I broke during my last confession.

I lied. *'Thou shalt not bear false witness.'*

I lusted. *'Flee from sexual immorality.'*

I tempted. *'Woe to the one by whom the temptation comes.'*

Sighing, I dress and tie my rope, feeling the knots dig into the bruised areas that they have been settled against for 23 and a half hours every day over the last seven days. This whole thing has put me in a bad place in my head all week.

While confessing, according to Father Michaels, not only was I being lustful, but I didn't confess my lustful actions. Normally, when I confess, there is a barrier between myself and Father, but not this last time. I was the only one there that morning, so instead of the confessional booth, Father took my confession in his office.

I was encouraged to kneel as I listed out my sins in front of him. He made me look at him while I spoke, to humble me in my humility of his judgement. I was there for so long that my legs had cramped, and I swayed forward to catch myself, almost knocking over Father when I hit his legs. He had grabbed hold of the back of my head and pulled my face further into his lap, pushed... *something* against my cheek, and I jerked back. His actions had made me feel uncomfortable, so I tried to quickly end my confessional.

He didn't let me and kept me on my knees while he accused me of lusting after him. I promised I wasn't.

He accused me of tempting him, so I asked how?

He accused me of making *him* sin through *my* temptation of flesh. I explained to him that I have no knowledge of the sins of flesh, so how could I tempt him?

Then finally, he accused me of failing to confess all my mortal sins. I had started crying by this point because I was so confused about what was happening. What had I done wrong?

He kicked me out of his office and sent me home. All of this culminated later that evening when he entered our home to inform my parents of what I had done and pulled out the rope. He tied each knot as he told them of each sin. All three of them then watched as I was ordered to tie it around my waste in penance to help prevent me from future sins, to stay chaste.

The longer I think about last week, the angrier I get as I jerk my tights up my legs.

Great. Another sin to confess. Wrath. One of the seven deadly sins that will only inspire further sin. I've pretty much hit the motherload this week according to my family. They sat me down last night to go over what I would be confessing to this week. I had to try and atone for *last* week.

According to them, not only am I lustful, but I'm prideful, greedy, and I didn't honor my father and mother, I *apparently* attempted to commit adultery with Father Michael - which still baffles me - and I'm a liar. *Oh!* also I'm a "coveter" because I covet what those have in a marriage bed.

Yeah, I'm adding wrath to my list today. At least I didn't kill anyone.

Stomping down the stairs to grab breakfast before heading to the church, I halt in the entrance to the kitchen when I see my mother and father both somberly sitting at the table in silence.

"What's wrong?" I ask because the look of disappointment that my father displays and my mother's sadness, is worrisome. I'm worried that I'm not going to like what they're about to say.

"Sit down, sweetheart." My mother indicates I should sit in the chair across from them.

"*Betty!*" he snaps at my mom. "We've already discussed this. We are not going to be coddling her through this. She's an adult now and must take accountability for her actions."

Confused, I look between the two of them. "What did I do?" I haven't seen them since I went to bed last night. I didn't have a chance to do anything.

"*Sit!*" I obey and spy an item on the table in front of me I hadn't noticed until now. "I have been in discussion with Father Michael and your mother since the incredibly embarrassing events that happened last week. I had hoped that we would have at least seen some growth from you, but we haven't.

"I apologize, father. I promise to do better. I've been uncomfortable with this rope on all the time." Looking to my mother, I soften my voice so she knows I will try to be better, "It really hurts mom; it feels like there are bruises across my entire stomach."

I know my mother empathizes with me, but she always concedes to my father's wishes. Pleading with her will get me nowhere. I stare at the contraption that's on the table while he keeps talking.

"The point of it was to give you a constant reminder to flee from your sins. You've only focused on how it's making your body feel. You're not grasping its purpose. As your parents, it's our duty to nurture you in discipline and instruction of our Lord." He points to the item. "This is how we've chosen to proceed."

I look at my mom, but now she isn't meeting my eye. Staring at the table again, I try to decipher what it is. It almost looks like one of those metal linked chokers that dogs wear that tightens when they pull on their leash. Only it doesn't connect in the same way. There's a hook on one side that goes through a loop on the other to join the ends. I've never seen it before.

"What is it?" I ask timidly. It doesn't look nice and I'm getting nervous.

"*It* is called a cilice. This is a tool used for repentance and atonement, and you are going to wear it."

Still not understanding, I ask him, "How am I supposed to wear it?"

"It's worn under your clothes, wrapped around your upper thigh like a garter. You'll wear this until we've seen that you're learning and have a desire to walk in the correct path. That's what your cord was *supposed* to do, but you're not allowing it to do its purpose. I feel that a more extreme measure needs to be taken." He's done answering my questions and is expecting me to obey him. "Put it on."

It takes a lot of effort to hold in my sigh as I reach forward and wrap my hand around to pick it up. I gasp at the sharp pain I feel and drop it, letting the links rattle as they hit the tabletop. "Pick it up, Faith. Put it on. Now."

Tears fill my eyes as I beg him. This thing is going to be excruciating. There are spikes all along the underside of the links that are each about a quarter inch long. The tips are slightly blunted, but if I bump it hard enough, it will most definitely puncture my skin. "Father, please. I swear that I don't need this. I will spend extra time doing community service and I will pray for-"

He puts his hand up to stop me from continuing. "Put it on, Faith," he orders me.

Shaking my head at him, I try again, "I can't... please. That's going to break my skin! I really can't. Please don't make me."

His face is turning red, and he uses his fists on the table to push himself out of his chair, standing now and leaning toward me. "*PUT IT ON! NOW!*"

I'm full on crying now and I look to my mother. "Mom…" I choke out. "Please don't make me."

She goes to open her mouth, but my father beats her to it. "Enough of this. Betty," he says her name as an order, and she must know what he wants because she sighs and stands up.

Father marches around to my side of the table and pulls me up from my chair, leaning me forward on my stomach across the table. "Wait! I'll put it on! I'm sorry," I beg but he ignores me and keeps his hand on the center of my back, pinning me down.

I struggle to convince him to let me up as I continue to promise that I'll put it on without complaint. I go unheard as he talks over me to my mother, "Run and grab me a pair of pliers and then come pull her tights down to put it around her left thigh."

"Yes honey…" She seems hesitant but, in the end, she listens. She always listens. My father is so much bigger than me that it's useless to try to struggle. If I stay still, maybe he'll realize that I'm trying to be good for him.

Relaxing my body under his weight, I continue to cry as we wait for my mother to run out to his workshop and find the pliers he asked for. He uses this time to give me lessons in penance, sin, and obeying.

"Let's start in Leviticus. Repeat after me. '*It shall be a holy convocation unto you; and ye shall afflict your souls.*' Say it, Faith."

Through choked sobs, I repeat, "*It shall b-be a holy convo-… convocation unto y-you; and…*"

"*And ye shall afflict your souls.*"

"*And ye shall afflic-flict your s-souls.*"

"'*He disciplines us for our own benefit, that we may repent from our evil ways.*' Psalms. Repeat," he orders. I stumble through the verse as my mother comes back in.

"Here Daniel. It's the only one I could find," she's talking in a monotone voice, completely checked out. This is what she does when she doesn't like something that he's doing but refuses to go against him.

"Her tights, Betty," he tells her, then has me repeat another verse. "*I chastise my body.*"

"I-I-I cha-chastise... my b-body." The words are getting harder to get out as he pushes harder on my back to hold me as I feel my mother pull down my tights and lift the bottom of my knee-length skirt. "M-mom! Please stop. I'll d-do it!" One more try. I plead with her.

"Now the cilice." He still ignores me. I hear the metal clink together as she lifts it and feel as it scraps around the front of my thigh, the points start digging into the skin. It's not painful yet, and I'm thankful. Maybe it won't be as bad as I tho-

I scream out as she grips the ends and connects them together at the back of my thigh. "STOP! It's g-going to c-cut my skin!" I don't think they know how tight it is.

My father releases my arms now that it's been secured. Immediately I try to reach back to try and loosen it and he smacks my hands away. "That's what I thought. Hands on the table, Faith."

I give up. I truly do.

Placing my hands on the table, I bow my head and wait. My mother slips her hand over mine to comfort me, but I pull it away and ignore her.

I wait as I feel my father lift my skirt once more and tuck it in to the back of my underwear.

I wait as he uses his pliers to twist the hook around the loop its connected to a few times so that I can't remove it.

Then I kneel and wait until my father finishes praying, "*My God, I am sorry for my sins with all my heart. In choosing to do wrong and failing to do good...*"

He finishes.

I repeat.

# Chapter 2

## *Arrow*

I see her walking toward me. She's young but fuck if she isn't one of the most beautiful women I've ever seen. She's struck me motionless.

White, blonde hair that hangs in thick waves almost to her waist. Softly rounded hips and high tits that are slightly too large for her frame. Fair, spotless skin that I don't even see a freckle on. Her creamy white skin looks as smooth as silk. I have the strongest urge to reach out and touch her arm, just to see if it's as velvety as it looks.

She's looking at the sidewalk as she walks. Does she walk with a limp? I can't tell. One moment I'd say yes, but then the next she walks as graceful as a dancer.

My cock ticks with her every step, and my mind releases its hold on my body. I stand from the table I'm enjoying my coffee at to approach her.

Shit. I moved too quickly and waited until she was too close. I scared the shit out of her. "Fuck!" I mumble under my breath and reach out to catch her as she turns too quickly and stumbles sideways.

Wrapping my hands around her waist, the first thing I notice is how narrow it is. I could probably wrap both hands entirely around her.

The second thing I notice are hard lumps across the front of her stomach as I pull her back toward me to stop her fall. What I *don't* expect is for her to cry out and curl over my hands to remove them from her stomach.

*What the fuck is that?* I open my mouth to ask exactly that, but she speaks first.

"S-sorry. Sorry. I didn't see you. I apologize." She backs up from me, barely flicking her eyes up to meet mine, but I catch them just long enough to see her pale blue-green eyes with a defined clarity that reminds me of clear ice.

"Fuck…" Jesus Christ. I didn't mean to swear at her. I was responding to the surprise of how distinctive they are. She flinches away before moving past me quickly.

I hear another soft, "Sorry." I'm frozen once more as I watch her walk away from me. I don't blink until she turns the corner, out of view, and then I lurch toward her instinctually before stopping myself.

Blowing a breath out, I run my hand over my face and marvel over the almost immediate regret I feel for not only scaring her, but for letting her walk away. It's probably the right thing, letting her go. I'm going on 42 and she doesn't look a day over 20.

Sitting back down, I try to drink my coffee again, but it tastes like ass. Looking back in the direction she went; my mind is made up.

"I have to know," I say out loud to myself, drawing the eye from the woman sitting at the table next to me, but I ignore her.

I throw a ten on the table, grab my bag, and follow her.

# Chapter 3

## *Faith*

I turn the corner after running into that man sitting outside a bakery. The moment he can no longer see me, I stop and catch my breath and try to ease the ache in my stomach from these stupid knots being pushed into the bruises they've caused.

Thank goodness that he didn't hit the choke collar. I refuse to call it by its name. I'm not opposed to doing penance for my sins, but to be forced into one for a sin I didn't know I was committing or even understand? Nope. I'm most definitely against that.

I walk delicately the rest of the way to church. The collar keeps digging into my skin when my thighs brush together so if I walk carefully enough, it alleviates a little of it.

I was supposed to go to confession earlier this morning, but with the intervention to fix me, I was delayed for a few hours. My father went to speak with Father Michaels immediately after he was done with me and has been there since. My mother said that he's going to wait for me and drive me home after I'm finished in the confessional. I'm thankful he's not going to force me to walk home. Thankful for small mercies.

I finish the rest of my walk, finally making it with minimal damage and pull the heavy door to the sanctuary open. The confessional booths are up front and tucked back into the corner, so that's where I need to go. Heading down the center aisle to find a seat on a pew to wait, I sit forward so only my bottom is on the seat.

There's a calming feeling that comes over me as I settle in. The pews aren't comfortable, not really, but that's not what calms me. It's the familiar dark wood, polished to a slippery shine that I've loved running my hand across all throughout my childhood and now adulthood. The wood is beautiful, the lines swirling under the lacquer, random knots littered throughout. To me, church services have been the only time where I've heard messages of God's love for us. It's the individual counseling we receive on the side that turns that love into hellfire, doom, and pain.

Twenty minutes pass, but I see no one. I haven't heard a sound echoing through the hall. My mother told me my father wanted me to come directly here to wait for him and Father Michaels. He had planned on speaking about my 'issues' in length before I arrived. I'm growing concerned that she heard him wrong. Maybe they're waiting for me in Father's office where he took my confession last week?

Unease overtakes me at the thought of angering them by not being where I'm supposed to be, making them wait on me. Rising from where I've been sitting, I make my way to the other side of the church where the offices are housed. Looking around, I still see no one as I walk, my gait feeling unnatural.

Father Michaels' door is closed, so I'm not sure if he's in counsel with someone or if he's somewhere else and the office is just locked up.

I rap my knuckles lightly on the door and wait a moment. Nothing. Shoot. What now?

Turning, I lean back against his door to contemplate where I can look next, but instead of finding a solid back support, I keep falling back as the door opens, not having been latched properly.

Two times today of stumbling, being caught off guard. Two times I've been able to avoid hitting the ground. Unfortunately, this is the first time that when I look up, I see Father Michaels' bare chest leaning over *my* father's bare back.

Three things happen in fast order.

My father's eyes open wider than I've ever seen them, filled with fear and horror.

Father Michaels' eyes narrow on me while the corner of his lip sneers up in anger.

*My* eyes hit the floor.

"Oh. Oh *God*. I'm... I'm so sorry." I'm scrambling for what to do right now. I've never seen... *Oh God, I'm going to be sick.* I shuffle my feet backwards as quickly as I can, keeping my eyes down, but desperately looking at the ground behind me and my path to exit and run from whatever this is. *What is this?*

"FAITH! Stop immediately!" Father Michaels shouts at me.

At the same time, my father shouts at me as well, "FUCK! Jesus Christ, Faith! What the hell are you doing?"

Shaking my head like I don't know what to do or how to answer them, I keep backing out, and try to make my apologies, "I... I'm so sorry... I thought... I didn't know. I'll-"

"I SAID STOP! Do *NOT* walk out of this room," Father Michaels yells again, while what sounds like him fighting with his clothes and belt, pulling them on... up? I don't know!

But I stop. It's instinctual. Self-preservation to keep the threat as calm as possible and not anger it.

"Shut the door," he orders me, the tone of his voice seething. He sounds enraged as he yells at my father, "Pull your Goddamn pants up, Dan."

"Sonofa - What do-" my father is talking as I shut the door behind me, shutting myself in with the two of them. I look longingly at the door with a desperate wish to escape.

Hissing at him, he says, "Don't open your mouth. FAITH!"

I jerk my head up when he barks at me and meet his eyes. The look of rage on his face is terrifying and I look to my father for guidance, but he won't meet my eyes. He's pale and shaking.

"Now. Let's sit a moment. Faith..." His voice is starting to calm down now, cajoling, like talking to a child that needs bad news to be sugar-coated. "I'm not sure what you think is happening here, but I assure you that you are incorrect."

I'm still in shock I think, because I cock my head at him, confused. Does he think I'm an idiot? "I don't think that I'm misunderstanding, Father," I tell him politely, non-aggressively. I don't want to displease him.

"Faith, your mother-"

"I said don't open your mouth, Dan," he orders my father, then redirects to me. "Yes, you are. We will discuss this no further. You've come here for confession. Your father and I were just discussing your most recent behavior and-"

I squeeze my eyes shut and cut him off, "Wait." Then opening my eyes again, I stare at both. I'm baffled. "Are you kidding me right now Father Michaels? *Dad?*" I *never* call him that. It's always felt disrespectful to me, like his position as the head of our household has earned him the title of father in the same way a priest is called Father as the head of the church.

"You will not speak to Father Michaels like that, Faith. I didn't raise you to be flippant and impolite." Ahh, now he's pulling himself back together.

"You didn't... ARE YOU FLIPPING KIDDING ME? Where on God's green earth do you get off talking to me about... when *you're-*"

"ENOUGH!" they both shout at the same time. I wrench myself backwards, away from the force of their raised voices, combined like this. All of it directed solely at me.

Father Michaels continues, "Enough. Clearly, you're being hysterical and think that something immoral is going on here. Like I was telling your father, this is clearly a bigger issue that's going on with you. These lust filled thoughts and actions have you seeing sin and immorality everywhere, including in the holiest of places."

Laughing out loud, I'm floored by what I'm hearing. "No. What I'm seeing is my father bent over for my Priest." *Oh, shoot.*

I instantly regret saying that. Lord Almighty, what was I *thinking*?

Pulling himself up to his full height, Father Michaels walks menacingly toward me, forcing me to step back until my back slams against the door. The dang thing is solid and stationary the way I had expected it to be the *first time* I leaned against it today.

"You will go home with your father. Go home, pray, and seek God's instruction. *Beg* him to open your eyes and heart to receive his admonishment and mercy. Consider what's been in your heart these past few weeks, and why you've been struggling to walk the path you're supposed to be following. I will come by this evening and sit down with you, your father, *and* your mother, to provide counsel and guidance." He turns his back on me, but before I lose sight of his face, I see him shoot my father a look that I'm not able to interpret. "Now go. I will pray as well."

"But-"

"Please Faith. No more," my father begs of me. He's never spoken to me like that before. Like he's lost control of a situation or lost the expectation that my mother and I will always defer to him.

No one says another word. My father simply grabs my elbow and pulls me all the way to the car, walking quickly and not allowing me to adjust my walk to ease the discomfort on my thigh. There are still no words between us when we pull into the driveway a short while later, nor when my mother catches us as we walk in through the back door.

"What's going on?" she asks.

"Not now Betty," he snaps at her and continues to drag me through the house until we reach the bottom of the stairs. This is where he finally drops my elbow and stares down at me. I'm not sure what emotions I'm seeing, but I know I'm not able to hide some of the judgement I'm feeling toward him. Or the audacity that he has to lecture me when he's... well, when he's doing *something* clearly very wrong.

There's a standoff between us, both of us waiting for the other to speak first. I don't give in. I simply turn away from him and walk up to my room. The room that has felt like home since the day I was born and now feels like a straitjacket, the tension surrounding it thick and suffocating.

I wait. And wait. And wait.

No one comes to my room for the remainder of the afternoon. No one comes to tell me it's time for dinner. No one comes when the doorbell rings after the sky is fully black. The sound of their voices is muted through the walls. I can't hear what they're saying, but I certainly can hear who's speaking.

Father Michaels has come to give his counsel.

# Chapter 4

## *Arrow*

I followed her to the church.

Slipping inside behind her, I found a spot in the corner of a pew at the very back of the sanctuary and watched her.

What is she doing? She's just sitting there. Praying maybe?

I'm enamored as I watch, her arm moving constantly while the rest of her stays perfectly still. It takes me a few minutes to conclude that she's simply sitting there, staring ahead and running her hand over the wood.

I'm not sure why I find this as interesting as I do. In my line of work, I find I need theatrics or action to keep my interest. A great mystery to unravel. But nothing has entertained me more in the past few years of my life than watching this girl doing nothing but run her hand across a wooden bench.

I'm about to get up and approach her when she abruptly stands, looks around, no notice of me, and walks to the other side of the space, and then disappears through a door.

Well, shit.

I hang around for a bit longer before deciding it'll be best to wait outside if I want to catch her rather than risk waiting here and her not returning.

I'm only outside for roughly fifteen minutes before I watch as an older, pot-bellied, *angry* man drags my girl out by her elbow toward the parking lot. She can barely keep her feet under her, and I would very much like to step in and tell him that the way he's man handling her is causing her discomfort.

I want to. Fuck do I want to, but there's no way I'll get there in time before they reach their car. Plus, it's clear this is her father. Not because they look alike, no. He's large, slightly overweight with a heavy brow, bulbous nose, and distinct lack of chin. It's simply their coloring. Her almost white hair is the same color as his even though his is thin and receding, along with the same fairness of skin.

The rest of her must match her mother, if her features are indicative of who she's favored. Her nose is pert, chin slightly pointed and rounded. Not sharp though. The curves in her face are softened, unlike her fathers. His face is elongated and oval. Her face is heart shaped with high cheek bones and thin arched eyebrows over those eyes of hers.

I close my eyes at that thought. I'm still stuck on them as well as the intense desire to drown in them.

When I open mine again, they follow the car which is distancing her from me, and I'm lost as to what to do now. How to find her, because I very much need to.

Quickly analyzing everything, my mind keeps focusing on the anger he carried. It doesn't take me long to decide what to do next.

They're at a Catholic Church, mid-week, with only one other remaining vehicle in the lot. People only go to church on days that aren't Sundays for a couple of reasons. It could be because they work there, or they are performing some sort of service work. *Or* they're meeting with the Pastor, well, Priest in this instance, for personal reasons.

My bet is on the latter because I doubt most people would storm out of a church in a fit of rage purely because the weekly newsletter didn't get out on time or had a few spelling errors. That means that the Priest is the one that's still in the building.

I would assume that a Priest wouldn't be too happy with the emotional state the girl and her father left in. The only chance I'll have to find her is to wait and follow the Priest, see if he goes to them.

I jog back to where I was having coffee earlier and pull open the door to the rental vehicle I'm using while staying here and start it up. Driving back to the church, I take a huge breath and release it in a sigh of relief. He's still here. It only took me 20 minutes to pick up my car and get back, but I would have been screwed if he had left during that time.

Settling in down the street with an unobstructed view of the front and side door to the church, as well as his vehicle, I wait.

Five hours later, I am still waiting.

Fortunately, I've been traveling in this car for over a week, so the back seat is stocked with snacks. Lots of snacks along with a suitcase and smaller duffel bag, laptop, jacket, and umbrella.

I'm fortunate that I have an abundance of patience. I've been trained to take the time necessary in any given situation. Those who try to rush the timeline end up getting skewed results. Me personally? I've never had a problem taking my time.

I sit up when I see who I assume is the Priest locking the side door, walking to the front and locking that door from the outside, and then head to his car. He seems to be unassuming, unimpressive in both looks and stature. What he does have, in abundance, is a commanding presence.

It wouldn't work on me, but with the way he carries himself, it's clear that he demands respect. I assume it's a quality that many in his position have. Without having met many priests, it's only an assumption I'm drawing. Based on opinion rather than fact.

We drive for no longer than ten or fifteen minutes to the other side of town. There are only three or four miles with lights in them, so we didn't have to start and stop too much. I perk up when he puts on his brakes and pulls in to the drive of a mediocre, split-level house. I can't tell if it's white or has a pastel hue. Either way, the siding is light in color.

The best part about this house is that the vehicle parked in the driveway is the same one I watched my girl drive away in.

Again, I settle in to watch and wait.

For her.

# Chapter 5

## *Faith*

What are they discussing? I can hear my mother every now and then, but mainly it's the two of them speaking in alternating rising and lowering voices. They are either arguing or having a very heated, passionate conversation.

I shudder at that. *Passionate*. Gross.

It didn't take me long to determine exactly what was going on while sitting in here with nothing but the memory of my father in subjugation for Father Michaels… in a *very* immoral way. Immoral in accordance with God's law.

Personally, I couldn't care less where someone finds their love. What I *do* care about is hypocrisy. That, and being thought of as stupid. It's infuriating.

I'm constantly overlooked or ignored completely because I'm introverted and a woman. I'm most comfortable in solitude, or around a very few people. I also get easily overwhelmed in high stress situations, like today. The calm is where I'm most at ease.

Anxiety is getting the better of me and I decide I can't sit here all night, not without knowing what's being said regarding what happened today along with whatever 'counsel' Father Michaels is supposed to be giving us. Also, I'm pretty sure that he had stated that there would be a sit down between all four of us, not just them.

Again, even at 21 years old, I'm still treated as a child.

Twisting the knob of my bedroom door as slowly as I can to minimize the sound of it unlatching, I slip out and tiptoe to the top of our short staircase. It comes out at the entrance of both the kitchen and family room. With the way the voices are moving toward me, it's clear they're in the family room.

Even with the low tones, now that I'm out here, I can hear them clearly. Father Michaels is reading scripture and I can hear my mother sniffling. Most likely she's sitting next to my father, hands in lap and quietly crying instead of giving any sort of input.

I'm not interested in the biblical verses Father is reading until my name is mentioned. I perk up to listen to Father Michaels' response to my mother's statement. It's the first thing she's said since I've stood here.

"But Daniel, it's *Faith*," she chokes out my name and I'm not sure what they're talking about. Or why she said that. What about me?

"Betty. Listen to me for a moment. I've studied scripture for all my life. God has given us this tool to use for the tough decisions." I hear him tap something, probably his Bible. "Everything we need is right here, telling us the correct path to take in every situation we may find ourselves in. Faith? She has lost her way. She's been lost for so long, probably longer than any of us realize, down this unnatural path that now she's seeing evil and sin everywhere. It's infected her mind. That infection is going to bleed into this household and will try and find its way to take hold of you as well."

"Well... I mean that hardly seems to warrant such a drastic-" she begins to argue. My father scolds her.

"Damnit, Betty, you're not listening!"

"Daniel, you need to calm down. It's not necessary to get angry, just try to explain your feelings about why this should be done." I contemplate what he's saying. Why should *what* be done?

Sighing, my father tries again, attempting to reign himself in. What my mother hears as anger, I'm labeling as panic. He's panicking over how to handle what I saw. "*This* is what we are trying to explain to you. We've been failing as her parents. Our job has been to teach her right from wrong and to discipline when necessary. We've been lax with her. We've lost our *own* fear of God and have brushed aside what we had assumed to be minor violations, but they've culminated into much greater, soul-destroying problems. How can we teach her if we don't have the fear ourselves?"

His voice is raised toward the end of his ramble to speak over my mother's increasingly loud sobs.

"Daniel, you did well explaining yourself. Let me take over for you, if I may?" Father Michaels asks.

"Please. I just… Damnit, Betty, would you stop crying? It's not going to help us right now." He's losing his patience.

"She's my only child!" my mother wails.

I feel the fear washing over me, taking hold and replacing all other emotions I had. She's never balked or fought this hard against a chosen method of discipline or punishment my father has ever decided to dole out. Father Michaels answers my question before I have a chance to let my mind run rampant. I don't think it would have ever made it to what they are debating and considering.

"It's all right here, Betty. You and Daniel no longer have the fear of God in you. In Proverbs, chapter 1 and verse 7, *'The fear of the Lord is the beginning of knowledge: but fools despise wisdom and instruction.'* Are you a fool, Betty? I don't think so. I'm here, providing you with the instruction, and you'd be foolish to ignore its wisdom."

My father seems to be a bit more confident now that Father Michaels has helped him along. "It's our responsibility to regain that fear, Betty. God tells us exactly how to find it through Abraham and Isaac's story. God commanded Abraham to offer Isaac as a sacrifice. 2 Samuel chapter 12, verse 13 and 14. *'The Lord also has put away your sin; you shall not die. However, because by this deed you have given great occasion to the enemies of the Lord to blaspheme, the child also who is born to you shall surely die.'* God is already going to condemn her to be taken from us anyway! By proving to God that we will obey, we offer her the same way Abraham offered Isaac."

Oh. My. *God*.

There's no way they are actually discussing this as a reasonable option. Absolutely *no way*!

My mother is still trying. "But we don't do sacrifices anymore!"

"Of course, we don't, Betty. You're missing the point here. When Abraham unquestionably followed God's command, what happened?"

"Umm... God gave Abraham a ram to sacrifice instead of Isaac," she answers, still sniffling.

"That's right," Father Michaels says. "Daniel, do you know *why* God gave Abraham a ram?"

"Because he recognized that even though Abraham was saddened about what he was to do, he feared God more," my father answers. It's obvious this whole thing is rehearsed. It's too clearly laid out like it's already been scripted.

"Exactly. A messenger stops Abraham from finishing the sacrifice by saying *'now I know you fear God.'* Do you see? It's not the sacrifice that's important here. It's the trial you and Daniel must face to ensure that you keep the fear of God alive within you."

"...Betty. God will save her if we know His fear."

More sniffling. I hold my breath as I wait along with both Father Michaels and my father for her response. I feel like it's an eternity before I'm straining to hear the words that inevitably shatter my faith in my church and my family.

"Al-Alright... I understand. If you think that this..." I stop listening as I head back to my bedroom, softly shutting the door behind me.

Quickly, I pull the only backpack I have out of my closet and begin to fill it with the barest of essentials I'll need for the next few days. My father and Father Michaels are clearly twisting these verses to justify shutting me up. If I tell anyone what I saw, they'll be ruined. Especially Father, he has the most to lose, the most motivation to get rid of me.

It's not my father's part in all this that bothers me the most either. A small part of me has always known that what he says is love isn't what love truly is. I'm not saying I'm fine with the fact that my father has no problem deciding that I must die in the course of one afternoon. It's my mother's agreement that crushes me. That small part that knew my father didn't love me never prepared me for the knowledge that she didn't either.

I have to leave. *Now*. I didn't stick around long enough to hear when this so called '*sacrifice*' was going to happen, but I guarantee it's not going to be next weekend after Sunday brunch. I have a small window of time to be gone from here, as far and as fast as possible.

Zipping my bag filled with a couple changes of clothes, I double check that my toothbrush and toothpaste have been added. There are a few other travel sized hygiene products, which I've loved collecting over the years from various motels, and my wallet filled with all the cash I have on hand. I've got several hundred dollars, not a lot, but enough to get me out of here.

I look around my room to make sure there's nothing else I'm forgetting. I see nothing else I need to pack, so I slip into my closet to change my clothes. I pull my dress off and the tights down, catching them on this stupid metal chain. I bite my tongue from crying out. I need to get it off.

Reaching behind my thigh, I try to find where the metal hook has been twisted around to clamp it on. After a couple of minutes trying to unbend it, I realize it's not going to happen. I can't push it down my leg either, it's dug so far into my skin that it will tear if I force it. The metal is too thick, my fingers too weak, and I have no more time to waste. I'll deal with it when I can.

I grab items to throw on in layers; a tank top, short-sleeved shirt, then a long-sleeved shirt with a sweatshirt over that. Unfortunately, the jacket I have is one of those thick woolen dress coats that would be impractical to wear right now. It's still mid-fall, so the layers alone will have to do.

I grab two thick pairs of leggings and pull each of them on. They're more moveable and act as a softer padding on my leg, plus jeans are too restrictive. Looking down my body, standing here in double leggings and my bra, I see the knotted cord.

*THIS* I can remove. Grabbing a pair of sharp scissors from my desk, it only takes me a moment to alternate between cutting and sawing before the ends separate and I'm free from it. I could have untied it, but cutting it has a certain air of finality to it. That relief gives me a massive lift of spirits and motivates me. I can survive on my own.

I can do this. I can do this. I can do this.

I repeat my mantra as I put on my tops, lay the cord on my bed next to the scissors I've tossed there, and grab my backpack.

Moving to my window, I look out into the darkness as I inch the moisture-swollen wooden frame upwards. I only need enough space to slide through feet first so I can hang down as far as possible before needing to drop to the ground. I'm probably ten or so feet up, only high enough to make my heart race a little as I release the sill and hit the ground not even a second later.

Pulling the hood of my sweatshirt over my head, I quickly look around to see if anyone is outside before running to the edge of my property and picking my way through the woods until I come out a few houses down.

Glancing down the street left and then right, I debate where I should go. Probably into town. If I head further into the country, it will only guarantee that I'll spend the better part of the night, and the next day, walking before I may be forced to sleep on the ground. I'll have more options if I go into town.

Decision made, I pick up my pace, half jogging and half running, as I move as quickly as I'm able. These blasted metal spikes are digging in so deeply that every now and then, as I'm moving, I can feel one of them slice into my skin.

I've dealt with pain before, I can grit my teeth through this for now. It won't be forever.

The further I get from what was once my home, the easier I start to breathe, even with the shortness of breath at my exertion to distance myself.

A train whistle cuts through the silence of the night, and I immediately know.

Call it God, call it faith, or luck, or karma. Whatever you call it, I immediately know that's where I need to go.

# Chapter 6

## *Arrow*

After sitting in my car outside that church for over five hours, I am ready to stretch my legs. Being 6'3 has its advantages. Sitting in any sized vehicle for five hours comfortably is not one of them.

My car may be visible to them, but where I lean against it, I know the shadows created by the trees have me hidden from the untrained eye.

These people have been sitting in the living room for close to an hour just talking. It's animated, but boring. I'm also disappointed because I haven't seen the girl yet. There are a few lights coming from various windows aside from where this meeting is happening, but I'm not sure which room she's in.

The older woman is crying now, and it looks like both men are trying to reason with her. I was correct in my assumption that she is the source of my girl's delicate features. Although her hair is a darker shade than the other two, it's still some version of ashy blonde. She's lovely, but pales in comparison to the girl hiding somewhere else in that house.

Movement to the right catches my attention and I focus my attention there to see what it is, and I'm floored.

*What the hell is this girl doing?*

I watch as the girl I saw earlier in the day, hair billowing around her waist, dressed in a good girl school uniform skirt and button up shirt, hangs and then drops from her window. Her hair looks like it's pulled back in a low knot at the back of her head, hidden by the hood of her sweatshirt. There's a medium sized bag on her back and she's dressed in dark, warm clothes. She's running.

Holy fuck. She's running!

Quickly, I pull my keys out and round the car to hop in. I don't give a shit what's happening in the house anymore. Well, that's not true, but it's also not my priority now.

I follow her direction to get a read on where she's going before starting my engine. I don't want her to know I'm here yet, and honestly, I'm really fucking curious. There's worry too, but the curiosity is outweighing everything else.

She slips into the woods, sticking to the edge for a few moments before disappearing. There's only one place she can come out at so I quickly pull up and park, shutting off the engine once more.

She for sure has a limp. It's apparent now as she approaches where I'm sitting and then rushes past me without looking in to see me sitting here. It's not obvious I'm in here, but I'm also not going out of my way to hide. I feel an urge to give her a lecture on staying aware of her surroundings, but it goes away when I see her face.

She's scared. She's scared and running, and fuck if I don't want to take that fear away from her. Getting this second look at her, I start to wonder if she's even 18. In regular clothes like this, she looks like a teenager, barely past puberty.

The growing concern that I'm now involved in a possible runaway teen situation is waring with the small amount of shame I have at being so attracted to her. I try to tell my cock that, but he feels no shame at all and couldn't care less what age she is, only that she looks like someone he desperately wants to be inside of.

For now, I won't dwell on that. I could be wrong, and it will end up being a moot point anyway. I focus on my concern instead.

Her pace only slows marginally by the time we make it fully into town. There aren't a lot of vehicles on the road this evening and it's going to become obvious very soon that I'm following her.

I want to snarl when I watch as she bumps into a man standing with a few others outside of one of the few local bars smoking. Her mouth is moving like she's apologizing again, must be a habit for her, ingrained to immediately say 'I'm sorry.'

That's not what I'm snarling at though. It's the dead man that's got his hand wrapped around her upper arm, trying to pull her toward him. The group are all taking turns, saying something to her. By the way she's pulling away and cowering from them and the looks they have on their faces, what they're saying isn't polite.

Again, ready to hop out and intervene, I'm halted when they release her, and she scurries away while they laugh at her retreating form. Fuckers are lucky I don't have time to stop.

She makes it to the other side of town before finally slowing down. Her limp is much heavier now. Her face is grimacing in pain as she leans against the wall of an abandoned building. She massages her lower left thigh. Maybe an old injury or disability?

We are in the industrial area. It's dirty, but there aren't a lot of people around. I also absolutely can't keep following in the car now. It has to be on foot.

We both look in the same direction when a loud whistle pierces the silent night. She stands a little taller and determination is set in her face. Pride fills my chest when I see her push back the fear and pain, everything is gone but that determination. She's saving herself, not waiting on a white knight to do it for her.

Now that I know exactly where she's going, I wait for her to get a decent distance away from me before hopping out, grabbing my bags, and landing on the ground. Reorganizing the items inside my duffel bag with only things I can't leave behind, I zip up the rest of my stuff, mainly spare clothes, into the suitcase and toss it in the trunk.

The only thing I add to my attire is my gun holster that is easily hidden under most of my shirts. I dig through the center console to grab my spare gun and pull my other from the holster I'm wearing around my ankle. I settle them against my upper body and throw the ankle cuff into the car.

Slamming the door shut, I lock it and pocket the keys. I'll throw them in the mail to send back to the rental company. I'm not worried about the cost of it being towed or damaged because I'm abandoning it.

Swinging my bag over one shoulder, I slip into the shadows and follow her. I catch up just in time to see her slip into the last train car, hiding herself in the shadows.

I'll follow as soon as she falls asleep.

# Chapter 7

## *Faith*

Groaning, I try to blink my eyes open when the flashes of sunlight strobe in my eyes, waking me up.

My body… oh God… it's so stinking sore right now that I just want to curl up and cry. My neck is stiff from using my bulky, misshaped backpack as a pillow. My stomach is tender to the touch from the cord I removed from my waist. Even though it *is* tender, it's a pain I welcome. The worst, my leg. It's absolutely *throbbing*.

After my run through town and then crawling up into this train car, it's past the point of tolerance. When I looked last night, it hadn't looked good, but it was better than it had felt. There was some dried blood where some of the points had punctured their way through. I was able to tear off a couple small pieces of cotton from my tank top to fold into a square and tuck in between the spots that were open. Not entirely sanitary, but it made a difference in comfort.

This morning though, there's a heavy throb working its way through the entire portion of my upper left thigh. Reaching down, I pull my pant leg up to look at my lower leg. There's no swelling and it's the same color as my right side. I let out a little sigh in relief that the blood flow hasn't been restricted. It's circulating just fine, probably why I can feel it so sharply.

"She's awake," a woman mutters under her breath. Jerking my head up at the sound of someone's voice, I'm shocked to see people in the car with me.

"About time. *Hey*, you!" the man sitting next to her calls to me. His voice is raspy, like he's been smoking for his entire life. "Benny, wake the fuck up." He nudges the third man that's stretched out next to them.

"Got dang it Chad, what the fuc-" he sees me staring at them, eyes wide. I'm so shocked that they're in here. I hadn't heard anyone moving around in here last night. Apparently, I was sleeping heavily, which is really terrifying now that I know anyone can just sneak up on me.

The first man, Chad, yells at me again, "Hey! I'm talkin' to you."

Quickly looking around the space, I see there's a fourth person sitting apart from the other three. Their body is big, so I'm assuming it's a man. He's got a hat pulled down covering most of his face. He must be asleep.

"Umm…" I say. I'm not sure what they want, just yelling at me to get my attention. Clearing my throat, I decide to be nice, my voice cracking on the first word, "Y-Yeah, hi. Umm… how are you?" I can't stop the swoop of my voice at the end like I'm unsure if I should be asking. Shoot, I'm tired. I rub my eyes.

A couple of them laugh at me. The woman's laugh is more of a cackle. I don't know how old any of them are, but they seem like they're around my parents' age. No one has said her name yet, but the woman speaks next, "HA! Well, how do you do? Care for a cup of tea?"

My face heats at their mocking. Chad mimics me next, "Right? Hey, Becca. Fancy a round of golf?" He nudges her, wiggling his eyebrows up and down before directing his attention back to me. "Whatcha doin' in here girl?" He's not laughing anymore.

"I don'-... I'm sorry. I d-didn't realize someone else was here. I-"

Becca snaps at me, "This is *our* car. Every'n knows it's ours. You don't get to just come in like you're own'en the place!"

"Spoiled rich girl," Benny grumbles. "She ought' to pay rent if you're gonna be in here. She looks like she's prob'ly got some money."

I glance over at the other man who's yet to say anything. He's still sleeping, arms across his chest, unmoving and completely relaxed.

Shifting my gaze back, I try to explain to them. "I really didn't know. I promise, as soon as we stop, I'll leave out of here."

"What about right now? You're in here now, you gonna pay rent?" she asks me.

"We're owed rent, imposin' on us, takin' up our space." I think that was Chad, but my sights are locked on the woman. She's sneering at me, clearly angry that I'm in here.

"Please, I don't have much with me. I promise I will leave the moment we stop," I plead with them.

"So, you *do* have money. You pay us now, we'll leave ya alone 'til we stop. You don't?" Chad shrugs like he couldn't careless either way. Like he couldn't care that I'm being given an impossible choice. "You can get off here."

I grip my bag tighter to my chest and shake my head as my eyes fill with tears. "I c-can't. I have to keep what I have. It's all I have," I whisper to them. *Please God, please let them have some empathy and grace right now.*

"You give us it now, or we'll come get it ourselves," Benny growls at me.

Choking back a sob, I keep shaking my head. "I-" I can't get anything out and I watch as they stand up, ready to act on their threat.

"You really want us to come get it from ya?" Chad scoffs. "You can pay us now, or how about we take the whole bag and then help you off here?"

"P-please..." I cry out. I quickly scramble to my feet so I'm not in a more vulnerable position on the ground and hold my hand out. "P-please don't. I really need-"

"Give us the fucking bag bitch," Becca grits out, holding her hand out for it. I don't move, just keep shaking my head no.

"Cunt's fuckin' stupid guys. Just go get the fuckin' thing," she says.

I tense my body and wrap my arms tighter around the backpack, quickly sliding the straps over my shoulders so it's more difficult for them to take it from me. Chad grabs the front of it and wrenches me forward as he tries to yank it from me. "Let it the fuck go!" he screams at me.

Benny reaches out to help Chad, but he barely grazes me when a fist flies into his face from somewhere behind Chad.

"*WHAT THE FUCK!*" he yells out, grabbing his nose and stumbling backwards into the woman. She screams as his body forces her to fall backwards on to her butt.

Chad shoves me to the side as he turns to face off with the fourth rider, who's most definitely awake now. I slam into a pile of junk along the wall and scream out when the collar around my leg stabs into the front of my thigh. Instantly I can feel a warm liquid seeping out and starting to run.

I hear fighting going on behind me, but I don't look, too focused on fighting back the shock of the pain. I can't lean forward to look down with my backpack hooked on the front of me like this. Glancing over at all the bodies, I can't make out what's happening through my tears. I can't see who's winning.

Huddling down, I cover my ears to block out the snarls and curses and the incessant scream from the woman, yelling for the man to stop. Squeezing my eyes shut, I try to stop the panic.

*Just make it stop. Please stop. Please stop. Pl-*

I scream when I feel a hand grip my shoulder and pull away. Crying out for who, I don't know. *I just don't want to be here anymore!*

"Hey. Hey. You're all right." It's the deep bass of the man who was sleeping in the corner. He puts his hand back on my shoulder and squeezes in a way to let me know he's not a threat. I stare up at him through wet lashes, not able to determine all his features except that he's got some dark facial hair on his face and he's thick. Like lumberjack thick, not extra weight thick.

"Come on, kitten. Let me help you up." I'm frozen. Sighing, he leans down to bring himself closer and lowers his voice, "I'm not going to hurt you, but they will if you don't come sit with me. Okay?"

Barely nodding yes, I slip my hand into the one he's holding out to me, and he pulls me up to my feet. Looking over, the three of them are sitting along the wall, Benny nursing his nose and Chad glaring at us. Becca has her back to us, so I don't see her face or what she's doing. They're all tense though.

"You good?" he asks. His arm slides around my shoulder and he leads me back to the area was he was sleeping at before the fight.

"Yes..." I whisper to him. I'm not and a pinch of guilt hits me for lying to him. I'm scared, upset, and now I'm bleeding, but I don't want him to feel like he needs to do more than he already has. "I'm so-sorry that yo-"

He chuckles at me and slips my backpack from my body to set next to his. "There's nothing to be sorry for. Come on, sit. This thing isn't going to stop for hours and you, my pet, look exhausted."

I'm flustered at the way he's speaking to me and my cheeks heat in embarrassment. "Where should I..." I look around. There is more stuff on the ground over here. A few crates, and some random pieces of wood and metal scattered around.

I look up with wide eyes when he doesn't answer and see him smiling down at me, eyes crinkled in the corners. It's an honest smile. He has honest eyes. I swallow back my words because I want to tell him his smile looks like what I would imagine Angel Gabriel's smile would look like.

His smile fades slightly and he rumbles a sound out. I'm not sure if it's a laugh or growl or what, but it's almost animalistic in nature. It causes the hair on my neck to stand on end when I shudder. Lord, my body is reacting strongly to his presence.

"Fuck. You..." he stops. Taking a breath, he releases my shoulder and sits back down where he was. His movements graceful and controlled. It's incredible to see someone who you'd think would be heavy footed because of their size move like a dancer or like one of those people who do martial arts in movies.

He gets himself comfortable while I stand, awkwardly, unsure of where I should be sitting. Does he want me to go back to where I was?

"Come here, kitten. You need sleep, as do I. I'll keep you safe." He holds his hand up to me. It's a polite gesture, like when a man holds the door open for a woman. He's holding his hand out to help me sit down without stumbling.

This time when I put my hand in his, I feel a connection zip through our hands, warming me from the inside. It's the calm that I'm always searching for. The rest of the tension leaves my shoulders and I move to sit down, wincing as the skin of my leg is stretched where I bend it.

"Are you hurt?" Kneeling now in front of him, I pause in my movement, still holding his hand.

I ignore his question because I really need him to know how much I appreciate his kindness right now. "Thank you so much. I'm so sorry you had to be involved in all of that, but you've helped me and I'm incredibly thankful for that." I gently tap my chest with the hand not buried within his. "Truly. It means… it means a lot," I choke a little, emotion overwhelming me once more.

That gorgeous smile is back as he studies me. "I want to tell you not to apologize again, but I can see that you want me to hear it. You're very welcome sweet girl. Come on now. Sit." He tugs me a bit and I fall forward into his lap.

He catches me before all my body weight hits him and I'm amazed at the strength he has when he lifts me up, turns me and settles me between his legs. They're bent, knees squeezing my sides and almost reaching my armpits.

I can't stop the shiver when I feel his hands and then arms slide around my waist from behind, one of his hands pausing briefly on my stomach before wrapping them fully around me and pulling me back in to his chest.

I'm surrounded, blanketed in safety. I can't stop the sob that tears from me at the relief he's given me.

He hugs me a bit tighter and settles his chin on top of my head. "I got you. Get some sleep my sweet girl." I think I feel a soft brush of his lips in my hair, and I don't even care that it may have been the first kiss anyone has ever given me.

I close my eyes and try my best to relax into him, to sleep like he's told me to, but I don't want to move around and annoy him. My heart is also racing at the fact that I'm being held by a man I've never met before, and I can't help but feel the excitement over that.

I tense when one of his hands releases me and his uses it to lay my head against his chest and strokes my hair that has come loose, and the side of my face.

He's holding me like a parent would hold a child to their chest to rock them to sleep or when they're scared. Then I feel the vibrations start up under my ear and I smile softly to myself.

He's humming me to sleep.

# Chapter 8

## *Arrow*

I'll be honest, I truly did not think I'd have this girl in my arms within 24 hours from running into her. I also didn't think that I would have fucked up as bad as I did within the first 24 hours of having seen her for the first time.

If she weren't passed out on my chest right now, I'd seriously consider throwing my fist into all those leeches' faces a few more times. What they got didn't even come close to what they deserve for scaring my kitten the way they did. If her sobbing hadn't crushed my heart the way it had while I was fighting them off her, I wouldn't have stopped until she and I were the only ones left in this train car.

I have a feeling that she wouldn't have liked for me to go that far anyway. She doesn't seem the vengeful type, not if her constant apologies tell me anything.

After spending almost the full night standing outside the train car, keeping the other homeless wanderers from entering, I was exhausted by the time I finally settled in the opposite corner from her once it seemed that no one else was going to approach for the night.

Apparently, I was wrong. I heard the commotion when we started moving and what I thought were just train sounds clanking and making a ton of noise, I hadn't noticed that some of it was those three slipping into the train car at the last moment. I allowed myself to get some solid sleep knowing that it was just the girl and me in here.

The rocking of the train car and white noise of speeding down a track, all combined with exhaustion, was why I didn't wake until I heard a man scream out *'Let it the fuck go!'* Immediately I was on my feet and saw my little girl being man handled by a couple of dirty pieces of trash.

White hot rage burned through me.

I only had to deliver a few well aimed punches to them both before they quickly got the hint that they had no chance with me. I was also just in time for my heart to be tormented by the sound of her defeat and pain in her sobs. Then fully shattered at the sight of her on the ground, curled in on herself and covering her ears for protection.

Fuck my life. She looked like a tiny kitten, scared and stranded, no chance to survive on her own in the wild.

Grabbing hold of her when I pulled her away from them, I briefly noticed that the large bumps under her shirt I felt yesterday were no longer there. I'll have to ask her about that later.

By the time she was settled in my arms, we were both relaxed. Peace surrounded the both of us as she sunk into my chest, purring under the stroke of my hand and the vibrations of my song for her.

I don't even know her name yet, but all of me has decided to keep her. She's mine and I'm sure she knows, even if it's just subconsciously.

I *really* fucking hope she's eighteen.

My mind is fighting the sleep that my body wants to be pulled into now that my adrenaline is coming back down. I don't want to risk her safety by giving them the opportunity to hurt her while I'm asleep, so I make sure that she's tucked far into my body.

She's in between my legs, leaning slightly on her right side. I scoot us a few inches to the right so I can brace my knee against the wall to support her and then attempt to tuck my left over her legs, locking her in.

When the weight of my leg tries to settle on her, she whimpers in her sleep, body stiffening slightly until I lift back up. Then she relaxes again.

try again. Same thing, except her whimper is followed by a groan this time.

Pinching my brows in confusion, I try to look at her leg but don't see anything. We're too far in the shadows to get enough light and she's wearing dark clothes. I shift her a bit more to her right and slide my arm out from under her heavy breasts that I'm really trying to not notice right now.

Slowly, I reach to run my fingers over her leg, looking for an injury. There must be something with that limp and her reaction to the weight. I start at her hip and press gently, watching her face as best I can for a response. Nothing.

I continue working my way down her leg until I get about mid-thigh. That's when I feel something hard under her pants. Just the slightest pressure has her brows furrowing. I follow it, trying to figure out what the fuck she's wearing, and find that it's got to be some sort of piece of metal that circles her entire thigh. It's not smooth but has dips and rises. It almost feels like a large chain.

I pull my hand away to scratch my cheek, running through all possibilities in my head when I feel something damp where my fingers touched. Pulling my hand away, there's enough light to see blood on my fingertips.

God *damnit*! Why the hell is she wearing something like that? I'm not sure if she knew she was bleeding, but I don't care. That thing needs to come off now. I need to find where the blood is coming from and stop it.

Shaking her awake, I try to rouse her as gently as I can. "Kitten. Kitten, I need you to wake up." I try to reign in my laugh at her complete non-response. This sweet thing is dead to the world. I try again and laugh a little more when there's still no movement. Honestly, I think she's fallen deeper under, her mouth parted slightly now with the barest hint of a soft snore.

I quickly wipe my hands on my pants to remove her blood before running them over her head to try and coax her awake. Kissing her crown, briefly taking an inhale of her shampoo, I speak a bit louder.

"Sweet girl. You need to wake up. Promise it won't be long." Ahh, now she's stirring.

"Kitten?" I ask when I see her eyelids flutter open and then tips her head back to gaze at me sleepily.

"Hmm?" A slow blink and then her lids start to drop again, even looking up the way she is.

"Open your eyes for me beautiful." Her lips twitch and then she does as I asked. Smiling at her, I have to physically stop myself from leaning down and brushing my lips across hers. "There you are. I'm sorry for waking you, but I'm worried. Your leg is bleeding pretty good right now and you've got a piece of metal wrapped around your leg. Wha-"

I stop talking as I watch her face completely shut down before she looks away from me and attempts to sit up.

Grabbing her quickly, I pull her back into me. I pin her with an arm across her chest and the other around her stomach and hold her to me, whispering in her ear, "I swear kitten, I'm not going to hurt you. Let me see what's going on and we'll figure it out."

Her head drops forward, her hair falling around her face as she shudders. "It's... Shoot." She turns to look at me and I'm again floored at how unbelievably alluring she is. A fucking knock-out. Jesus Christ.

"It's what?" I push.

"It's just... it's really flipping embarrassing." She's looking away again and picking at a seam line in my jeans. I'm not sure she realizes she's touching me, but it makes my chest expand at the knowledge that she's at least somewhat comfortable with me.

"No judgements from me. Tell me... please?" I ask her.

She looks so ashamed as she explains, "It's called a cilice. This one sort of looks like a thick metal chain that sort of reminded me of a dog's choke collar. Anyway, its worn by someone who wants to do penance for a sin they've committed." I'm not really following.

"So... I'm not sure I understand. What does it *do?*"

She blows out a breath. "What it does is cause a constant discomfort to remind you not to commit that sin again for whatever you're doing the penance for. If that makes sense? I don't really know for sure... I've never had to wear one before."

I jerk back at that. "You *had* to wear it? I thought you said it's if you wanted to do penance? Also, penance for what?"

It's hard to fully see, but I can tell she's blushing when she mutters under her breath. I don't think she wants me to hear. "...myfathermademe..."

I raise an eyebrow at that. "Your father made you? Why don't you just take the damn thing off now if it's hurting you? That's not why you're bleeding, right?" Fuck, I got distracted from the whole reason I woke her up to begin with.

"I can't..." she whispers.

"Sure you can. Look, I'll turn my back and block you from the others in here. Just do it quick and-" I stop at the whine that escapes from the back of her throat like a wounded fucking animal. "Jesus, baby... What is it?"

Her eyes are watery with unshed tears, and she's got her mouth clamped shut like she's fighting to hold her words in. I pull my feet under me, squat in front of her, and cup her cheeks just in time to wipe away the first tear as it rolls down her cheek. "Come on kitten. You have to help me understand."

Sucking in a rattly breath, she shakes her head no but makes me understand anyway. "I can't get it off. My father, he... he did something to it. Twisted the hook or something and I can't get it off. I tried."

My nostrils flare in anger and my fingers grip her face a little harder. She tries to pull back from me, but I stop her. "Sorry... sorry. I'm not going to hurt you. I'm not mad at you." My mind races to figure this out. "Would you let me see it? Maybe it's something I'll be able to undo."

"Umm... al-alright. It's just..." She trails off and doesn't finish her thought.

"It's just what?"

Whispering again, she says, "You'll see my underwear…" I bite my cheek so I don't laugh at her. God she's cute.

I clear my throat, so I don't laugh when I speak. "Listen to me. I'm a grown man and can assure you that I will not be scandalized by a pair of panties. I'll also promise to do my best to not look as much as possible. I'm not going to ask you if this is all right. It's going to have to be. We need to get the cilice off and I also want to see where you're bleeding to try and stop that as well."

Breathing a sigh of relief, she stands to pull down her leggings and gets them down to just above her knee. I'm still squatting down, but I grab hold of her hips, briefly look at her pert ass covered with a simple pair of white cotton panties and pull her a step over into the light.

*I'm going to kill her father.*

My anger scared her earlier, so I don't say anything this time. Thankfully, she has her back to me and can't tell that I'm barely holding it together. She's shivering slightly, either because she's cold or the fact that she's out of her comfort zone, standing here with her pants halfway down her legs. Either way, I try to distract the both of us while I see what I can do to help her.

"So, kitten. I feel like we've skipped quite a few steps over the last hour. Tell me about yourself. What's your name?" I run my finger along the bottom of the thick chain links to clear some of the blood away so I can see what the hell I'm dealing with.

"Oh! I'm so sorry. That was rude of me to not introduce myself. My name is Faith Holton."

A shudder runs through her when my fingers graze her skin over the top of this *thing*. I try slipping a finger under one of the links and find that I can't. It's incredibly tight, her skin puckered around it, almost like there are indentations spread out.

"Faith… your name is beautiful. What does it mean? Well, I know what 'faith' means, but does it have another meaning as a first name?" I lean forward to try and see, my eyes widening when I realize that there are fucking spikes lining the entire inside of this thing, digging into her skin.

"My name means faithfulness and loyalty, or to trust. What's yo-"

"Faith… there are spikes under this and cutting your skin open."

She pauses a moment. "…I know."

Grinding my jaw, I find where it's been joined together and see that the hook has been twisted around the loop it goes through several times. Reaching into my pocket, I pull out my keys to try and leverage it under the end and push it up. "I'm sorry kitten, I'm going to try my best not to hurt you, but I need to try and pry this open… How old are you, Faith?"

I'm able to work the flat side of the key under the end, and I slowly begin to bend it up before slipping the key out and then sliding it on the other side to follow the direction of the bends. Her leg jerks forward when I start to push the part that's right up against her skin back down.

"Shh... I'm sorry baby. Keep talking to me."

"I'm uhh... I just turned 21 a couple of months ago." I raise my eyebrows at that. I'm surprised that she's in her twenties. She looks younger.

"You look young for your age. Are you going to college?"

"I hear that all the time. It's because of my height. It's deceiving." I continue to work the hook around as she tells me that she attended a two-year technical school to receive her Associates for Business Administration, but she hasn't found a job yet. She asks me what I do for a living.

"I work for the government. I do investigative work for the NCAVC." I don't want to intimidate her and tell her that I'm basically a profiler for the FBI.

Fuck, this is taking forever. It's not helping that she's bleeding and causing the key to slip in my hand every now and then. I know this is painful for her, but her resilience is impressive.

"What's the NCAVC?"

"It stands for the National Center for the Analysis of Violent Crime." Last turn and this thing will be off her.

"Oh... wow. That sounds like... is it dangerous?" She's hesitant to ask and I only briefly wonder why.

"Not normally. It has its moments though. *There*!" I say as the hook is finally freed. "I'll be careful removing it. It's digging in pretty good. Again, very sorry for causing you additional pain."

"It's fi-" she cries out as I slowly peel it away from her skin. "I-It's fine. It'll b-be better when... it's off." She sounds like she's trying to not cry. I quickly finish and then toss it on the floor a couple of feet from us. Grabbing a clean t-shirt from my bag, I wrap it around her thigh and tie it to stop some of the wounds from bleeding more than they already are.

"We need to keep pressure on this for a bit. I don't have any bandages with me. My shirt isn't necessarily sanitary, but it's clean. It'll have to do for now. I know you'd like to redress, but I'd like for you to stay like this for a bit, sit with me again and let me keep hold of the shirt and keep pressure on it."

It looks like there are a few shallow cuts scattered around her thigh. The main source of her problem is the outer side of her thigh where it must have pierced the skin when she fell. A few could probably use a stitch or two, but it's most likely too late for that now.

"I feel like a terrible inconvenience to you. It will probably be okay if I do it, don't you think?" Sweet Faith has such a tender heart, never wanting to be a burden. Soon she'll realize that this is my pleasure, never a burden.

"Nope. Don't argue." Sitting down again in the same position I was before, I take hold of her hips and pull her back down to me, sliding my hands up to her waist to pick her up and set her across my lap this time. When I have my hands on her waist, I note that I was right yesterday. My thumbs and fingers touch.

"Thank you for all you've done... again. It's such a relief to have that off." I know she's still sore, but her entire body is more relaxed now that she's not in constant pain. What her father did has got to be some sort of crime and I'm going to investigate it for her. This is unacceptable.

I wrap my hand around the side of her thigh, pull it toward me, and cradle her in my arms at the same time.

I can't stop myself this time. I lean down and brush a kiss across her cheek and then place another small one at the very corner of her mouth. She sucks in her breath and gazes up at me, frozen in shock. I don't point it out to her.

"Again, you're very welcome kitten. Now, close your eyes and get some more rest. We have a long trip ahead of us and you'll need your strength."

I watch her close her eyes in compliance, and her face continue to soften as she allows herself to go back under.

"What's your name?" she whispers.

"Arrow."

# Chapter 9

## *Faith*

I didn't get to think about Arrow's name until after I woke up, sprawled face down on his chest, my hair in his face. The jerking of the train pulled me out of sleep and as I looked up, he was grinning at me.

Leaning back against his duffel bag, he has one arm tucked under his head and his other wrapped around my back, holding me to him. How long has he been looking at me? I blush and bury my face back into his chest to get myself centered.

"We should be stopping soon, and I'd like to leave as soon as we do. I don't want you staying any longer than necessary, not with those punctures in your leg. We need to get to a hotel and get you cleaned and patched up."

*Well, that's embarrassing. Am I that dirty?* I pull myself up and try to subtly smell myself to make sure I'm not super gross right now. "You're fine, kitten. I meant your leg." He's chuckling at my apparent panic. I'm more relieved than embarrassed now that I know I don't smell.

"I would have felt terrible if you had to deal this long, laying like this." I try to lift up from his body by pushing myself back from him, but the moment I put pressure on my left knee it sends a deep ache all the way up through my thigh and I groan.

Arrow immediately pulls me back on to his chest, concern etched on his face. "We *really* need to get you out of here. Just stay where you are until we fully stop and then I'll help you, all right?" Nodding, I agree and settle back in, able to enjoy it now that I'm wide awake.

"Sorry," I mutter, then ask him what I meant to right before I fell asleep. "Where'd the name Arrow come from? I've never heard it used as a name before."

"My parents are sort of free-spirited people. Not hippies or anything, but they didn't have a problem going against the norm. I have an older brother named Archer, and they decided to keep going with the theme."

"Is he your only sibling?" I would have loved to have a sibling growing up, someone to talk and play with when I was little. Maybe a sister I could've shared clothes with or a brother that would've played in a fort outside with me. My parents had me late in life and decided that one was enough.

"He is. He's just about 4 years older than me. My parents had planned on more, but after I showed up, they felt they had their hands full with the two of us. We were rambunctious."

He pulls me into him tighter as the train car takes one larger shudder and then finally comes to a complete stop. The feeling of being a burden rolls through me when I realize that I've only got a few hundred dollars to pitch in for a room. "Arrow?"

He's watching the other three as they ignore us and make a quick escape off the train. "Hmm?" When they're gone, he looks back to me, "You ready to get out of here?"

"I uhh... Shoot," I bite the corner of my mouth and try to explain without sounding like I'm a sob story, "I don't really have much to put in for a room or anything. I thought maybe I'd find a shelter when I got far enough away from home."

"Put your arm around my neck. I'm going to stand up with you and see if it's easier for you to put weight on your leg that way. Also, don't worry about the room. You hold on to your money. I have plenty to cover it."

"That's not fair to you! It should be even," I protest. If he pays for the entire thing, it'll add one more thing he's done for me on my shoulders. There are so many at this point that I have no idea how I'll ever be able to repay him. I can't even think of how to compensate him for the protection he's given me.

"Baby, look at me," he waits until I'm looking up at him before continuing. "I'm aware that you're in a tough spot right now. I may not know why, I'm gonna be asking about that by the way, but you don't need to worry about me and being fair. It's not going to hurt my bank account to cover a room for however long we need it. Will you accept that I just want to help you?"

Chewing on the inside of my cheek, I try hard to come up with an argument. I've always tried to help others when I could without expectation of the favor returned. It's the accepting it myself part that's difficult for me.

"I can see your mind whirling, pretty girl. Will it help to tell you that it's not just that I want to help you, but I *need* to help you? It'll make me feel like I'm completing my purpose. Let me take care of you… Please?"

My pulse picks up when he calls me pretty. I know he's simply being kind, but after my proximity to very large muscles for the last four or five hours, I can't help my reaction to it. I feel like I'm thirteen, developing my very first crush.

For now, I can let it go. I'll find some way to thank him before we part ways. Maybe I'll try to get his phone number or address and use them later. "I'll try not to argue for now."

"Thank you, baby." I freeze when he places a kiss on the corner of my mouth, hardly enough for me to enjoy, before he pulls away. "I'm going to jump down first. Hand me the bags and then I'll help you out."

He sets me down like giving me my *actual* first kiss was no big deal. I'm sure he's kissed girls so many times that the one he just gave me most likely means nothing to him. Just a 'whatever' type of gesture. Maybe it's a normal thing and I just didn't know.

I feel like an idiot when I realize Arrow is standing down on the ground, holding his arms out for the bags. "Oh! S-Sorry!" Looking around, I quickly grab the bags and hand him one at a time. I'm trying to ignore the throbbing of my leg, the ache steadily growing more noticeable the longer I keep my weight on it. He doesn't need a girl following him around, whining the entire time.

He holds his arms back out to me to help me down. Grabbing his shoulders, I feel his hands wrap around my waist. "You apologize a lot, don't you?"

"I uhh... I guess. I don't mean to do it, really. Sorry..." I flinch and then sigh. It's a terrible habit, and I know it makes me seem like a pushover. He chuckles as he helps me down, and I hold in the groan when the pressure of his hands on my stomach digs into the bruises covering it.

"Hey, are you okay? Is it your leg?" He's looking down at me as he throws both of our bags over his shoulder, and my eyes widen in shock. This is the first time I've been able to really see him in the light and at his full height.

My first thought is spoken out loud, unintentionally but understandably because it's *so* true. "You're *beautiful*." I want to do a face palm when I feel my face instantaneously *explode* in heat, the red scorching its way up my face. Who does that? Who *says* something like that out loud?

I watch as his smile grows even wider than it just was. "Well kitten, I happen to think that you are as well. Stunning really."

I dig my teeth into my bottom lip to stop the unexpected giggle trying to work its way past my vocal cords. It doesn't stop the smile from quirking my lips up, and I look down at the ground to save myself from the intensity of his stare.

Arrow slides a finger under my chin and tips my face up to stop me from hiding. "You don't believe me now, but you will in time."

Furrowing my eyebrows, I study his face to determine his sincerity when something clicks, and my eyes widen in surprise. "I've seen you before! Yesterday, outside of Bert's Deli! What are you doing here? On the train I mean."

This time he seems surprised. What are the odds that we'd meet yesterday and then again less than a day later, huddled in an empty train car, leaving town. It can't be just a coincidence.

"I'll explain when we get settled. It's a longer conversation than I want to have standing here. Come on, kitten." He grabs my hand and leads me toward the town we've arrived in.

It takes us about thirty minutes of walking to find a place that he deems decent enough for us to stay. I only made it about twenty minutes before he picked me up and carried me, stating that he couldn't stand watching me limp any longer.

With the bags thrown over his shoulder, he hugged me, had me wrap my legs around his waist, and then slipped his arms underneath my bottom. I don't think he realized where he was touching me, so I didn't say anything. I just hid my face in his shoulder with the excuse I didn't want to obstruct his view. The last ten minutes are spent enjoying the excuse I must stay close.

Another fifteen minutes later, and Arrow is dropping me on the only bed in the room, staring down at me with his hands on his hips. There were no rooms available that had double beds, so after verifying with me that I'd be okay sharing, here we are with a single king.

"All right, kitten. I'm going to need you to take off your pants."

# Chapter 10

## *Faith*

I freeze. *Uhh... what?* I can't even... I can't thi-

Arrow bursts out laughing, and I jolt from the unexpectedness of the sound. "I'm so sorry, but fuck you're precious. I promise I'm not laughing at you. Faith, sweet girl, I want to look at your leg and make sure it's not getting worse. I didn't get a good look in the train car; it was way too dark."

I can't stop it. The tears try to escape my lids and I do everything in my power to keep it contained. Between yesterday with my family, the exhaustion from traveling the way we have, the drama from this morning with those people that wanted to take my money, I think I'm filled to the max with emotions. Humiliation is apparently my breaking point.

"I-" my voice cracks. I stop trying to speak.

"Hey, hey. None of that kitten." He's stopped laughing and is crawling on to the bed next to me and then I find myself wrapped up in his arms. "Shh, I didn't mean to upset you. I swear, I just find you incredibly endearing." He runs his hand over the back of my head and holds my face into his neck while I try to explain.

"No. You're fine. I'm just… I think I'm ill-equipped to handle… well, I guess to handle you." At this point, I'm so far out of my comfort zone that I just need him to understand me.

"Don't try to handle me. Be you and let me be charmed." I wipe my eyes and give him a small smile, so he knows I'm okay to move on from this. "Will you let me take a look now?"

Sighing, I pull back from him to try and stand up. "Are you sure? I could probably look it over in the bathroom if you're not comfortable with seeing me like that."

Shaking his head, he's still smiling when he mutters, "So precious." Moving over to his bag, he starts digging through it and pulls out a first aid kit. "I'm fine. I've always got a little first aid kit with me. This should tide us over until I can get to a store. Go on Faith, let's get this done."

Delaying is pointless, so I suck it up and carefully slide my leggings back down, hissing through my teeth when the elastic waist rubs against it. I've taken off my sweatshirt and long-sleeved shirt already, leaving me in just my tank and t-shirt, plus my underwear. There's no going back now.

"Lay down for me." I do and he pulls away the shirt he used to wrap my thigh. Wiping the area with some disinfectant wipes, he fills me in on my condition, "This doesn't look *too* bad, but you're going to be sore for a little while."

"I suppose that's a good thing. I don't think I could get away with going to a clinic right now, not without giving them all my information." I close my eyes and try not to flinch when he wipes some of the areas that are opened with the wipes, causing an instant burning sting.

Looking at me like he's going to take me to task, he gently scolds me, "Yeah, I'm going to need you to tell me about that in a minute. Jumping a train like you did was dangerous kitten."

"Isn't it just as dangerous for you as it is me?" I'm sure he means well, but I truly don't think I had any other choice at that moment. "Why *were* you there? You said you'd tell me." I open my eyes and look at him when I direct that last question at him.

Flicking his gaze to mine before focusing back on my leg, he gives me an answer I wasn't expecting. "I followed you."

"*What?*" I try to sit up, feeling uneasy with the thought that maybe I shouldn't have just followed him without question. His hand on my shoulder pushes me right back down to the bed.

"Relax. I probably shouldn't have said it like that." Tossing the last wipe onto a pile of other dirtied ones, he grabs a tube of antibiotic cream and starts to dab it on my wounds. He keeps talking as well, "You know we ran in to each other yesterday. Sorry about that by the way."

"It's fine. Go on please."

"After I bumped into you, I was instantly fascinated by you. Captivated even. You walked away from me, and you were only gone for a few minutes before I was overcome with the urge to find you. Like if I didn't, it would be one of those regrets that would forever eat at me."

Okay, that was sweet and not alarming so far. He waits for a moment, and when I say nothing, he continues.

"So... I followed you to a church. You were sitting up in a front pew for a while and I just observed you for a bit, trying to figure out why I felt the need to be there. I had just decided to approach you when you got up and left the room. I waited for a bit longer, but when you didn't come back, I decided to wait outside for you."

"I didn't see you. You didn't say anything when I left." I wince when I remember how I left the church. "Nevermind..."

Frowning at me like he's angry, I know he saw me and my father. "Yeah... so you know why I didn't approach you. You and your father took off in the car so quickly, I didn't know what to do. I was pretty bothered about the whole thing, so I went on a limb to see if the Priest-"

"Father Michaels," I tell him.

"To see if Father Michaels, whom I assumed was a part of whatever was so distressing between you and your father, was going to seek the both of you out."

Raising my eyebrows at him, I'm surprised that he went to such extremes just off a random feeling. "That seems like extreme measures on a what-if."

Shrugging, he gives me a sheepish smile, "Honestly? When I first saw you, I thought you were the most beautiful woman I've ever seen. I couldn't not try."

I think Arrow is the first person to tell me that he found me beautiful, and he's now said it a few times. My face heats at his compliment. "Umm... Thank you," I mumble.

He's amused with me when he smiles broadly, "I'll tell you anytime you want to hear it kitten. Anyway, I figured it was a long shot, waiting on the Pr-... Father Michaels, but it was my only option at that point. So, I did."

Wait.

"You followed him to my house and then followed me when I left?" Does he know what they were talking about? "Did you hear them talking?"

"I did end up outside your home, but no, I didn't hear them talking. I could see him speaking with your father and the woman I assume is your mother. At that point, I was just curious because they were animated. I had planned to come up with a reason to come back the next day to try and talk with you and would have left had I not seen you drop out of your bedroom window."

"Why didn't you say anything outside? Or when we were on the train?"

His eyes soften. "Faith, baby girl, you looked terrified. You were running, looking behind you like someone could have been following. Had I approached you, a stranger in the middle of the night, you would have been scared to death. I stayed back to make sure you didn't get into any trouble and kept an eye on you until the train left. I dozed off when it started to get light out, and then we were on our way. The rest you know."

I'm stunned speechless. His explanation calms the nervousness I felt when he first told me he was following me. Plus, I'm relieved that he decided to because I'm sure this morning would have had a much different outcome if he hadn't been there.

"There, you're all set for now." He pats my leg and grabs my hand to pull me to a sitting position. He's got my leg wrapped loosely with some gauze to stop the cream from rubbing off on the blanket.

"It's crazy that you did all that, but I feel really blessed you did. Thank you for going out on a limb for me. I don't know how I'll ever be able to repay you."

"You don't need to repay me. I was gl-" he stops speaking and narrows his eyes when he looks down toward my stomach. I ran a hand through my hair and my shirt must have lifted. Flicking his eyes up to mine and then back down, he grinds his teeth, fury in his voice, "What the hell is that?"

My bruises from the knots. I tug my shirt back down and look away. "It's nothing."

I jerk back when he raises his voice at me, "Don't tell me that's nothing. Your fucking stomach is practically black and blue! Lift your shirt, Faith."

Shaking my head, I pull it even lower to hold tight around my hips. Seeing what my father did to my leg was bad enough.

"I'm not messing around, lift your fucking shirt." He's so *angry* and it's pushing my anxiety up a notch.

"I don't want-"

He doesn't let me finish. Arrow reaches forward and pulls the bottom of my shirt and wrenches it from my hands, lifting it up almost to the underside of my breasts. "HEY! Stop! It's not anything!" I say in panic as I try to wrestle my shirt back down.

I'm unsuccessful, so I try to twist away from him to hide my stomach and give him my back. I freeze when a loud growl erupts from his chest, and he grabs the back of my neck and pushes me face down to the bed.

Crying out, I reach back to pull his hand from me when he barks at me, *"STOP MOVING!"* My body immediately follows his order even though my mind is telling me that I'm in an extremely vulnerable position with a stranger twice my size.

My shirt is yanked all the way up to expose the length of my back. *"Who the fuck has been beating you?!"*

Crying harder, I beg him to please let me up. He ignores me and repeats his question, refusing to move until I talk. So, I talk and pour out everything, face down on the mattress, which is being soaked by my tears.

*"My father!* My father did. Since as long as I can remember. When I was little, I was punished for not obeying the rules or

arguing with either of my parents. As I got older, if I committed a grave sin against God or my family, I had to pay my penance. 2 Corinthians, chapter 11, verse 24 and 25. '*Five times did I receive forty stripes, save one. Thrice was I beaten with rods.*' Breaking one of God's commandments required judgement. So, I would receive 39 lashes before I was forgiven. '*But he is merciful and will forgive their sins; and will not destroy them.*' Moses allowed the head of the house to use a rod as long as it didn't cause death."

Arrow is silent. He must expect me to keep explaining, so I continue.

"The bruising on my stomach is from a knotted cord I was to wear for committing three grievous sins against Father Michaels, God's appointed mouthpiece. He told my parents that I was a liar and lustful and that I had tried to tempt him into adultery. I wore a cord with three knots to remind me to stay pure and chaste. I took it off before I left." I have nothing left to bare myself to him with.

He hasn't said a word the entire time I've been talking. Well, *crying* and talking. I'm not sure what else he's waiting for, and I can't see his face. I don't want to fight him anymore; he's not hurting me. This quiet is only giving me time to remember everything that happened as it all flashes through my head.

Finally, he speaks, "Is this why you ran?"

Pausing, I debate on whether I should tell him the worst of it. Would he have to do something about it because of his job? Will he think me weak, like a pushover, that I let everything go so far? Will this be the thing that makes him think I'm too much trouble, so he'll wash his hands of me?

All the answers to my questions are an '*I don't know.*' I won't lie to him, but I could tell him that I don't want to answer. In the end though, there's really no point to keep it to myself. I must have faith in him. So, I decide to give him the rest of my truths.

"I ran because Father Michaels convinced my parents that I needed to die… and they agreed."

# Chapter 11

## *Arrow*

A man can only take so much.

Hissing through clenched teeth, I ask the only question I can to make sense of all of this, "*WHY?*"

"Because I walked in on Father Michaels and my father in a very, uh… *compromising* situation." She's sniffling now, no longer letting out those gut-wrenching sobs.

"So, by 'compromising situation,' you mean…" I just want to be clear with what exactly is going on.

She snorts and I feel the force of it through the back of her neck. *FUCK!* Quickly I release her. I hadn't realized I was still holding her down. "Shit. Sorry kitten." Scooping her up, the guilt turns in my stomach when I see how red and puffy her face is from crying so hard. *Jesus Christ.* I don't even know how long I stayed frozen, pinning her like that.

Running the back of her hands across her eyes to wipe away the remaining tears, she nods in acknowledgment of my apology and answers, "By 'compromising situation' I mean exactly what I think you're assuming. They were..." she blushes, this time I think because she's embarrassed to say the words. "Uhh, they weren't wearing and clothes and Father Michaels... he was, umm..."

I'll spare her. "I got it." The look of relief on her face makes me feel a tiny bit better after the way I reacted to seeing her back. God, there are a couple dozen thin, slightly raised lines across her back. All almost perfectly horizontal and spread from her shoulder blades to the top of her ass.

"So, you walk in on your father and Priest doing the ugly. How do you get from that to running because they want to kill you. Seems like an overreaction, you know?"

"Honestly, it's all convoluted. Father Michaels and my father concocted this whole twisted plan and presented it to my mother, using scripture to support their reasoning. Obviously, taking verses out of context can support anything you want it to. They convinced my mother that I've completely lost my way and they failed as parents because they're no longer afraid. I dunno... I don't think I can even fully explain it because it makes absolutely no sense. What I *do* know is that I immediately packed a bag and left when the three of them agreed that sacrificing me was for the greater good. Clearly, they just didn't want me to tell anyone what I saw."

It's mind-boggling that they all bought in to it. "Sounds like a cult."

She blows out a breath, frustrated. "I'm not so sure it isn't. I've felt off about what he's been preaching for a while now. I think I just stayed because it was familiar. I knew what to expect from them, well I *used* to know what to expect. I've never really been out on my own before. My parents expected me to stay with them until I eventually met someone and started my own family."

I try not to tense at the idea that there could be someone out there that she belongs to. "Soo… does that mean that you have someone waiting on you?"

She snorts again, like it's ridiculous of me to even ask. "Hardly. I've never dated anyone before. I haven't even kissed anyone until you."

My brows try to hit my hairline. "Kitten, I haven't kissed you yet." I'm pretty sure I would have remembered licking those lips of hers.

"You kissed me right here." She points to the corner of her mouth. My heart melts to think that a small peck was her first kiss.

"That wasn't a kiss, that was just a little peck on the cheek." The flash of disappointment I see on her face has my pulse picking up slightly. She wouldn't be disappointed unless she had wanted to have that first kiss.

"Oh. Okay," she pauses awkwardly, and I want to fill the silence, but she beats me to it, "So, yeah. No, I mean. I hadn't been dating anyone. I hadn't been prepared to be on my own suddenly like this, obviously. I have money, but I'm afraid to go to the bank right now. I'm not sure if that's a way my parents could know where I'm at, and I figured better safe than sorry. So here I am."

I need to back up a moment. "Faith, did you want that to be a real kiss?"

I bite my tongue when her mouth opens and closes. She wasn't expecting me to ask her that. "I'm sorry. I just misunderstood what it was, that's all." She waves her hand like she wants to brush it off, but I see her trying to be tough, like it's no big deal.

"I'm going to kiss you for real, kitten. That way there's no confusion on whether I gave you an actual kiss or not." Yup. I'm gonna kiss the fuck out of this girl. Her inexperience is fueling me like a drug, and every time she says something innocent in its simplicity, I want her even more.

She's unpracticed, so it makes her incredibly honest in her response to me. "I… uhh… you don't have to." She lets out a giggle before she can catch it, and then presses her lips together to silence it. She doesn't know what to say.

Cupping the side of her jaw and neck, my fingers press into the divot at the top of her neck. I run my thumb over her cheek to follow the pink blush back to her ear where it's turning red. Tipping her head back slightly, I lower my mouth to hers, gently setting my lips there a moment. Diving in would probably be a little too shocking right off the bat.

Her lips are soft, and I barely move mine over hers. My eyes are open, studying her face to make sure I'm not making her uncomfortable. Hers are squeezed shut, like if she opens them, it might go away. Pulling back an inch, I wait for her to look at me.

Eventually, her eyes open and she releases a huge gust of air, "Wow... That was-"

I take advantage of her open mouth and kiss her more forcefully this time, sliding my tongue in a bit to touch the tip of hers. She squeaks between our joined lips at the contact and pulls her tongue back like she's worried she made a mistake. She didn't and I can't stop the small smile playing on my lips as I chase her tongue with mine to let her know it wasn't a mistake.

Her eyes shoot open at the unexpected contact. *Fuck me.* She's going to be the death of me. The fact that just the touch of my tongue shocked her makes me feel like a fucking caveman at the thought of showing her more. More, like other places my tongue could go.

Lifting my other hand, I cradle the back of her head as I deepen the kiss. I let my eyes slide shut when hers do, instinct taking over. Gripping her hair in a fist, I tilt her face so I can dip deeper, exploring as much as I can. She tastes pure. Fresh, like drinking crisp, ice cold water from a stream.

Her tentative hand that touches my chest directly over my pounding heart, followed by a soft moan, breaks me. Without pulling back from her, I lay her back on the bed and then lay down next her.

My cock is so fucking hard right now, it's painfully pressing up against the zipper and trying to find its way into her. I do my best to ignore it as I kick up the intensity another notch.

Her hand is trembling on my chest. Nipping her bottom lip, I love the gasp she lets out. I move her trembling hand to wrap around my neck and she grips me to her.

I know I'm probably moving her along to fast, but I can't stop myself as I move my body over hers more fully to settle between her legs that she widened on instinct for me. She may not know exactly what she's looking for, but her body is seeking it.

Grinding my cock into her pussy, she tears her mouth from mine and cries out, "Oh my God!" I groan when I grind again, running my mouth along her jaw and then down her neck, grazing my teeth in my path. Her hips lift, seeking a relief that I'd be willing to bet she's never gotten before.

Grazing my teeth once more over that same spot, I feel her pump her hips up again. I want her out of control for me, not thinking, only feeling. Running the flat of my tongue over her racing pulse, I suck gently and then bit down.

"Arrow!" Wrapping both of her arms around my head, she keeps her body moving under me and it makes me go wild for her.

"I'm going to make you come for me, my sweet girl." Licking my way back up her neck, across her jaw, and then up the side of her face. Before I attack her mouth again, I growl at her, pumping my cock against her cunt, "You taste so fucking sweet. I can't wait to taste the rest of you."

The tremors racing through her make my body snap, my cum shooting from the head of my cock and filling the inside of my jeans.

I continue to grind into her as each pulse washes over me, soaking in the scream that tears from her throat that I swallow as I continue to attack her mouth. She falls apart under me, shivering violently. Every twitch of her body has my cock releasing another small spurt of cum, draining everything I had stored.

We slow our kiss, changing it from heavy possession to a more relaxing, amorous kind of kiss.

I pull back to look down at her and see tear tracks running from corners of both her eyes, the path flowing into her hair line. I'm not worried about these tears though.

Faith awards me with the most breathtaking smile I've seen on her yet. It's pure joy, and I put it there. Giving her a quick kiss, I give her all my focus. "You okay, kitten? Was that okay?"

She nods her head yes so quickly that I want to worry about whiplash. "It was... I can't even describe... just *wow*." The flush on her face is probably a good mix between her orgasm and a shyness now that we've both come down.

Chuckling, I tease her, "That good, huh?"

"I think I saw *God*," she whispers to me.

I'm ok with being compared to God. One last kiss for now. I deliver it and then move from the top of her, careful not to put any weight on her thigh. "Did I hurt you at all? Your leg or stomach?"

"No. Although, I wouldn't have even noticed if you had," she sighs, then blinks one of those slow blinks that happens when trying to keep your eyes open.

"Good." I move to stand, and she comes further awake, looking worried that I'm moving away from her. "Shh. Stay right there. I'm going to clean up, change right quick, and then come back."

"Clean up?" Her head tilts in confusion. Holy fuck me sideways.

I point at my cock. "Yes, clean up. I came as well. It'll get uncomfortable if I don't change." Ahh, now she's following. Her eyes go round as saucers. Laughing, I head into the bathroom, quickly wipe down and then change into another pair of boxer briefs before flipping the light off and walking back to the bed.

She's tucked herself under the blankets and moved all the way to the side. If she's never kissed anyone, then I know she's never slept next to anyone before. Another first I'm going to enjoy getting from her.

I slide into bed next to her and move toward the middle. "I'm keeping you on me for the night. We have a long day tomorrow, so let's get as much sleep as we can."

I wrap my arm under her breasts, careful to avoid her bruising and pull her into me. Rearranging her so her back is pressed to my chest, she asks, "What are we doing tomorrow?"

This right here? I've made up my mind. This is how I'm sleeping every night for the rest of my life. I can't stop kissing her.

"We're going to keep moving you further away from your home, then figure out what the fuck we're going to do next."

"Where did you want to go?" I like that she's relaxed about letting me make the calls.

"I'm taking you back to *my* home, if that's all right with you?" I should be nervous, but I'm not. I think she's just as affected as I am.

"Where's your home?" she asks through a yawn.

"I'm taking you to Virginia, near Quantico."

"Holy Shit!"

*Oh my God... I think that's the first time I've ever heard her swear.*

## Chapter 12

### *Faith*

It took us nearly four days to make it to his home. I've never left my state before, so making the drive cross-country was incredible. I couldn't close my eyes, not wanting to miss anything. I live a couple hours north of Sacramento, California and he lives in Quantico, Virginia.

I saw the Sierra-Nevada Mountains, salt flats in Idaho, the Rocky Mountains, and then the rolling hills in Wyoming. Every state felt like I had arrived in on a new planet. I knew that there were different types of climates and environments but knowing and then seeing are two completely different things. Every mile we drove, every site we saw, confirmed two things about myself that I didn't know.

First, I hated living at home and was apparently more than ready to live on my own.

Second, I want to see more. I want to travel and explore places I'd never dreamed of visiting in the past.

Well, there is a third thing, but just thinking it has my cheeks flushing hot. Third, I'm desperate for Arrow. The conversations we have about serious *and* mindless topics, his smiles that make me want to scream at the power they hold over me, his kisses that remove everything else from around me, his body and mind and eyes and voice and-

"I have to know, what in the hell are you thinking about right now? Because your face went from cream to tomato in like thirty seconds." He's laughing at me again.

It only took me spending time with him for another day to learn that he's not making fun of me. He truly enjoys my lack of knowledge in *certain* areas and watching me discover new things seems to be his new addiction. He's on a mission to introduce something new to me every day. His only stipulation was pants must stay on for now.

So, I haven't seen 'it' yet... I'm dying to. I've felt it and it's like a flipping log in his pants that shifts and moves without even touching it sometimes. My parents never let me attend health classes in school, nor did they take it upon themselves to educate me either. All this means is I've never seen one, not even in a picture and I really really *really* want to see his.

"Seriously, I have to know. It's like watching a kid see Disney for the first time and then dreaming about it after they've left." The other thing that Arrow has been teaching me: I shouldn't be afraid or nervous to tell him what's on my mind, he's never judging me.

"I was just thinking about last night and that I'm really curious about… that." I point at his lap. Not being afraid is still a work in progress and using words to describe his parts has been uncomfortable. Obviously, I *know* them. I just don't feel right saying anything other than 'penis' out loud, and that's hardly sexy.

My train of thought has me zoned out again, staring at the thing that's at the front of my mind, and I blink myself out of it when I see it move and get bigger under his clothes.

"Sweetness, he's very curious about you as well." His voice has a husky quality to it, and I shiver when it rolls over me. "Soon. I'll introduce you real soon." He winks and gives the road in front of us his full attention again.

Shoot. Now my nervous energy has excitement thrown in the mix. Soon. I smile to myself and let my thoughts take over again in the comfortable silence.

The sun is just setting hours later as we finally make it to his home. It doesn't take us long to grab showers while waiting on food to be delivered. Apparently, Arrow has been traveling for a few weeks, so there's not much food in his fridge.

Curled up, cross-legged on his couch, my knee is touching his thigh as I pick at the salad I asked for. After eating fast food and junk during the drive, I was craving something cold and fresh.

"Are you not hungry?" he asks me. He ordered the same thing I did, saying it was a good idea to go light tonight, and had just picked up his fork to dig in.

I'm *not* hungry, but only because my stomach is twisting, really flipping nervous to ask what I've been trying to gather the nerves for. I have to get it out, but what if he laughs or says no?

"Baby?" Setting down his food on the table and then grabbing mine to do the same. He grabs my hand, "What's wrong? If you don't like-"

"*Can I see it?*" I just blurt it out, practically yelling. I grimace when it comes out like that, and I try again more calmly and with a quieter voice, "I, umm… I can't stop thinking about it. Can I?"

Reaching out, he picks me up and carries me right to his bedroom on the other side of his single-story home and drops me on the bed. "You may, if that wasn't obvious." He winks and grabs the back of his shirt to pull it over his head.

Sucking in my breath at the sight of his chest and flat stomach, grooves and lines detailing every muscle he's clearly worked hard for, I keep watching. He toes off his shoes and socks, leaving him standing in his jeans at the end of the bed.

"Come over here, kitten." I scramble across the blanket and sit in front of him, eyes lasered to his growing bulge. It's right *there*. "I'll let you explore under one condition."

Flicking my eyes up to his face, I can only stay there a moment before I'm drawn back down like a magnet. "What's your condition?" My tongue peaks out to touch my upper lip.

"You use a word to say what *it* is. I don't care what you say. You can call it a cock, dick, prick, shaft, or willie. I don't really like the last and prefer one of the first couple, but I want to hear one of them." He presses his hand to it while he's speaking. Maybe it's hurting him or it's uncomfortable.

Looking back up at him and staying there this time, I lick my lip before meeting his condition, "Can I… May I see your c-cock?" The stutter was unintentional, but I know it'll get easier.

His eyes are heated, and his lip is tipped up on one side. "You want me to take it out? Or do you want to do it?"

"You… please."

Reaching down, he slowly pulls his zipper down, loosening his pants to hang lower on his hips. Then he slides his thumbs in the waist band of his boxer briefs and lowers them. I watch as he reveals his member to me, and my mouth salivates.

It's beautiful. Long and thick, darker toward the tip where it becomes larger again. Leaning a little forward to see, my eyes widen when I see a drop of fluid clinging to the end and then follow it to the floor when it falls. There's already another gathering where it fell from. There's a large vein on the underside of it and I follow it to the base of the shaft. I'm not sure what I had expected, but I think reality is much better than my imagination.

"Babygirl…"

"Hmm?" I'm still analyzing and taking him in when I hear a groan come from him. It snaps me out of the trance I was in.

"Babygirl, touch me." What? I thought he was only going to let me look. The other nights when I touched him, he pulled my hand away and told me not yet.

"I can?" Groaning out a laugh, he runs a hand down my cheek in a tender touch.

"You can. I'd *really* love for you to explore. Experiment with it, see what happens when you touch it in different ways. Play, kitten."

Nodding my head yes, I reach out and brush my fingertips along the side and watch in fascination as it bounces away from my touch. I do it again and giggle when it bounces again. "It's so weird how it moves like that."

"It's involuntary," he laughs, then clears his throat. "Try wrapping your hand around it and squeezing."

Wrapping my hand around the middle, I find that my fingers can't fully touch. I'm surprised by the texture. It's different from the rest of his skin. "It's so velvety!" I run my fingers over him again, a little harder this time, to enjoy the sensation of how smooth it is. He almost reminds me of the silky fabric on the pews at church.

Arrow doesn't say anything, just watches as I squeeze him. I'm intrigued by the fluid that comes out, so I gather some, bringing it closer to my face to get a better look.

It's perfectly clear, not sticky. Almost like water. I let my curiosity take over and I touch my fingertip to my tongue, curious if it tastes like water as well. It doesn't at all, but it also doesn't taste bad. A little salty and earthy, slightly sweet even.

"Christ Faith... you're killing me." He's panting a little bit now and I'm worried that I'm doing it wrong, so I pull back.

"Sorry, did I do something wrong?" I don't want to make him uncomfortable.

"God, not at all, kitten. It's just fucking sexy as hell watching you taste me like that. Did you mind it? The taste, I mean." I watch as he wraps his fist around the base and strokes his hand up and then back down once, more fluid pushing from the head.

"I didn't mind. It's interesting, but doesn't taste bad at all." I wonder what I would taste like between *my* legs. I'll have to check that out later.

"You want to try something else?" he asks me.

I nod my head yes as he strokes himself. I'm fascinated by all of this.

"Try using your mouth. You can use your tongue to lick and put your mouth around the head to suck. Pretty much anything you can do with your hand, you can also do with your mouth."

Cocking my head, I decide I want to, but I don't how to start. "How do you like it to be done? I want it to feel good for you too."

"I promise, whatever you do will feel great. I can guide you this time if you want."

"Please."

"Open your mouth and stick your tongue out a little bit." I do what he says, and he moves his hips closer, letting the end of his cock run over my tongue, spreading the clear fluid around so I can taste more of it.

"I'm going to hold you while I move. Put your hands on my thighs and if you need me to stop or slow down, just tap my leg or push me back. Okay?"

"...Okay," I whisper.

Placing a hand on each of his thighs, he cradles my head with both of his, and moves his cock closer to me. "Open up, kitten. Wider this time."

Opening my mouth again for him, I relax my jaw and he slides himself in, going further than before. He moans as he pulls back slightly and then pushes back in. The intimacy of this has me tingling between my legs, wetness starting to leak out, dampening my panties.

I look up to watch his face as he strokes into my mouth. I'm loving the different expressions I see there. Pleasure, relief, pain, tension... It's all there.

"That feels so good... Fuck, it's hard to hold back." I can feel his hands trembling slightly. I think he's restraining himself to not hurt me. I really like this, and I want him to totally relax as well.

Pushing back on his thighs slightly, he quickly slides out of my mouth when he steps back and releases me. "Sorry, did I go too deep?" His cock is glistening from the saliva in my mouth and looks delicious.

"Not at all! It's just… you don't have to hold back. You're not hurting me. I really like this," I tell him.

"Are you sure?"

"I am. I'll let you know if I need you to stop. Move however you want."

My stomach flips in excitement as he quickly comes back and pulls me toward him, bumping the tip into my lips. I allow him to slide back in and I move my tongue around the underside a bit to try and taste more of him.

"Wrap your lips around me tighter. If your teeth graze me, it's all right… just try not to bite." My mouth is full, so I just nod my head and do my best, sucking slightly harder, swallowing him in further.

He yells out louder when I do that, "*Fuck!* Just like that baby… keep doing that for me." I do and he groans.

He grips my hair and starts thrusting, gradually moving harder and more quickly into my mouth. I feel him hitting the back of my throat, making me gag slightly. He pulls out of my mouth but doesn't release my head. "I'm going to angle you better so I can go deeper. Relax your throat and breath through your nose. Okay?"

I barely get out 'okay' before he's sliding back in, tilting my head up slightly. This gives me a better view of his face as he watches himself disappear over and over into my mouth. Whispering to me, he praises me, and I flush at the compliment. "You're doing so good kitten. You're making me feel so good. I don't think I can hold back; your tongue feels amazing."

He's thrusting so hard into my throat that my eyes are watering. I try to remember to keep breathing through my nose. Saliva leaks from my mouth, dripping down my chin and neck. His panting sounds have me moaning around him, which makes him pound harder, pressing his cock into my mouth as deep as he can go.

"I'm going to come kitten. Do you want me to pull out?" he stutters out, never slowing down his hips. He tastes so good, and I really don't want him to finish without me being a part of it, so I shake my head to tell him I don't want him to.

"God *damn* Faith… fuuuuuuck. I'm going to come. Swallow as much as you can." My hair is being pulled tighter in his fists and he doesn't slow down, but his thrusts become erratic as he nears his completion.

I wrap my hands around the back of his thighs to pull him closer and steady myself. A few last thrusts and then he holds himself deep in my mouth, grinding his pelvis into my lips as I feel the first pump of his cock and then warm fluid in my throat.

He growls as he pulses a couple more times, then pulls back slightly and punches forward again, like he needs to feel my tongue again. When he briefly pulled back like that, a jet of his cum floods my tongue and I'm able to taste even more of him.

He shifts his hand and presses in again by pulling the back of my head toward him. One last pulse and he releases the rest of his breath through a mix of a sigh and moan, resting in the back of my throat a moment.

I nuzzle my nose into him, enjoying the closeness like this. Loving that I was able to give him pleasure, and really excited to try this all again.

"Fuck..." he mutters and then pulls himself free from me to look down at the aftermath of the state he's left me in.

We watch each other a moment. I'm still gripping the back of his thighs and he's still holding my face, running his thumbs through whatever fluids are left around my mouth and chin. "You okay, my sweet Faith?"

"I'm okay. That was really... I really loved that, Arrow." His eyes soften and he chuckles at me. Reaching over to grab his shirt, he starts to wipe my face down, cleaning himself from me as best he can.

"I *also* really loved that." Leaning down, he presses a kiss to my lips and then slides his tongue into my mouth. My lips are swollen and tender from how hard he used them, but I don't want the kiss to end.

Speaking against my lips, he murmurs softly, "I can taste myself on you." He dips in again a few more times until we slow and end the kiss.

He lets out a rattled breath and then stares at me. I can't keep the smile from my face, and he returns one just as big. Standing up to his full height, he narrows his eyes at me, and that smile turns more predatory, causing my pulse to pick up.

"Take your pants off for me and lay back. I'm going to show you what *my* mouth can do."

# Chapter 13

**4 weeks later**

## *Arrow*

The last month with Faith has been incredible. About a week after she had been settled into my home, I had a talk with her to make sure she was okay with the age difference between us. I also asked her if she was sure she wanted to stay here or if she was feeling like she wanted to move out on her own.

My *intentions* with that conversation were to let her know that I'd support her in whatever choices she made. She went from a home where she was controlled her entire life, directly into mine. I just wanted to make sure she wasn't only doing what she thought I wanted.

The conversation did not go as planned. I learned two things during that talk. First thing was that with this girl, what you see is exactly what you get. By that, I mean that if she's acting like she's happy here and telling me that she's happy here, she really is happy here. She doesn't play games like so many other women do where they'll act one way and then blindside you, wanting something else the entire time. Faith is incredibly honest.

The second thing I learned is that her tears crush me. Not the tears she sheds when she's touched by something, nor the tears I've watched multiple times now run down her cheeks when my cock is in the back of her throat. No, the tears I'm talking about are the ones when I've unintentionally hurt her.

Turns out, when I asked her, *'Are you sure you're okay with staying here? I'm a lot older than you, and I don't want you to feel like you owe me anything to stay.'* What *she* heard was, *'Are you sure you really want to stay? I'm not sure that the age difference is going to be something we can always handle. I'm not into messing around with someone that's doing me a favor.'* Or something like that.

She burst into tears a moment after I brought it up. I wasn't even fully focused on her, cooking dinner and trying to figure out what to do next on the back of the box. I had to throw everything on the counter and turn off the burners to rush over and scoop her up into my arms and soothe her. She thought I was asking her to leave.

It took her a solid half an hour to get herself back under control from the emotional upheaval I created. We didn't eat dinner that night. I took her back to our room and laid with her, kissing her, petting her head, assuring her that I wanted nothing more than for her to stay here. She didn't believe me right away and thought I was just saying it because she got emotional. I wanted to kick myself in the ass for that whole evening. I felt terrible for unintentionally making her doubt how I felt about her.

Probably not the best move on my part, but that was also the same night that I told her I loved her. I explained that I wanted to tell her and was just making sure she was on par with where I was. Oh, she was. After declaring my feelings, she laughed at me. *Laughed* at me. Apparently, she assumed that I knew she was in love with me, and she already knew I was with her. Like I said, this girl doesn't play games.

Since then, we've been going strong, building this new life together. I haven't fucked her yet, but we've certainly done pretty much everything else. Losing her virginity is a huge step, and we both wanted to make sure she was completely comfortable. There was no hurry, besides the ache I feel in my cock pretty much all the time because it wants inside her tight pussy *so* badly.

Pulling my shirt on after my shower, I walk into the kitchen to see her lovely ass swinging back and forth, peeking out from under one of my t-shirts, while stirring something on the stove. She's got music playing softly. I assume it's so it wouldn't bother me while she let me sleep in late after a long night on a job.

Sneaking up behind her, I wrap an arm around her waist and match her rhythm, pulling her closer with each sway of our hips. My cock is hard as I grind into her and the good mood dancing she was doing before turns into something erotic. I graze her breast with my other hand, and she wraps an arm around my neck to look up and behind her into my face.

"Morning babygirl," my voice rumbles out, rough from using it for the first time today. She kisses me in greeting, and we continue to dance a few more minutes before a loud knock on my front door startles us.

"What the fuck? It's Saturday morning." Who the hell is here this early? They're about to get their ass beat for interrupting my time with my kitten.

Wrenching the door open, I pull up short when I see two police officers along with Faith's parents waiting on my front porch. I'm only momentarily surprised, but I knew this was coming. I didn't tell Faith, but I started putting together what I could to take care of her father and that asshole of a Priest.

Guess they got to us first.

"*Faith!*" her mother cries out, seeing Faith standing behind me. She tries to run toward her, but I block the doorway to stop her.

"Where are your pants!?" her father snaps. "Lord have mercy, she's been tricked by this... this..." I roll my eyes when he points at me. "This *man*. Faith! Go get some clothes on and come here immediately."

"Not happening," I growl at him. I check to make sure Faith is alright, and then turn to the officers tagging along. She's just shocked, not too upset or scared at the moment. "I'm know why you're here. I'd invite you in, but those two are not welcome in my home." I point at Betty and Daniel Holton.

The male officer clears his throat, a little confused that I'm reacting the way I am, "I'm Officer Kent and this is my partner, Officer Nelson." He points to the female next to him. "You're Arrow Matias, correct? With the feds over at NCAVC?"

I bare my teeth at Faith's father when his eyes widen almost imperceptibly. Apparently, he didn't know I was a Federal Agent. "That's right. So, I'd ask how I could help you, but I know why you're all here. Faith and I will step outside in a moment, if you don't mind waiting?"

"That's absurd! You can't leave her in there alone with him, he kidnapped her!" He's turning red in the face, clearly pissed.

"He didn't kidnap me!" Faith interjects, clearly moving past her shock and stepping up next to me. I slide my hand onto her waist and push her behind me slightly so I can keep myself between her and her parents.

At the same time, her mother asks to anyone listening, "What's the NCAVC?"

"Please Mr. Matias, Miss Holton, would you step out here so we can figure out what's going on?" Officer Nelson asks us. These cops aren't being aggressive, so I nod my head before looking at Betty.

"The NCAVC is a department of the FBI called the National Center for the Analysis of Violent Crime. Pretty convenient, right?"

I direct that last question at Daniel and get pleasure as his face blanches.

I let him sit with that a moment. "We'll be right out." Then I shut the door on them and quickly wrap my girl up in my arms. "Are you going to be okay with this?"

She's clinging to me, shaking with the adrenaline, but assures me she'll be okay, "Yeah, I'll be all right. I'm not scared of them, not really. It's more just nerves from the confrontation. It's the altercation that's scary. What if they make me leave?"

"I'll be right with you. I can tell you right now those cops know something's not right. You're an adult and have choices. They can't really make you go anywhere without being arrested, which neither of us will be, because we've done nothing wrong. Jump up here and let me hold you a moment before we get dressed."

I walk her back to our room with her legs wrapped around my waist. Grinning at me, she shows me just how not scared she really is, "You know, I think I'm most disappointed at the interruption in the kitchen. I like the way you dance with me."

Chuckling, I give her a fast, hard kiss. "Oh kitten, we were about to stop dancing anyway." She giggles at that, and then we hurry to throw some clothes on.

"Let's get things straightened out now that everyone is dressed," Officer Kent says to all of us once Faith and I are outside on the porch. She's standing in front of me, leaning back for support and I've got my arm across her chest, gripping her shoulder. "Miss

Holton. Your parents filed a missing person's report about five weeks ago, and they haven't heard from you since. We found Mr. Matias's rental vehicle abandoned in town and were able to verify through a few different hotels' security feeds that you two have been traveling together. Would you please explain what's going on?" He looks quickly to me before focusing back on her.

Daniel speaks before Faith has a chance. "What happened is he's fooled her into coming here to take advantage of her!" I swear to God, this fucker needs to shut the fuck up. A smartass remark is at the tip of my tongue before my girl steps up and takes hold of the situation... and she's pissed.

"Noo... what *happened* was my father and mother, along with the Priest at our church, decided that I needed to be put up as a sacrifice for *their* greater good." My eyes may or may not have widened just a touch, surprised at the venom in her voice. My kitten has some claws, and I'm here for it.

"Excuse me... *what?*" Kent asks, eyes narrowing on my girl. I could sort of see why he'd find that disbelieving, but a low growl escapes from my throat anyway.

"Watch your tone, Officer Kent," I warn.

"I meant exactly what I said." She looks at her father and directs her next question to him. It's a beautiful thing to see how she stands up for herself, but also doesn't act disrespectful. "Father, would you like to tell mom why you and Father Michaels came up with the idea?" She looks to the officers, "The idea about the sacrifice. I can assure you that mother won't lie to you about it. If she's anything, she's honest. *Right* mom?"

Betty's eyes are filled with tears. "I thought- "

"Betty. Shut. Up," Daniel spits at her. "This is ridiculous. You need to arrest him and allow us to take her back home. She's not prepared to be on her own."

Everyone ignores him except for Betty. She presses her lips together and looks at her hands. "We aren't going to arrest someone for bringing someone to their home if that person went voluntarily, Mr. Holton. What I do want to know is what the hell you mean by 'sacrifice'?" Betty flinches when Officer Kent says 'hell'.

"My father and Father Michaels convinced my mother that they should all present me as a sacrifice to God. My mother will tell you it's because they told her that it was necessary to endure a trial for the sake of all our souls. What my father *should* tell you, but probably won't admit, is that he and Father Michaels wanted to silence me after I saw them together."

Crickets.

Then a cough. "*Saw* them together?" her mother squeaks out.

Faith's eyes only marginally soften toward her mother. "Yes, mom. The day I left, when I went to confession, I accidentally stumbled in on the two of them in a very inappropriate and compromising position."

Betty shakes her head like she doesn't believe her or doesn't understand. This woman is delusional. "I don't know what that means!" she cries out.

"Mom, Father Michaels had dad bent over his desk... they were naked. Shall I continue?" I snort out a laugh at her candidness. A month ago, she wouldn't have been able to be that blunt, even though she still won't swear or talk crudely. I love her for it.

Betty snaps her head to look directly at Daniel while he shakes with rage and then seethes at my girl, "You disrespectful little-"

"*Enough*," I snap. "Officers, I would appreciate if you would escort these two from my property, though I wouldn't let them go very far. I'll come by the precinct Monday morning with the file I've started on these two as well as Donovan Michaels. You'll find there's a lot more to all of this."

Office Nelson looks to Kent and then back to me. "We uhh... we're probably going to need to see both of you on Monday. We'll have some more questions. For now, we apologize for taking up both of your times."

Both of us wait and watch as Daniel and Betty Holton are escorted to the squad cars. They don't allow either of them to drive the vehicle they arrived in. "We'll have this towed within the hour," Kent calls out to me.

I nod to him and then hold my girl to my chest as we watch the four of them leave. We don't move for at least ten minutes after they're out of sight. I want to give her the time she needs to figure out where her head's at after what just happened.

She finally sighs loudly and relaxes her body.

"What are you thinking, kitten?" I expect that she'll be battling with feeling guilty for getting her parents in trouble and what was the right thing to do. This has got to be emotionally draining.

"Is it bad that I feel bad?" she whispers out.

"It's not bad to feel any way you want to feel. You're entitled to handle it all anyway you want. Is there anything you need from me?" I kiss her head and give her a gentle squeeze.

Turning in my arms, she wraps hers around my waist and sets her chin on my chest to look up at me. "Will you do one thing for me, Arrow?"

"Yep. What do you need?"

"I'd *really* like for you to…" she trails off and blushes but doesn't take her eyes from me. I grin mischievously. Her inability to say naughty words is one of my favorite things about her.

I encourage her, "Say it, Faith. No one can hear you but me."

She chews on her lip, deciding. Then, finally she asks me for what she wants.

"I'd really like for you to fuck me."

# Chapter 14

## *Faith*

"Fuck yes I will."

I squeal as he grabs me and throws me over his shoulder to take me inside. He doesn't stop until we get to his room, sliding me down his body to my feet next to the bed.

Reaching my arms up, I curl them around his neck and bring him in closer. I'm convinced that Arrow is the world's best kisser. They're addictive. We've spent hours just making out and touching.

I love how patient he's been, waiting for me to be ready. I'm pretty sure I have been, but maybe I was just waiting for there to be nothing from my past hanging over my head. I am nervous about it, but it's a good nervous. I know I won't regret giving myself to him.

Quickly, we separate and pull our clothes off, then slam our bodies back together to continue kissing. I moan as his fingers thread through my hair, letting him take control and position me where he wants me.

"I'm not going to be able to go slow, kitten. I feel like we've been doing foreplay for a month." I don't blame him. I don't want to wait either. The need for him to fill me is building intensely.

"I don't care. Please, Arrow... "

He lifts me, and then turns to sit on the bed with me on his lap. His cock is pressed against me, my pussy lips already slick and spreading to welcome him.

I can't stop the rock of my hips, rubbing my clit long his shaft. The friction is hot and my need for him ramps up rapidly. He's kissing my neck and chest, biting my nipples while I grip his hair to brace myself as I move.

We both freeze and jerk our eyes to look at each other. I've slid far enough forward that I caught the head of his cock at my entrance. He's *right* there.

"Babygirl..." He's pulsing against me, and I can feel his muscles working to stop from thrusting inside me. "If you need a mo-"

I slide his throbbing head inside me. No more waiting. We both groan at the feel of him being inside of me. It's just a little bit, but still further than we've gone so far.

Arrow pulls me against his body by wrapping both of his arms around me like a hug. Hugging him back, I bury my face in his neck and cry out as I let my weight and gravity pull me down and I feel him break through my virginity.

It isn't as painful as I had heard, but it's uncomfortable. Arrow runs one of his hands down my hair to soothe me, giving us both a moment to process that this is finally happening.

"Faith, look at me." Leaning back, I give him my eyes. He smiles sweetly and wipes away the few tears that escaped when I took him in me. "You move when you're ready. It'll feel better the more you move but take your time. I'm not going anywhere. Does it hurt?"

"No, not really. I just feel full. It's different than what I had thought it would feel like," I tell him. I don't want him to think I'm in pain; I'm not. It's just a throbbing that's buried deep from being touched where I hadn't before.

"Do you trust me?"

I giggle. "Of *course*, I trust you. I love you."

"I love you too." Flashing his teeth, he gives each nipple a quick lick and then nip, then focuses back on our conversation, "I'm going to move you now. I'm going to make you feel *really* good. Ready?"

"Y-yes... Okay." It's not that I'm scared, I just think my body is starting to shiver because of the sensation of all of this.

"Hang on to me, kitten," he whispers. I suck in air and hold my breath as he grips my waist to lift me slowly, then lets me sink back down.

"Oh Go-" The sound is stolen when he lifts and drops me again, a little more quickly this time.

"Fuck your pussy feels good. I'm gonna speed us up. Tell me if you need me to change something," he's panting, fighting for breath. His hips are rolling, grinding up into me.

Nodding my head yes, I gasp when he flips us to lay me on my back, never slipping out of me. Then I cry out again, calling for him as he starts to slide his length in and out of me, stroking every nerve I didn't even know I had inside of me.

"Christ... I swear next time will be longer. You feel too good... too tight..." Grunting into my hair, he grips my shoulders and shoves into me harder, making my body jerk up the bed before sliding back down when he pulls out.

Each thrust, he circles his hips and grinds into my clit, sparks shooting through me to settle deep in my lower stomach. *"Arrow...* I think I'm going to come." I'm not sure what sensations I'm feeling. It's like the other orgasms he's given me, but this one feels bigger, more potent. It's going to break me.

"Let go baby, let me feel you fall apart around me."

Kissing me deeply, he strokes his tongue in my mouth to the rhythm of his thrusts into my body. I'm dancing on the edge of it but can't let myself fall and I cry into him mouth, begging for something, "I c-... I *can't!* I'm trying..."

Arrow growls at me and pushes up from my body. He hooks my legs over his arms, then leans back down to spread me wider and tilt my hips up further. *There...* The head of his cock is hitting a spot inside me every time our bodies slam together.

Crying out more, I squeeze my eyes shut against the reaction my body is having, impossible to resist the explosion he's driving me toward.

"That's it sweet girl... there you go," he praises me when the first flutters of my orgasm tear through me and I fall apart for him, shaking under the powerful drive of his cock.

He roars out as his movements become uncontrolled and one final thrust and hold into my body has a deluge of heat filling me, my body sending extra sparks of pleasure to bury me.

I'm dead... I can't think...I'm-

"*Faith!*" The sound of my name snaps me out of it, and I suck in a huge gasp of air, filling my lungs with precious oxygen.

"Holy..." I sigh and look up into Arrow's face as he slowly lets my legs fall to the side and relaxes on top of me. "I love you... thank you."

His deep rumble of a laugh shakes my body as well. He kisses my nose and then brushes the hair from my face and then cups my cheeks. "Thank *you*, beautiful... now, give me a minute to come back to earth and then I'm going to show you what it's like to..."

Grinning, I listen to him dirty talk in my ear about all the ways he's going to take me for the rest of our lives.

My heart beats for him as I realize that he's my favorite verse. He's wiped away my tears, protected me from death and sadness, and took away my pain.

Arrow is the first one to finally show me God.

# Bonus Epilogue

## *Arrow*

"My dishes for two days against your trash for one week, David," says Adam.

Adam is the oldest of our boys. 13-years-old and already towering over his mom. He's got a few more inches to catch up to me, but I have no doubt he'll get there. 9-year-old David has passed her as well, and Noah is right at the same height. Little Seth is only 6, so he has a few more years.

Faith desperately wanted a little girl, so we kept trying. Unfortunately, Seth's birth went sideways, and she ended up needing a c-section along with a hysterectomy to stop the bleeding. So, fifteen years of marriage gave us four healthy, sweet, sassy, and *extremely* exhausting boys. Mischievous to a fault.

"That's not fair! That's five more times of doing a job!"

"Yeah, but taking the trash out only takes like 5 minutes. Doing the dishes is at least 20 if you have to put them away first!" Adam argues with David.

Noah adds in his two cents, "I don't wanna pick up my room."

"We won't have to. That's the whole point!"

*What the hell are these guys talking about?*

"Momma's gonna be mad," Seth informs his three older brothers. He's the baby of the family and just as protective of his momma as I am.

Walking into the house after being gone for two weeks was supposed to be filled with hugs and kisses. Instead, I had to search the house for my family only to find my four boys huddled in the loft, spying on Faith while she picks up their playroom.

The room is *trashed.*

I had every intention of asking them to go help, but once I started hearing their whispering, I just had to stick to the shadows to find out what they're up to.

I get my answer after only a few minutes.

"Whatcha think she'll say?" asks Noah, my 7-year-old. Cocking my head while staring at the backs of theirs, I try to figure out what he's talking about.

Whispering, David lowers his voice, "What if she says *shit?*"

I bite my tongue. If Faith heard that, she'd lose it.

Adam informs them, "If she says *shit*, I say it's a double win. *Crap*, *dick*, or *piss* are for a regular win. *Shit*, *damnit*, and *ass* should be doubles."

Noah giggles, "What if she says… you know… the 'f' word?"

The other three boys turn to him with wide eyes. David gulps. "Dude… if she says *that*… we're all screwed."

Now it makes sense.

These little assholes set her up. It's working too. I can hear Faith grumbling to her-self, complaining about the disaster she's trying to organize.

"Oh man... she's about to find-" Adam's voice cuts off when we all hear her yell.

"GOD *DAMNIT!*" My humor evaporates quickly. My wife very rarely swears, and when she does, it's normally at my encouragement when we are alone and I'm teasing her.

This, though? This is bad.

"Fuck," I say under my breath, but apparently it was loud enough that the boys heard me. They all stiffen and quickly turn around to see me standing behind them.

"*Dad!*" Seth cries out and rushes to me, throwing himself into my arms.

"Hey buddy," I say and pick him up to give him a hug. Looking over his head, I give the other three a stern look. "What the hell did you guys do?"

Even though our boys can test our patience to no end, overall, they have good hearts. I can see the guilt filling all of their faces now that they've realized they've pushed their mom too far.

Adam steps forward. "Hey dad! Mom said you weren't gonna be home until to-morrow night?" He's trying to distract me, but it won't work.

"I finished early and wanted to surprise you all. Thank God I did because you all were about to get into some serious trouble!" Setting Seth down, I look the four of them over. "I'm going to rescue your mother. You four get your asses down there and take care of whatever it was that she just found. I'll get her out of here."

Sighing, they nod their heads, acknowledging that they hear me. Following them down the stairs into the main room, I close my eyes when I get a better view of the nightmare Faith has been dealing with. 'Goddamnit' is right.

I head over to my wife and over my shoulder, I call out, "Fix this. *Now*. Then get to bed and I'll see you all in the morning."

Faith whips her head up to me when she hears me, and I can see her fighting off tears of frustration. "Arrow…"

Picking her up, she wraps her arms around me and I kiss the side of her head. "I got you kitten. They're going to fix it."

"Sorry mom…" Adam says to her. I can tell he feels awful, as do the rest of them.

"Yeah, we're really sorry. We were just playing around and trying to be funny," Noah adds.

She looks around the room and just shakes her head. "Boys, this is bad. What were you think-"

I cut her off with a quick, hard kiss to her mouth. "Don't worry about it right now. They're going to take care of it. Aren't you?" I ask them, raising an eyebrow.

"Right now," David assures the both of us.

"Perfect. Get it done. We'll see you in the morning." Faith wiggles from my arms and goes to each one of them.

No matter how frustrated or angry she gets, she'll never go to bed with them thinking she's angry or without telling them she loves them. Saying goodnight to each of them, she hugs and kisses them, whispering something in each of their ears that the rest of us can't hear. There are some smiles, and Noah's lip trembles a little when he gives her a hug.

"I love you guys," she calls to them after I sweep her back up, and then carry her to our bedroom.

Shutting the door behind us, I sit on the side of the bed, keeping her in my lap.

"Hey sweet girl." I brush her hair back and look her over. She's tired. I hate that for her and I'm glad that I get to give her some news that will cheer her up.

"Hey…" Smiling up at me, she closes her eyes, soaking in the feel of my fingers running over her face. "I thought you weren't home until tomorrow?"

"Surprised?" I chuckle.

Leaning in to kiss me, she rests her lips against mine. "Very surprised. I'm so happy you're here. How'd everything go?"

I'm not always allowed to fill her in on my investigations, but she knew what this one was about, that it was going to be rough. We were following up on a few murders of some teenage girls who were found in the state over and it led us to a huge trafficking ring. Thank

God we were able to get the information we needed so they can prosecute.

"As good as it could go. It's done, though, which is all that's important."

Sighing, she seems happy at that news. "When do you leave again?"

"I don't."

Furrowing her brows, she leans back to look at my face. "What do you mean?"

I roll her over to her back on the bed and then crawl over her, pressing my hips into her when she spreads her legs to cradle me. "I *mean*, I talked to some of the department heads and told them I wanted to take a step back from field work. They'll still call me in, but only on a consultation basis."

I watch for her reaction to the news while she processes what I'm telling her.

"Wait, so that means that you're not traveling anymore? No more trips?" I can hear the excitement in her voice.

Grinning, I kiss her again, this time sliding my tongue along her lips, encouraging her to open her mouth for me. "No more trips, kitten," I whisper.

This woman has been an angel, staying home and raising our boys, alone, during the times when I have to travel for my job. I know it's been rough for her, and I knew it was time to take on a different role. "Are you happy about that?"

Groaning, she wraps her arms around my neck and hooks her legs around my waist. "So happy," she mumbles.

Pulling back, I hold her face and look her over. "So, happy girl... the boys wouldn't *dare* to interrupt us right now, which by the way, do you know what they were doing?"

Huffing out a laugh, she relaxes into the bed. "Trying to make me crazy?"

Chuckling, I smirk at her. "Your children were betting on whether they could get you to swear. They wagered their chores depending on the offensiveness of whichever word you used. They got as far as wondering if you would say *fuck*," her eyes widen, and I continue. "The *Goddamnit* scared the shit out of them. They didn't expect that as a possibility."

Laughing softly, she bites her lip at me. "I feel pretty bad about it."

"Don't. But, back to what I was saying... now that the boys are occupied for the night, how do you think we should celebrate the good news?" I wiggle my eyebrows at her.

"Well, we could celebrate by doing the f-word..."

"You know I want you to say it first." I laugh at her narrowing eyes.

"I believe I've already sworn enough for one night, don't you think?"

I shake my head. "Never... I want to hear you tell me what you want me to do to you, kitten. Would you like me to make you purr?"

Her eyes flash with heat even while her face turns a soft shade of pink. Over a decade and a half together and my girl still gets shy on me.

"Baby... tell me you want me to lick your pussy..."

I laugh at her adorable kitten growl, but she listens. "Arrow, my love... *Please*, would you lick my pussy?"

I thrust my hardening cock against her, our clothes the only thing stopping me from sliding inside her. She groans and arches her back off the bed from the contact. Holding myself pressed up against her, I still until she looks at me again.

"Now, tell me you want me to fuck you after I make you cum all over my tongue." I ache to taste her; I just need to wait for the words. It's our game and I know I'll win. I always win.

"Darn it, Arrow. Will you just do it and stop teasing?" She thrusts up against me, so I pull my hips back, denying her the friction.

"Uh uhh, sweet girl. I want the words." I shake my head at her like I'm disappointed and she rolls her eyes.

Reaching up, she grabs my face and pulls me down to her, nipping my lip just enough to give me a little bite of pain. "Arrow... I *need* you to lick my pussy. I need you to eat me until I cum all over your tongue, and then I'm desperate for your hard cock to fuck me until I scream."

"*Yes!*" I growl at her. "Get your pants off and spread your legs for me."

Standing up, I quickly wrench my clothes off while she fights with her own. Her panties are just making their way to her feet when I crawl back on the bed. Yanking them from her, I shove her knees open and pin them wide to the bed and stare down at my wife's glistening lips. She's so wet that I could slam into her now without hurting her, but a promise is a promise.

Laying between her legs, I curl my arms under her thighs and rest my hands on her stomach to hold her in place.

After running my nose along her skin, I nip just above her clit before looking up at her. Our eyes meet and hold while I lean into her and give her clit an open-mouthed kiss.

Gasping at the contact, I can feel her body shudder under me. I spread her lips open with one hand and dance a finger across her opening to tease her.

"P-Please Arrow…" she begs, and the sound of her voice turned on like this is music to my ears.

"Just a minute… let me enjoy the view." I run my tongue up once from ass to clit and then pull back to continue running my finger over her. "I love you so much, kitten, and I'm so glad I got to come home early to this…"

"Babe?"

"Yeah, sweet girl?"

"I love you too… now please, make me fucking cum."

I grin, and then lean in, giving my wife exactly what she asked for.

# THE COMPLETE INNOCENCE BOXSET

The End

S. E. Green

THE COMPLETE INNOCENCE BOXSET

# EDEN

## S.E. Green

S. E. Green

# From the Author

I live for music, so I often get inspired by many contemporary songs and artists when I write. While some books that I write are inspired by multiple songs, this one was a one song repeater for me. It just sort of sucked me in a put me in a particular mood - one that I hope you feel when you listen. It's called **Experience** by *Ludovico Einaudi*.

Also, as a side note, this story came to me while I was actually playing this song on the piano. Eden is my first pianist that I've written – she won't be my last. There's something so erotic about playing, putting your emotions and body into playing, particularly when someone is enraptured while watching you play. When I play, I day dream... well, I day dream while I drive as well. The scene that popped into my head is at the end of Chapter 1 where Marcus is in a dark room with her, listening to her, completely enthralled and Eden crawls into his lap. This piece by Einaudi is also extremely dramatic, so to me it feels like someone is running away from something that just irrevocably changed their life. Not a lot, but it's what grew this story. I hope you enjoy Eden and Marcus!

S. E. Green

# Trigger Warnings

Please know that there could be some triggering topics addressed that include **verbal abuse and neglect (both as an adult and child), violence.**

Having experienced abuse in my past (one sexual assault and one physically abusive relationship), I sometimes draw from how I felt and recovered from it. Everyone reacts differently to trauma, so if you doubt that my character(s) reacted in a believable way, please keep in mind we are all wonderfully different. My therapist told me that our bodies tend to subconsciously protect itself the best way it thinks will keep us the safest. Please seek help if you are being hurt or have been hurt in the past. We all want you safe and feeling loved!

S. E. Green

# Chapter 1

## *Marcus*

"You are fucking late," I growl.

Joseph and Thompson stand up a bit straighter when they realize I'm pissed. I don't give either of them my attention and continue sipping a twelve-year-old Redbreast whiskey on the rocks. It's not my favorite, but it's the best they serve here. The tumbler the bartender poured it into is made of thick glass, which is probably a good thing right now since I'm irritated. Squeezing a glass until it breaks would be an annoyance no one wants to deal with.

"Mr. Costa. We apologize, we had to wait on the prin-" Joseph clears his throat before continuing, "...on Miss Altera. She had planned on bein' here over 45 minutes ago but took her time gettin' out the door."

"We had no chance of tellin' ya," Thompson adds. These two aren't my favorite employees. They're a bit rough around the edges and kind of slimy, but perfect for where I've got them assigned.

Grunting, I throw back the rest of my drink and stretch my arms across the back of the booth to study the two brothers. My ankle rests on my knee and I know that they see me as relaxed, unworried, and uncaring. They're wrong. I'm on edge and have been since they told me earlier today that Leo Altera's daughter was going to be out and about tonight.

"Where is she?" I saw these two fools walk in through the front door ten minutes ago, alone, with no girl.

"She went in through the back, Sir." At least Joseph is *trying* to ease my displeasure with the two of them. Thompson doesn't seem to care. He hasn't stopped starting at the women dancing in the center of the club, their short dresses showing off their tits hanging out.

That's odd. "Why would she go in through the back? And why did *you* not follow her in that way?"

"'Cuz she ain't plannin' on clubbin'. Said somethin' 'bout a back room and meetin' with a friend... Figured we could check things out here, ya know?" This moron is giving me a fucking headache.

Pinching the bridge of my nose in frustration, I try to keep my temper in check. "Thompson?"

"Yeah, boss?" He's finally giving me his full attention.

"*Vattene dal cazzo*," I hiss, giving him a hard look as I tell him to get the fuck out. He doesn't understand Italian, but he's not so ignorant that he can't figure it out.

Mumbling, he turns and walks back to the public part of the club, disappearing.

Focusing back on Joseph, I wait a moment before talking, making him uneasy. He fidgets, unsure if he should say something or stay silent.

"Tell me about the girl," I finally demand. Honestly, I don't want to be here all night. Wasting time in a place like this, when I could be meeting with more important people, is frustrating. Besides, everyone here is only interested in drinking and dancing and fucking. I'm not against the fucking part, or the drinking part, but the socialization makes my skin crawl. Too many fucking people in here.

Nodding quickly, Joseph fills me in, "There ain't a whole lot to her. She's not around in the house a lot. Altera doesn't bring her around his people when he's meetin' with them. She's got a fancy car and fancy clothes, a bit stuck up too. She doesn't talk to anyone when she's out of her room, except when she asks to go somewhere."

I'm not impressed by what he's told me so far. Nothing is interesting enough to give me any ideas on how to use her to take down Altera. "Tell me about her personality. What kinds of things does she like? Where does she go when she does leave?"

Blowing out a breath, he thinks for a minute. *Cazzo*, this is going to take for fucking ever. "Joseph, I do not have all fucking night. Talk now or get the fuck out of here."

"S-Sorry Sir. So, yeah… Her name is Eden. I think she's 19. The other guards made a comment about her being legal and all that, but I don't think she's been for a while. Anyways, I've only seen her interact with people a couple times. I saw one time when she was talkin' to her dad, Altera, about some performance or something. He was pissed and yellin' at her. She was cryin' and supposedly had an anxiety or panic attack. I don't know the difference between 'em."

Frowning, I think that over while he continues.

"She stutters a lot too when she's talkin'. Honestly man-" I raise my eyebrows at his familiarity. "Uhh... I mean Sir. She don't do a whole lot. She's just in her room or traipsin' around in short little dresses, teasin' the men. She ignores everyone else in the house, like won't even look at us or nothin'. I think she's just a young spoiled princess who hangs around the house and lives off daddy."

Tapping my finger on the arm rest, I consider what he's told me. Basically, if I want to use her, I'm dealing with a spoiled, lazy teenager who thinks she's better than everyone else. *Fottimi...* Fuck me.

Sighing, I stand up and straighten my jacket, buttoning the bottom and smoothing my hand down my chest, removing any wrinkles I may have caused while sitting and waiting. "Show me the girl."

"Yup. Okay. She's uhh... she's in one of the closed off rooms they use for private parties and stuff." I follow him as we leave the VIP area. Weaving my way around the edge of the club, I ignore the few women who approach to try and garner my attention. I'm not opposed to meeting beautiful women; I'm just opposed to beautiful women chasing me down.

At this point in my life, I'd rather enjoy the hunt. Throwing themselves at me is the first way to get me uninterested.

"Some of the other men that Altera had guardin' her said that she comes here a lot. She'll sometimes stay for hours in the backroom. Supposedly, she's friends with the cook's wife or the club manager's wife or somethin'. They let her do her thing when they don't need the room."

Nodding that I hear him, we stop in front of a set of double doors. Joseph hands me a key. "What is this for?" I ask him before taking it.

"One of the bouncers gave it to me. Said it's for this room. She keeps it locked so people don't bug her, but this way we can get in there if we need her. Otherwise, we just gotta wait 'til she's done and take her home."

Fucking weird, but alright. I take the key and slip it into the slot, turning it gently. I don't know what the setup is in there, but I'm just going to slip in and get a read on her. Maybe talk to her, but I don't know what good that'll do at this point.

Joseph starts to walk away back toward the club, so I stop him. "*Dove cazzo vai?*"

"Uhh... what?" Rolling my eyes at him, I let out a frustrated breath. I keep forgetting that these guys are new and don't fucking understand me.

"I said, where the fuck are you going? You need to stay here. *Rimani qui.* Guard the door so I am not interrupted."

I don't wait for him to acknowledge me. He knows to listen, otherwise he'll be working elsewhere. I slip into the room, letting the door softly snick shut behind me.

Instantly, the throbbing music from the club is muted, only the pounding of the bass left. That pounding disappears when I hear the ethereal notes filling the room now, all coming from the piano pushed into the corner on the opposite side of the room from me.

"*Bella...*" I murmur. I haven't seen the girl yet, but the song she plays is beautiful. Haunting notes blanket my thoughts as I slowly move closer, still out of sight from her.

Finding a seat in the middle of the room, I pull one of the chairs that was lifted and placed upside down on the table. I internally cringe when the metal on the legs of the chair scrape across the floor and the piano comes to a grinding halt. A mash of chords sounds, like she slammed her hands down on all the keys.

Sitting down, I situate myself before focusing back on her. She must have been leaning over the keys before, but now she sits ramrod straight, her wide eyes pinned on me. I must have startled her, and I feel a twinge of remorse, but I push it away.

Sitting forward in the chair, I lean both of my elbows on the tops of my thighs and my hands hang between my legs, loosely clasped. We study each other for a moment.

She's not angry I'm in here, but not happy either. She seems uncertain about my presence, more than anything. She's a lovely little thing. Even in the dim lights I can see she's gorgeous. Dark, almost black thick hair is tied in a loose braid and slung over her shoulder where it hangs down to below her perky little tits. Her eye color isn't clear, but they look dark and are rimmed with thick lashes.

Those eyes haven't moved from my face. Either she can't see all of me, she's not interested in what she sees, or she's just scared and afraid to move. What I do know is I want her to keep playing.

"Continue," I order her, my voice coming out lower and harsher than I had intended.

She flinches when the sound of my voice cuts through the silence and then promptly looks away to stare back down at the piano. I'm more than twenty feet from her, but I can see her trembling from here. *Fottimi...* My intentions weren't to scare the girl.

I clear my throat and try to speak a little more gently. "I apologize. I will not interrupt you again, but I would very much like to listen... if that is alright with you, *stellina*?"

A gentle voice whispers through the room back to me. "Stellina?"

My lip quirks slightly at her question. "'Yes. It means little star. Please, do not let me stop you."

She doesn't say anything else. Doesn't acknowledge my answer. She simply places her hands back on the piano and picks up where she left off when I interrupted her.

The longer I listen to her, the more mesmerized I become. I'm not sure if I have any conscious thoughts while she plays, shifting flawlessly from one song to another. No music in front of her, only a few brief glances in my direction, almost looking for approval in a way.

I'm not sure what to make of her. I'm intrigued, that's for certain. Enraptured, she's incredibly beautiful. Ensnared, her talent is indisputable. Is she spoiled? I can't tell. Nor can I tell if she's entitled or lazy. I doubt lazy though. Lazy people don't practice for so long that they would acquire this level of skill. A tease? She's certainly alluring, so possibly.

What I do know is that I'm fascinated.

## Chapter 2

**1 month later**

## *Eden*

Looking at the clock, I see that it's after 10 pm. Dad normally wants me in my room for the night by 8 so he can meet with his 'business associates' in private. Private meaning everyone but me, which truly, I'm okay with. I'm not interested in investments and upcoming businesses in the area. I also don't know 'who's who' in our city.

Slipping out of my room to grab something to drink from the kitchen, I make it downstairs before Thompson intercepts me. He's been trying to antagonize or corner me lately, making lewd comments and gestures. I've told my dad that I'm not comfortable having him following me. My skin crawls every time he's around.

Dad just brushed me off, in front of Thompson *and* his partner, Joe. I wish he hadn't done that because now he think he has free reign.

"Hey girl… what's daddy's princess doin' walkin' around here so late? You lookin' for somethin'?" I shudder when he licks his lips and comes closer to me, forcing my back to hit the wall.

"I'm just going to get a-" I try to tell him I'm just getting a drink, but he doesn't let me finish.

"I think you're lookin' for somethin' to get ya ready for the weekend, aren't ya?" I look at him in confusion, not sure what he's talking about. He does that a lot, most of my dad's men do that. Talk about things that make no sense. I know what they're implying, I'm not entirely in the dark, but some of the suggestive remarks don't make any sort of sense. Like now.

Trying to move past him, I shake my head and ignore what he said. What's this weekend? "I'm just going to get a drink. I'll be quick."

Grabbing my arm, he turns me and pushes me back into the wall. His body is pressed against mine, and I try to hold back a gag at the revolting smell of stale cigarettes and body odor.

"Don't be a lil' bitch. Daddy's all busy right now, so tattlin' on me ain't gonna be an option. You tried to get me fired! For what? Reactin' to your fuckin' teasin'? Walkin' around this house like you own the place." The longer he talks, the louder he's getting.

"I swear I wasn't try-" I cry out and close my eyes when he slams his hand into the wall right next to my head.

"Thompson. Man, the hell are you doin'?" I breathe a sigh of relief. I don't particularly care for Joe, but he doesn't make me feel uncomfortable like Thompson does. He just doesn't like me much.

"Just talkin' to the fuckin' princess about deliverin' on promises she keeps makin'." He looks down at my chest before sneering, his rancid breath blowing out across my face. "Tits hangin' out, askin' for attention. Been a long time since you got fucked, or somethin'? Desperate for my cock, aren't ya?"

He emphasizes his question with a grind on my body, something hard pushing into my belly. My tongue is stuck to the roof of my mouth, throat closed up and dry. He's so close, and I don't know how to get him to back up.

"Come on brother, you're gonna piss off the boss," Joe tells him, sounding bored like he doesn't really care one way or the other. I'm surprised that they're brothers. They don't look a thing alike. I had no idea they were related. I try to plead with him with my eyes, but I can't tell if he sees me. My eyes are blurry, pulse beating rapidly in fear.

"I don' give a fuck if the boss is pissed. Doin' bullshit babysittin' on a fuckin' cockteasin' slut who thinks she's too good for everyone around her." He thrusts into me again when he calls me a slut, teeth gritted.

I try to push him away but he grabs my hands and slams them on the wall above my head and shoves his face into mine. "Don' fuckin' push me you fuckin' bitch. Fuckin' WHOR-"

"What the hell is going on in here?"

I sag in relief at the sound of my dad's voice, and I cry out for him to help me.

"Sir, he was just messin' around. Didn't mean anything by it," Joe explains. He sounds less bored now, worried for his brother. It's hard not to be angry at him for not stepping in earlier.

Thompson quickly squeezes my wrists, grinding the bones together before releasing me and pushing himself away. He gives me a murderous look before turning to my dad. "Yup... just messin' around. Eddie here was sneakin' around the hallway, and I figured I'd give her a little scare, since she ain't supposed to be here."

"*No!*" I sob out. "That's not... that's not what I..." Sniffing, I rub my wrists. "I just wanted a drink of water." I get so tongue-tied and clam up whenever an altercation occurs around me.

"You're messing around... calling my daughter a bitch and a whore? *That's* messing around?" He looks at Joe. "Is he for fucking real?"

Awkwardly laughing, Joe rubs the back of his head and looks around as a few other of my dad's associates come into the room. "You know how guys can be. It's late and I'm sure he meant nothin' by it."

"Ahh." Dad just shrugs like it's no big deal and my heart falls when he, once again, doesn't intervene for me. "Thompson, come over here a moment."

Thompson smirks back at me before strolling over to him. There are six people in the space now, not including me, and I inch back toward the doorway to the kitchen. I just want to get out of here.

Glancing back at them before leaving, I watch, horrified as my dad pulls out a gun and shoots Thompson in the center of his forehead.

Silence.

His body drops to the ground with a loud thud and nobody moves. "Fuckin' asshole." Dad looks to everyone around him before adding, "don't fuckin' lie to me, it pisses me off. Fucking Costa wouldn't put up with this bullshit."

*Oh my God...*I don't know what to do!

Quickly looking around the room to make sure no one is watching me; I notice that Joe is looking at me with so much hate in his eyes that I shrink in on myself.

I know they are... *were* brothers, apparently, but I don't know why he'd be angry at me for what his brother did. A shiver runs through my body as I start to hyperventilate, watching as the blood pooling around his head spreads across the floor.

"*Eden*!" I snap my head up when my dad barks out my name. "Go get dressed and come to my office. I need to talk to you." He doesn't wait for me to agree when he mutters something under his breath to a man I don't recognize standing next to him. Then he turns and walks out, everyone else following him except for Joe.

"You're fuckin' dead... look what you fuckin did!" he hisses through his teeth, keeping his voice low enough that dad can't hear him. He takes a step toward me and I can't stop the flinch and my step backwards, away from him.

Whispering, I can only croak out my words, "I-I'm s-sorry. I d-did'n-"

"I don't give a *fuck*. Run to your room and listen to daddy." He lunges toward me and laughs cruelly when I let out a small noise and fall back into the wall. Turning from him, I run through the kitchen and out the back door.

I hear his laughter as my bare feet hit the grass, wet from the sprinklers earlier this evening. I only briefly register that I'm in a nightgown, not wearing any shoes, and it's freezing outside.

My heavy breathing keeps the air misting in front of my face, allowing me to see how fast I'm panting as I run toward my only safe place. Even though Wild Sides is a dance club and bar, the owners have never minded me using the back room they save for private parties.

The night floor manager, Johnny, is married to one of my tutors, Mrs. Anna. She knows, from spending hours at my house, that I'm not comfortable there. The only thing dad really allowed me to do was learn piano, aside from the tutoring and homeschooling I received. Unfortunately, the piano at home is in the center of the house and my dad's office is connected to that space. Which means I don't get to use it if he's in an important meeting, or there are a bunch of people walking around.

My house is *always* filled with people…

I run until I make it to the back door of Wild Sides, slamming my hand on the door until one of the employees sticks his head out, looking around before catching site of me.

"Jesus…" he mumbles, before shutting the door on me.

I know I look a mess. It's probably close to 11, I'm in a white nightgown that looks like a spaghetti strap dress and tears running down my face. Dizziness overtakes me when I fight the sobs trying to break free as I catch my breath from my run.

A raspy voice lets me know that Johnny is here. "Eden! What the hell, girl? Are you alright?"

"N-n-no… c-can I use m-m-my r-room?" I can't stop the trembling as I hug myself, trying to self soothe. A trick I learned when I was younger, upset, and dad was busy. He was always busy.

"Your feet are bleedin' girl! Tell me what's goin' on." He pulls his phone out of his pocket as he mumbles something that sounds like '*I'm gonna call him*', but I'm not sure.

Shaking my head, I ask again. Beg him this time. "P-P-Please Johnny… I just… p-please let m-me." The end breaks on another sob.

Running his hand down a scruffy cheek, he looks at me a moment before giving in. "Yeah, okay. Just stay in there for a while.

I don't need anyone seeing you runnin' around like this. Want me to call your dad?"

"*No...* No, please d-don't. I j-just n-need to... to go..." I can't get anything else out. Thank God, he lets me in. The door to my room is down a hallway that most of their patrons don't use.

I slip into the room and shut the door on Johnny, feeling slightly bad for being rude, but I need to be alone. I need to figure out what happened tonight and what I should do.

Stumbling through the dark over to the piano, I sit down and wince when the backs of my thighs come in contact with the cold bench. The floor is slick under my feet and my hands are locked into fists on my lap, gripping the ends of my nightgown.

Forcing them to unclench, I stare at my shaking hands before covering my face with them, hiding away from everything. I drop my forehead on the keys, the discordant notes ringing out through the space. The noise breaks me and I let go... and sob.

I'm not sure how long I sit there, crying on the only thing that's brought me any joy, in the only space I've ever felt safe. But it's not enough. I can feel the anxiety attack coming on, overtaking me and I desperately try some of the methods that I've read. The ones that tell you stimulating pressure points can help slow your heart rate and trigger your nervous system into calling down.

I use my thumbs to press into the tip of each of my fingers, pushing hard until I feel a small sting of pain. Over and over again, I dance my thumbs across my fingers, then dig them into my thighs to stop them from shaking, but nothing is helping.

Jerking my head up, I look at the door when I hear it open and close a moment later. I see *him*.

I don't know who he is, but he's always here. For the last few weeks, every time I've come here, he's shown up within thirty minutes of me. Never saying anything, just sitting in the middle of the room at an empty table with a glass of something that he sips until I'm done playing. Then he always tosses the rest of it back and leaves after giving me a nod of acknowledgement.

He's another constant. A constant presence that I didn't know I needed until he was always there. Maybe I came here because I had hoped he'd be here, I'm not sure.

I watch him through my wet lashes, still breathing heavily. He pauses near the door, inspecting me with a furrowed brow. Without taking his eyes off me, he strolls over to his regular seat. My eyes follow him, begging him for something I don't know I need.

Settling in his regular spot, he places his hands on his lap and leans back in the chair, watching me.

My breath picks up, the calm I was trying to find starting to fade away, and I know I need to do something. Jumping to my feet, he shifts almost imperceptibly at my movement. I just... I *need* him.

My feet falter a moment, but they quickly find themselves directly in front of him, and I'm looking into his face. Up close, he's elegant... handsome, but everything is hidden behind his eyes. I can't identify what he thinks of me right now, but at this moment... I don't care.

I choke back another sob and see his eyes soften toward me. Still, I hold back, even though I want to go to him the rest of the way.

"*Topolina?*" His deep, sonorous voice breaks down my last barrier, and I go to him.

Closing the last few feet of distance, I inch my way slowly onto his lap, curl against his chest and press my face into his neck.

He's stiff, holding his arms out to the sides like he doesn't know if he should touch me. He may not want to, but I feel this urgent compulsion to use him. Like I just know that he's here for me, and only me.

Holding on to him, I cry silently into his neck. I can't stop the shudders from wracking through my body, but I can at least control my sound. I beg in my head over and over, *please please please...* desperately wanting him.

I need a hug. I need him to hold me. I need *him*.

Finally, I feel his arms slowly wrap around my body, pulling me into him. Closer than I was able to get on my own.

"I have got you *piccolo mia*."

Finally, I can breathe.

# Chapter 3

## *Marcus*

After getting a call from Joseph that Thompson was dead, and *then* one from John that my little mouse was in her room again, my mood was fucked.

Joseph informed me that her father, fucking Altera, shot Thompson because he had an altercation with my *topolina*. His explanation was that Thompson was simply telling her that she needed to go back to her room, on orders of her father, and she refused. Leo got involved and just took him out.

I'm certain that's not the whole story, but Joseph was adamant that this little girl was to blame. Then, with the call from the night manager here at the club telling me that she was in her room, I had to come and find out what happened.

I've spent the last month watching her. It's become an obsession. All of the employees here know now that they're to call me the moment she steps foot within the building. Every night she's here, I come. I watch her. I *want* her, but I still haven't figured out who she really is.

Is she the spoiled princess that my men and her father's men think her to be? Or is she simply sheltered, and not used to interacting with people? Naive? My gut is leaning toward the latter, but I need to find out for sure.

Walking into the room, I hesitate when I see her, disheveled and shaking, sitting on her bench. My initial instinct is to go to her, but I hold back. Even though I've been a constant presence in here, she still doesn't know me. So, I sit and wait to see what she does.

My stomach turns at the look of longing she's directing at me, especially when she walks to me and stands in front of me. She looks a mess. Only in a slip of a white nightgown, dirty feet that may have a bit of blood mixed in there, and hair wild around her shoulders. It's been tangled in the wind and strands are stuck to her face, damp where her tears have soaked her cheeks. And she's pale.

Not sure what she needs or what I can do for her, I call her name. Well, I call her my little mouse unintentionally, and that must have been all she was waiting for. I suck in a breath and freeze when she climbs into my lap and curls up like a *piccola gattina*. A little kitten that has yet to show her claws if she has them.

I can feel the heat of her tears on my neck and the trembling of her body tucked into mine. A feeling of rightness overtakes me and once I unfreeze my limbs, I curl my arms around her and hold her tightly to me.

"I have got you *piccola mia*." And I do have her, my little one. I feel her shiver when she hears me speak.

Feelings of empathy wash over me as I soak in her fear and sadness, a great desire to fight off her demons. I just need to know what or who they are.

After running a hand up and down her back for a while, feeling the subtle bumps of her spine and the curve of her waist, my mind starts to track in a different direction as my cock stirs to life.

Gripping her arms, I try to pull her back so I can get her to look at me, but she whimpers, turning her body to wrap her legs around my waist, seemingly afraid that I'm trying to move her from my lap. She grips me harder and fuck if I don't feel the heat of her pussy directly on my cock. *Merda.* This is not helping.

I only have so much strength and she's a beautiful woman, so I don't try to move her again. Instead, I kiss the top of her head and begin to ask my questions.

"*Bella*, tell me what has happened." My voice comes out a little lower than I had intended, but between the pressure on my cock and finally touching her, it can't be helped.

She chokes out another sob and squeezes me tighter, silent for a moment before I hear her speak in a tiny, broken voice, "M-My dad… he… I can't go h-home."

"Why can you not go home? What did your dad do?" I know, but I want her to tell me. Maybe a test to see if she's a liar.

She looks up at me, her champagne brown eyes lined with thick, wet lashes, suck me in. She whispers like she doesn't want anyone else to hear even though we're alone in here, "He did something b-bad... and Joe-"

"Joe?" What did Joseph do?

She sniffs and rubs the back of her hand across each eye. "He was so *mad*, but I didn't know! I just wanted..." She looks down at my chest and picks at one of the buttons on my shirt. "He was s-scaring me... wouldn't let me go. I d-didn't want him to..."

I pull the back of her head into my chest again and soothe her while she cries again. "Tell me *topolina*, who would not let you go?" Her father? Did that fuck Joseph touch her? My grip on her head tightens, accidentally pulling the roots of her hair. She doesn't complain, the only reaction she has is her breath falters slightly.

"...T-Thompson. H-He was hurting me, rubbed on me..." Her body shudders in revulsion before continuing, and the more she talks, the more my rage takes over. She explains what he did, holding her against the wall, cursing at her and saying he was going to fuck her. Then tells me how her father shot Thompson and then what Joseph said to her.

I believe her. She wouldn't be this shaken if she was trying to intentionally get someone hurt. Joseph is going to be a problem, but I'll deal with that later. "That *pezzo di medda*, I will fucking kill him." Piece of shit had better run, the same way he told my little mouse to run.

The whole time she's on my lap, she continues to try to dig her way into me, trying to get closer. Her pussy grinds on my cock as she grips her thighs around my waist, and I hold back a groan as I dig my fingers into her back.

I can't stand the friction anymore, so I grab the sides of her face and force her to look at me. "My *topolina*, you are asking for trouble if you keep moving like that. *Cazzo*, I can only take so much." I groan out again as her body shifts once more against me.

I feel her body stiffen slightly as we stare at each other, my eyes flicking across her face, trying to read what she needs from me. Her quick glance at my lips tells me all I need to know, and I crash my lips into hers.

Forcing her head back, I use my thumb on her chin to pry her mouth open and slide my tongue into her mouth, tasting her for the first time. My kiss doesn't start off slow, it's frantic from the start because of my need for her. It's obvious she's unskilled, which is another thing my men may have gotten wrong, but I don't mind. I take advantage of her unschooled mouth and teach her exactly what I want and *how* I want it.

I feel her sigh against my mouth as she wraps her arms around my neck, tentatively holding on at first, then gaining confidence the longer we kiss.

I have to feel her. Her body is shifting ever so slightly against my hardness, a tease to how she'll move if I were inside of her. Sliding my hands from her face, I run them down her sides and grip her hips tightly, most likely bruising her. Using her body, I grind her along my cock, back and forth to get the friction I need, never slowing down with my tongue in her mouth.

"Please…" she murmurs, asking for more.

Thrusting up into her again, she gasps, and my final restraint breaks.

I can't stop my hands from gripping her nightgown and lifting it to her waist, bunching it with one hand while I use the other to dip into the back of her panties to grip one cheek. Dancing my fingers down the crack of her pert little ass, I find my way to her heat, scorching from all of the movement. She's absolutely drenched with desire.

I rumble out another groan as I feel her slickness, and attack her mouth again, leaning her back slightly, forcing her chest to thrust out against mine. "Hold on to me *il mia piccola amore*. I need you little mouse."

Not waiting for her to respond, I wrap my arms around her waist and feel her grip my neck tighter. Her legs are like vices around my waist when I quickly turn her and set her on the table behind us.

Her eyes are wide, looking up at me when I place my hand in the center of her chest to lay her back along the table. My gaze takes in her hardened nipples standing out through her thin nightgown, her trembling body, and her shaking hands as she reaches for me. Her lips are swollen from taking her mouth so aggressively, and she hasn't looked more beautiful.

Keeping my eyes locked on hers, I reach under the bottom of her gown and grip her thin, soaking panties, tearing them from her and tossing them aside.

Looking down at her exposed pussy, I can't stop my tongue from licking her taste off my mouth. I quickly wrestle with my belt and pull down my zipper to pull my cock out. Fuck, it's painfully hard.

Grabbing her knees, I push them open, spreading her so I can more easily line myself up. In one quick movement, I shove my way into her tightness without pausing, burying myself deep.

The moment I enter her, I look up into her eyes and see them widen with shock and then fill with tears from the pain as I tear through her innocence.

She stays completely silent. *Cazzo!* She was a fucking virgin, and I just took her like a woman who's been fucked hard before. How the fuck is she still a virgin? My men made it seem like she's… well, it doesn't matter now. They were wrong.

"*Mi dispiace tanto amore mia…*" Fuck. *I am so sorry my love*, I say to her and then again in my head, as I attempt to wipe the tears running down her face.

I move to pull my hips back to pull my cock out of her, knowing that it's hurting her, but she stops me. "*NO!*" she sobs out, "Please d-don't. I need you."

I'm pissed at myself and don't intend to sound so gruff when I speak to her. "I did not know you were untouched, little mouse. I would not have…" I trail off as I watch her curl in on herself at my words, and pull away from me.

"… Sorry," she whispers. Trying to push herself up from the table, I can feel myself begin to slip from her body, and I panic.

"Do not move, *topolina*." I push forward and reseat myself inside her pussy, grinding myself against her clit, and she cries out. Reaching down, I pull one of her legs up alongside of me and lean over her, placing my arms on either side of her so we are face to face. The movement helps me keep her pinned to the table and makes my eyes roll when I feel her muscles flutter and squeeze my cock. *Cazzo*, she feels amazing.

"I simply meant that I am sorry for taking you the way I did. Had I known it was your first time, I would have gone slower. I am not mad at you, *stellina*. I did not give you the chance to tell me. Please, give me a moment. You are incredibly tight and…" I groan again and place my forehead against hers when I feel her clench, pulling me in further. "*Ti senti così bene…* so good."

I can't stop my body from pulling back and then plunging into her again. Her pussy is so fucking hot, my cock feels like it could be scorched.

"It hurts…" she whimpers.

I hate that I'm hurting her, it wasn't my intention. When I start to move, I know it'll feel better for her, but I need to distract her right now. Wrapping my arms under her, I pull her up into my chest and lift her from the table. Keeping myself imbedded inside of her, I take the few steps back to my chair and sit down gently so I can keep her face to face.

"*La mia bambina...* I will try not to hurt you." Kissing her softly on the lips, I keep my arms wrapped around her upper body, my cock still buried deep.

She moans more and more the longer we kiss, her hips involuntarily starting to circle on my lap, grinding her clit into the base of my cock. "You feel so good..." she whispers to me.

"Take what you need from me, my little mouse." I don't hold back the thrust when I push myself into her, quirking my lip at the loud gasp and shriek she lets out.

"Tell me when you are ready for me to move..." I place a kiss to her lips, cheek, and then I lick up her neck until I reach her ear. I wind her hair into my fist and tip her head back so she can only look at me and nowhere else.

"I... I'm ready," she murmurs, part question and part statement.

Growling low, I grit my teeth. "Little mouse... I want to hear you scream for me."

# Chapter 4

## *Eden*

I hold on to his neck tightly, burying my face into it as he pounds into me. I don't know if my body likes the feeling of something stabbing into me, each thrust sending a sharp wave of... maybe pleasure? Pain, but I'm not sure if it's pain because it hurts, or pain from being so overstimulated.

The tears continue to roll down my face the entire time I'm panting into his neck. I'm not really crying anymore, not like I was earlier, but this closeness I feel toward him is paralyzing. I can't move except to hold on to him.

He has his arms wrapped around me, one around my waist, the other running up the length of my back before holding the back of my neck in a firm grasp. He's leaned back slightly in his chair as his hips continue to thrust up into me at a fast pace, our skin slapping together obscenely.

Our bodies are slick, and I cry out each time he slams inside of me. His sounds are almost terrifying, animalistic sounds reverberating through his chest as he growls words in another language. I don't know what he's saying, but I can recognize that it's Italian.

"*La tua figa si sente così bene... Cazzo, sei stretto. Sei mio... Nel momento in cui ho scopato nella tua figa vergine, sei diventata mia, topolina...*" He's speaking as he licks into my mouth, pulling my hair to tilt my head to the side and biting my neck.

"*Gesù Cristo*! I am going to cum," he grunts into my ear. I'm weeping as he pounds harder, grinding his body into mine, causing sparks of pleasure to force its way through the pain of his thickness.

My body feels out of control as it squeezes around him, searching for something unknown. The sliding in and out is creating so much heat and wetness that I can feel myself dripping onto him. "I... I don't know what's h-happening..."

I feel like I'm spiraling, and I don't know where I'm going to end up. I just know that if I keep holding on to him, I'll be okay.

"You are going to come for me, my sweet. Come all over my cock..." He groans and then kisses me again, thrusting his tongue into my mouth and wrapping it around mine. I can hardly keep up with the ferocity of his mouth before he rips away and pushes my head back to his neck.

Panting and crying out, my hips are moving over him, searching for the fall off the ledge that I'm balanced on. "*Please!*" I beg him.

Roaring, he stands us both up and bounces me onto his hard length, and the change in position pushes me over the edge. I shatter into a million pieces, screaming out as I pulse around him.

He slams into me a few more times before sitting back down and pulling my hips back and forth as he grinds. I can feel him swelling and pulsing as a warm rush of heat fills me.

I'm still twitching and shaking as he slows down the movements, breathing heavily over my head, still pinning my face into his neck. I can't help but dip my tongue out to taste the saltiness of his skin from all our exertion.

Moaning at the feel of my tongue, he runs his hand down my back and grips my ass cheek, squeezing and releasing like he can't control the tension in his hands.

I sigh as my body relaxes and melts into him. I couldn't decide before whether it was pain or pleasure. There definitely was pain, but the pleasure was indescribable.

We don't speak for a while and simply sit here like this, his body still inside of mine. Lazily, I run my fingers down the back of his neck, a small smile gracing my lips when his body shudders at the light touch.

Wincing, I realize that I don't even know his name, and he doesn't know mine. I suck in a breath to ask, but before a sound comes out, the door to the room slams open and we both jolt at the noise.

Peaking over his shoulder, I see two men I've never seen before striding inside, halting when they see us. I can't help but dip my head to hide. God, he's still inside of me and there are strangers staring at us!

I cringe when one of them starts to speak rather than leave us be.

"Mr. Cos-"

"*Vattene dal cazzo!*" he hisses without looking at them, holding me tightly to his chest to keep their eyes from seeing me. He's still fully dressed, so maybe they don't know what's happened in here?

"But there are men-"

"*OUT!*" he snaps at them once more. They both mumble something, and then the door closes.

"I'm sorry, topolina. They will not come in again." He tilts my head back to look me over, concern etched on his face. "Are you okay? Did I hurt you?"

I can't help the smile that grows on my face. Here he is, asking if I'm alright after the way he took me, and I can still feel him twitching inside of me. I bite my lip and try to hide my giggle. "I'm alright, I think. I can't really feel my toes, though." I look down at them and cock my head to the side. "Is that normal? To be numb like this?"

A chuckle runs through his chest, making it shake, and I can feel the movement on the tips of my nipples. "I suppose they could be, but I am not certain. We should probably stand you up and get you righted." He looks around us and then sounds a bit frustrated. "*Merda*! I ripped your panties."

"I'll be fine." When I say that, I remember why I'm here in the first place and my mood plummets. Then it drops even further when

I think about the fact that we don't know each other. "I uhh... I should probably introduce myself... I suppose. I'm Eden?"

"Eden... It is a beautiful name for *la mia piccola stella*." He brushes his lips along mine, and whispers what I suppose was what he just said, "My little star." The compliment makes me turn bright red. Needing to change the subject, I try to redirect.

"Umm... thank you. So, what's your na-" I'm cut off again, this time by the ringing of his cell phone.

"*Cazzo*! Everyone is trying my patience tonight. Let me help you stand *bella*." The phone continues to ring as he grips my hips and stands me up, his length slipping from my body and I wince at the ache it causes.

His phone stops ringing for only half a minute before starting up again. He growls this time, standing up to tuck himself back into his pants, and hits the answer button. Placing the phone on speaker while he zips up and tucks in his shirt, I almost instantly begin to feel uneasy when I hear a familiar voice on the other line.

"What?" he barks out, angry that he had to answer the phone.

"*Sir. Altera is fuckin' pissed cuz that bitch Eden ain't back home yet. Did you go to the club to find her? I need to find her before the other guards-*"

I can't stop the horror from slicing through my gut. That's Joe! I don't... I don't understand why he'd be calling this man?

"*JOSEPH*!" He looks to me, and his eyes widen when he sees whatever look I have on my face, then looks back at his phone. "I will call you back."

He presses the button to end the call, staring at it a moment, seemingly trying to decide what to do with me.

The moment he looks back at me, I can't stop from taking a step back. Nor can I stop the tears from falling again at the betrayal. He was *mine*! He was *my* peace and *my* person away from all of the crap at my home.

Holding his hands out to the sides like he's showing me he's unarmed, he softens his voice, "Eden... *topolina*."

Shaking my head, I whisper, "Who are you? You know Joe... You know my dad?"

He takes a step toward me. I take a step away, my body beginning to tremble.

God, I feel like an idiot. A really big one apparently, as now I'm feeling the fluid he spilled inside of me run down the inside of my legs. I look down and suck in a gasping breath as I watch it run. His eyes are looking at the same place mine were when I look back up at him.

"Eden, please. Let me explain... *Mi dispiace tanto amore mia.*"

My voice comes out a little strong, but I can't stop the crack in it. "Who *a-are* you!?" I demand.

Clearing his throat, he breaks my heart a little more. "My name is Marcus Costa. I am a business man here in the city, for now at least, until I go back to my home in Italy." I know that name. I've heard my dad and other men in the home say it like it's a curse.

"You know my dad?" I know his answer, he only confirms it with a nod of his head.

"I do, but it-"

"And you know Joe... oh God... did he send you to get me?" This time I back up more than just another step.

"*Merda*," he says under his breath, then runs his fingers through his hair. "It is not what you think. Yes, I know Joseph. He works for me..."

I don't stick around to hear anymore and take off toward the door. Joe sent him to find me. Joe, who thinks it's my fault that his brother died, sent Marcus Costa to come find me. The man who's been in this room for the past month, watching me, has known who I was the entire time. That means Thompson probably works for him too.

I'm not going to stick around to see if he blames me as well.

"EDEN!" I hear him yell out, but I ignore it as I grab the handle to the door to find my escape.

Hands wrap around me, and I scream out as I'm wrenched backwards into his chest. "NOO! Let *go*! I didn't mean for Thompson to be killed; I swear it!"

I'm begging and crying; afraid he's going to do what he most likely came to do. Get revenge for the loss of one of his own.

"*Christo* Eden. That is not… FUCK. Would you please let me explain?"

I fight him, my head dizzy and my eyes blinding me with uncontrollable tears. "Please don't hurt me!" Sobbing out, I continue to beg him, "*please* Mr. Costa, I promise I did'n-"

He flips me around to face him, wrapping his arms around me once more. I can't push him back from me, he only holds me tighter to him.

"Shh shh, *la mia bambina*. I need you to calm and listen to me for a moment."

Heaving out great sobs, I give up. He's so much stronger than me and is refusing to release me. I don't know if I feel worse now that I know he's not who I thought he was, or earlier this evening when I watched Thompson die and Joe threaten me.

My heart keeps breaking. The only thought I have is, '*but he was my person.*'

# Chapter 5

## *Marcus*

Holding onto Eden as she fights and sobs in my arms makes me feel like the lowest piece of shit. I knew she didn't know who I was, and I knew that I was being deceptive. Never have I claimed to be a good man either. I see what I want and I take it, especially if it's being offered in the form of a sweet little mouse who is taking a piece of my heart every moment we spend together.

"*Mia dolce e innocente ragazza.* I know I have hurt you, but please calm and give me a moment to talk." I'm not above begging because those tears are grinding my guilt into my stomach.

Kissing her head while she's stiff in my arms, I wait for an answer from her, but she says nothing. Leaning down, I pick her up so she's eye level with me and still in my arms, unable to escape. "Look at me sweet girl…"

I study her, my eyes running over her face, and watch as a multitude of emotions take turns in her expression before finally settling on misery. I did that, and I can't stop the sigh as my breath flutters over her face.

Leaning my face in, I gently brush the tip of my nose against hers. Glassy eyes meet mine, and I finally have her attention. Speaking to her as softly as I can, I explain.

"I am sorry if you feel tricked. It was not my intention, I swear it to you, *bambolina*." I continue to talk to her in a low voice so if someone were in here, they wouldn't be able to overhear my assurances. Nor would they notice that I've never spoken like this to anyone before. "Yes, I know who you are. I have known since I came in here the first night. *Per favore piccola*. I did not know that this is where we would find ourselves."

She shakes her head like she doesn't want to listen to me. The fighting has calmed down, but my little mouse is still stiff in my arms. "Why does Joe work for you when he also works for my dad? ... Are you g-going to hurt m-me because of what happened to T-Thompson?"

"*CAZZO*! NO!" She's shaking like she's truly afraid of me. Taking a step forward, I push her against the door. "I believe you when you say what happened tonight, and I will take care of Joseph. You have no need to worry about him."

"...Why though? Why any of this? Who are you?" It's a fair question, but there's not an easy answer.

"I told you I am a business man. I watch for failing companies needing a buy out for their properties. I purchase those properties, fix them, and then sell them." I hesitate before continuing, but I need to know. "Do you know what your father does?"

"... He's a landlord," she whispers.

"Yes and no. He threatens and blackmails people in this city and charges them for 'protection'. Because of his interference and dealings with so many people and companies, I have found that he is halting my deals through threats on the other party. Do you understand? He is stalling my business and costing me money, all to force them to stay in business and continue padding his pockets."

I'm not sure if I should have told her as much as I did, but I need her to understand that I'm not the bad guy in this scenario... well, not the *only* bad guy.

She looks away from me and quickly wipes away some tears, sniffling to get herself under control. "I don't know anything about the stuff you said my dad does. He makes me leave when he has people over. I can figure out Thompson and Joe being there at my dad's. Why have you been here with me?"

And here is where I'm going to lose her. *Fottimi.* "I will not lie to you. When I first learned of you, well... I thought to find a way to use you against your father. I..." I trail off. What can I say? I have no excuse.

I watch another tear slip down her cheek, and a wave of sadness and dejection washes over her. "Eden..." I murmur her name.

Her next question digs deep, her feelings hurt enough that she can't look at me. Instead, she's looking over my shoulder when she asks, "So tonight... this was... was because of who my dad is..."

"No, that is not what tonight was. Tonight is-" She interrupts me.

"Would you be here if it weren't for my dad?"

My natural response is to say no, that's not why I'm here, but I think about her question. My mistake is the pause before answering. She shuts down before I'm able to formulate an answer.

Her voice is emotionless. Quiet. Distant. "Would you please set me down, Mr. Costa?" Her body limp like she's given up.

A rush of panic hits my chest and I hike her up further on the wall, pressing myself closer. "No *mia topolina*. You call me Marcus. Do not shut me out. I do not think like I did a month ago. I would not have taken you the way I did tonight if I had." I'm growling at her, angry at myself for fucking this all up.

Her tears keep flowing as she finally looks at me. "You were supposed to be my person... my constant outside of everything at home. You took that away when you took me-"

We are pushed back slightly when someone tries to shove their way into the room. "WHAT?" I bark out at whomever is interrupting us. I set her down so the door doesn't hit her a second time, and she takes advantage to scurry away and distance herself from me.

"Mr. Costa!" Joseph shoves his way into the room and slams the door shut behind him. "Some of Altera's men came here with me. I sent them to the other rooms first to look for the girl so I could get here alone." He looks around the room and I know the moment he lays eyes on Eden. They narrow and the hate he has for her is palpable.

"Get the fuck out of here," I hiss at him, redirecting his attention back onto me. "You and I will speak later. Now go."

"Fine. But what are you gonna do with *her*?" he asks with a sneer in his voice, like speaking about her is disgusting to him. "She fuckin' got Thompson killed!"

"*Vattene dal cazzo*!" I order again, but it's too late. The doors burst open a second time and four of Leo Altera's men pour into the room. The rage is beginning to overtake me, and I want to lash out at everyone in here. I need them to leave so I can fix the mess between me and my sweet girl.

Looking back at her, I see her cowering from all of the testosterone in the room. Christ, she's practically naked in her nightgown, just fucked for the first time and surrounded by six angry men. This is the first time I am unsure about what to do.

"All of you need to stop!" I yell into the room, using my voice that makes grown men cower. Everyone freezes while I walk over to block Eden from their view.

Speaking under my breath so only she can hear, I plead with her, "*Topolina*, please stay here or come with me. I do not want you to leave thinking incorrectly about my intentions with you. I have not explained myself properly. Will you come with me?"

One of her father's men must have moved in behind me because he overhears my question to her. "Not gonna happen, Costa. Mr.

Altera ordered us to bring her home. Miss Altera, we need to go *now*," he snaps at her, and I growl at the tone he's using with her.

"Do not speak to her like that," I hiss. "She does not need to go with you if she does not wish to." I say this loud enough for everyone to hear so she knows she has options.

"Don't matter. Her daddy says we take her home, we take her home. Miss Altera, you come with us or I carry you." I'm stuck because I could force it, but they don't know Joe works for me. He won't be for long, but I still need him at the moment.

I watch as Eden curls her shoulders over to hug herself, and staring at the ground, heads out of the room without a word. "Eden. You and I are not done speaking." She needs to know this isn't over, not until she understands that she is mine.

The blank look she gives me before one of the men pushes her to keep walking guts me. She looks hopeless, like I'm just another man that has disappointed her. Used her. Taken advantage of her naivety.

I swear to myself I'm going to correct my mistakes and make sure she knows that she is mine to own. That she is mine to protect.

*Che lei è il mia cuore.* That she is my heart.

She cannot go on thinking that I've used her body for devious reasons. I'm pissed at myself for allowing her to leave thinking the worst of me. My little girl needs to know that I will always keep her safe and loved.

I fucked up. Now I need to figure out a way to fix it.

# Chapter 6

## *Eden*

My dad has been screaming at me for the past twenty minutes over the fact that I left the house and didn't go find him like I was told. He's threatened to lock me in my room, beat me, told me he doesn't trust me, and accused me of being a 'spoiled little shit' that is going to have to pull her own weight now. I'm to start helping the family business.

I'm to do my duty.

Some of his men are in the room with us, including Joe. He's been fighting back his laughter as I continue to be berated. Not laughter as in ha-ha, but the type where he's enjoying my misery. The phone has been in his hand the entire time as well. Every time my dad turns his back, Joe is texting.

I briefly think about letting dad know that Joe, well… Joseph, according to Mr. Costa, is here spying. Briefly. Then I remember four hours ago when my dad pulled out a gun and shot Thompson for a lesser offense. So… I keep my mouth shut. I refuse to be the reason another person dies.

"Are you fucking listening to me, Eden?" my dad shouts, jerking my attention back to the present.

I answer quietly to not give him any more reason to be angry. "Yes, dad."

"Good. Goddamnit! This whole evening has been a shit show because of you. Did you tell anyone while you were out? Because what happens here in the house *stays* in this fucking house." He comes closer to me, glaring down and hovering as a way to intimidate. It's working. "Did you fucking *betray* me, Eden?"

I to force myself to not look over at Joe when I answer him. "N-No dad. I swear, I didn't." Wincing, I close my eyes when I hear Joe snort from where he's standing along the wall.

Dad turns to him, "You got something to say?" I shudder and watch wide eyed as he pulls his gun back out of his pocket and holds it to Joe's head. "Please, tell me. What are you finding so *fucking* funny about all of this?"

Joe stands up a little straighter, no longer smirking at me and nervously looking at the gun. "No! Nothing Mr. Altera."

Dad cocks the gun and presses it further into his forehead. "You sure? Cuz your brother sure had something to say. Give me a reason. *Please*. I'm really wanting to fucking shoot something tonight."

"Dad..." I call him gently to distract him from Joe. It was a mistake.

He whips around and marches back over to me and pushes the gun into my head, darling at me. He's furious with me. "And *you*," he hisses. "*You* are going to prove to me that you're with me. You understand me girl?"

I'm shaking, eyes focused on the barrel pressing into the area between my eyes. "Y-y-yes d-dad... *please* d-don't..." I beg him. I'm pretty sure I'm beyond terrified that my body can't even generate tears at this point.

"You should be fucking scared, taking off like that. *What the fuck were you THINKING?* And fucking *Marcus* Costa, Eden? How the *fuck* do you know him?" The gun is pressed harder into my skin. I'm frozen. Cold. I see nothing but the solid black barrel and his finger on the trigger.

"I-I don't know him! He... He was just l-listening to m-me play. I d-didn't know who he w-was!" *Please dad, please please believe me!*

Bending his elbow so he can step closer to me and keep the gun to my head, he growls, "Well he certainly fucking knows *YOU*. I got a nice little call from him before you got back, tell me that he wants a trade. You for the east side territory of my city." An evil grin spreads across his face. "Guess what, Eden?"

"W-What?" I croak out.

"He's gonna get you. He thinks he's getting you for a nice *long* weekend, but you'll only be there long enough to get what I need. He's coming tomorrow evening. I suggest you get a good night's sleep *daughter* 'cause we've got a lot to go through tomorrow. Also, pretty sure you're gonna have a busy fuckin' night."

Finally, he pulls the gun away, but doesn't back up. "You're going to be my whore. *That's* how you prove your loyalty to me. Spread those fucking legs and bend over anytime Costa asks you. When he gives you a break, you get me info. Got me, girl?"

Unable to speak, I just nod my head. I'll agree to anything right now.

"Get the fuck out of here, and go to your fucking room. *Fucking listen* to me this time!" Dad finally turns and storms out of the room, his men following. Joe is the last to leave, but he doesn't look at me.

Finding myself alone, I take a shaky step back and my foot slides slightly. Looking down, I realize I've peed. I didn't know I did it, and the sight of the puddle on the floor and my damp legs is what finally makes the tears come.

Looking around, I don't see anything I can use to clean up, so I run to the kitchen, grab a towel, and then hurry back to the family room. God, this is embarrassing… I'm nineteen years old and I'm peeing my pants. Granted, I've never had a gun held to my head before, so I think I'm allowed a little bit of grace.

Cleaning up the floor quickly, I hurry to my bedroom. I don't make eye contact with any of my dad's men that I pass. My eyes stay on the ground until the door snicks shut behind me, and I can relax.

I hurry to the bathroom and lock myself in, relaxing even further now that there are two doors separating myself from the rest of the household. I'm frantic to get clean and wash this damn day off.

Between watching a man get murdered by my own dad, running barefoot through town in chilly temperatures, losing my virginity which I can't even process right now, and then everything with Mr. Costa and dad. I'm just... it's too much.

The tremors in my hands make removing my clothes difficult, but I am able to manage. Looking in the mirror, I realize that I have to process the fact that I had sex tonight. I also need to process the fact that we didn't use a condom, and I'm not on birth control.

I stare unblinking, fixed on the inside of my thighs where they are tinged pink and sticky with the remains of Mr. Costa... Marcus, I suppose. I guess I'm allowed to use his first name if I'm staring at his cum drying on my legs.

Unsure of how long I stand and stare at my reflection, I'm finally pulled out of whatever trance I was in when the steam covers the mirror and I can't see the evidence of recklessness.

He was my person... and he took that away from me.

That thought sinks in and I choke out a distressed, painful sob. He was my *person*, and it was all a trick. A way to play on Leo Altera's 'supposed' weakness. His stupid, naive daughter who, turns out, means absolutely nothing to the man who helped give her life.

Shaking my head, I climb into the shower to wash away the dirt and grime, along with the pee, shame, and embarrassment. I watch as the water gradually turns from a light brown to clear, the evidence at least visibly gone. Physically, I can still feel it when I reach between my thighs to touch the bruised and swollen skin from where he took me. As I gently wash that area, the soap stings where my skin feels raw. Am I still bleeding?

It wasn't like what I thought it would be. Initially, it hurt and made me wonder why women want to do it all. Although the closeness was something I wanted more than anything. I wanted to crawl into him, and I feel my cheeks flush at that thought. What he must have thought of me, behaving like that. Crawling into his lap and clinging to him.

After working my way through a shower, my body trembling so violently that I was barely able to open my bottles to get my shampoo and wash it out, I step to dry off and dress, again, into a nightgown. I noticed that my towel was tinged a little pink when I dabbed it against my lower lips. I am still bleeding, but only slightly. That knowledge makes my stomach twist; I still feel such acute proof of him, when he most likely won't feel anything of me.

Forcing my mind to move away from these thoughts, I crawl into bed with an extra blanket to keep me warm. I'm freezing now, because of the adrenaline crash maybe. I can't stop shaking. Trying to blank my mind, I visualize my fingers playing a slow, tender song on the piano that's meant to soothe me.

I'm startled when I hear my phone vibrate on the table next to my bed, and I reach to see what the noise is from. I rarely get notifications, especially this late. I'm shocked to see a text waiting for me from an unknown number.

***Unknown***: *Mi scuso per l'italiano, è più sicuro. Ho bisogna di sapere se stai bene. Per favore, topolina... Dimmi che non sei ferita... Che non ti ho fatta male.*

Furrowing my eyebrows, I read through the gibberish, confused until two words stand out, *l'italiano* and *topolina*. This is Marcus Costa, texting me in Italian. Why would he write in Italian? Clearly, I don't speak it, and I'm sure he knows that.

Highlighting the entire text, I copy and then paste into a browser to translate. I don't know what to think of what he's said.

***Unknown***: *I apologize for the Italian, it's safer. I need to know if you're ok. Please, little mouse... Tell me you're not hurt... That I didn't hurt you.*

Biting my lip, I consider what to do as I analyze each line of his text. '*I apologize for the Italian, it's safer.*' I'm assuming in case my dad reads my phone, which he's never done. I don't think he's ever cared enough about who I'm talking with.

'*I need to know if you're okay.*' Nope. I'm definitely not okay. I'm not okay with anything that happened tonight.

'*Please, little mouse... Tell me you're not hurt... That I didn't hurt you.*' This makes me hesitate and only serves to confuse me more.

I am hurt, and he did hurt me, but what is he referring to? I suppose it doesn't really matter because the answer would be yes across the board. Physically, yes, he *did* hurt me. I'm sore, bleeding from skin rubbed raw, so tender to the touch that I could barely use a towel to dry off. But am I upset about it? Physically, no. Mentally and emotionally? I sure the hell am.

If he's referring to my feelings though, then the answer is still yes. That is a box I don't want to open and unpack right now. I can't deal with the fact that a man twice my age screwed me because he's angry with my dad. That's just… it's just so incredibly *insulting*. I'm not sure how anyone could have made me feel more unimportant. Un*worthy* of basic human decency.

My dad has always forgotten about me, neglecting my needs as his child. I grew used to it. But this? Someone going out of their way to use me in such a cruel way? This makes me feel inhuman. Like I don't deserve compassion or to be treated like I'm worth something.

The tears begin to trek their way down as that thought devastates me.

**Unknown**: *Bella piccola stella… rispondi per favore*

I don't need to translate his next text; I get the gist. I tell him the truth.

**Me**: *No*

# Chapter 7

## *Marcus*

**Topolina**: *No*

*Fottimi.* I'm not sure why I even asked her those questions. I knew the answer, but I had hoped. It's distressing and heartbreaking to hear her confirm it.

I had called her father within minutes of her leaving with his men. It was a risk, letting him know that I knew Eden, but it was the only thing I could think of to keep her safe for the time being. She'll be heading back home where her father, who just killed someone tonight, and Joseph, whose brother was the one who got killed, are both waiting to get her alone for a few minutes.

At this point, I don't care about the business side of shit and Altera's meddling in my deals. There are plenty of other opportunities. What I do care about is getting her out. So, I offer something he wants for something I want in return. The city for Eden.

I should be hanged for even speaking the words of trading her like a piece of meat, but if Altera knows to what degree I'd go to for his little girl, he'd take advantage of it. For now, I get her for a long weekend to use however I want. He's whoring his daughter out to get me gone.

When I've got her in my home, then we can have the conversation I wanted to finish tonight and figure out what she wants to do down the road. My hope is she'll want to stay with me. She called me her person tonight. What she doesn't know is that she's *my* person as well, I just didn't realize it until my little mouse was taken from me.

> *Joseph*: *Princess is gettin her ass reamed for leavin tonight. I'm stickin around to make sure she don't try an sell me out.*
> *Me*: *What is he saying to her? Is she ok?*
> *Joseph*: *Bitch is fine... unlike my brother... he's sayin a bunch of stuff like she betrayed him and wantin to know what she told people when she left. Called her a whore to, had to bite my tongue at that to not laugh. lol*
> *Me*: *Has he told her about my call to him yet?*
> *Me*: *Joseph*

He's stopped texting me and I frown at my phone. It's driving me crazy to not know what's going on over there.

*Me*: You had better update me the moment you are able because you and I have more to discuss.

*Joseph*: Sorry boss. Fuck me... Altera is a crazy mother fucker. He just held a gun to my head when I laughed about her sayin she didn't betray him. Kinda funny cuz I'm preeeeetty sure I saw her good an fucked tonight. Haha

*Me*: Joseph. Listen to me very carefully. You and I? We are not friends. We are not old pals that gossip like two little old ladies. Do your fucking job. Watch the girl. Do NOT touch the girl. Do you understand?

*Joseph*: ...She's the reason my brother's dead, BOSS. I'm not lettin that go.

CAZZO! I can't pull him out because then I have no eyes in there, especially now that she has her father's full attention. But trusting him to leave Eden be? Gone is my hope that he will stay away. He's out for her blood. Making a quick decision, I decide I'm not going to wait until tomorrow to pick up my *topolina*. It's well after midnight, I simply said I wanted her 'tomorrow', which, technically, is now.

*Me*: You WILL stay away. I am coming to get her now. You have the weekend to get me as much information as you can. Do not fail me. You will not like the consequences.

*Joseph*: U comin NOW?

*Me*: Watch yourself, Joseph.

After calling my driver and telling him where I want to go, I message the head of my security team to grab a group of his guys and follow me to Altera's house. I grip my phone and go out to wait on my driver. My phone alerts me a few times and I see that it's Joseph, but I ignore it until I'm on my way. Picking back up, I read his messages and I see. Fucking. Red.

***Joseph***: *If you comin now, I should probably tell ya that Altera is fuckin raging tonight.*
***Joseph***: *After he held the gun to me, he turned it on her.*
***Joseph***: *She pissed herself lol*
***Joseph***: *You want me to grab her or follow daddy?*
***Joseph***: *Boss?*
***Joseph***: *Imma go with him. He's takin' us all to his office. Message when I can.*

He held a fucking gun to his own daughter's head. This *pezzo di medda* is going to hurt. I just need a plan. I'm glad I didn't wait until the morning to go get her.

The drive takes much longer than I had hoped. Eden lives only about fifteen minutes from the club, but I'm at least another twenty in the opposite direction. Anxiousness is eating at my stomach, every minute feeling like ten.

His security doesn't hold us up for very long at the gate and within moments of arriving, we are pulling up in front of his home. I button my jacket as I walk to the door, not slowing my stride. I know his people are watching. Waiting to open the door for me. Three steps from the door, I smirk as I'm proved correct.

"Mr. Cos-" I interrupt the older man who opened the door to greet us.

"I'm here to speak with Altera. Tell him to bring the girl." He doesn't move and my patience is running thin. I want to see my girl. "*Adesso!*" *Now*, you fuck.

Walking past him, my men and I find our way easily enough to a sitting room where I see a beautiful deep cherry red baby grand piano. I furrow my brows, curious why she would go so far from home to play when she has this.

My question is answered almost the moment it crosses my mind as I watch Altera and a couple of his men, including Joseph, walk out of an attached office. I wouldn't want to stay in here either.

I raise one eyebrow when Altera addresses me with a bold arrogance that he's not entitled to have. "Marcus. I'd say welcome to my home, but considering the hour and the fact that we were supposed to meet tomorrow night, I'm not so sure why I'm getting the pleasure of your company."

Sliding my hands into my pants pockets, I give the impression that I'm relaxed and don't find him a threat. "I am certain that when we spoke, it was this date that I was to acquire the companionship of your daughter, was it not? I am here to retrieve her."

Blustering, his face turns a slight ruddy shade of red. "I don't think so, Costa. We agreed for tomorrow night. She's not ready anyways." He waves at me like he's going to walk away when he adds, "Come back tomorrow, she'll be ready then."

"I do not think so. I get her now or the deal is off. I have more money than you Altera, I can outlast any of the roadblocks you throw my way. Are you willing to risk yours to find out? I want her now and I have already sent for someone to retrieve her."

"Are you fucking kidding me? This is my goddamn house you piece of-" He doesn't get to finish because I'm front of him in a flash, hand around his throat.

"I think you misunderstand me and the threat I pose to you, *Leonard*. Do not test my patience right now, I am not in the mood," I growl at him, trying my best to reign in the hostility I'm feeling. "*Non scopare con me*, Altera. You will not like the outcome."

I squeeze slightly, feeling the rigidness of his Adam's apple bob under my palm, before releasing. Stepping back, I slide my hands back into my pockets. His eyes are shooting daggers at me, but he says nothing more. "Now, bring the girl in here."

"Sir." I hear a voice from the other side of the room and we all look to see another one of Altera's men standing just inside the room. His hand is wrapped tightly around Eden's upper arm, and it takes a lot of will power to stop myself from walking over and snapping each one of his fingers that dig into her skin.

She's looking at the ground, not meeting anyone's eyes. There's a new nightgown draped over her, and she's wrapped in a robe that looks hastily tied. Barefoot, hair still damp from a shower, and pale.

*Cazzo.* She looks terrified. Of me? Or is it her father? Probably both right now, considering how things were left between us and then what happened with her father when she returned home.

"*Topolina*," I gentle my voice slightly, but not so much that people in here will guess that this little mouse is going to be a weakness for me.

The guilt at how I took her, the pain I caused her, aches inside of me as she flinches at the sound of my voice. She doesn't look at me, nor does she look at her father. Her gaze stays down, frozen, emotionless. Detached.

I'm in part to blame for her current state. *Mi dispiace tanto amore mia...* so sorry. I can't speak out loud, but I'll make her believe me soon enough. This is going to get worse before it gets better.

"Eden. Mr. Costa is here to take you with him. Do you want to go with him now, or wait until later when we had *originally* planned?" Rolling my eyes internally, I want to scoff at his clearly leading question.

"I don-"

"*Topolina*, go get your jacket and put some shoes on. You do not need to bring anything else along. I do not want to waste time here any longer." I don't let her say no. Getting out of here is priority.

"Now wait a fucking second. If she doesn't want to go right now, she doesn't have to!" her father snaps at me.

"Do you or do you not want the East side of the city?" I glare at him.

"Of course-"

"Did we or did we not agree that she will be mine for the next few days, to start on this date?" I continue asking.

He growls at me, "Yes, but we-"

"I will hear no more. A deal was struck, I have come to collect. Eden, shoes and jacket. Now *per favore*."

I want to yell to her that I'm not trying to scare her, but this is necessary. Every time I speak to her father, her shoulders curl in on her a little more. Altera's man pulls her out of the room, barely allowing her to keep up, taking her to get her things.

Looking at Altera, I glare at him. "We will not be interrupted. If we are, the agreement is over. I will have her home by midnight, Sunday evening."

Sneering at me, he looks me up and down before trying to throw an insult. "Sure, Costa. Enjoy her... That's what you're paying for right?"

I move to take a step forward, but I hear a muttered '*Sir*' behind me, pulling me back from slamming my body into this *pezzo di medda*. I'm unsure which one of my men stepped in, but I will find out and thank him later.

I ignore Altera's snort of laughter and wait for her to return. It only takes another minute or two, but she's pulled back into the room. This time though, they don't stop until she's in front of me, eyes still down and body stiff.

"Release her," I order the man next to her, and I glare at the white bloodless spots on her arm where he was squeezing.

Wrapping my arm around her waist, I pull her into me and whisper into her ear while starting at her father, "*Topolina*, do not be afraid of me. We will talk once we are gone."

I don't know how she's responding because I can't see her eyes, but I do give her a gentle kiss under her ear. Then, standing up straight, I face her father hopefully for the last time.

"No contact." I turn Eden around and guide her out the door, away from that fuck of a father, and into my vehicle.

"Babygirl…" I begin, once we are seated.

Eden says the only thing that I think could make me feel heartbroken.

"Please Mr. Costa… please don't hurt me."

# Chapter 8

## *Eden*

My plea to Marcus Costa is accompanied by a drumming pulse in my ears as my heart races. If dad is afraid of this man, I should be too, right?

I can't stop the flinch my body unintentionally decides is necessary when he moves quickly onto my seat. What I didn't expect was for him to pick me up and place me on his lap, arranging me back to how we were in the club.

My body shudders when he wraps both of his strong, solid arms around me and pins me to his chest. There is no escaping, even if I wanted to. The thought *I don't want to escape* makes itself known before flitting away. I shouldn't want to. I don't want to be one of those girls that is desperate for the men that don't love them back the same way.

"My treasure… *tesoro mia, per favore*, no. Please. Never do I want you afraid of me. I will not and never would hurt you." The despair and misery in his voice takes me aback.

"But I thought… My dad said you both made a deal for me. I was a business trade." I think it's that fact that makes me feel the worst. It's barbaric.

"*Si*. We did, but it was the only way I could remove you from the house quickly and safely. I know what your father is capable of, and I also know what happened tonight after you got home." He can't keep the fury out of his voice when he speaks about that. How did he know…?

"…Joe?" It's a silly question, of course it was him. I watched him on his phone the entire time dad was screaming at me.

He gently grips my face to make me look at him, his eyes bouncing around my face like he's making sure I'm okay. "Tell me you are okay, *il mia cuore.*" *Il mia curoe*? I want to ask but he continues, "Joseph said that your father scared you enough that you…" he trails off but isn't able to hide the quick glance to my lap.

My face flares a deep shade of red in embarrassment. I can't believe Joe told him that. I'm mortified. Clearing my throat, I can't keep my eyes on his when I answer, "I'm fine."

"You are *NOT* fine! You do not need to be ashamed. You do not need to lie to me because you are embarrassed. I imagine it was terrifying, and I am sorry I was not there to stop him." He's earnest when he says this, but I still don't know what his intentions are with me.

"It really doesn't matter. What are-"

His lips silence me when he crushes his against mine. It's a desperate kiss, not as heated as at the club, but like he's trying to convince me of something. I don't kiss him back right away, but a quick nip to my bottom lip has me gasping, allowing him entry into my mouth.

Just as I begin to reciprocate, he pulls back just enough to break contact with my mouth. Under his breath, I hear him again say something in Italian, "*Io ti brama...*"

Barely shaking my head, I ask, "What does that mean?"

He looks at my lips with a hint of a smile and leans in to kiss me again, more gently this time, for just a moment. "I crave you... that is what it means," he says when he pulls back again.

"Mr. Co-"

"Marcus. Please *bella*, only ever call me Marcus." There's that desperate look again.

I sigh. "Alright." Clearing my throat, I ask him what I've been trying to since we got into this car, "Marcus..." He grins at my use of his name. "I don't know what you're expecting of me. Before, when... *that* happened, I didn't know you had this connection with my dad. I didn't know you knew me, and obviously you have these plans. I can't stay in the dark here, not knowing what to expect."

Blowing out a breath, he leans further away from me so we can speak, but keeps me on his lap. I'm not sure when I moved, but I'm straddling him now with my knees planted on the seat on either side of his waist. His knees are spread, forcing mine to stay wide. My cheeks burn a little remembering what happened when we were in this position earlier.

"*Topolina*, I have *no* expectations of you. You are free to make your own choices when we get to my home. My only request is that you stay there for the time being while we figure out what to do about your father." He's clearly angry with my dad, but he's keeping himself in check for me.

"So, no expectations. What is it that you want then?"

"You." I blink at him. I think he short circuited my brain because I have no idea what that means.

"Umm... but I'm-"

"*Il mia topolina*. You are my little mouse, Eden. *MINE*, if you will let me keep you." He tilts his head to the side like he's waiting for an answer.

I blink again.

"It is alright, *il mia cuore*. As I said, no expectations. But that does not mean I am going to back off. The first thing that needs to happen is for me to explain what happened earlier this night. Let me say what I need to before you speak, *sì?*" I'm okay moving on because I can't wrap my head around that. It's almost ridiculous to believe that he'd want someone like me. I'm half his age, inexperienced, and have never been out on my own.

"Okay," I croak out. I doubt I could say anything else right now anyways.

"I have been in the city for over a year. I told you already what I do for a living. Your father has been a thorn in my side since the beginning. The moment I have the opportunity to move on a property, he has threatened the seller to back out of our deal. I thought to send a couple of my people into his home, *your* home-"

"His home... sorry for interrupting." It's important that he knows that it isn't my home. Dad has full control there and I'm restricted quite a bit on my freedom there.

"His home. I had Joseph and Thompson work their way onto his team almost immediately after I realized your father was going to be a problem. Their job was to seek out anything I could use to stop him from continuing to interfere. I *am* sorry, *topolina*. It is true that I had initially thought to try and use you to combat him, which is why I first started coming to your room at the club. I would like to know how that began, by the way."

Nodding, I let him finish.

"Very quickly, my interest in using you against him faded. Instead, I became enthralled by you. I did not know what to make of you and I wanted to know you. I just was not sure of the best way to make it happen."

"What do you mean you didn't know what to make of me?" It seems a bit cryptic and vague.

Sighing, he scratches his cheek. Then grabs my hand and holds it against his chest while he explains, "What I meant was that, obviously my men had a misunderstood perception of who you are.

Initially, the belief was that you were a spoiled princess who toys with men and looks down upon those below you."

I jerk my head back and try to pull my hand away. He doesn't allow me to retreat. "*Rimani qui*, Eden. Stay. Please, let me finish."

Biting my lip, I nod a bit more hesitantly this time.

"I do not believe that. I am just saying, that is what they told me. Earlier this evening, when I showed up in your room, and you were in the state you were in, I knew they were wrong about you. I also knew that I could not trust what Joseph said about what happened with Thompson."

My throat tightens and my eyes water at the reminder of my part to play in Thompson's death. Whispering, I must ask him, "Joe?"

"Joseph will be dealt with. When you crawled into my lap tonight, I knew that you felt the same as I did. My need. *La mia brama*. My longing for you. *Princepessa, Il mia piccola amore, that is what happened between you and I. I swear to you, I did not try to deceive you."

He looks back and forth across my face trying to read my expression, not getting an answer.

"Do you believe me, *topolina*?" His voice is raspy with a hint of emotion behind it.

"...Yes," I answer and nod at the same time. He pulls me back into his arms, wrapping them around me tightly. I feel a kiss on the top of my head as I lay my ear on his chest, listening to the steady drum of his heart.

We both absorb the silence and reconnection for a small amount of time before I decide to continue our talk. "So, what now? I'm only here for the weekend-"

He growls at that. *"Non ti rimanderò indietro."*

My lip quirks up. I think he doesn't realize when he's speaking Italian or English some of these times when he gets upset. "English, per favore?"

A quick kiss to my lips is his apology. "I said, I will not send you back. I want you to stay with me. Come home with me, to my *actual* home."

"Where's that?" I don't know where he lives here, and we've been driving for a good thirty minutes at this point. "On the south side? That seems like where we are heading," I muse, glancing out the window.

He chuckles. "No. This home here is only temporary. I find I do not want to stay here much longer. I only want to stay long enough to deal with your father, then I would like to take you back to my home in Italy. It is in Matera, near the end of the boot." Smiling, he glances out the window. "We are just about to my condo."

A little insecure with the knowledge that he wants me to actually go to Italy, I awkwardly ask how serious he is about us, "So, umm... if you want me to go with you to Italy... does that mean that we, you and I, are... umm..." I blush and look down. God, this is embarrassing, but I've never had a boyfriend and I don't even know if that's what he would be to me. "...My, umm... boyfriend?"

"No." My stomach sinks. I feel like an idiot misreading what he wants. "No *bella*, I am not a boy." I look up at him when he grips my hair at the back of my head in his fist and prevents me from looking away. "You can be my little girl if you would like, but what I would like between us is something bigger than that. I am not your boyfriend. I am simply yours."

His fist grips harder when he says that. "Do you understand me, *piccola mia*?"

My breathing is getting heavy the longer he holds onto my hair and his eyes focused on mine. "Y-Yes… I understand you." Licking my lips, I look at his. With him holding me this way, it's like a pavlovian response… my hips want to shift over him.

Sliding his hand that's free down my waist and then lower, he grips my hip and jerks me closer to him. This time, I feel and recognize the hardness for what it is. Marcus isn't moving me, but he is holding me firmly against him with persistent pressure.

He sits up straighter so that we are face to face. The tug on my hair forces me to look up at the ceiling of the car. The sharp bite to the side of my throat, followed by the fire trail up to my cheek from his tongue, has a shudder rocketing through my entire body, forcing me to tense up.

The second bite to my chin has a soft moan escaping from my mouth as it parts, trying to keep up with the speed of my breath. This time when he chuckles, it sounds sinister. He allows me to face him again so he can take my mouth. Unlike before when there was a sense of desperation in his kiss, this one is full of a crazed hunger that has my head spinning.

"Eden..." he groans into my mouth. Christ, he tastes so good. The flavor a mix of sin and lust and an almost violent need for control. "Eden... we have stopped. *Cazzo*, I fucking need you again. Will you let me have you?"

Kiss.

"Let me own you?" he growls.

Kiss, then a sharper nip to my lip.

"*Ho bisogno di assaporarti, banchettare con te...* I need to eat all of you." Groaning, he pulls his mouth from me and rests his forehead against mine.

I close my eyes, enjoying the brush of his breath on my face. Licking my lips, I enjoy the taste of him. "Yes, Marcus," I breathe out.

Keeping me on his lap, he knocks on the window which alerts the driver to open the door. I go to move from his lap but he stops me. "*Topolina...* I cannot put you down." Then, pressing his lips to my ear, he lets me know why in a low voice only I can hear, "my cock is trying to fight its way to you, do not deprive it of your heat. Wrap your legs around me."

He shifts his way out of the car and stands us both up. I tighten my legs around his waist and hips, my arms tighten around his shoulders when I dip my face into his neck.

"Good girl, little mouse..."

S. E. Green

I tremble for him under his praise.

# Chapter 9

## *Marcus*

It only takes me a minute or two to get us up to my floor and into the condo. I briefly glance at the clock and notice it's after 3 am. *Merda*, I need to get her into my bed so she can sleep off everything that's happened in the past six hours or so.

That thought vanishes the moment my little mouse squeezes me tighter, pressing her nose into my neck to subtly scent me. Digging my fingers into where I'm holding her to me, I can barely keep the hunger at bay for the last few feet into my bedroom.

Crossing the threshold, I use my foot to kick the door shut and slam her body to the closed door. The puff of air and then hitch of breath I feel where the contact forces it from her lungs is what releases the shackles of my restraint.

I brace her up by pinning her with my lower body, and grind my cock into her center. Precum is practically dripping from the head of my cock, aching to tunnel its way into her tight pussy.

Taking her mouth again, our kiss is heated while I hike her legs further up my sides, opening her for me. She works the hem of her nightgown up to her waist while I reach between us to free my heavy shaft from the constraints of my pants.

"*Sei mio*, Eden. *MINE!*" I growl out the last as I reach around her ass, grip the side of her panties and yank them to the side. Exposing her pussy to the air, the head of my cock finds its home almost immediately.

She's soaking. It's the only thing that would have stopped me.

Slamming my thickness all the way inside her, I roar into the room at the same time she screams to the ceiling. "*Così stretto, bella!*" She's so fucking tight!

Pulling my hips back, I thrust up just as hard as the first time, reveling in her whimper. "Is this too much *topolina*?" I ask through gritted teeth. I'd ease up if she needed me to, but my need to fuck her hard makes me feel feral.

She presses the pillow of her bottom lip between mine, moaning and shaking her head yes. *Grazie dio...* I let my lust takeover and pound into her, bouncing every time her pussy meets the root of my cock. The sound of her cries egging me on to speed up, fuck her harder.

I slip my arm under one of her knees and pull it up to open her wider, letting me in deeper. It's like I can't get close enough as I grind her to an orgasm. Hanging on to me, her hands are digging into my back with nails piercing my skin.

The fluttering of her pussy and the pain of her fingers has my own orgasm bubbling up. "Love..." I groan, my lips working over her face like I can't consume enough of her. "I am going to fill you, little girl..."

"Oh God... Marcus. I'm... I'm going to c-cum," she cries out. I already have one of her legs pinned up and out to the side, so I do the same with her other leg, angling her for constant pressure on her clit. I drive my cock in and out of her, aiming for her g-spot.

I speed up, quickening to an almost violent pace. Her groans and shrieks of pleasure wash over me until, finally, she explodes off the edge, pulsating over and over as I steadily fuck her.

Finally, I can feel myself hurtling off the cliff with her, my balls erupting and filling her with my cum.

Two, three more thrusts and I hold myself inside of her, the last few jets emptying out all that I have. Groaning, I lean my head against her shoulder, my hips involuntarily twitching every time an aftershock of her own orgasm squeezes me.

Unmoving, we are both frozen except for the panting of our breaths, chests heaving from the exertion and intensity of coming together. *"Sei il mia tutta*, Eden. *Everything..."* I tell her, leaning my head back to look at her. I smile to myself when I see that she's still got her eyes squeezed tightly, apparently still drifting off wherever I sent her.

"Sweet girl, I am going to lower your legs." Slowly, I set her down.

She laughs under her breath when her legs tremble like a new born fawn, gripping my biceps to keep her standing. "My legs are shaking like crazy."

I kiss her gently and then pull her into me and then let out a sigh of contentment. "Let me clean you up and then we can both lay down and get some very much needed sleep. *Sì?*"

"Alright." She blushes when we both notice the slickness covering the inside of her thighs. Mumbling, she adds, "…I suppose I could use another shower."

Leading her to my bathroom, we both quickly wash our bodies with minimal touching. I do let my fingers graze over her body a few times, particularly when she washes her chest, and her nipples stand at attention. I have yet to really explore those and I plan to devote a lot of time there in the near future.

Once I have her settled under my sheets wearing one of my t-shirts, we relax into the bed and lay facing each other. My lips tilt up as she runs the pad of her finger over my lips, staring at them. I nip her finger and she jolts but keeps touching.

"I know you are tired, Marcus, but I want to tell you something because I think it may become a problem." She seems hesitant but isn't fully shying away from whatever she needs to tell me.

I reassure her. "You do not need to worry about telling me anything."

"Well, after you called my dad and made the deal-"

"Sorry about that. You do believe me that I do not view you as simply property to be traded, correct?" It's important to make that point so she has no doubt.

An easy smile for me graces her lips. "Yeah, I do. I'm sorry I didn't give you a chance to explain earlier, after we…" she gestures between the two of us. "…well, after that. With Joe bursting into the room, my fear took over and there was just a lot going through my head right then."

Leaning forward, I kiss the tip of her nose and then forehead. "Do not apologize, *topolina*. I should have told you who I was before we made it to that point."

Nodding, she moves on, "So, after you both made the deal and his guys had brought me back home, he informed me of what was going to happen. He said that he promised me to you for the weekend, but that I'm only staying long enough to get information. He wants me to find out anything I can about your upcoming plans. Like what you plan to do next." She bites her lip, done speaking it would seem, and waiting for my response.

"I had expected that, little mouse. Your father would never send you here without strings attached. The question we need to answer is, what do we from here?" It's awfully adorable that she was worried about this.

"I'm not really sure. He's not going to accept that I didn't get anything." Her hands shake slightly as she thinks about his anger. I grip them and pull her closer to me so our bodies line up all the way and tuck part of my leg between hers.

She relaxes into me and breathes in my scent again. I won't tell her I notice; I don't want her to stop. "What would you like the final outcome to be? If you had a choice on how everything turned out, what would you want?"

"I don't want to go home." My little mouse shouldn't be afraid of her home. I will never put her into a position to fear coming home to me. *NEVER*.

"What else?" I encourage her to keep thinking about it.

"I, umm... I like the idea of staying with you." She blushes. Fuck if that doesn't make me crave her more. "And I don't want my dad to be a part of my life anymore. He's never seen me as more than an inconvenience. Something sometimes seen but never heard."

My brow softens at the knowledge that *il mia cuore* has spent her life feeling like a burden. Another vow I'll make to her. "Not with me, Eden. Never with me." I fall just a little more for her when her breath hitches at my promise.

"He shouldn't be allowed to kill someone and just walk away like he didn't do anything wrong," she whispers.

Anger courses through me. I didn't particularly care for Thompson, but he certainly didn't deserve to die the way he did. "I very much agree with you there. Aside from Joseph, I don't see any of his men turning on him if we were to report him."

Her eyes light up. "We have cameras!"

"Security in that part of the house? Are you sure?" My pulse picks up as an idea forms in my head.

Vigorously nodding, she says, "Yes, I'm positive. He had them installed a few years ago when he thought someone was stealing from him, or stealing information maybe? He never really told me, just things I overheard. I have also heard him say that he needed 'get rid of the tapes' before as well. Not often, but he's said it. He will probably have his IT guy do it as soon as he thinks of it."

"*Merda.* I'm going to see if my security team can get in remotely and gain access to the security footage. If we can get him on tape for killing Thompson, we could turn it over to the police and let them deal with him. Are you against any of that?" Eden doesn't make me worry about her answer for even a second.

"*YES*!" she blurts out. "I don't want him to be hurt, but this is okay. It's the right thing to do."

"Then we have a plan for now. You rest here while I go speak with my security team. You are exhausted." I slide out of the bed and lean over to kiss her head. Grabbing new clothes from my drawers, I toss them on and notice that she's watching me. I can't help but take a little longer sliding my shirt on and finally chuckle when I think I hear her actually gulp. "Truly, I wish I could stay here and enjoy your eyes on me a little longer."

I laugh outright when she covers her head in embarrassment. Striding over, I pull back the blanket and plant my hands on either side of her head to look down at her. Even in the darkened room, I can see the fire crawling up her neck and across her chest. "Do not be embarrassed, little mouse. I promise, I want to stare at your body just as much. It makes me feel good to know that you find me attractive."

"I just... I didn't even realize I was staring until you started laughing. I zoned out." She gives me a sheepish smile.

Sliding my hands under her shoulders, I drop further onto my forearms, bringing me a hairsbreadth from her mouth. "I enjoy it... do not feel you need to ever stop." I kiss her hard, working us back up and then pull back quickly, both of us heaving. "I will be back shortly."

"That's good because I'm sure you're just as tired as I am," she says softly with a yawn, already sinking back into the bed.

"Sleep well *il mia topolina*." I kiss her again and then go to call my guys. I want to hurry back and enjoy having her in my bed for the first night.

Once I set my team to task and get back into my room, I see that Eden is fast asleep. I quickly strip and slip into bed next to her. Immediately she rolls toward me and nuzzles into my neck, letting out a soft, relaxed sigh.

I wrap her in my arms, enjoying the press of her breasts against my chest and fall asleep to the knowledge that this contentment, this *girl*, is my future.

# Chapter 10

## *Eden*

"*CAZZO!*" I flinch when Marcus yells, anger lacing his voice. He sees me when I do and sighs. "Sweet girl, I apologize. It is just frustration."

"It's okay, just startled me. So, what does this mean?" I ask, not following along with what the issue is. We were eating breakfast when Jeffrey, the head of Marcus's security, arrived to tell us that he couldn't get into my dad's security system.

Jeffrey gives me a patient smile, which calms my nerves. Normally, when I ask for information, I'm ignored or I'm answered, but they're irritated about it. "What it means, Miss Altera-"

"Call her Eden," Marcus says sharply.

Jeffrey nods his head. "Eden. It means that right now, the feed from your father's system is not connected to the network. If it were, we'd be able to access all the files he has stored. It's most likely there, we just have no way to get to it."

"Ahh… so what do we do?" I look at both of them, Jeffrey still patient even in the face of Marcus's anger, and Marcus grinding his teeth and glaring at him.

"No," Marcus hisses.

"Mr. Costa, if you want the feed, someone has to connect the security system to the network. She's the only one that can get close to that room without rousing suspicion. I'd suggest Joseph, but with what happened with his brother, I don't trust his stability." Everything he's saying sounds reasonable, but by the look on Marcus's face, he disagrees.

"*Fottimi…*" he growls under his breath. "There is nothing else we can do?" he asks Jeffrey before looking to me. "Sending you back worries me. I do not trust your father."

"He's not a nice person, but he's not going to do anything. He's never hurt me before; he simply ignores me. I don't mind doing it." Nodding my head to Jeffrey, I add, "if you'll tell me what to do."

"*He held a gun to your head!*" Marcus yells at me, causing me to flinch again. The instant he sees it, his face falls and he pulls me onto his lap. "*Bella*, again, I am sorry for yelling. I promise I am not mad at you. I would *never* hurt you. The thought of you being hurt scares me."

"I can do this, Marcus. I promise… If Jeffrey can tell me what I need to look for and what to do, I can just go there and wait for him to go to another part of the house or leave. None of his people should be in the house when he's gone except for two or three. They know his office is off limits, so they won't go in."

"Will you be able to get in, Eden?" Jeffrey asks.

"I know where he keeps the spare key. I've seen him use it a few times." I assure them both.

Marcus is silent as both Jeffrey and I wait for him to either agree or come up with another issue.

Finally, his shoulders ease a bit. He grabs my face and tips my head down so he can kiss my forehead. "Fine... *FUCK*, I do not like it but I understand that there are no other options. Jeffrey, you make sure you tell her everything you can with as much detail. I do not want her in there only to be caught while trying to figure things out."

"I will. Honestly, it'll be pretty basic." He looks back at me, "Eden, let's go to Mr. Costa's security room and I'll show you what type of equipment you'll be looking for and what you need to do. I'll also send you with a cord in case there isn't one there."

"*Every* detail you can, Jeffrey," he grits out, still holding me with his lips brushing against my skin. Drawing my attention back to him, his eyes soften, "Are you *sure* you will be okay doing this? I need you to be incredibly careful and do this as quickly as you can so that you can leave immediately afterwards."

A light smile to him for reassurance, I nod my head, "I promise. I won't risk myself. If I can't do it, I'll just get some things and then leave again."

Grunting, he doesn't say anything else, just jerks his head to the door to indicate that Jeffrey and I should go so I can learn what to do.

It only takes an hour or so for Jeffrey to feel completely comfortable that I know what to do. It's really not that hard, it turns out. Simply connect the storage drive to the router. He said that he, Marcus, and another couple of the security team will be near, but out of sight, watching to see if I'm successful or not.

We spend the remainder of the morning together, relaxing and talking about superficial things like favorite books, movies, songs, etc. The more I learn about him, the more I realize that even though we have a big age difference, we have a lot of things in common. I love that he talks to me like I'm his equal, and not like he's just indulging a silly little girl.

"*Il mia topolina*, this is the list I want you to give to your father. There is just enough truth to it that he will not question it, but also does not give him anything that could hurt me or my business if things do not go as planned." Marcus gives me a list of different names and companies, written in his bold, blocked penmanship. It suits him.

Looking around for more paper, I see a scrap of paper and grab a pen from his desk. "I should write this down myself, like I saw it and copied from something you had. I'm sure you don't just leave lists like this lying around, right?"

He chuckles, then leans forward to wrap an arm around my waist. "You are correct. This is a good idea. Are you ready to go there, *topolina*? You can still change your mind." I can hear the worry in his voice, but truly, I'm not scared to do this.

"Marcus…" Turning in his arms, I tuck myself in to look up at him. "I'll only be there for a short period of time. I'm going to do this, then sneak right back out of that house and head out on foot where I know none of his men ever are. I doubt I'll even be there for the night."

"Will you do me a favor?" His eyes bounce between mine and I can see the please buried within them.

"If I can, I will," I promise him.

"Will you keep your phone on you? I would like to connect a call before you head in. Just slip it in your pocket. This way, if something happens, I will know to come immediately."

That actually makes me feel much more at ease with all of this, and the tension I didn't know I was holding, eases from my shoulders. Nodding, I give him a full smile of teeth and squinty eyes. "Absolutely. I love that idea."

Hi eyes brighten at my smile and he can't keep his hidden. "Perfect, *il mia piccola amore*."

Curious, I tilt my head and ask, "What does that mean? Il mia piccola amore." I'm starting to pick up the meanings of a few words, but that's because of common sense or he's told me already. He said this before, but I haven't figured out this particular phrase yet.

Pulling me into him further, he kisses my cheek, temple, and mouth before saying, "it means 'my little love.' Does that bother you?"

Blushing, I hike my shoulders up to my ears like I want to hide it from him. "N-no… it doesn't bother me."

"Good. We should go now. I assume afternoons are pretty quiet over there and probably the best time for him to be out of the house."

Grabbing my nightgown that I arrived in from his bedroom, I throw it in a bag along with a toothbrush and hairbrush. We want it to look like I'm coming back, like we are done and he's just sent me on my way.

Marcus and I stay mostly silent except for a few times where he asks me to repeat the plan to assure him that I'm not forgetting anything. Gripping his hand, I hold it tucked between my thighs like I'm not going to allow him to let go. He gives me a few comforting squeezes, clearly sensing my nerves.

We pull up to the front of my house and Marcus kisses me quick and hard before releasing me and slipping to the other seat in the back. We thought it would be better if he wasn't seen. It should look like I basically just got a ride home.

"Slide your phone into your pocket, topolina. I want to make sure I can hear you when you are speaking before you get out." He wags his phone at me and then holds it up to his ear. I slide it into the pocket of the sweatpants I borrowed from him. It won't be obvious even if my dad does look for it.

"Thank you for thinking of this. The phone in the pocket thing. I don't think there's going to be any problem, but it really does ease some of my nervousness. I've never done anything sneaky before… that's the part I'm nervous about. Well, that and I don't want to let you or Jeffrey down." I wind my hands together to ease the tension. I want to go to him, but know I have to wait until I get this done.

Pulling his phone down, he stares at me a moment before the door is opened to allow me to step out. "*Il mia piccola amore*, be careful. I will not be far until this is done." I give him a quick nod, unable to say anything because I see my dad at the door, waiting for me. "*Ti amo*," I hear whispered just as the door shuts.

My heart kicks up and I want nothing more than to turn around and dive back into the car with Marcus. I know what that means… did he really mean to say that? Was I supposed to hear him? Even though I don't allow myself to go back to him, I do turn my head and watch him drive away. I can feel my eyes watering at the rush of emotions that hit me all at once. Happiness, importance, panic, nervousness, anxiety… the list could go on, but my thoughts are interrupted when I hear my father.

"Are you fucking kidding me right now? The fuck are you doing back here already?" He stomps down the steps and speeds toward me. I can't stop myself from taking a few steps back, the natural instinct to flee from the threat.

"Dad, I-" I try to explain. He doesn't let me.

"What the fuck is so wrong with your pussy that you couldn't even make it 24 hours before he's ready to get rid of you?" Leaning into me, I can feel spittle hit my face when he sneers at me, "You better have not come home empty fucking handed, Eden."

"I-I didn't! Dad, I got you names… please," I whisper, those watery eyes from Marcus' whispered *I love you* are turned into tears f fear. He's been mad at me before, but nothing like this. Ever since he killed Thompson in front of me, he's been so much more hateful. Reaching into the bag I'm holding at my side, I dig for the list we made, and I bump the phone in my pocket and I relax a bit knowing that Marcus is right there listening.

It's like my did does a complete one-eighty when he realizes I'm holding a slip of paper out to him and his eyes widen in glee. Whipping the paper from my hand, I pull my arm back to my body as he opens it up to read it over. His glee turns to annoyance and then to disgust and loathing. "…This mother fuc-… *Brett*! Get the fuck over here!" he screams out over his shoulder. Then he turns from me and races back into the house. I'm completely forgotten.

I can hear him yelling at his guys, ordering them to get different people on the phone. Making it into the house, no one notices as I slip into the kitchen so I can hear what's happening. After about fifteen minutes of chaos, dad finally yells into the phone, "*I'm going to be right fucking there you piece of shit. Fucking turning your back on me? Let's see how well THAT works out for you*!"

There's a crash as something is thrown against a wall, followed by dad giving an order that couldn't have come at a better time, "Get everybody the fuck down to Pierce's place! Tell them to wait until we get there. Fucking *EVERYBODY*!"

Holy crap. Who the hell did Marcus put on that list?

It only takes ten minutes before dad's guys are all clearing the house, leaving me alone in the silence. I don't move for a few minutes, listening to see if anyone is going to come back in, then I pull my phone out and whisper into it, "Marcus?"

"Yes, *Bella*? I am still here with you." I shiver as his voice rumbles into my ear, like he's whispering. Well, I suppose he sort of is, but I can't get distracted.

"Umm... did you know that was going to happen?" Confusion laces my question. I've never seen dad freak like that before.

He chuckles darkly, "I had hoped he would react like that. Andrew Pierce is one of his biggest pay days. To lose him would put a serious dent in your father's income. Plus, it is not a short drive to the location. You have about an hour and then I want you to come back out. Let me know when you are finished."

Breathing a little easier, I feel good about the time I have. "Will do. I'm going to go do it now."

Jogging into the family room where dad's office is connected to, I tilt one of the paintings to the left, pull the plain silver key from the tiny hook it's on, and then put the frame back in its place.

It doesn't take me long to sneak in and find the few pieces of equipment Jeffrey had shown me. I only had to reassure myself one time with a question I sent through Marcus to him, and then it was done. Not even ten minutes, it's done and they are already doing their snooping.

Locking the door from the inside, I pull his office shut, replace the key, and then run up to my bedroom to grab a few items that I don't want to leave behind. There isn't much. Dad never really gave me anything. Just little items from moments in my life I've collected along the way.

"Marcus?" I ask when I'm ready to leave.

"Eden, please tell me you are leaving now." He sounds so worried that I feel a sense of belonging that I have never felt before. Someone cares. He *is* my person. I wasn't wrong about that and I couldn't be more grateful.

"Yes," I whisper. "I'm going to head out the side door and into the woods. It's only a small walk but comes out on to a country road about half a mile away. No one will see you pick me up there."

"Hurry *topolina*," he orders.

With clothes changed and a backpack slung over my shoulder, I sneak out the side door to head into the woods. I'm not even ten steps into the leaf covered forest floor when I hear a twig snap and a voice filled with so much vitriol, my heart stops.

"Lucky me... I'm *so* fuckin' glad I finally got you alone you fuckin' whore."

Joe.

Shit.

# Chapter 11

## *Marcus*

*I'm going to fucking kill him.*

"Drive. Faster," I hiss at one of my employees at the wheel. Jeffrey is in the front seat next to him, holding onto his computer while trying to get the footage we need as the driver takes a corner a little too sharply.

"They were heading the same way she had originally planned to before he turned off her phone, Mr. Costa. I think our best bet is to go to the spot we were going to pick her up anyways and head into the woods that way. We've got another team coming from the other direction. He can't get far with her."

Jeffrey is trying to be reassuring but that's not what I'm concerned about. "I am positive that Joseph is not intending to take her anywhere. He blames her for Thompson…" I trail off, getting ready to open my door and head toward her the moment the car comes to a stop.

"Fuck," he mumbles, then I hear him speaking to our guys on the phone, updating them to let them know that Joseph is unhinged.

*Cazzo*, I should have gotten rid of him right after Thompson died, and I feel like I'm failing my little mouse.

Finally, the car comes to a quick stop and the three of us pour out of the car and take off into the woods, spreading out to cover more ground. I'm running as fast as I can, ignoring the little whips of thin branches snapping across my arms and face.

I hear a distant, but clearly feminine cry and all three of us whip our heads to the right and immediately change directions.

"Get your guns out, fucking shoot him. No matter the excuses," I snarl. They both murmur their acknowledgments

I can hear them now, my little love is tripping through the brush, crying and Joseph is mocking her. "Awe, fuckin' cunt scared? You should be," he yells. He's so focused on her that he doesn't hear us until we're right on top of him. "I don't give a fuck who you're spreadin' your legs for. They can all kiss my fuckin' ass…"

"P-Please Joe," she begs. "I d-didn't want him to…" She hiccups out a sob, "…to get him h-hurt. M-My da-"

"Your fuckin' *dad*? Really? Had you just opened your God damn mouth and fuckin' said somethin', he wouldn't ha-" His head jerks in our direction when he finally hears us.

The three of us pull up short when he pulls out a gun and grabs Eden, putting her right in front of him, gun to the back of her head. "D-Don't come any closer you fuckin' pieces of shit!" he screams at us.

"Joseph." I've got my gun pointed at him, as does Jeffrey and the driver. Dan? Don? I don't fucking care at this moment. "Put the gun down. This will not end well for you if you hurt her." I try my best to sound calm and reasonable.

It doesn't work. His eyes are wildly looking between the three of us before glaring back at me. "Not gonna end well? It sure the fuck won't. This whore got your guy, MY BROTHER, killed. What do you do? You *FUCK* her."

"Marc-" she sobs out at me. I try not to look at her face because I need to focus on this dead man.

"*SHUT THE FUCK UP YOU CUNT!*" He smashes his gun into the side of her head before holding it to her temple once more. She cries out from the pain, and then starts sobbing harder, trembling under his gun.

I. See. Red.

"*Sei fottutamente morto,*" I hiss at him and cock my gun, holding it steady, trained on his forehead. I'm almost positive I could make the shot, but I won't risk her.

"Shut up you Italian fuck!" I want to roll my eyes at his attempt to insult me, but all I can focus on now is the barrel of his gun against my little mouse's head. Two fucking times within forty-eight hours has she had this happen to her. "GOD DAMNIT! ARE YOU FUCKIN' KIDDIN' ME?"

Joseph looks down and starts screaming about the fact that she peed again. *No shit you idiot. What do you expect when someone is held at gunpoint?* "Fuckin' pissing everywhere like a motherfuckin' child."

"Joseph," I snap at him to get his attention. "Look at me. You hurt her; you are not getting out of here alive. You let her go, we can talk." I'm lying. He's going to die tonight.

He looks around at us, finally a hint of fear in his eyes, but he doesn't give in. Wrapping his arm tighter around Eden's throat, he squeezes, forcing her to turn her head to the right so she can breathe easier.

I see Jeffrey motion to her out of the corner of my eye to drop down on his count. Now we just wait for the right timing.

"You are gonna kill me anyways. I'll fuckin' take her with me," he yells at us. I can hear the fear in his voice.

"Not necessarily, but I can promise you that if you hurt her, I will draw out your death and make it as painful and I can. Let. Her. Go. Joseph." I don't shift my eyes away from him when I see a few of my men sneaking in behind him.

He must hear one of them because he quickly turns his head to look behind him. Jeffrey and I both yell for Eden to drop. The second she moves, I pull the trigger.

Joseph is dead before he hits the ground.

"Make sure he is dead," I order my guys as I run over to my girl. When he fell, she hadn't been all the way down so she flew back with him.

"Eden, *il mia cuore*, come here sweet girl." Dropping on my knees next to her, I pull her into my arms. She's a trembling and sobbing mess. Some of Joseph's blood hit her face in a speckled mist, along with the trail of blood where he hit her temple. "I am so sorry you were hurt, love. Shh, it is all over."

She throws herself into my body harder, causing me to fall back onto my ass. "M-Mar-c-cus," she hiccups. "Pl-Pleeeease… I want to-to go."

"We will, I swear it. Let me look at you to make sure we can patch you up at home first." I try to pull her head back from my chest to look at the side of her head, but she won't move. I try to just turn her to face the other direction, which she allows me to do. Running my hand through her hair, I hold her as I inspect where that asshole hit her. It's swelling, which is cutting off the blood from flowing.

"I will have my physician look at you at home. Come *il mia cuore*. Wrap your arms around my neck and I will carry you to the car." She's such a tiny little thing that standing takes no effort with her added weight.

"Th-Thank you for c-coming to get me."

I stop and look down at her. "I will always come to get you. *Ti amo, bella.* Always."

She is still clinging to me with all the strength she has, and I hear an '*I love you too*' muffled from her face pressed into my shirt along with the tears that haven't stopped flowing.

"I know you do, *topolina*."

I tell my men what to do with Joseph before leaving. The walk back to the car goes by quick since I'm so focused on her, and before I know it, I have her curled around me in the seat while we wait for the driver to take us back home.

"Baby girl… look at me, *per favore*."

She looks up at me through wet lashes, eyes swollen from crying so hard. "I need you to know that this will *never* happen again. I will not allow it. I meant what I said back there. I do love you, very much. I felt it well before I had you, spending all that time with you in your space." Leaning down, I give her a soft kiss before continuing, "You are my everything, my priority now, my life. *Sì?*"

She nods her head and whispers, "*Sì.*"

Eden doesn't need to tell me she loves me again; I know she does. I knew the moment she curled into my lap, seeking comfort from me when she couldn't find it anywhere else.

Jeffrey and a few others approach the car, carrying Joseph's body. Nodding my head to the back, they move him back there. I don't want my little girl to see him again. This night was already more than she should have ever experienced.

"You all did well, thank you for your help in getting her back," I say to them. "Truly, it is more than I could ever repay, but I will try my best."

They acknowledge my thanks and promise, not making a big deal out of helping us out. Another vehicle pulls up behind us and that's where they stick the body, away from us.

"Are you ready to go home, *il mia piccola amore*?" I ask, placing a kiss on her head and lifting her up slightly to bring her head closer to mine.

She tucks her face into my neck, breathes in deeply and then lets out a shuddered breath.

"*Sì.*"

# Chapter 12

## *Eden*

Six weeks.

It's been six weeks since the night Joseph tried to kill me. I've had a few nightmares, but Marcus has been there every time. He's *always* there when I need him. Every day, I think it's impossible to love him as much as I do at that moment, but then the next day comes and I fall even harder.

He is a hard man, stoic even, and has control over everything in his life, his business, and his men. But with me? Never. It doesn't matter who he's with or speaking to, the moment I walk into the room or pass by his door, his eyes soften for me and he waves me to him.

Giggling to myself, I remember telling him just this morning that I think I've spent more time sitting in his lap than I do my own chair. He told me that he doesn't know why I sit on chairs at all when he has a perfectly good lap.

It's strange, the roles he and I have taken. There's no doubt that he views me as his equal, his partner. But there's also this dynamic between us where I get a sense of almost a parental type of comfort. That's not to say that he makes me think of my dad, he does *NOT*. I think it's more of the combination between our age difference and the way he takes care of me.

If he had his way, I'd never walk again. Marcus loves to carry me when he wants me to be in a different spot. Curling up on his lap while he's working is one of my absolute favorite things to do. Sometimes I'll just lay my head on his chest and listen to his heart beat over the sound of his computer keys clicking away on his computer.

The naturalness of it is what surprises me the most. When he's holding me like that, he'll touch me and pet my hair in a way that seems almost more soothing to him than me. Like he gets comfort from the act of touching me. When he makes a phone call, he will wrap an arm around me and then lean back in his chair while he speaks to whoever called him.

Out of all of this, the affection and attention, the conversations, both serious and superficial, the most incredible part has been in the bedroom.

Well, not just there I suppose. There's the office, the kitchen, the bathroom, the-

"*Il mia topolina*, what has you turning red and smiling like that?"

The sound of his voice still does something to me every time he speaks. I'll never get enough of it. "Umm, I was just thinking about… well, about you and me." I bite my lip, trying to hold back a grin.

Raising an eyebrow, he slowly walks over to me and stops when we are only inches apart. "Please, tell me what in particular about us?" Reaching up, he tucks a lock of my hair behind my ear and watches his hand as he runs it down my bare shoulder.

A ragged breath escapes, my nipples hardening already at just his small touch. He smirks as he watches them stand out under my tank top. Running a finger over one, then the other, he pinches harder than I was ready for and I let out a loud gasp. "Are you going to tell me, *bella*? Or do I need to persuade you?"

Clearing my throat, I tell him the truth, "I was just thinking about how you… you know…" I point down to between my legs.

Chuckling darkly, he grins at me. "You mean when I licked your pussy until you came all over my tongue? Or did you mean when I fucked you so hard you were not able to walk afterwards?"

"Okay, well now I'm thinking about *that*." Glaring at him, I close the last bit of space and press my nipples against his chest. I can feel how hard he is pressed against my belly. Biting my lip, I look up at him, trying to play it off like I don't notice.

Growling, he pulls my hips closer and grinds against me, and then tilts my head back further to take my mouth with his in an aggressive kiss. "*Io ti brama*, Eden. Fuck."

I've been learning Italian and I know he's telling me that he craves me. He's insatiable and I am not one to complain. "*Ti amo*, Marcus," I tell him between our kisses.

He grins wickedly, and kisses me hard once more, wrapping his hand into my hair. "Show me how much, Eden."

Holding my hair in his fist, he watches as I suck in air, already so wet that he would have no problem slipping into me with ease. He still holds me, and I keep my gaze on his face. It's his other hand, though, that has my attention. I feel him working it between us as he loosens his belt, the clank of metal the only sound in the room over my heavy panting. Then he releases his cock to rest heavily against my stomach once again.

"*Suca, bella*," he tells me as he tips my head forward again to stare at his cock. My mouth salivates, knowing how he'll taste in my mouth, and I'm quick to fall to my knees.

He doesn't release my hair from his fist, and instead uses it to guide my mouth over his length, driving into my throat quicker than I had anticipated. Quickly, I adjust and enjoy his flavor and the sounds coming from deep inside of him.

I love that I can make him feel so good like this. Even though I'm on my knees, it makes me feel powerful, like I could bring him to *his* knees if I wanted to.

Sucking him into my mouth for a few minutes, I run my tongue along the underside of his shaft and press the head to the roof of my mouth, sucking hard. He can't hold back the drive of his hips when I do that, and he thrusts into my mouth five or six times quickly, then wrenches himself free.

"I need to be inside you, my little mouse." He uses my hair to pull me back up and then bends to lift me, tossing me over his shoulder as he heads to our bedroom.

Laughing, I reach down and try to slap his butt, but I can't quite reach because he's so tall.

He growls at me and gives my bottom half a dozen quick smacks to the underside of the cheeks and I cry out, the pleasure he gives me through that little bite of pain is always my undoing.

Moaning, I grip his shirt as we head into our bedroom, desperate for him now. It's like that every time he spanks me. Instantly wet and out of control for him.

I fall to the bed when he flips me back off his shoulder and I scramble up further as he immediately puts a knee on the bed, pursuing me. "My little girl is a brat this evening. What should I do about it?"

He stops me from moving further away by grabbing my ankle and jerking me back toward him. Breathless, I squirm under him to try and rub my legs together to ease some of the ache there. "I-I don't care Marcus. Please, I just need you so bad," I beg him.

"Hmm... Well, you have two options then. I can either spank this pert little ass until it's beat red and hot enough to warm us all night, or..."

"Or?" I ask. No matter what he says, I know it'll be a tough decision.

"*OR*, I can flip you onto your stomach, spread those cheeks wide open and work my cock into that little ass of yours. Which would you prefer, love?"

I blank. We haven't done that before. Well, he's played back there and it's *always* felt amazing. I'm nervous because of how large his cock is, but I know he won't hurt me.

"Choose, or I will choose f-"

"*Both*," I blurt out.

His eyes widen slightly and then a look of hunger fill them. "Fuck. Yes."

Flipping me over quickly, he lands a dozen hard smacks all over my bottom until I'm dripping wet, lifting my ass to meet his hand on the final few he delivers.

I feel his weight come down on top of my back. His cock nestles between my legs and slides between my lips to wet himself. The head of him bumps my clit each time he slides up and I groan, trying to grind against him.

His hand grips the back of my neck and I still. Leaning over to place his mouth next to my ear, he tells me in a low, husky voice, "You will stay still and not move. I do not want to hurt you and I already feel close to losing control." He punctuates that with a small thrust, driving his cock up and between my ass cheeks, the wetness allowing him to glide the head along my small entrance.

He presses against it firmly, like he's going to push inside of me right now. I can't help but tense up and he stays still, not retreating but also not pushing forward.

"I am going to go get some lube. Spread your little ass for me so I can get you ready. Do you understand, *il mia piccola amore*?"

Thank God my face is pressed into the mattress because it feels so embarrassing to expose myself like that, and my cheeks are heating. A sharp smack to my pussy has me jolting forward and crying out.

"*Adesso.*"

I obey and he's only gone a moment before I feel the bed dip between my legs again. He runs his tongue from my pussy all the way up to my asshole, and then down again. He repeats this a few more times and I'm trembling, trying to keep my hands where he told me to.

Finally, I hear the snick of the tube and cool liquid flows from the top of my crack, and runs all the way to my soaking center. Tossing the tube to the side, he uses his other hand to spread the slick fluid over all of me, running his hand over and over my ass, with enough pressure to remind me what is about to happen, but gently enough to relax me.

Sinking into the mattress, I enjoy the way he's making me feel. "Marcus… that feels really good," I whisper to him, turning my face to the side so I can peak at him. His eyes are fixed on his hand and looking at the most private parts of me.

"I only ever want you to feel good for me, *bella*," he says, then circles his finger around the hole, pressing firmly as he circles it. I gasp when I feel the tip of his finger dip inside before pulling back out.

He repeats this over and over until there are steady sounds of pleasure coming from my mouth, and he's got one finger thrusting all the way inside at a steady pace. "Take a breath for me, baby girl. Then blow out."

I do and, on my exhale, I feel him add a second finger, not hesitating this time like he did with his first. I cry out at the burn of being stretched like this. He doesn't add another finger until I'm used to the burn and shift back against him.

He scissors his fingers, stretching me wider to get a third finger in. My pussy is throbbing for attention. This feels so much better than I expected. "Please Marcus, I want to come so bad…" I groan out. All my embarrassment now completely gone.

"Oh, you will," he says. I can hear the strain in his voice when he adds, "We both will, little mouse." Pulling his fingers out of me, I cry out for him to come back.

"Hush. Patience, love," he laughs. "I am just getting more lube. I am much larger than those three fingers."

Holy shit. I shake as he comes back over me and lays against my back again. Grabbing each one of my hands, he wraps his around them and stretches my arms in front of me as he pins them down.

My legs widen to allow him to settle between me and his heavy cock rests against my throbbing core.

His entire body is covering me and I can feel the small thrusts of his hips, ready to slide inside of me. "Ready, love?" he asks, kissing the side of my face and then biting the side of my neck.

I nod yes. I can't speak. I'm nervous, but also so turned on that I feel like I'm going to combust if he doesn't do something soon. That thought had just crossed my brain when I feel the head of his cock pressing against my small entrance.

"Take another big breath and push back against me. It will feel uncomfortable at first and burn slightly, but I swear to you it will feel better quickly." He's growling low, holding himself against me with that steady pressure, but not pushing forward yet.

Sucking in a deep breath, I've barely had time to release it when I feel the head of him breach my ring of muscles. He doesn't thrust in quickly, but he also doesn't stop.

I cry out at the burn. He releases my hands and tucks his arms under me, hugging himself to my back, but he doesn't stop. He's relentless as he slowly continues to widen me, going deeper and deeper until I feel his body resting against my ass.

"Baby girl," he whispers and wipes the stray tears from my eyes. "You did so good, topolina. So good for me," he adds, groaning into my ear.

"It… it burns," I tell him, my voice cracking.

"But does it hurt? It will burn until you get used to feeling me there, but if there is actual pain, I need to know," concern lacing his voice now.

I take a moment to analyze my body and realize that yes, it does burn. A lot. But pain? No, there isn't any pain. I try to shift my hips a bit to get more comfortable and I feel him slide out a bit and then back in. I gasp loudly and then groan. I do it again and it feels even better. The burn is still there, but it's accompanied with a new type of pleasure from nerves I didn't know I had.

"That feels so good when you move like that. I am going to start moving. I will go slow at first, is that okay?" I can feel how tense he is, trying not to move until I'm ready.

"Yes, please…" I groan out and then shift my hips to drive him in again.

"I am going to hold on to you. You just enjoy the ride baby girl and let me do the work."

I scream out when I feel him pull all the way back until the head is the only part of him left inside of me, and then a steady push back inside. Still slow, but faster than when he first went in.

"Oh fuck, you are so fucking tight…" he grits out. Pulling back, he does it again and again until I'm steadily crying out for him to fuck me harder.

By the time I feel the stirrings of a different kind of orgasm building, he is thrusting into my ass almost as hard and as quickly as when he is inside my pussy.

"I need you to come. I cannot hold out my longer. Your ass is so tight, you are sucking me in."

Marcus slides his hand under me and rubs at my clit hard, no build up, just hard and fast until he forces me over the edge. I wasn't prepared for the quickness of it and I scream into the bed as I fall apart under him.

He pounds into me the entire time I orgasm, prolonging it until he slams twice more inside me and then comes. I can feel him pulsing and filling me as he yells and curses out in Italian. Words I don't know yet and I smile to myself as I enjoy the feeling of him filling me.

Finally, we both come down from the intensity of that entire thing and I can't stop from giggling as he slides out of me.

"What is so funny, *il mia topolina*?" I can hear the smile in his voice so I know he's not irritated.

"That was just… wow, Marcus. We just did that! It wasn't what I was expecting."

"Better or worse than what you had expected?"

"Better. *Much* better." Peaking over my shoulder at him, I give him a sly grin. "I can't wait to do it again!"

Laughing, he pulls me into his chest and kisses my temple. "Neither can I, love."

# Chapter 13

## *Marcus*

It only took a couple of months for Eden's father to finally face all of the consequences from his actions. A little parting gift from me to him was Joseph's body being left inside his home, hidden away so when the cops came after they received the surveillance footage, they had a second body to charge him with.

Once his arrest made the news, the other people he was screwing over came out of the wood works, providing additional evidence of blackmail, embezzlement, assault, and even a few more murder accusations.

Mr. Leo Altera is a *pezzo di medda*. Thank God his daughter fell far from the tree.

The two of us are on our way to go out for dinner. Nothing fancy, but intimate enough that we'll be alone, undisturbed and unobserved by other guests.

I'm pulled out of my musings when I feel Eden's hand glide over the back on mine, drawing my full attention on to her. "Is everything okay? You seem really distracted right now."

Turning my hand in hers, I grab it and pull it up to my lips, placing a few kisses on the back of her hand. "*Sì topolina*, everything is just fine." The look of concern on her face has me softening my features and pulling her into me. "I swear babygirl. I was only thinking. Nothing is wrong." Nothing *is* wrong. Not really, I'm just a little nervous on how the conversation could go tonight.

She squeezes my hand, and we are silent for the remainder of the drive. After we arrive, we are shown to our booth tucked in the back. Eden slides in first and I follow, sitting close so our thighs touch. I order drinks and an appetizer and then ask the waiter to leave us for a bit.

"Okay… something is clearly bothering you. You have been silent th-" Cutting her off with a quick kiss, I cup her cheeks and look at her. "Marcus?" she whispers.

"My little love… You know how much I love you, yes?" I ask her and I immediately regret how I phrased that when a look of panic overtakes her. I stop her before she can say anything, "That sounded bad. It was not supposed to. I am trying to ask you if you would come back to Italy with me? To my home there?"

Her eyes bounce across my face a moment before they light up with amusement and happiness. "You're an ass! I thought you were going to tell me some terrible news!"

Chuckling, I kiss her. "No, not terrible news. I was only nervous that you may not be ready to leave here yet. I have concluded everything I sought out to do here. Now that your father is dealt with, there is nothing keeping us here. Unless *you* want to stay?"

I can see the answer on her face before she even tries to answer. There's a glow of excitement radiating from her that's blinding. Squealing, she throws her leg over my lap to straddle my waist and hugs me tight to her. "*PLEASE*! Oh Marcus, please please *please* can we go? Like right now? You're not messing with me?"

Ignoring the few people who can see us, I fist her hair and bring her lips to mine. Speaking against them, I swear to her, "I will never mess with you *il mia topolina, il mia cuore*."

"I desperately want to go to your home!" Kissing me again, she holds my neck in her hands and presses her forehead to mine. "There is nothing for me here. There never has been. I want to go wherever you'll take me."

"Babygirl, you are perfect." Kissing her, I add, "I am nothing without you."

"You are everything, Marcus. *Sei la mia anima gemello…*" she whispers.

My heart flips when she speaks to me in Italian and I kiss her to show her everything I'm feeling.

'*You are my soulmate.*' And she is mine.

# Bonus Epilogue

## *Marcus*

"*Topolina*, come here a moment, please."

*Il mia piccola amore* is laying on her stomach on one of the chaise lounges furnishing the balcony attached to the master bedroom in our home, turning pages to a thin book.

"Give me a minute, I'm almost done," she calls over her shoulder. Her feet are in the air, ankles crossed and she's mumbling words under her breath as she reads.

Going over to her, I sit beside to her and place a hand on the curve of her lower back. It still fascinates me that my hand spans the entire width of it, and I can't help pressing my fingers into her skin, massaging along her spine. "What are you reading?"

Peaking over her shoulder, I raise an eyebrow at the children's picture book. She turns her head, her chin resting on her shoulder, and hides her book. "Don't look!"

I grin at the blush crawling up her cheeks and tease her, "babydoll, don't be shy. Will you show me what you are reading?"

She tucks her book under her chest and lays on it. Then, biting her lip, embarrassment laces her voice, "...I don't want to show you. It's embarrassing."

Reaching out to her, I tuck a stray lock of hair behind her ear. "*Il mia cuore*, you should never be ashamed of anything with me... Show me, *per favore*."

Sighing, she pulls the book out and hands it to me. Wringing her hands together, she watches as I flip through the pages. It's a children's book for early readers. My heart turns over when I realize that she's trying to read a children's book in Italian. "I just... I'm trying to learn the words. It's easier to speak than it is to read. We've been here almost a year and I want to get more proficient.'

I set the closed book on my lap and lean over to brush my lips across hers. "I think this is a good idea. I will try to find you some books that they use in schools if you would like to learn how to read and write Italian, my love."

Nodding her head, she gives me a small smile, her eyes sparkling in the bright afternoon sun. When we are outside like this, her eyes take on a warm chocolate brown color that allow her enjoyment to shine out of them.

"*Per favore*. What did you call me for?" she asks, changing the subject.

"Ahh, *sì*." Setting the book on the lounge, I stand and pull her up with me. "I have something to show you. Come with me."

"Oohh," she laughs out. "Is it a surprise?"

"Possibly." I kiss her quickly, take her hand and lead her downstairs further into the house. Walking her into one of the sitting rooms, I keep my body in front of hers so she doesn't see what I got her right away. "Close your eyes, *bella*."

Giggling, she does as she's told. Pulling her in front of me, I tuck her body into the front of mine and place my hands on her shoulders. "Okay… open your eyes for me."

I know the moment she does when I hear her large intake of breath, gasping at the item that's in the center of the room.

Covering her mouth, she cries out, "Oh my *God!* It's a piano!" She cranes her neck back to look up at me, and I see tears glistening in her eyes. "You got me a piano?"

Flashing my teeth at her, I give her a single nod. "I got you a piano. Do you like it?"

"Holy shit…" she breathes out, and then looks back at the Bösendorfer baby grand piano. I can tell she's itching to play it and I'm just as anxious because I have *another* surprise for her.

"Would you play for me *topolina*?" I encourage her, turning her and guiding her toward her gift.

"…ohmygod…" I can tell she's overwhelmed. She's missed playing since we moved to Matera. I could have bought her a regular piano, but I wanted to get something special for her.

"Sit, *il mia piccola amore*. Play something?"

Her eyes are zeroed in on the keys and she slides onto the bench, running her fingers across the polished keys. I pull the bench out further, lift her up so that I can sit, and set her on my lap. At the sound of her giggling, I bite my cheek to stay focused on the task at hand.

"What would you like me to play?" she asks, sweetly.

"Anything, little girl. Just play for me." Placing my hands on her waist, she situates herself and then begins to play the first piece I ever heard her play back at the club last year.

I bite back a groan when her swaying to reach the notes grind her ass into my cock and I can feel it getting hard underneath her. As the song grows, her hands drift further up the keys and I bite my lip when I hear the clanking noise that rattles through the piano.

Her playing falters, but she doesn't stop. Pushing through the song for another few phrases, the noise rings again through the piano and this time, she pulls her hands away. "Oh no…"

"What is it?" I ask. I know what it is.

"I umm… I think there's something wrong with the piano."

"Hmm… I am not sure why? It was just delivered less than an hour ago," I tell her. The look of confusion on her face is adorable as she peaks inside the body of the instrument. The guys that delivered the piano set it all up and lifted the cover so it was fully open allowing us to see all of the strings and internals.

She runs her eyes over everything but doesn't see what I've hidden in there. "Why not keep playing? Maybe it was nothing," I say, trying to keep the teasing out of my voice.

"Alright..." she mumbles. Settling back into my lap, this time I do groan and she gives me a flirty smile and adjusts a second time on purpose, rubbing her ass against my cock. "You okay there, Marcus?"

I grunt, "Good.... I am good." Kissing the back of her head, I wrap my arms around her waist and settle my chin on her shoulder. "Play for me *bella piccola stella*... my beautiful little star."

Smiling to herself, she picks up where she left off and again, hears the thunk of something rattling around inside. This time, she stands up quickly and leans over to look inside. "Honestly Marcus, there's something in there!"

"Well, look inside. You can see if there is anything there."

I watch as she moves out from between myself and the piano and around the side where she rests her stomach against the part that curves inward. Leaning the upper half of her body in, I follow her.

She doesn't see me move behind her by a couple of feet to wait on her.

It doesn't take long before I hear her murmur, "What the hell is that?" And then she reaches in to pick out what I've hidden. It's my queue.

"...Marcus, what is th-" she turns around and stops talking when she sees me.

I'm down on one knee.

"Baby girl... come here." I coo to her, holding a hand out.

Her breath hitches when she realizes what is happening and she whispers, "Oh my God…"

"You are my everything… *sei il mia tutta, topolina.* You deserve to be given the world and all the good things I can give to you. Before I met you, I was not living… I was only existing. I know I should ask, but I am not going to. I *need* you." Her lip is trembling and I push through the unpracticed words I want to say. "*Ti amo, bella. Ti amo… sposami picolla…* Marry me."

Her hand is shaking as she grips the ring with diamonds set in a star pattern surrounding another chocolate brown diamond. The color was the closest I could find to match the color of her eyes.

Sobbing out, she throws herself into my arms and I sit back onto the floor and hold her to me. It's like she can't get close enough when she wraps her legs around my waist, her arms around my neck with her fingers digging into my shoulders.

"Sweet girl… you are not supposed to be crying little love." Pushing her hair back from her face, I look down into her already swollen red-rimmed eyes. "I hope you know how much I love and adore you. You are my sun… my warmth… and my heart."

She can only nod her head yes, unable to pass any words through her lips. Tilting her head up, she plants wet, salty kisses all over my cheeks, nose, lips, and eyes before tucking her head back into the crook of my neck.

"I hope this means yes, *si*?"

"Y-yes…" she croaks out. "*Sì*, Marcus. *Anch'io ti amo…* I love you too!"

Smiling to myself, I hold her tightly to my body, enjoying the way she fits so sweetly against me. I rock her gently for some time before I feel her shoulders start to shake.

Looking down, I worry that she's crying, but when I find her face, I see that she's laughing.

"What is so funny, *topolina*?" I ask her, kissing her temple.

Giggling, she smiles widely at me. "Did you buy the piano for me just to put a ring in it?"

Chuckling, I shake my head. "No little girl, I bought you the piano because I want to hear your music. It just happened to show up on the same day that I had planned to give you your ring."

"Oh *shoot!* I forgot the ring!" She leans away from me and peals the ring from the palm of her hand where it's indented her skin from squeezing it so tightly.

I take it from her and slide it onto her ring finger on her left hand. Once it's settled in place, I press it against my heart. "Perfect."

Kissing the back of my hand, she asks, "when did you want to get married?"

"I have an appointment for us tomorrow. There is no reason to wait, is there?" I cock an eyebrow at her.

Biting her lip, she shakes her head slowly, "No… no reason to wait. I'm umm… I don't know what to say about all of this. You caught me off guard, but you have to know that I'm really excited. I don't feel like I'm good enough for you…"

"Stop right there. You are beyond perfect for me," I assure her.

"I just mean, I feel really lucky to have you and I'm going to be selfish and keep you all to myself… if that's alright?"

Kissing her again, I trail my lips across her cheek to her ear, "*Topolina…* it is *more* than alright."

The End

# Glossary of Italian Terms/Phrases

**'adesso'** Now

**'bambolina'** babydoll

**'bella'** beautiful

**'bella piccola stella'** beautiful little star

**'cazzo'** fuck

**'fottimi'** fuck me

**'Gesù Cristo'** Jesus Christ

**'Grazie Dio'** Thank God

**'il mia cuore'** my heart

**'il mia piccola amore'** my little love

**'il mia topolina'** my little mouse

**'la mia bambina'** my baby girl

**'la mia piccola stella'** my little star

**'merda'** shit

**'per favore piccola'** please baby

**'pezzo di medda'** piece of shit

**'piccola mia'** my little one

**'piccola gattina'** little kitten

**'rimani qui'** stay here

**'sì'** yes

**'suca'** suck my cock/dick

**'stellina'** little star

'topolina' little mouse

'Così stretto, bella.' So tight, beautiful.

'Dove cazzo via?' Where the fuck are you going?

'Io ti brama.' I crave you.

'Mi dispiace tanto amore mia.' I'm so sorry my love.

'Non scopare con me.' Don't fuck with me.

'Non ti rimanderò indietro.' I won't send you back.

'Rispondi, per favore.' Answer, please.

'Sei fottutamente morto.' You're fucking dead.

'Sei il mia tutta.' You're my everything.

'Sei la mia anima gemello.' You are my soulmate.

'Ti amo.' I love you. (intimate)

'Ti senti così bene.' You feel so good.

'Vattene dal cazzo.' Get the fuck out.

'Ho bisogno di assaporarti, banchettare con te.' I need to savor you, feast on you.

'La tua figa si sente così bene... Cazzo, sei stretto... Sei mio... Nel momento in cui ho scopato nella tua figa vergine, sei diventata mia, topolina...' Your pussy feels so good... Fuck, you're tight... You're mine... The moment I fucked in your virgin pussy, you became mine, little mouse.

**'Mi scuso per l'italiano, è più sicuro. Ho bisogna di sapere se stai bene. Per favore, topolina... Dimmi che non sei ferita... Che non ti ho fatta male.'** I apologize for the Italian, it's safer. I need to know if you're okay. Please, little mouse... Tell me you're not hurt... That I didn't hurt you.

S. E. Green

THE COMPLETE INNOCENCE BOXSET

# LILY

## S.E. Green

S. E. Green

# From the Author

I live for music, so I often get inspired by many contemporary songs and artists when I write. While some books that I write are inspired by multiple songs, this one was a one song repeater for me. It just sort of sucked me in a put me in a particular mood - one that I hope you feel when you listen. It's called **Gravity (Day 1)** by *Ludovico Einaudi*.

Also, as a side note, this story came to me while I was actually playing this song on the piano. The song has always had a feeling of sadness to me, through the entire piece, and it was one of those moments that while playing, I had the urge to mope. A little 'woe is me' period of time, but there was absolutely nothing wrong. It was silly, but when I play, I day dream… and I had a daydream of being ganged up on for something that wasn't true, or something that I wasn't doing. Being misunderstood. The scene that popped into my head is basically all of Chapter 1 and 2. Sometimes, you just want to feel like a victim, and that's how Lily came about for me. I hope you enjoy Lily, Fallon, and Rhett!

S. E. Green

## Trigger Warnings

Please know that there could be some triggering topics addressed that include **physical abuse, death of a parent, and violence (all only discussed as past events).**

Having experienced abuse in my past (one sexual assault and one physically/verbally abusive relationship), I sometimes draw from how I felt and recovered from it. Everyone reacts differently to trauma, so if you doubt that my character(s) reacted in a believable way, please keep in mind we are all wonderfully different. My therapist told me that our bodies tend to subconsciously protect itself the best way it thinks will keep us the safest. Please seek help if you are being hurt or have been hurt in the past. We all want you safe and feeling loved!

THE COMPLETE INNOCENCE BOXSET

# Chapter 1

## *Fallon*

*"Sweetheart. Are you and Rhett on your way?"*

Damnit. I forgot about the family dinner that mom and dad had asked us to come to tonight. They always do a get together every time they take in a new foster kid. It's a way to make them feel welcome and to get to know everyone. I appreciate what they do for these kids, but it's getting to the point that they've gotten more bad ones than good. Kids that are stealing from them, disrespecting them, sneaking out at night, and just overall getting into trouble. Assholes. That's what they are. A bunch of unappreciative fucking assholes.

I sigh, not wanting to disappoint her. "Yeah... we might be a little bit late, though. Sorry, we both sort of forgot about it."

*"Fallon! I talked to you twice about it and I know for sure that your father sent a reminder text just a couple of days ago. Did you really forget?"* I wince at the sound of disappointment in her voice. Mom doesn't ask for a lot, but when she does, we always try to make it happen.

Cindy and Jeff Miller, aka mom and dad, have been a part of my life since I was 9 years old and Rhett's since he was 11. He and I were the first two foster kids that they took into their home after they spent years trying to have children of their own, unsuccessfully. By the time I was 14 and Rhett was 13, they offered to adopt us, and we quickly accepted.

We are the only two they've ever adopted. We went from Fallon Barr and Rhett DeMuro to Fallon and Rhett Miller. The two of them saved our lives and we will forever be grateful. Which is why we show up to every welcome home dinner they throw for each kid they bring home. Some only stick around for a couple of months, some a couple of years. The only thing they all have in common is that they never stick around forever.

It's hard to watch my parents get disappointed every time it doesn't work out with one of the kids. Mom feels like she failed them and dad tends to dwell on what he could have done better. Was he too hard on them? Not hard enough?

The group they have now is a mix. The seven-year-old girl, Pearl, is alright. She's not bad per se, she just has a *lot* of energy. Bouncing off the walls, exhausting mom and dad who are in their early sixties now. Kevin and Carleigh are a set of thirteen-year-old twins that are out of fucking control. We've already heard of a few times that they've snuck out or gotten pissed and destroyed stuff in the home. Carleigh has cornered Pearl a few times now and they are at the point that they are going to have to separate them. Either find a new home for Pearl, or a new home for the twins. I know they would choose the twins because they would view them as the ones that need them the most.

Now they've gone and added a fourth. A seventeen-year-old girl who's almost aged out of the system. They've never taken this many kids at once, so we don't know why they've taken her. Rhett and I have both tried to tell them that it's probably time to retire from the fostering, but I don't think they ever will. Their hearts are too big, and it kills us to see them taken advantage of over and over again.

Focusing back on my mom, I try to reassure her, "I swear mom, it wasn't intentional. We just got really busy at the shop and lost track of time. We'll clean up quick and head over. Be there in an hour, tops."

*"You better. I'm going to push dinner back to wait on you boys. It's important. Lily is having a hard time and I think making her feel welcome will really help her out. It's been hard to get her to connect."* I roll my eyes as Rhett walks over to me, furrowing his brows. Mom and her damn bleeding heart. I'm sure this girl is just pissy about being moved to a new home. They always are.

"Who are you talking to?" he whispers, and I mouth '*mom*' back to him.

"Fuck! Dinner tonight!" he says a little louder and mom hears him.

*"RHETT! Watch your mouth! You know better than that..."* she scolds. We both snicker because she really does hate swearing.

I put the phone on speaker as he comes closer to join the conversation. "Sorry ma. I'll watch my tongue when we get there."

"Let us let you go. We'll close up and head over," I promise her. The sooner we get there, the sooner we can leave. Not that we don't want to spend time with the parents, but I don't have the energy to be patient with those twins tonight.

"*Alright. Drive safely, see you soon.*"

"You need us to pick anything up?" I ask, wanting to offer an olive branch for disappointing her by being late tonight.

She pauses while she thinks, "*Nah, I think we have everything. Just bring yourselves. Love you boys!*"

"Love you too, mom," I laugh at her use of 'boys'.

"Love you!" Rhett yells out as he starts to walk away. I hang up and stick my phone in my back pocket.

"This is going to fucking suck." I run my hand through my hair and scratch the back of my head, looking around at the mess we've got in here. "Think we should just leave this and get to it tomorrow?"

We have a shop where we rebuild and customize bikes. People bring in their frames, tell us what they want, and we hunt down the parts to make it happen. It's been decently lucrative, and we always have a few projects going at once.

Rhett stops and looks around too with his hands on his hips. "I fucking hate doing that, but we probably should. Dad is already going to get on us for upsetting mom by being this late." He pulls the tie in his hair out, and then knots it back up.

"You need to cut that shit," I tell him, nodding at his hair that's almost to his shoulders.

Flashing his teeth at me, he laughs, "The fuck I will! It flows better in the wind like this and the ladies love it."

He's not wrong. Throw in the tattoos and piercings with the long hair, women drool over him. I don't have any problems getting my fair share of pussy either, but he's got the Jax Teller from Sons of Anarchy thing going for him that make them cream.

Forty-five minutes later, we pull into the driveway of the home we spent half our childhood in and park the truck behind mom's Dodge Caravan. We aren't even to the front door yet and I can hear Carleigh screeching through the shut door.

"Jesus Christ," Rhett groans. "I really fucking hope it's only her that-"

He stops when we hear Pearl scream back at her and then feet pounding like someone is running. I glare at Rhett, "Spoke to soon, you fucker."

Opening the front door, we walk into a battlefield. Dad is standing in the middle of the living room, holding the two girls apart while they try to go at each other.

Rhett immediately walks over to help. Standing at 6'2, he towers over the girls, and even dad who's only around 5'10. "Knock it off you two," he growls. "Grow up and stop the damn screaming!" Rhett really doesn't have patience for that kind of crap.

"You can't tell me what to fuc-" Carleigh starts to growl at Rhett.

"*Carleigh!*" mom yells from the kitchen. "We don't use that kind of language in this house. Come in here please and give me a hand. Pearl, grab the dishes and set the table please."

"For fucks sake…" Carleigh says under her breath, and I want to shake the attitude out of her.

"Come on kid, let's have a nice dinner without the bickering. Alright?" dad pleads with her, then looks to Pearl. "Please?"

Pearl is bouncing on her toes, nodding her head quickly. "Alright, Mr. Miller. Sorry!" Dad smiles at her and then looks to Carleigh. That's when Pearl sticks her tongue out at the other girl and Carleigh's face turns red in anger.

"You little-" She lunges for her.

"ENOUGH!" I bark at them, stopping them in their tracks. "Just do what they asked. For the love of God…" I sigh.

Glaring at each other, neither says anything else as they walk into the kitchen. Looking around, I see Kevin sitting on the couch playing a video game, ignoring everyone around him. Walking over to him, I nudge his foot to get is attention. "Hey, Kevin. Why don't you go see if there's anything you can do to help as well?"

Of course, I get the eye roll from him, but at least he doesn't argue when he gets up and mutters, "whatever," under his breath.

"Jesus, dad," Rhett says. "Are they like this all the time?"

Dad sighs and sits down, running his hands over his face. "Lately, yeah. It was a little calmer before, but since Lily came to stay here, it's got those girls all worked up and bickering nonstop."

"She's giving you a hard time too?" I ask. This is all too much for them if they're dealing with four of them like this.

Shaking his head, he answers, "Lily? No. She doesn't fight with them. Well, not really. She keeps to herself in her room most of the time. The others are pissed because they think she should be out here doing her share of the chores. They think she's getting special treatment."

"Well, *shouldn't* she be helping?" Rhett asks, and I agree.

"It's not that she doesn't help. We just don't have her out here doing chores where she's in the middle of everything. She gets overwhelmed with the noise and chaos. Lily helps with other things like folding laundry, or outside work."

I scowl at him. "Sounds to me like she just doesn't want to do the crap jobs. You can't let them walk all over you guys, dad."

"Fallon, it's fine. She's adjusting. This is a big change."

Rhett laughs without humor, "Dad, she's playing you guys. You gotta put your foot down right away, *then* if you want, start to back off once you've established that you're in charge. Letting her dictate how she wants to do things is giving her the power. She won't respect you two."

"Just give her a chance, please," he asks of us.

*"DINNER!"* mom yells, then I hear, "Thank you for your help, Lily."

Dad's eyes widen and then he squeezes them shut when he realizes that Lily has been in the kitchen the entire time we've been talking, and mouths *'shit'*. Hell. No. This girl is not going to have dad acting like he has to watch himself in his own home.

"Come on boys," he says, then to us says quietly, so others can't hear, "Hopefully she didn't hear any of that."

Shrugging, Rhett isn't worried. Neither am I. "Don't stress about it. Nothing was said that couldn't be said in front of her," I assure him, not softening my voice. I'm not worried about being overheard.

He whips his head to me and scowls. "Knock it off Fallon." I'm a little taken aback by that. Meeting Rhett's eyes, I can tell that he and I agree. This girl needs to be taken down a peg and learn that she doesn't get to control how things are run in this house.

Walking into the kitchen, I see long, brown hair with a flash of green in it turn the corner before I see mom and head over to greet her. "Hey mom," I say, leaning down to kiss her cheek. "It smells really good in here."

Standing on tiptoes, she gives me a kiss on the cheek. "Hi sweetheart." Then she looks over my shoulder and the gentle smile she has on her face drops away, turning into a scowl that could melt butter. Smacking my arm, she hisses at me, "Are you kidding me

Fallon? That little girl heard every word you and your brother said out there!"

My eyes widen at her. Cindy Miller has never once gotten on me like that before. Rhett and I have always helped with all of the kids they bring into their home. "Mom! Look, I'm sorry if we hurt her feelings, but seriously, you can't do special treatments and not expect the others to get bent out of shape over it."

She blows out a frustrated breath and swipes her hair off her forehead with the back of her arm. Looking at me for a minute, she just lets her shoulders slump and I don't like the defeat she's feeling right now. "Just... would you please bite your tongue tonight? It's been a huge adjustment for not just her, but all of us. The way we normally handle the other kids isn't going to work with this one. Alright?"

It takes everything in me not to argue with her, but it's obvious she's exhausted. "Yeah, fine. I'll try." She raises an eyebrow at me. "I said I'll *try*. But Rhett and I won't sit back and watch these kids walk all over you."

She just shakes her head and steps around me. Over her shoulder, she says, "Grab the salad bowl for me, please." Then she disappears around the corner into the dining room.

"This is bullshit, Fallon," Rhett says under his breath, coming to stand next to me. I agree but keep my mouth shut.

Walking into the dining room, I see that everyone is seated with an empty chair at the end of the table and one next to the girl with the green streaked hair. Moving to sit next to her, mom jumps up quickly. "Fallon, honey. Sit over here by your dad. He's missed you."

What the hell? She scoots around the table and slips in the chair next to the new girl. Rhett sits in the chair at the end of the table, to the right of where mom is now sitting, and I take up her seat between Carleigh and Pearl. Awesome.

Getting settled, I finally get a chance to see the newest addition to the family. Sadly, all I see is the side of her head and a partial profile as she looks away from all of us and stares at the table, picking at the napkin folded underneath the silverware.

"Lily, honey. I'd like you to meet our sons, Rhett and Fallon. They live over in Pennburg and have a motorcycle shop there." Mom has her hand rested on the back of Lily's chair and the girl is leaning forward to prevent mom from touching her. Green-brown hazel eyes, void of all emotions, briefly look at me and then over to Rhett before she takes them away from us and redirects her focus back to where it was before mom spoke to her.

No words, no reaction, no acknowledgement. Nothing.

Rhett snorts, clearly irritated. "Nice to meet you too." I see her wince a little at Rhett's tone. Good, she *should* know she's being rude.

"It's nice to meet you, Lily," I try. I gentle my voice the best I can and mom throws me a thankful gaze. We wait a moment and still nothing.

"Lily?" mom urges her, but the girl just ignores her.

"Don't bother mom, it's fine. If she doesn't want to be polite and say hello, it's no skin off our backs. Let's eat, yeah?" I tell her, a little embarrassed at the fact that it's Carleigh that snickers at my comment.

Dad and mom are looking at me like they want to choke me. Rhett shakes his head. Pearl and Carleigh start to bicker over my lap and Kevin reaches to grab the spoon from the mashed potatoes bowl and starts piling them onto his plate.

I'm ready to go home.

## Chapter 2

### *Rhett*

*Unbelievable.* Lily has my parents wrapped around her finger. The brief view I got of her face showed me that she's gorgeous. I was surprised at the little nose piercing she's got as well. Her hair is thick, almost black with a streak of sage green woven down the right side of her head. Hazel eyes, delicate features, and almost flawless ivory skin.

She's wearing a little bit of makeup, but it looks like it's only really her eyes lined with liner and mascara on her lashes. She's tiny. Not short, though. She looks like she's around mom's height, which is 5'5". It's her frame that's tiny. Lily's arms are so thin that I can see the hint of her shoulder bones poking out and her wrists look fragile. Too thin, but that's the thing that's in right now. Girls are so concerned about their weight that they starve themselves to have what they think are perfect bodies.

It's frustrating to me when someone doesn't eat because they think they need to only be 110 pounds. People should be more appreciative of the food they're provided. I know what it's like to be without and I've never put my nose up at a good meal.

I feel bad for Fallon sitting between those bickering girls. The frustration with them is radiating off of him and I can tell he's going to snap soon. We've worked ten 12-hour days in a row and we're both exhausted. Dealing with these little shits is the last thing either of us want to be doing, but we promised mom and dad.

Classifying Lily as a kid may not be entirely fair, but we were told she's only 17. Everyone is chatting, filling their plates, or asking for something to be passed to them. Kevin is already digging into his food, shoveling it in faster than everyone else can fill their plates.

Except Lily. She hasn't moved, hasn't reached for anything. Well, her eyes have moved. I've noticed her watch the dishes as they make their rounds. Clearly, she's hungry, but she's being stubborn and not accepting anything.

Mom keeps asking her if she'd like something and the only thing I've heard her say since we got here has been, 'no thank you.' Dad tries to encourage her to eat when she's said no for the third time. "Lily dear, try some of the meatloaf. Just a little bit. It's one of the things Cindy makes best and it's delicious."

Fallon watches her with a scowl on his face, and his jaw clenches when she sighs and then hesitantly reaches forward with her fork to poke a small slice of meatloaf and put it on her plate. It's sickening watching mom light up just because this ungrateful girl is trying her food. Mom puts a croissant on her plate without asking and Lily just stares at it like it's going to bite her.

"Please try to eat a little for me, Lily," mom speaks softly to her.

Finally, this girl does something other than look away and say no. She gives mom a forced grin and picks up her fork, looks around, eyes lingering on Fallon and then me before cutting the smallest of pieces from the meat and placing it in her mouth, chewing slowly.

This goes on for the next twenty minutes. Everyone has finished their plates, some having finished off seconds, and Lily is still working on that tiny piece of meatloaf with mom staring at her from the corner of her eye. I'm getting fed up and my appetite is completely gone watching her get catered to.

"*ENOUGH!*" Fallon roars from the other side of the table, glaring at the two other girls who have not stopped fighting since we all sat down. "You two have *got* to stop all this damn fighting! For fucks sake!" He slams his hand down on the table.

Lily jumps in her seat, dropping her fork to her plate and dad shouts back at Fallon, "FALLON! Come on. Knock it off with the language, *please.*"

"Girls, enough of this or you'll be done eating for the evening," mom scolds.

Lily looks at her like she's horrified at what mom said, then quickly stands up, picking up her plate with her.

"Lily honey, I didn't mean they wouldn't get to eat honey. Please, sit down." Mom's tone changes quickly to try and appease

Lily. She ignores mom and keeps walking toward the door with her plate like she's going to go back upstairs.

"STOP, Lily," I say. I don't yell, but my voice is firm.

"*Rhett...*" mom hisses at me, but I ignore her. I can hear Fallon arguing with dad over allowing her to leave the table like this. Glaring at Lily, I see that she's stopped walking and is staring at me, holding her plate tightly, unmoving. Good, it's nice to see that she's capable of listening.

"Do not walk out of this room with that plate," I tell her. I feel a little bad because she clearly looks petrified of me, but I don't back down.

I wait.

She doesn't move, seemingly frozen to her spot. Finally, she looks around the room at everyone silently watching her. She takes another step in the direction of her room and I lose it.

Standing up, I plant my hands on the table, leaning forward to level my glare at her. "You eat at the table or you don't eat at all. That's the rule." I had expected mom and dad to back me up on this, but I'm surprised at the turn everything takes. Lily's eyes fill with tears as mom jumps up to yell at me for being mean.

I can't help the shocked bark of laughter that escapes me at mom's accusation. Fallon jumps in to defend me, "Really mom? You guys are letting this little girl get away with being rude like this? She shouldn't get this much special treatment!"

I watch as Lilly sucks in a breath and walks back toward the table and I take a relieved breath that she's listening. It's only for a moment because she completely bypasses the table to head to the kitchen. She sets her plate on the counter next to the sink without even cleaning it off and walks quickly out of the room, not looking at anyone. The next moment, I hear her feet pound upstairs, and chaos completely ensues.

"Kevin, Carleigh, and Pearl. Go to your rooms for just a bit. We'll call you when you can come out. It won't be long," dad barks at the other three and I'm shocked at how quickly they all scatter, leaving plates behind.

Fallon and I are both standing, mom has her forehead resting in her hand, shaking her head back and forth in frustration, and dad is grinding his teeth while staring at us.

"You fucking idiots," he grits out, and then sits down heavily like the weight of the world is on him.

I'm shocked. "What the hell is going on? Why are you two acting like this?"

"You both are letting that brat get away with behaving like that? Ignoring everyone while you're trying to be kind. Ungrateful. *Rude* even." Fallon is shaking his head and looks at me to back him up. I'm right there with him.

"Expecting the others to follow different rules than the ones you are giving her is absurd! Besides, what the hell is she even doing here? Lily looks like she's days away from aging out of the system!

What, she couldn't hack the last place she was at? They had to get rid of her that quickly that they couldn't wait an extra couple of months?" I add in and Fallon finishes up for me.

"That ought to tell you both something, if someone didn't want her that bad that they couldn't even wait a few weeks for her to turn 18. You all are bending over backwards for this girl. She's got to be playing you! At this age, she knows how to work the damn system!" He's getting pissed all over again and breathing heavily.

"What the hell is wrong with the two of you?" dad asks, looking at us like he doesn't recognize us.

Mom loudly sighs, and shakes her head at us. "Neither of you know what you're talking about. Neither of you know what that girl has been through! The damage you've do-"

Mom whips her head around and snaps her mouth shut when we all hear a soft voice clearing. Lily peeks into the room, not looking at either Fallon or myself. I open my mouth to confront her again, but dad stops me by hissing under his breath, "don't open your goddamn mouth, son."

"Lily, honey..." Mom jumps up and tries to approach her but stops when Lily stiffens and takes a step back.

"Umm... I just-" She quickly looks at me and my brother before back to mom, "just w-wanted to apologize... I w-won't behave like that again. I swear..." She's whispering by the time she trails off.

My mom looks crestfallen, and Fallon and I both watch on in confusion.

Shaking her head, she says, "No, sweetheart. *No*. You have nothing to be sorry for. Are you still hungry? Would you like me to make up another plate for you?"

Lily looks at us once more and takes another step back. "No, thank you. I just... I'm sorry," her voice cracks and then she turns and walks away again.

Everyone is silent while we listen to her footsteps retreat again up to her room. Fallon breaks the silence, "What the hell is going on?"

"What's going on is that Lily lost her father when she was 13 years old. She had no family to take her in, so she went into the foster system. She was sent to a home that already had another five children living there when they got her out of there." Mom looks to dad, who nods his head for her to continue, then she faces us again. "These people beat and starved all of those kids. Refused to use the funds they received from the state on the kids. A lot of them came in and left, but Lily didn't. She was there for 4 years. Abused for speaking and taunted with food. Starved."

"What do you mean taunted with food?" I ask, feeling a little sick at mom's description of Lily's background.

"I mean that they would give her food, then when she would start to eat, they'd take it away, punish her for eating it, or would just eat in front of her without allowing her anything. She's underweight, although she *has* put on a few pounds since getting here. You both…" she breathes heavily and grinds her jaw like she doesn't know what to say to us.

"Mom," I say. Fuck, what do I say? "I'm sorry. Had I known, I wouldn't have gotten on her like that. It just seemed like you guys were catering to her."

"We have spent the last two weeks trying to encourage her to eat, let alone eat with us! Half a dozen times has she eaten in front of us. She gets overwhelmed, particularly with the others here, so tonight was especially hard for her. Not only were you both being horribly mean to her, but you also threatened her *food*!" We both wince when we realize how badly we messed up.

Fallon sighs, running his hand over his face, scrubbing it like he can wipe tonight away. "We'll go apologize to her. Get her to come back down and finish her dinner."

"No," dad says.

"No?" I ask. "We should at least apologize to her!"

"We really are sorry," Fallon adds.

Mom just shakes her head, putting her forehead back into her hand. "No, boys. You know we love you both, so *so* much, but we only have her for another month and we need to do our best to get her ready to be on her own. Just… I need you guys not to come back until she's gone."

"Are you serious?" I ask. I'm floored that they're reacting like this. "Fallon, help me out here."

He's just standing with his hands on his hips, staring at our parents like he can't believe what he's hearing.

"Your mom is right. Lily has already told us enough times that she wants to get out of our hair the moment she's able. Let us help her as much as we can. It'll only be a month."

I growl quietly. I don't feel right about any of this. I especially don't feel right just leaving and not making it right with Lily. I'm not usually this much of an asshole and I'm disappointed in myself for misreading the situation so poorly. Fallon and I both did, but we only have ourselves to blame. Our parents tried to get us to stop and we didn't listen.

"Come on boys, let me walk you out. Say goodnight to your mother," dad says, standing up and adjusting his belt.

They're both exhausted and we've done enough damage tonight, arguing with them is only going to make things worse. I silently tell Fallon to let it go for tonight and we can take it up later.

After kissing our mother goodbye, dad walks us outside without saying anything. I get in the driver's side, start up the truck and roll down the window. Dad leans against the door and looks at the both of us.

"Look, I know you both meant well, but tonight was bad. That can't happen again, especially around Lily." God, he sounds so disappointed in us.

"Dad," Fallon says, "let us try to fix this. We feel fucking awful." He squeezes my shoulder when he includes me in that, and I just swallow down the lump in my throat.

He looks to the house a minute like he's thinking and then studies us. "Maybe. Not now though. Let's see if we can at least undo tonight and get her back on track. Let us know when you get home. I love you boys." He slaps the door and steps back, sliding his hands in his pockets.

"Love you too," I mutter and then back out of the driveway to head home.

The two of us are silent for most of the drive, both lost in our own thoughts. I keep replaying the whole evening in my head and now I see her reactions to us for what they were. It makes me sick to know that I scared her like that, and I know I'm not going to be okay until I can at least apologize to her.

"Fuck, Rhett," Fallon mumbles.

I nod my head at him, "I know, man."

"She's a beautiful girl, though," he adds, like he didn't mean to say that out loud and I give him a slight smile, thinking back on the first time I looked at her.

"Yeah, she really is."

# Chapter 3

## *Lily*

"Lily, sweetie. Come sit and share some cookies with me," Cindy asks, waving me into the kitchen as I walk by with a small box to take out to my car.

Biting my lip, I look at the front door longingly. It's not that I don't like her, it's that I feel like a terrible inconvenience to the entire family. "Would you mind if I took this out first?" I ask her, holding the box up to show that my hands are full.

She smiles at me, but it doesn't quite reach her eyes. "Sure, go ahead. Do you need any help?" I can't tell if she's asking to be kind or because she's ready for me to go. I can never tell. She and Jeff have repeatedly told me that I'm welcome in their home for as long as I'd like, assuring me I am not, nor have I ever been, a burden.

*"We only have her for another month and we need to do our best to get her ready to be on her own. Just... I need you guys not to come back until she's gone."*

And then, *"Your mom is right. Let us help her as much as we can. It'll only be a month."*

Swallowing back the sick feeling of being unwanted, I turn to Cindy to reassure her, "I'll be fine. It'll only take a moment and then I'll be back." Hurrying out the door, I don't wait for her response and set the box on the floorboard in the trunk.

Staring at the first of about a dozen boxes I need to load into my car, I can't help but be nervous for the new big change coming in my life. Tomorrow is my birthday and I plan on heading out first thing in the morning. The lease has already been signed in a small apartment complex on the south side of Pennburg. Not the nicest area, but I've lived in worse. I managed to purchase a used car that'll get me where I need to go for the next few years, and I have enough savings to cover at least three months of expenses in case something happens with my job. I'm ready. I'm prepared. But *fuck* if I'm not scared.

Slipping back into the house, I take a deep breath before heading into the kitchen to sit with Cindy. I still find it uncomfortable to eat with them, but I am getting better. It's much easier when it's one on one.

"Did you make these today?" I ask her, the scent of freshly baked cookies floating through the air. "They smell amazing." Sitting next to her, I can see that my compliment makes her happy. That's good, it's not my intention to make her always feel uncomfortable. I feel like more often than not, I *do* make her feel awkward. Especially after that terrible dinner last month when her sons were here.

I close my eyes when I hear their voices again, yelling at me for being rude and ungrateful, calling me a brat. Then Cindy and Jeff asking them to stay away from their home until I'm gone. That's the main reason I need to leave tomorrow. I refuse to stay one day longer where they don't allow their sons to visit.

"I did. I made them this morning. There are some extras packed away for you to take, if you'd like?" She really is a kind lady, and I *will* miss her.

"I'd be happy to, thank you." Taking a cookie from the plate she pushes toward me, I nibble at it after subtly looking at her to make sure it's okay. I know in my head it is, it's just sometimes tough convincing my body of it.

"Of course! Listen, I wanted to ask you something and I need you to know that the decision is entirely up to you." My hand freezes with the cookie in my mouth as I look to her.

I force myself to swallow the food in my mouth and then clear my throat. "Umm, okay? What do you need?"

She reaches forward and squeezes my hand I've rested on the counter. "Well, it's about Rhett and Fallon." I suck in a breath and she squeezes my hand again reassuringly. "They would very much like to come to dinner tonight to help celebrate your birthday and be a part of seeing you off."

My heart was pounding at the beginning of her statement when she mentioned that they wanted to come, but the fact that they only want to come to see me off? That knowledge hurts. I clear my throat once more and squeeze her hand before pulling mine away, clasping the other in my lap.

Cindy looks a little confused by my withdrawal and straightens. "Lily?"

"It's f-fine... if they want to come. This is your home, and they're your sons. It shouldn't be up to me for you to have them over for dinner." I fight my emotions hard to stop the hurt from showing up on my face. If I'm unsuccessful, she doesn't call me out on it.

"Lily, that's not what... honey, it's important to us that you are comfortable. Fallon and Rhett both felt like they made a mistake when you all met, and they have been asking to come to-"

"Cindy, please. Honestly. It's not a problem. I'm sure both you and Jeff would like to see them as well. I would never expect you to keep them away. They are your family. I'm going to finish getting my stuff together. I do want you to know that I have appreciated everything you and Jeff have done for me. Opening your home when it was already so full really meant a lot. Thank you so much." Standing up, I give Cindy a quick hug before backing away.

"You're a special girl, Lily. We really wish you wanted to stay longer." I know she feels like she has to say that, it's one of those things that people just say because it's the polite thing to do. "I'll let the boys know that they can come. We are planning to eat around 5:30. Let me know if there's anything I can do to help you."

"I will." Smiling once more, I head out of the kitchen and back into my room. I stay there for the rest of the afternoon after I finish loading my car. I'm leaving with a few extra things that I hadn't expected. Yesterday morning, I came to my room and found a few bags holding a towel set, bed sheets, a four-person set of dishes, and also a small box containing a couple different sized pots and pans for cooking.

Last month, I would have tried to give them back, but I know that they really do care about not just sending me off to fend for myself. I didn't lie to her when I said that I appreciated everything they've done for me. They saved my life and I'll be forever grateful to them.

I look at the clock when I hear a couple car doors slam. Seeing that it's almost 5 in the evening, my nerves start to pick up. I've already heard the others moving around the house and sometimes passing by the door to my room, so I know it's got to be *them*. I really wish I could just stay in here until it's time to leave in the morning.

Listening, I hear them chatting and laughing along with their parents and the other three. Another pang of hurt, this one stemming from jealousy, stabs my chest. I've heard the other kids talk about the boys and how they've done things with them and taken them places. It's like the two boys accepted everyone else immediately, problems and all, but with me it was an instant dislike. I push the thoughts of *what's wrong with me* away when I hear a loud knocking on my door and then Carleigh's voice yelling out.

"Lily! Cindy said it's time to eat so get out here. We're fucking hungry!" God, I will *not* miss this girl.

"Carleigh, for the love of God, would you watch your mouth?" I can hear Cindy scold her, probably yelling from the kitchen.

Carleigh is mumbling, "Yeah yeah," as she walks away from my door to head back downstairs.

Shit. I sit down a minute to get my nerves under control. It's silly to let them affect me so much. Their opinion shouldn't matter anymore because by this time tomorrow I'll be settled into a new apartment, on my own, with no one to answer to or anyone to judge me. Still, I'm not looking forward to hearing about my failings described to the two people who have come to mean a lot to me, even if I find it difficult to express it to them.

*You're better than this Lily. You're not a coward. Don't let the opinions of strangers dictate how you feel about yourself.* A little self-talk and motivation never hurt anyone. Taking a deep breath, I force myself to head down there.

By the time I make it to the bottom of the stairs, I can hear everyone gathering in the dining room, setting things on the table and moving chairs around. "Seriously, is she gonna come down anytime soon?" Carleigh whines.

I freeze when I hear the new voice answer her, knowing it's either Fallon or Rhett. "Carleigh, leave her be. We'll all get to eat soon enough."

Gripping the bottom of my shirt, I realize I can't do this. I can't face them again. Not with their comments and judgements and *anger*. My stomach is rolling and my appetite is completely disappearing. No way can I eat in front of them.

"Hey there, Lily." My body jolts to the side, away from the voice behind me, like I've been electrocuted, and I slam my shoulder into the wall. *Fuck!* That hurt. "Shit. Sorry, I didn't mean to scare you."

Looking around, I see that it's Fallon, standing only a few feet away from me, studying me with creased brows. Nodding my head, I will my heart rate to slow down. "It's o-okay." Christ, that's embarrassing, like falling down the stairs in front of a bunch of people.

He takes a step closer to me, not taking his eyes from my face. "You sure? You hit the wall pretty hard." He starts to reach out for me and that's all I need to hurry myself along.

"I'm alright. Thank you." I hurry to move into the dining room, away from Fallon and find my regular seat next to Cindy.

"There you are sweetheart. I hope you brought your appetite because the girls and I put together a feast!" Cindy reaches her hand out and pats my thigh once I'm settled. I avoid looking around because I don't know where Fallon and Rhett are sitting, and I'm going to try my best to stay off their radar this time.

"Hey guys," Jeff says as he walks into the room. "It's nice to see you here," he tells them, stopping behind me and bringing his hand to rest on my shoulder. Leaning down to catch my eye, he softens his voice and gives me a gentle smile when I look up at him. "Happy birthday Lily... well, happy a-day-early-birthday!"

Keeping my voice low, I thank him, "Thank you, Jeff. And you too Cindy, this all smells really good." I squeeze the hand she still rests on my thigh and I know that's all she needed, since she lets go after that.

Pearl shouts out at all of us, "We helped too, Lily! I made the garlic bread." This girl has an incredible amount of energy, but she has a sweet heart. Looking over at her, I give her a genuine smile.

"Thank you, Pearl, and you too Carleigh. It means a lot," I tell them and then shoot my eyes to my right when I hear an intake of breath. My eyes lock onto bright blue eyes directly in front of me. Rhett.

He's staring at me like he's never seen me before and my smile for Pearl falters, then falls from my face. Movement to my right has me seeing Fallon pulling out the chair at the end of the table. Gulping, I realize that I'm stuck at the end of the table with both of them.

The nerves are back tenfold and I don't know how I'm going to get through dinner tonight. *Please Lily, don't fuck this up again.* I beg myself, closing my eyes to calm down.

Once I open them again, I see that both of them are still staring at me. Not with anger this time, at least not yet. More like they're uncomfortable being around me. Also, not what I want.

Sucking it up, I force a smile and look back at Rhett, noticing his eyes widen almost imperceptibly. "It's umm… it's nice to see you again, Rhett." Looking over at Fallon, I include him as well, "and Fallon. Sorry about earlier. Thanks for coming…" Trailing off, I feel odd about thanking them for coming to their own home.

At least now the niceties are out of the way. There's no way they can complain about my manners, and once I get through this meal, it'll be over. Looking down at my plate, I see that it's already been made up. A massive piece of lasagna, Caesar salad, and some garlic bread with melted cheese on top.

I almost feel a little queasy over the amount of food piled on my plate and I look over to Cindy, panicked over how much food this is. There's no way I can eat all of this, and I don't want the guys to think that I'm wasting food.

Leaning over and whispering to me, Cindy tries to be encouraging, "Just do your best. The girls made up everyone's plates. Just eat what you want and we can wrap the rest up for you to take for leftovers. Alright?" She reaches over and tucks a piece of my hair behind my ear.

I try not to nod like crazy and attempt to blink those damn tears away… again. I'm really fucking overwhelmed right now, and the two giant men across and to the right of me are the main reason for it.

"Everyone, dig in!" Jeff says, *thank God*, and moves the attention away from me. Picking up their forks, most of them dive into their meal without hesitation.

I pick mine up slowly and notice from the corner of my eye that neither Rhett nor Fallon have started eating either. Stabbing a piece of lettuce with my fork, I bring it to my mouth and chew. It should be amazing, but all I can taste is sandpaper.

"So, Lily. Tell us about your plans," Fallon says, finally picking up his fork and taking a bite from his own plate.

Fuck my life. Here comes the inquisition.

# Chapter 4

## *Fallon*

Watching Lily take a bite of her dinner is enough to show me that Rhett and I were so wrong last time. It's clear that she's uncomfortable eating around people and it just reminds me again how much of an ass I was last time we were here.

I can also tell that she's uncomfortable sitting here with the two of us which hurts more than I would expect it to. The impression we made on her was bad enough that just saying hello to her in the hallway had her jumping and running away as fast as she could.

My plan was to wait out in the hallway to try and catch her alone to apologize for the way we treated her, but it didn't feel right when she was staring up at me with fear. *Never* would I think that a woman would be afraid of me. At least not like this.

The two of us have been talking with our parents regularly since we left last month and have learned quite a bit about Lily through their updates. They never did get her back to the point where she wasn't afraid that they would take away her food or punish her for eating it. Instead, she eats very little with the family and then takes food that mom has slipped to her up to her room to finish eating alone. She trusted them before we came, but not anymore. That's on us. It's also on us to make it up to her.

It's quite noticeable how much she's changed in a month. She's still thin, but there's a softness to her now that radiates health. It's a relief to see.

It's clear that it took a lot of effort to thank us for coming when we sat down. But she *did*, and it's just another example of how badly we misread her. It's obvious that she's sweet, and our parents clearly adore her.

Taking a bite of food, I look at Rhett and see him staring at her. He was caught off guard when she smiled at him and seems tongue tied now. Her smile completely transformed her face from lovely to absolutely gorgeous. Clearing my throat, I try to start a conversation so she can learn that we aren't bad guys.

"So, Lily. Tell us about your plans," I ask, taking a bite of mom's lasagna. So good.

She works her throat a moment, maybe not expecting the question. "I'm moving into an apartment over in Pennburg where I've got a job lined up to start next week." I knew this from dad, but I like that she's answering me.

"What will you be doing?" She'll be an administrative assistant at a small accounting firm while also going to school. Again, information from dad.

Chewing on her lip, she looks at mom again like she's unsure of why I'm asking. "Umm, just some filing and answering phones." She goes to take another bite, but not before checking to see if Rhett and I are watching her. We are, and another rush of guilt hits me when I watch her hand tremble as she forces another piece of lettuce in her mouth.

"Pennburg?" Rhett asks, then points between the two of us. "That's where we have our shop. Where in the city will you be living?"

"In an apartment building on the south side of town." I wrinkle my brows, there aren't a lot of decent places there and it's got a higher crime rate than any other parts.

Looking at dad, I ask, "Have you seen where she'll be staying? That area of town isn't the greatest."

"I haven't. She found the place by herself and got signed up with a lease. Enrolled in school there, too." He smiles at Lily, clearly proud of her and I watch as she flushes. I didn't know that and I can't help the surprise.

"Really?" I wince when I realize she took that the wrong way when she stiffens, a little scowl on her face. "That's great!" I tell her. Fuck, why is this so hard? That sounded fake as fuck.

"Thanks," she says, a hint of sarcasm laced in there.

Mom rubs her back reassuringly and Lily gives her a more natural smile, even if it's barely there. "She did good. Has funding all lined up. Her place is within walking distance of both her job and the school."

Scratching his jaw, it's clear to me that Rhett is just as concerned about where she'll be living as I am. "That's great that you've got it all planned out. That your car out in the driveway?"

"Yeah, I bought it last week so I'd be able to get around after I move." Mom's smile falters when she mentions moving. I know she doesn't want Lily to leave yet and hasn't been able to get her to even consider staying awhile longer.

Carleigh joins the conversation, "And I get her room when she's gone!"

"*What?* That's not fair!" Kevin says, looking to mom. "Seriously? Why does she get it? I'm bigger than her! I need the space."

Sighing, mom tells him, "Nobody is moving rooms. Where would she stay when she comes to visit if you take her room?"

Carleigh whips her head around to look at everyone and then glares at Lily, "Wait, you're gonna come back here?"

I watch as Lily looks embarrassed at the question, like she's hurt that the two of them don't care she's leaving. "Of course, she'll come visit," Rhett steps in. In an attempt to redirect away from Carleigh's rude comment, he asks Lily, "So, mom and dad told us you were moving. What time are you leaving?"

"Not soon enough," that little asshole mumbles and I've never wanted to strangle someone so much.

"Carleigh!" I snap at her. "Come on, there's no reason to be mean."

"He's right honey, you need to be aware of how your words can hurt someone's feelings," mom adds.

"But it's not fair that I'm stuck sharing a room with Pearl just because she showed up. I'm the one that had to move!" she whines, looking around for support.

Lily's face is turning red and she's gripping her napkin, clearly upset with the direction this is taking. "Enough Carleigh, or you can leave the room," dad tells her, and she finally shuts up.

I try to get back on topic, "Rhett and I have lived in Pennburg for a while, are you sure that's where you want to go? Have you looked at other areas with schools?" I really am concerned about where she'll be staying. "You don't want to stay here awhile longer to check out other options? I'm sure you could still do school from here as well."

There's a flash of something in her eyes when she looks at me this time, not nervous for once. "Yes. I'm positive. It's where I want to go."

Rhett is still glaring at Carleigh when he asks a bit more aggressively than I'm sure he intended, "So when did you say you were leaving, Lily?"

"Rhett," I say under my breath to get his attention. He doesn't realize it, but the way he asked sounded like he wanted her to leave.

I know it's not what he meant, he was just trying to get back on topic after Carleigh's rudeness and didn't temper his tone.

"What?" He looks at me, then at Lily and immediately sees she's misunderstood him. "*Fuck*," he whispers.

Mom grabs her hand that now has white knuckles. "Honey, that came out wrong."

Lily shakes her head and pulls her hand from mom's and mom looks despondent when she pushes her chair out to stand up.

"Lily, sweetheart…" dad calls to her and she gives him a tight smile.

"It's alright," then turning to mom, "Thank you for dinner. It was really good and I would love to take it with me if it's not a problem." Mom tries to say something back but Lily doesn't give her a chance when she turns her eyes on us. "Look, I know you both aren't thrilled I'm here and I'm sorry that you got banned from coming home because of me."

Sucking in a breath, I look at mom and she looks sick. I don't think she knew that Lily knew about that. Lily doesn't stop. "I can't change the fact that my birthday isn't until tomorrow, so I'm *so* sorry that I'm not out of your hair sooner than you had wanted."

Shaking his head, Rhett starts to tell her she's wrong, "No, Lily that's not wh-" but she interrupts.

"Pennburg is a big city. You don't need to be bothered that I'll be living near you, I promise, I won't get in your way. Just… give me a damn chance to leave. I'm literally leaving as *soon* as I can for you guys. I don't know what your problem is with me, but it's not necessary to make it so obvious that you want me gone." Swallowing, she looks between the two of us and I watch as her face turns pale when she realizes everything she just said.

Looking at mom, she's shaking. Then she whispers, "Sorry…" and leaves the table. Again.

I'm frozen a moment, trying to figure out when everything went ass up. "Boys…" mom chokes out, and it's enough to get both Rhett and I moving.

"We'll fix it mom," Rhett says and both he and I rush from the table to follow Lily upstairs.

Making it to the closed door of her room, I grab Rhett's arm to stop him from just opening the door and walking in. I can hear her in there, so under my breath I tell him, "Just wait a minute." Leaning toward the door, we hear a sniffle. We both stare at each other, saying nothing. I know we are on the same page.

Grabbing the handle, he pushes the door open to her room and I follow, shutting it behind me so we'll have some privacy. Rhett is looking around, "Where-"

Both of us spin when we hear her gasp and see her sitting on the floor against the wall next to the door.

"*Goddamnit*," I say under my breath. It's obvious she's been crying. She's staring at us, eyes wide as saucers and fucking petrified.

"Lily," Rhett says gently, "I wasn't trying to imply-"

He stops when her breathing picks up, and she's looking back and forth between the two of us. She's panicking and us towering over her like this is causing it.

"Baby girl, no," I tell her, and stop when she holds her hands up to us to ward us off.

Choking on a sob, we watch as she squeezes her eyes shut and begs us, "I'm so sorry. I shouldn't have spoken to you like that. I swear, it won't happen again. I'll stay up here and I'll be gone by morning. P-Please…"

I can feel the same look of horror that's on Rhett's face, spread over mine. The fuck did those bastards do to this girl?

Swallowing back bile, I tug on my short beard and look to my brother, but he's breathing heavily, frozen in his spot. I know that he recognizes the same trauma in her that he and I both experienced from our childhoods prior to being taken in by mom and dad.

I can't stand here another second with her thinking that we would, or are capable of, hurting her, particularly in the way she's obviously been hurt before. It's apparent our height isn't helping, so I make a quick decision and ignore the quick thump of my heart knowing that I'm about to touch her.

Coming closer, I lean down to pick her up and move to her bed to sit with her as quickly as I can. She fights me, pushing my arms to let her go, but I hold firm. Sitting on the end of her bed, I flip her around to straddle my legs so I can look at her face.

Rhett is close behind and sits next to us, and then we both wrap our arms around her until she realizes we aren't going to hurt her.

# Chapter 5

## *Lily*

I'm stunned when Fallon picks me up from my spot and sets me in his lap, sitting down himself. *What the fuck is happening right now?*

After my embarrassing outburst at dinner, the only thing I could think to do was run. I was so ashamed for having talked to them like that. I only have twelve or so hours left here, there's no reason I couldn't have just kept my mouth shut. I just snapped at the fact that, with still not knowing me, they seemed so insistent that I leave, or at least not go to their town.

I wasn't expecting them to follow me and barge into my room. Panic took over everything else I was feeling and I just reacted. Both of them are so much taller than most men, like 6'2 or 6'3. If you combine that with their broad shoulders, thick arms and thighs, the beard on Fallon and the piercings and tattoos on Rhett, they're intimidating.

So was my old foster father. Maybe not as wide as these two, but he still towered, and when he towered, I got hurt.

When Fallon picked me up, it was what pushed me over the edge and I fought. His arms are too strong to push away, but I tried my hardest to get my hands under his to try and pry them from me. Crying out, I squeeze my eyes closed when I feel my body spin and find myself straddling his lap, his legs so wide that I can feel the pull in my hips.

He's got his arms wrapped around me, one arm across my upper back, the other my lower back and I'm pressed to his chest. I try to push him back once more and when I do, I feel Rhett's arms slide in front of me as he wraps himself around my back.

I'm pinned. I can't *breathe*.

"Let *go!*" I yell out, but they ignore me. I can hear them both speaking to me in low, hushed voices. What they're saying is escaping my ears. I can't hear anything over the sound of blood rushing in my head and the pounding of my heartbeat.

They keep me like this for I don't know how long, until finally a few of their words start to break through to me. '...*Safe... it's okay... won't hurt you... you're alright...*' One of them is running a hand through my hair and pushing it back from my face, there's another wiping tears off my cheeks and speaking his words against my forehead.

I begin to calm down and take a moment to catch my breath, but still come back to my original thought. *What the fuck is happening right now?*

"Baby..." Fallon coos at me. "You're okay. You've done nothing wrong."

Rhett picks up, "we aren't going to let you go until you've calmed down, until you know we aren't here to hurt you." He runs his hand through my hair again, it must have been him doing it the whole time. "We aren't angry with you, not at all."

Fallon runs his hand over my wet cheeks again before slipping it under my chin to tilt up so I'm forced to look at him. "Take a breath and hold it." He sucks in air to show me what he wants me to do and I copy him.

After doing this a few times, I calm a bit more, but my throat is still so tight that I know I can't say anything yet. He continues breathing with me and Rhett is still stroking my hair. "There you go... just like that. Feeling better?" Fallon asks.

I give him a stiff head nod but keep my lips pressed together. I can feel the vibrations in Rhett's chest that's plastered to my back when he speaks next, "We're sorry that it came across like we were pushing you to leave here. That wasn't it at all. Our parents have kept us up to date on you since we botched the *last* time we met, and we really were curious about your plans. No ill intentions, we swear."

Looking over my shoulder, I can see the honesty in his eyes. I try to give him the benefit of the doubt, nodding my head. With a small but genuine smile for me, he continues, "I'm going to let you go now so you don't feel so squished between us." Fallon chuckles and I feel the vibrations from *his* chest at my front.

Releasing me, he doesn't move away, just sits back on my bed and gets more comfortable. I move to slide off Fallon's lap and am surprised when he doesn't loosen his hold the way Rhett did.

Looking at him, I give him a confused look and he laughs again. "I like having you here, plus it's easier to talk. This way, if you get upset again, you'll already be right here."

Clearing my throat, I look at him and then Rhett. "I'm not really sure what to say… I am sorry for the way I spoke to you. This is your home, and it was-"

"No Lily," says Rhett, "this is *your* home. We've been gone for over fifteen years. We should have been put in our places last time we were here."

"Well, we *were* put in our places, but by our parents. We are really very sorry for assuming the worst of you. It's not an excuse, but we are just protective of them. They've had a rough go of it for the last few years with some of the foster kids they've taken in and we were already on the defense," says Fallon.

"It's fine," I whisper. It is I suppose. "No harm done."

"It's not fine, but thank you for not holding it against us. And we did do harm to you. They said you struggle with food and we made that worse by the things we said." I stiffen when Rhett says that, embarrassed that they've talked about my eating habits.

Pulling me into him, Fallon lays my head against his chest but keeps my face turned toward Rhett. "Don't be embarrassed by it. We understand more than you know. Both Rhett and I came from situations where food was limited and we found ourselves hungry a lot."

"Which is why we should have picked up on what was happening and not making assumptions." Rhett leans forward so he's more in my line of sight and runs his hand down my spine.

The touch makes me shiver, causing goosebumps to pop up on my arms. I see a flash of heat cross his face before he locks it back up, and Fallon tightens his arms marginally. Both of their reactions, even though they were subtle, make me aware of the predicament I'm in.

I'm still on Fallon's lap, legs spread open and over his and the entirety of my body is pressed along the length of him. Just from his steady breathing, I can feel his muscles rolling under his skin, along his chest and in his arms.

Rhett meets Fallon's gaze for a moment. I'm not sure what they communicate, and I don't ask. Whatever it was has Fallon relaxing his arms. I take that as a sign that he's ready for me to move away from him, so I put my hands on his chest to steady myself as I stand up. My toes have barely hit the floor when Rhett grabs my waist and arranges me on his lap the same way I was just on Fallon's.

Leaning back, I look at him, "What are you-"

He buries my face into his chest, and I can hear the smile in his voice when he tells me, "I wanted my chance to hold you as well." *Shit.* Fallon is still laughing when I look at him. He's leaned back, bracing himself on his arms while watching us. When he sees me looking, he winks.

My face explodes with heat, and I squeeze my eyes shut. I feel a soft kiss at the top of my head, then a rumble, "You going to be okay?"

I move to pull back, and just like Fallon, Rhett doesn't budge, keeping me locked into him. I sigh, "Yes. Maybe we all just over reacted. I'm probably on edge too… with moving to be on my own for the first time."

"Do you need any help? And are you sure you're going to a decent place?" I can hear the concern in his voice, and Fallon agrees.

"It's not too late to decide to stay longer. I know they wouldn't mind you staying however long you needed to," he says.

This time I pull myself away, and Rhett reluctantly lets me go. Standing in front of them, I wrap an arm around my body to hold onto an elbow while looking between the two of them. "It's not a bad place. Obviously, it's not going to be amazing. I'm only eighteen and a lot of places won't rent to someone my age. But it's affordable and the location is convenient."

I can see that they don't love that answer, but there's nothing really to argue about. It's all the truth and reasonable. "What about needing help?" Fallon asks.

Shaking my head, I give him a smile. "No. I've only got a few boxes of stuff. I doubt it'll take me more than 15 minutes to take it all up. The place has a few pieces of furniture already and I'll work on getting whatever I need after I see what's there.

Rhett furrows his brow, "You haven't been there yet?"

"That doesn't seem like a good idea," Fallon says, adding in his opinion.

"No… but I've seen some pictures of the types of units they have and did my research. There weren't any horror stories or anything and the guy that manages the building seems nice." I'm trying not to get defensive. These are all the same questions that Jeff had when I had discussed my plans with him and Cindy.

They look at each other and then, like twins, they both sit up and lean forward, fully focused on me. Both studying me, I decide to study them right back. It's like we are in a standoff, waiting to see who will break first. It's confusing and I can't really keep the look of displeasure with their arguments off my face.

Rhett cracks first and drops his face to laugh, rubbing his hands over his face before looking back at me with a raised eyebrow. "You're a stubborn thing, aren't you?"

"Umm… not normally, no…" my serious response to his question has Fallon laughing now as well.

I think I hear him say, "She's something else," to Fallon and Fallon say, "Adorable," but they both speak at the same time and over each other so I can't be sure.

My face heats a bit more now, standing here under their scrutiny, and I want us all to move past this. Looking away from them, I let my eyes wander over my room. It's so bare right now. I didn't fully make it my space because I knew I wouldn't stay long here, but the few touches I had put on the space are now boxed away. It's the first room that's been *mine* since dad died and there's a comfort here that I'll miss.

"You look sad," says Rhett, and I turn back to face them both.

"In a way I am. I'll miss this room. Maybe it's the safety I felt in here, but it's the first time I felt any measure of 'home' since I was 12. It's a little bittersweet to see it empty and packed up." I can't help my eyes watering at the emotional rush from dumping that on them, so I smile to show I'm not *only* sad.

Rhett stands up and takes the few steps to me, not caring about being inside my personal space. My neck has to tip back pretty far to look up at him, waiting to see what he's going to say.

Cupping my cheek gently, he studies me. "Don't be a stranger to them. I promise you that you mean a lot to both of our parents and they are going to be worried for a while. Besides, you're not going to be able to fully get away, we live awfully close to you." This time *he* gives me a wink, leans down to kiss my cheek, and then pulls me into a hug. Speaking into my hair so only I can hear, he mumbles out, "I really am sorry for treating you the way I did last month and for the misunderstanding tonight. You're a sweet girl and I wish we had the last month to get to know you more. Easily fixed though."

"What do you mean?" I pull back from the hug, putting some distance between us. Both of them have this presence that can feel overwhelming in double doses like this.

"I *mean*, we're not going to be strangers. You'll have to suck it up." Grinning widely, he laughs at the shock on my face. Brushing his thumb over my chin, he looks at it and says, "…something else," to himself.

We stand there silently for a few moments, Rhett's eyes looking over my face and I can't help but feel a rush of heat in my cheeks at the look of interest in his eyes. Well, at least I *think* it's interest. I'm not sure since I've never really experienced it before.

"We're going to be staying the night here tonight so we can be with them to see you off and also help you with your move," Fallon tells me, coming up behind Rhett who clears his throat and moves away so Fallon can take his place in front of me.

"You really don't need to waste your time. There's not much to do," I argue.

"It's not a waste of time and we want to help. Besides, we owe it to you for being assholes." My mood sinks a little, but I don't allow it to change my expression. He bends down to give me a hug and a kiss on the cheek as well. "Sleep well and we'll see you in the morning."

"You too… both of you," I include Rhett.

"Goodnight Lily," he says and then I watch the both of them leave my room.

I release a massive breath when I'm alone again. That was… I don't even know what that was. Clearly, they feel bad, and I appreciate that they apologized. There is a feeling of disappointment that they are insisting that they help me as repayment for what happened.

I had planned on leaving early anyways, maybe I'll just sneak out a tad earlier. They don't need to help me just because they feel bad.

Grabbing a sheet of paper, I write a quick note thanking Cindy and Jeff for everything they've done for me. A sentence saying goodbye to the twins and Pearl, and then one letting Fallon and Rhett off the hook for tomorrow. Then I change into a sleep shirt and change my morning alarm for an hour earlier than I had planned.

I'll just touch bases after I've settled into my new apartment.

# Chapter 6

## *Rhett*

Shutting the door to Lily's room, I turn to Fallon with a raised eyebrow, "That went... well?"

Huffing out a laugh, he shakes his head at me, "Yeah, I think so." Jerking his head in the direction of the stairs, we head back down to find mom and dad sitting at the kitchen counter, the other three kids absent.

Mom's eyes are glassy like she's been crying, and she looks up at both of us when we walk in. "*Please*, tell me she's okay?"

"What happened in there?" dad asks.

Fallon takes a seat next to mom and gives her a side hug while I lean back against the counter with crossed arms. Fuck, what a night. "Don't worry ma, she's alright. She got the impression from tonight-"

"Combined with last time we were here..." Fallon interrupts.

"Yeah, combined with all of that visit, that our questions were to push her out of the house and that we weren't happy with her moving to our town." Mom's eyes widen and she opens her mouth to say something, but I just hold up my hand. "She doesn't believe that now. We explained that we truly were asking because we wanted to know and had no ulterior motives."

Looking at Fallon, I nod for him to continue. "We also apologized for how we treated her last month. She seemed like she was okay, so I think we are good."

"Good," dad says. "I'm sure that was important for her to hear."

"Yeah, but I've got to ask… do you know details of how that last foster home treated her? I know you mentioned the food thing and that she suffered some abuse there, but do you know any other details?"

Mom shakes her head, "Not really. Her case worker just gave us the brief overview. Their biggest concern was lack of nutrition and encouraged us to work on that. She was physically abused, but to what degree we aren't sure. Lily was adamant that there was no sexual abuse, so that was a relief. I assume she was most likely smacked around quite a bit though."

Tilting my head to the side, I think about that and then look to Fallon. "That would make sense." Our parents look at me questioningly, so I fill them in on what happened when we first got in there. "When she was sitting against the wall when we came in, we were both standing over her and she panicked, held her arms out to stop us and apologized like we were going to hit her or something."

"…Jesus," dad mutters.

Fallon squeezes mom's shoulder when she starts to cry quietly. "We worked through it, and I think we left her knowing that we would never hurt her. Even got a couple hugs out of her!" he teases.

Mom whips her head up to look at him, then to me. "Really? Because I've been working with her for a while, and she just started to accept physical affection from me recently. She's pretty closed off."

I want to puff my chest a little at that. Dad eyes both of us like he's figuring something out, but he doesn't say anything. "I dunno, but it worked out okay, I think. We're going to stick around for the night and help her move in the morning, check out this apartment she's moving into."

Fallon asks, "Have either of you gotten any information on it? Been by there at all?"

"No, well, sort of yes. She showed me the listing and asked for some advice. It doesn't look awesome, but not too bad either. We tried to convince her to stay longer, but she wasn't hearing it. At her age, I think it's about the best we could hope for," dad says, scratching his cheek and leaning back in his chair. "You boys are going there with her?"

"That's the plan," says Fallon.

"I don't like the area she's in. It'll make me feel better to at least see it," I tell them and I can tell that both are relieved about it. "We're going to try and get some sleep. I'm sure that Lily will be up with the sun, ready to head out."

Mom stands up and gives Fallon a kiss on the side of his head and then walks over to me, arms open for a hug. I wrap her up and reassure her, "We'll make sure she's alright mom. Don't worry too much."

Stepping back, she cups my cheek and nods her head. "You two are good boys. Be kind to her."

"Promise we will. Night ma." I kiss her cheek.

Dad jerks his head at us to wait a moment and while she heads out of the room.

"What's up dad?" I ask him.

He's got his arms crossed, studying the two of us. I look at my brother with a raised eyebrow and he just shrugs his shoulders. Finally, dad leans forward and clasps his hands. "You boys are interested in her, aren't you?"

Fallon's eyes widen a fraction and I can't stop the smirk from crossing my lips. "Yeah... we are. Well, I am. Fallon?" I look at him.

He's scratching his beard while he considers what he should say. Then, slowly he nods his head and answers, "...Yes. Obviously, we don't know her well yet, but there's something about her. I feel enough that I'd like to pursue it." He studies dad, then asks, "is that going to be a problem for you or mom?"

"No. I just need you boys to go slow with her. I don't think she has much of any experience in the dating scene and with two of you, it will probably be overwhelming for her." I can hear the concern in his voice so I rush to ease his mind.

"Dad, we would never push her. We'll help her with the move, stick around for a bit to make sure she's settled and then from there, see if this could go anywhere."

"Good," he nods and then stands up. "Good. You both are good guys, be good to her. I don't think she's had much love in her life for a long while. I think you both would be good for her."

Smiling at him, I give Fallon an elbow and jerk my head over my shoulder. "Let's get some sleep. Night dad."

"Night dad," Fallon repeats.

"G'night boys. Thanks for making tonight right for her." He smacks us on the shoulder as he walks past us out of the room.

I follow Fallon to get some sleep, feeling really good about how this night ended.

Waking the next morning, I shake Fallon to get up. It's still dark out, but I want us both up and ready to go so that Lily doesn't have to wait on us.

It only takes us about 20 minutes until we've got a pot of coffee going and we are settled at the table to wait for the rest of the household to get moving. I can't help the smile from spreading when I hear light feet coming down the stairs. It's clear that our Lily is trying to sneak out.

Raising an eyebrow at me, Fallon holds a finger up to stop me from saying anything and we both wait, trying not to laugh when she turns the corner and stops with wide eyes looking back and forth between the two of us.

"Good morning, Lily. You're up early." There's a smile behind his voice and I bite my cheek as we watch the blush spread across her face.

Clearing my throat, she jerks her gaze over to me, and I ask, "Would you like some coffee?"

"Umm… no thank you. Why are you up this early?" Yeah, she was trying to sneak out on us. I'm not upset about it, but I am curious as to why.

Fallon beats me to answer her question, "We wanted to make sure we were ready to go so you weren't waiting on us." Taking a sip of his coffee, he watches her over the rim of his cup.

"You guys really don't need to help me. I'll be fine getting there."

"We know you'll be fine," I say. "We still would like to help."

Biting her lip, she considers us. "I don't want you feeling like you have to. You don't owe me anything."

Confused, I tell her, "Lily, we don't feel like we owe you anything. We *want* to help you. Please, let us?"

Sighing, she rubs her forehead like she's getting a headache. "Alright… I just don't want you to do it because you feel like you're obligated." Looking around, she walks over to a spot on the counter that's empty and sets down a folded piece of paper.

"What's that?" Fallon asks her.

I can't stop my body reacting to how gorgeous she is when she looks back at him over her shoulder with a small smile. "It's a note for Jeff and Cindy. I didn't want them to make it a big thing while I was leaving this morning, so I had planned to head out before anyone got up."

"Ma will want to say goodbye, Lily," I tell her gently. It's not my intention to guilt her, but mom would be hurt if she snuck out.

Shoulders slumping, she picks the note back up, folds it and puts it in her pocket. In a soft voice, she says, "I'll wait for her…"

I look at Fallon, but he hasn't stopped staring at her. I know him well enough that he's really interested in her and is trying to figure out how he wants to handle it. Finally, he feels my gaze on him and meets my eye. I smirk at him and he smiles back. We are definitely on the same page.

Looking back at her, I watch her find a seat at the table, oblivious to our silent communication. Reaching forward to grab her wrist and her attention, I wait for her eye contact, then reassure her, "It'll mean a lot to her. You'll still be able to sneak out since she's always the first one down here." I give her a gentle squeeze and then pull my hand back.

She stares where my hand just was and then rubs it with her hand, placing them both in her lap.

The three of us wait until ma makes her way into the kitchen. She looks between all of us. "What's going on?"

Jumping up, Lily walks over to her and looks uncomfortable for a moment before leaning in and wrapping her arms around our mom. She looks at us over Lily's shoulder, eyes filling with tears while she hugs her back and squeezes. She pulls back only slightly before cupping Lily's cheeks. "You will *not* be a stranger, you hear me? Let me know as soon as you get settled in tonight to let me know you're okay." Then mom leans forward to give her a kiss on the forehead.

Nodding, Lily whispers, "I will. I promise. Thank you for everything, Cindy." She squeezes ma's wrists and then pulls away to go outside. She doesn't look at either of us as she quickly wipes her eyes and then heads outside to her car. We've got her parked in so I'm not worried that she'll take off.

Biting her lip, ma looks at us helplessly. Fallon gives her a quick hug and then I do the same, promising we will watch out for her.

When I get to the truck, Fallon is leaning down to talk to Lily through the window. She nods her head and he brushes a knuckle against her cheek. Smiling, he backs up and hops in the truck next to me.

"What'd you say to her?" I ask.

Smiling, he buckles up as I back out of the driveway to give her enough space to back out so we can follow. "I got the address to her apartment in case we lose her, and told her she did good with mom." He puts in the address, and we settle in for the thirty-minute drive to her new place.

Once we get off the highway and start driving through Pennburg, I find myself glaring at the area. The longer we drive, the more and more pissed we become. "Are you fucking kidding me?" I mutter when we make the final turn onto her street.

"Rhett, she cannot stay here." He's grinding his teeth while looking around at all the shady people hanging around outside. There's garbage in the street, music pounding from somewhere, and there are a few buildings that look like they're condemned.

"I *know*," I growl, throwing the truck into park when we stop in front of a three-story building that doesn't look any better than the rest of them here. Fallon is out of the truck before me and I hurry to catch up to him.

"Baby girl, you cannot stay here," he's saying before I've even made it to them. I watch her face harden and she squares her shoulders.

"This place will be fine for now, Fallon. I don't plan on staying forever, but it'll get me by." I know she thinks she's being reasonable, but I don't feel good about leaving her here.

"Rhett, help me out here. Tell her this is a bad idea and you agree with me."

I'm ready to argue with her because I absolutely agree with him, but she's quick to stop me. "Look, I haven't even been inside yet. This is my choice. Besides, I've been in a lot worse, I can handle myself."

I bite my tongue and try my best not to push her. "Open your trunk so we can grab your stuff." It's all I can say right now and Fallon is glaring at me. I just shake my head at him to let it be for now.

Relaxing, she thanks me as we all grab stuff and empty out her trunk. She really doesn't have a lot and all of it can be carried in one trip. Staying silent, we follow her up the stairs to the third floor. They're at least clear of debris but haven't seen a broom in a long time.

We continue on to the end of the hallway where she's the last door on the right. I can hear a loud TV from one apartment and another has a couple fighting with a baby crying. There has to be zero insulation between these walls because you can hear everything.

When she opens the door to her new apartment, the first thing I see is the condition of the furniture. Stained and torn. I also notice movement of some creepy crawly in my peripheral. Fallon sets the boxes he has down, and I stack mine on top of them.

"Lily, set your stuff down," I tell her.

She listens and puts it on the counter, looking around with furrowed brows, clearly not expecting this either.

Muttering to herself, she says, "I'm going to have to ask a-... *HEY!*" She yells out when I pick her up from behind, turn her and throw her over my shoulder. "What are you *doing*?"

She grabs hold of my shirt to keep steady when I turn and walk out the door. Passing by Fallon, I ask, "Can you get it all?"

"Yep," he says, and I keep moving, ignoring her demands to be put down.

Lily is *not* staying in this shithole.

# Chapter 7

## *Fallon*

Thank God Rhett took control of the situation because I'm about to lose it. I cannot believe the state of this apartment. Lily seems to be a smart girl with a good head on her shoulders, so there's no way this was what she was expecting.

After rearranging everything we've carried up into a way that I can grab it all, I have to bite my cheek to stop myself from laughing out loud at all the protesting and yelling that she's doing. I'm glad to see that after our talk last night, she seems less afraid to make herself heard around us.

Once I catch up and set the boxes on the back of the truck, I finally release my laugh when Rhett smacks her butt to stop her from fighting him. "Stop fighting me, Lily. Fallon, grab her keys out of her pocket."

"What in the hell are you-" she starts demanding when she feels me reach into her back pocket to grab her car keys. *"Why are you taking my keys?!"* Lily has her head turned to look up at me and is fighting her hair out of her face.

Squatting down, I bring myself eye level. "Lily, you are absolutely *not* staying here. Aside from the fact that you're in an incredibly dangerous area, that place should be condemned."

Rhett adds his two cents, "There's no way we can let you stay here."

Her eyes a filling with angry tears and her chest is heaving with heavy breaths. "It's *my* apartment. I've already paid for it! You don't get to just decide that I'm not staying here."

"Yeah… yeah we do," Rhett says and storms over to the passenger side of the truck, yanks the door open, and pulls her from his shoulder and plants her in the seat.

He wrestles the seatbelt over her while she smacks his hands. "Rhett! *Stop it!* What do you think you're doing?!"

Ignoring her, he looks quickly over to me before finally getting her buckled in. "Fallon, take her and the truck to the house. I'll drive her car." Hopping into the driver's seat, I toss the keys to him. Lily tries to catch them out of the air but Rhett is faster.

"Give me my damn keys! You can't *do* th-"

He grabs the hair at the back of her head and pulls her to him as he crushes his lips to hers, silencing her protests. I'm surprised for only a second before it transforms into jealousy and wanting. I'm not angry at him, I just wish I was him right now.

She isn't kissing him back. Lily is completely frozen, eyes wide with shock.

Pulling himself away, he looks her over for a moment before grinning and then shutting the door. Her eyes follow him to her car as she subconsciously touches her lip with her fingers. I watch her profile until Rhett is in her car and she looks over to see me staring at her.

Wrenching her hand away from her mouth, her face turns bright red, embarrassed by what just happened. I start the truck up and pull away from the building, then reach over and grab the hand she had on her lips, and squeeze it.

"You alright?" I ask her.

"...*No*..." she whispers. Swallowing deeply, she fumbles through her disjointed thoughts, clearly confused. "I... umm... what did... Rhett and that..." She coughs and then tries again, "w-why did he do... *that?*"

I really want to look over at her, but I keep my eyes on the road when I answer her, chuckling at how flustered she is, "Well, you're very beautiful Lily." I can't help but wonder how many times she's been kissed, because if her shock from that quick one from Rhett tells me anything, it means she may not have kissed a lot of guys before.

Her manic bark of laughter startles me and I glance over at her to make sure she's alright before back to the road. "Why is that funny?" I ask her.

Shaking her head, she looks away from and back out the window. "It's not funny, the opposite really... it's just absurd."

"Are you upset that he kissed you?" If she is, I'll have to let Rhett know he needs to back off. Lily doesn't know it yet, but we're going to put her up in a room at our house. I don't want her uncomfortable staying with two grown men who clearly have some interest in her.

I peak over when she doesn't answer and see her face turning red with embarrassment. Yeah, she didn't mind the kiss and I'm pretty thrilled about that. "You don't need to be embarrassed, Lily." I can't help asking my next question. "Have you kissed many people before?"

The blush deepens to a darker shade of red and she whispers, "No... I, umm... yeah, no."

Huh. Interesting. Raising a brow, I keep my voice gentle so she doesn't feel put on the spot, "Lily..."

Turning to me finally, she meets my eyes briefly, "What?"

"*Have* you been kissed before?" There's no way this girl hasn't been chased by at least a few guys by now. Again, her answer surprises me.

She mutters, "Nope," under her breath.

I'm surprised by the possessiveness that overtakes me at that knowledge. If she's never kissed anyone before, then that means she's most likely innocent in other aspects as well. Most likely a virgin. It's unintentional when I blurt out, "Are you a virgin?" I wince the moment it's out of my mouth because it's really none of my business.

Again, no answer. She just clears her throat and keeps staring out the side window, twisting her hands together. I have my answer and I make a mental note to let Rhett know before he tries to act on anything again. We don't want to scare her away.

I'm not sure what to say so I change the subject, "So… you're planning on a business administration degree. What do you want to do with it?"

Her shoulders relax slightly and I know the new topic was the right decision. "I don't have anything specific, I just thought that it was a generic enough degree that will open up the most job opportunities for me. Plus, it's only a two-year degree so I won't have to deal with a large student loan payment."

Nodding my head, I tell her, "That's reasonable, but if you weren't limited financially what would you want to do? Your dream job?"

She chews on her lip as she thinks my question over, "I'm not really sure. I've never given it much thought honestly."

Pulling up to our house, I throw the truck into park and face her. "You should give it some thought. I get making the practical decisions for the future you expect to have, but having that dream in the back of your mind may influence your choices to eventually get you there. I'm just saying, think about it."

She gives me a small smile, "I'll think about it." We both climb out as Rhett pulls up behind us in her car. Nervously, she wrings her hands like she's not sure what's going on or what the plan is. I grab her hand and walk her into the house with Rhett behind us.

"Can I use your bathroom really quick?" she asks me.

I point her in the direction of the upstairs bathroom. It will be the one she would end up using if she is willing to stay here. Plus, it'll give me a few minutes to talk to Rhett. "Up the stairs, second door on the left."

She thanks me, looks sideways at Rhett, and then heads up. I watch her until she disappears around the corner and turn quickly to Rhett. "Look, we've only got a minute, but you need to know a couple of things. We gotta take it easy with her. That kiss? I'm pretty certain that was her first kiss."

"What do you mean 'first kiss?' No way has she never kissed someone before, Fallon." He looks at me like I'm being ridiculous and I'm shaking my head almost immediately.

"I'm certain. I think you shocked the fuck out of her. I'm also positive that she's a virgin."

"Umm, that drive was like 15 minutes long. How do you go from 'Hey, we're basically kidnapping you to move you into our house' over to 'have you ever fucked anyone before?'"

Laughing softly, I take a second to listen for her movement upstairs, and when I hear the floor creak, I know it's safe to keep talking. "I know, it just sort of came up. I didn't mean to ask her, but she was red as a tomato after you shut the door on her and I was trying to be nonchalant about it. Also, fuck you man... kissing her like that! What *was* that?"

He grins, a little cocky about it, and then shrugs. "I dunno, I couldn't help it. She was fighting me and trying to knock my hands away from her seatbelt. I like her fire and I didn't think about it. Why, you jealous?" He laughs.

I scowl, "You know I am you fucker." He stands up a little straighter at the same time I hear her footsteps coming back down the stairs.

"You want something to drink, Lily?" he asks her with a smile. She's nervous again, her shoulders rigid like she's not sure what she should be doing.

"No thank you. I'm sorry if I sound rude, but why am I here?"

Taking a deep breath, Rhett and I look at each other again before I do my best to explain in the most non-confrontational way that there's *no fucking way* we are letting her stay in that shithole. We want her to stay here with us. "Lily, we have an extra room that you're welcome to take for however long you want to stay here."

"We don't feel comfortable with you in that apartment, and if mom and dad knew the condition we found it in, they wouldn't be okay with it either," adds Rhett, and then he winks at her. "Besides, the parents got you for this long, it should be our turn now."

"Umm... but you guys don't know me. Why would you... why would you even *want* to?"

"Baby," I croon, "look at me." I wait until I have her eyes before continuing. "I know we didn't give you the best of first impressions, but we really do want to. You're smart, beautiful, seem to have your head on your shoulders, and there's just a feeling that we both have that it's important. That *you're* important."

She bites her lip and looks at her toe as she digs them into the floor, thinking over what I've said. Rhett and I both watch her, waiting on an answer or reaction or *something*. He gets impatient. "What's your concern, sweetheart?"

"I don't feel right about just staying here…" She looks at Rhett and then me, watching for our reactions. "But I do agree that the apartment was worse than I had expected. I won't stay without contributing. I want to pay rent, help cook and clean, yard work, or anything else you think would be fair."

I can tell that he's about to argue with her, but I beat him to it. "That's fine." He glares at me but once I explain, he'll be on board. "Why don't we just agree to the same rent you had planned at the other place? That way you don't have to change up your budget. We can work the other stuff out later."

She's embarrassed again when she tells us, "I'm not sure you'll be okay with that. That apartment was pretty cheap, mainly because it was all I could afford and because of my age."

"What were you supposed to pay them?" Rhett asks.

"Umm… $350 a month," she mutters.

"I don't think that place is even worth that much. But let's stick with the $350, I'm good with that if you are, Rhett?" He's still pissed that I'm okay with her paying us. I try to widen my eyes when she isn't looking at me to get him to just go along with it.

"...Fine. Is that okay with you, Lily?" he asks her.

"What about utilities? And food and—"

"Nope. Just the $350," I say. "We can work out the food stuff later. For now, let's just agree to this and play it all by ear, yeah?" I'm really hoping she won't have any more arguments.

Sighing, she looks between the both of us again while she tries to decide. "I just… why? *Why* would you even want me here? I don't get it. Why do you care?"

I ignore my own instructions that I just gave Rhett about taking it easy and walk over to her. Standing in front of her, she tips her head back to look up at me. I cup her cheek with one hand and when she stiffens and straightens up a little, I grab her hair at the back of her head with the other.

Sucking in a breath, her eyes are wide and I flash her a quick smile before leaning in and pressing my lips against hers. My cock hardens almost immediately, just by the touch of her lips to mine and I know that this is going to be something. Her, Rhett, and I.

Brushing my mouth across hers, she gasps and I take advantage and slip my tongue into her mouth, tilting my head to the side to deepen our kiss. She's unsure at first but I relax when I feel her grip my wrist to hold on to me. Rhett clears his throat, reminding me to not get carried away. I pull back and give her one more soft kiss.

Without releasing her, I wait for her to open her eyes that she shut at some point. When she does, I can't stop the gravel in my voice, deepened from being turned on. "*That's* why, Lily. Are you okay with that?"

"With us?" Rhett adds.

Looking over my shoulder at him, she swallows and gives him a slight nod.

"We'll show you your room and bring your stuff in, alright sweetheart?" he continues. I'm still holding her face and staring at her. I'm having a hard time pulling away from her.

"Al-Alright." She looks back up at me and gives me a little half smile. Running my thumb across her cheek, I drop it and then force myself to let her go.

"Let's get your stuff and you can settle in," I say.

She takes a step back from me, puts her shoes back on and heads outside.

"Why do you want to let her pay us rent?" Rhett is quick to ask.

I shake my head at him. "There's no way that little girl is going to be okay staying here for free. We'll just throw it into an account for her and once she's comfortable enough being here with us, we'll give it back."

"...Huh. That's a good fucking idea."

I smirk at him. "That's because I'm fucking brilliant. Come on, let's get her shit inside."

# Chapter 8

## *Lily*

Two weeks.

I've been here for two weeks and I still don't know how I'm feeling about staying here.

The first few days were fine, if maybe a little awkward for me. I didn't want to intrude on their space and routines, so I made sure to keep all of my stuff in the guest room they had open for me. The upstairs has four bedrooms, two that each have their own bathrooms and Rhett and Fallon are in both of those. The other two rooms were set up as a guest room and office, plus the bathroom. It's a nice set up and I'm glad that they don't have to deal with my stuff in the bathroom.

After a few days, they encouraged me to put my touches around the house, but I've been hesitant. Not because I'm not comfortable here, but I'm not sure that *they* still want me here.

We have, I think, a decent routine going. They won't let me pay for food, so I make sure that I do as much cooking as I can. I put lunches together for everyone in the morning. They go do their thing in their shop and I alternate between going to classes and my part time job.

Normally I'm home before them, so I make sure they have something ready for dinner. Over the past couple of weeks, they've been gradually coming home a little later every night. It's to the point now that sometimes they don't get home until close to 8 at night.

I'm still struggling to eat in front of them, so I've been making myself something light to eat before they get home. Neither of them has said anything so they must be okay with me not joining them for dinner.

They said that they've got a few projects that they need to get done and have apologized for the late hours. I get it, I really do, but I can't help but feel like maybe I'm an unwelcome disturbance to their routine. Neither of them has been rude or stand-offish toward me, it's just… I think I'm friend zoned.

Touching my lips as I try to read a few chapters for one of my classes, I can't stop my mind from wandering to that first day when they both kissed me. It was my very first and second kiss I've ever gotten. It was also the last time I was kissed.

I *thought* that they were implying they were interested in something more than friends, but at this point, I don't think so. I feel stupid for misreading the entire situation and can't help but wonder if they wanted this to be more temporary that I had originally thought. I haven't been looking for another place, but maybe I should be?

Biting my lip, I can't stop the disappointment from seeping in. The time I have spent with them, I've learned a lot. They're both extremely close to each other. More than just brothers, but best friends as well. They're both hilarious and constantly telling jokes and teasing each other as well as me. Rhett is more laid back than Fallon, but Fallon has a bit of a sweeter temperament.

Rhett plays the guitar while Fallon likes to sit and draw in a sketchbook during the few times we've been able to all hang out. They've told me stories from when they first moved in with Jeff and Cindy and a little bit of their backgrounds. Fallon was removed from his parents when he was 7 after CPS was called a few times when he came to school with bruises and the teachers were concerned.

Rhett was surrendered by his mom when he was a toddler, so he doesn't remember anything about her. He was in a few different foster homes before he found his way to the Millers. Both of them were the first children they took in and the only ones they adopted.

The more I learn about them, about how strong and resilient they are, and how much they love their family, I fall for them a little more. The crushes on them are growing for me, but they seem to have pulled back.

The loud knock on the door to my room jerks me from my thoughts. "Lily?"

It's Fallon. I didn't hear either of them come into the house and looking at my watch, I'm surprised that it's only 4 and they're already home. It's Sunday and last weekend they worked late both days. "I'm here, door is unlocked," I call to him.

He sticks his head in and gives me a grin. "Hey! We got done early. Mom and dad called to see if we'd all come for dinner. I'd ask if you want to go, but they said we had to bring you, so you have no choice." He snickers.

Smiling softly, I shut my book. "Sure. Now?"

"Yup. Mom wants us to come as soon as we can so we don't have to eat late."

"It won't take me long to get ready. Should I just meet you guys there?" Standing up, I stretch my back from being bent over my book for so long. When I look back over to him, he's frowning at me and my smile falters. "What?"

"Lily, you're not going to meet us there. You're riding with us." His brows are still furrowed while he studies me.

"Oh. Okay, are you sure you don't mind me riding with you guys?" I don't know why I feel weird about riding with them. Maybe it's the feeling like I'm just tagging along, I don't know though.

He widens the door and steps inside, still looking at me like he's confused by me. "Why would we mind you riding with us?"

"We gotta get going!" Rhett yells from downstairs and the interruption saves me from having to answer Fallon. He hasn't taken his eyes off me though so I give him another quick smile that feels a little forced.

"I'll get ready quick and be down in just a couple of minutes," I tell him while grabbing my bag to take with me into the bathroom.

"Lily..." he starts, but doesn't finish.

"Five minutes, tops. Promise." I sneak past him and hurry into the bathroom to wash my face and freshen up quickly. By the time I'm done, I can hear the two of them talking downstairs but their voices are low enough that I can't understand them.

After changing, I hurry downstairs only to find both of them sitting at the counter, talking low and seem to be having a somewhat heated discussion.

"Is everything okay?" They both stop talking and look over at me, neither of them smiling. I can't stop the tension from tightening in my shoulders. Are they mad at me? "I didn't mean to take so long getting ready..." I trail off when their gazes harden more. Yeah, they look pissed.

"Sweetheart-"

"Baby-"

They both start talking at once and then Fallon nods to Rhett indicating he can go first. "Lily... there's no need to apologize. You didn't do anything wrong."

Biting my lip, I nod at him.

"Are you okay going there for dinner with us? Don't feel like we are forcing you to go," Fallon says.

I deflate at that. "Do you not want me to go? I'm fine staying he-" I stop talking when they both stand up.

"I'm going to go call them." Fallon grabs his phone and walks into the other room.

Rhett is still standing and hasn't moved from his spot. My stomach is twisting because I don't know what I did to piss them off. Taking a step back, I try to hide the emotion from my voice, "I can, umm... I can go back upstairs if you-"

Curling his finger at me, Rhett signals I should come over to him, but I'm frozen. Dropping his hand, his nostrils flare in frustration. "Would you come here please?"

Swallowing, I move over to him, nervous about why he and Fallon are so mad at me. I can't stop my eyes from watering, knowing I've fucked up somehow. I stop a couple feet away from him and he just sighs before walking to me, grabbing me around the waist and setting me up on the counter.

"What are-"

"Shh..." he silences me.

"But why-"

"Lily, don't talk for a minute. We are waiting for Fallon." He places a hand on either side of me, boxing me in so I can't get back down without having to push him away.

Staying silent, I fight back the tears and the knot in my throat. *Fuck.* We wait in silence except for when I sniff and then clear my throat. Rhett's finger comes under my chin and lifts my face to his but I just can't look at him. I can't see him angry or irritated with me because I won't be able to hold it together.

"Baby girl," he murmurs. "Look at me, beautiful." I squeeze my eyes shut until I hear a whispered, "Please…"

I open my eyes and meet his cobalt blues and see him deflate, the anger completely gone. "I told them we'd come next week," I hear Fallon say and I try to turn my head to look at him, but Rhett has my chin in a hold and won't let me look away from him.

"You guys don't have to cancel! Honestly, I can just stay here if it's a problem." My eyes widen when Rhett's gaze narrows again on me and I hear a growl come from Fallon. *What the hell is going on?*

"Brother…" Fallon says.

"I know. I'm trying to debate on how to fix this." Rhett is still looking at me but he's talking to his brother. He studies me a moment and then says to him, "What do you think? Should we just talk about this and explain that we want her here and apparently fucked up by giving her some space to get comfortable?"

Fallon moves over to stand next to Rhett who shifts to the right a little to give him some room. "We could do that. *Or*, you and I could kiss the shit out of her until she figures it out that way."

Rhett's lips tilt up on one side to smirk at me while he considers it. My mouth opens to argue but he crashes his to mine in a hungry kiss that sends my head swirling. This is so much more than the last one he gave me and I can barely keep up. He pushes my knees apart to slide his body between them, getting closer to me. Wrapping his arms around me, he slides his tongue along mine. Nipping my lip, I gasp at the sting, while he runs a hand down my back and his fingers through my hair.

All thoughts leave me as he devours my mouth over and over again before wrenching away from me. I can't stop my body from following him, unintentionally looking for him to come back. Rhett is breathing heavily when he grips my face and turns me to face Fallon. "Your turn," he says.

Fallon doesn't give me a chance to catch my breath before he fists my hair to pull my head back, my mouth dropping open at the pain of it, and replaces Rhett's mouth with his. His kiss is so much different than Rhett's, but no less potent. Fallon is controlled, powerful and aggressive, where Rhett has a wildness to him that I feel could consume me if he were to let himself fully off his leash.

Rhett hasn't moved from between my legs and while Fallon continues to kiss me, I feel Rhett grip my hips to pull me further towards the edge of the counter. He's pressing his body into mine and I feel a hardness between his legs that I've never felt before, but my body is telling me that it's a very, *very* good thing that I want.

I don't know how long they kiss me, both of them going for a second round. At this point, my nipples are so hard they hurt poking into my bra. I'm dripping wet between my legs and my heart is racing so fast that I place my hand there a moment to make sure it's not exploding out of my chest.

Fallon is the first to say something, "Baby, you are very much wanted here."

"You're *needed* here," Rhett adds, "and we're sorry that we didn't make that clear."

"I thought I misunderstood everything when you brought me here... that maybe you were wanting me to leave or that I was in the way," I tell them, then chew on my swollen lips, tender from how rough their kisses were. Trying to think of what to say next without sounding immature, Fallon pulls my lip from being torn apart by my teeth.

"You didn't misunderstand anything sweet girl. We thought we should back off and take things slower for you. We didn't want you to feel pressured."

"We want you so bad that we had to keep ourselves at work to make sure we didn't just pounce on you the moment you were around us. We're sorry for confusing you and making you feel unwanted and unwelcome. That's on us." Rhett looks so apologetic and I feel bad. I don't want them to feel guilty about anything.

Shaking my head at them, I set out to give them reassurance, "No, please. I've-" I yelp when he hoists me up and I instantly wrap my legs around him to stop myself from falling.

Fallon laughs at my right and Rhett is grinning so big, his smile almost hurts it's so beautiful. He walks us away from the counter to head out of the kitchen and I stop him. "Wait! What... Where are we going?"

He starts moving again and Fallon answers my question, "Upstairs so we can *not* continue to back off. Clearly it was a mistake and we are going to remedy that. If you're okay with that?" he asks me. "You decide when you're done for the night. We won't go any further than you're ready for, whether that's just a little kissing and cuddling…"

"Or letting us strip you, eat you, and then fuck you," Rhett adds, picking up his pace a little, taking the stairs two at a time. He's carrying me like there's no effort at all on his part.

I gasp at his words and stare at him to make sure he's being serious and not just teasing. When I see the heat in his eyes and the same reflected in Fallon's, my face flushes from the excitement that starts to twist in my chest.

Wrapping my arms tighter around his neck when he reaches for the door to his room, I bury my face into his neck and peak over at Fallon. He's still looking at me like he wants to devour me and it gives me a little confidence.

As Fallon shuts us into Rhett's bedroom, I whisper to them my agreement.

"I'd really like to try the second option."

# Chapter 9

## *Rhett*

Lily's whispered agreement is what both Fallon and I have been waiting for.

We fucked up by kissing her and then stepping back when we first brought her home. We thought we were being smart by giving her space. We figured most people, especially someone who has never been in a relationship, would be overwhelmed.

What we thought was giving her time to adjust and get used to being around us, she took as our disinterest. Throw in working late hours, eating separately, barely saying hello and goodbye in the mornings and evenings, I don't blame her.

When she thought we were all going to dinner tonight separately, like she was just an afterthought, I was pissed. Not at her, but at myself and Fallon. Ma has been asking how she's been doing here and we figured everything was fine. Dad knows that we're interested in her and has asked us a few times where we all stand. He even mentioned that we should probably talk to her, but we thought we knew better.

I'm sure Fallon told them that we needed to straighten some things out with our girl and that we'd see them another night. Tonight is for us, so I focus back on feeling her body pressed against mine when I hear the snick of the door shutting behind us.

My cock is throbbing, pressed against her center while her body is wrapped around mine. I drop her to the bed and she lets out a little squeak. Fallon is already standing next to me and we both pull our shirts off at the same time.

"Option two it is." Fallon laughs, throwing his shirt on the floor. He and I have shared a few girls before, but never one where we both were interested in them long term. It's been a learning process but, at least in the bedroom, we know how to work together without getting in each other's way.

I watch as he crawls onto the bed, forcing her to scramble back slightly. I take my time removing the rest of my clothes, all except my boxers. Leaving them on for now will help to not overwhelm her.

"Lay back for him sweetheart," I order her, and she looks at me with wide eyes. It's obvious that she's nervous but she doesn't seem like she wants us to stop. Both Fallon and I will check in a few times before we get to a point where there's no going back.

I get impossibly harder when she obeys my command and lays back with Fallon hovering over her. "Good girl," he says to her and runs his hand from her neck, down her chest between her breasts and then settles on her waist as he brings his lower half to press against her.

Licking her lips, she accepts his kiss with a soft moan and widens her legs to let him get more comfortable. He runs his hand under her shirt and moves down to kiss her stomach as he reveals her skin to us. I don't have the patience to only watch so once he releases her mouth from his, I take my place next to them and turn her face towards me and capture her tongue with mine.

Fuck she tastes so sweet. "I'm going to pull your shirt off, is that okay with you?" I ask her, leaning back a little to watch for any signs that she's unsure.

"Yes, please..." she says without hesitation. Grabbing the bottom of her shirt where Fallon has it bunched in his fist, I slide it up and over her head, pulling her hair to fan out over my pillow. Fallon gets to her bra before I do and I watch as he releases the center front clasp and her perfect tits spill out from the cups as it falls away from her.

She's got a hand in his hair as he begins to feast on her pebbled nipples and she giggles into my mouth when I start to kiss her again. "What's so funny?" I ask, keeping my lips on hers and run them over her cheek to her ear where I nip the lobe.

"Fallon's beard tickles," her soft voice sounds shy but playful.

Smiling into her skin, I rub my scruff against her neck and laugh with her when she starts to giggle again.

"Know where else it can tickle?" he asks her, before sucking her other nipple into his mouth and making a popping noise when he releases it before looking up at her. "Baby?"

She shakes her head, "No… where?" Her chest is heaving with her quick breaths and I can feel her stomach trembling as I run my hand below her belly button.

Fallon gives her a sly grin before reaching for the button on her jeans and snapping it open. "I'll show you, if you'd like?" I can hear the teeth of her zipper as he pulls it down, then his eyebrow raises at her, waiting for an answer.

She nods her head quickly. "Y-yes…" Fallon looks to me, so I move up and slide in behind her. Looking back at me, she furrows her brows. "What are you…"

I wrap her hair up in my fist and force her to watch Fallon as he pulls both her jeans and underwear from her hips and down her legs. I bite her ear again and whisper, "I'm going to hold you while he tickles you, baby girl."

Sucking in a breath at my words, she settles her ass against my leaking cock and I groan while pressing myself against her. Her body shivers at the combination of my length grinding into her and Fallon's mouth running up the inside of her leg.

He presses her knees open to widen for him and I release her hair to grab both of her knees and lift them over my legs. Spreading my own wider, she tenses when she realizes how exposed she is. She's blushing as she reaches to cover herself, but I stop her by wrapping my arms around hers and pinning them to her chest.

"Don't move, Lily," he says, then gets off the bed to pull his own clothes off. He doesn't wait like I did to remove everything and strips completely naked. She gasps when she sees his cock for the first time and I chuckle at her reaction.

"Have you seen a cock before, sweetheart?" I ask her. He waits for her answer and smirks as he strokes himself a few times, staring at her spread open for him.

Her breaths are shallow and she can only shake her head no. Fallon rumbles out a laugh himself. "I'll show you more later. Right now, I need to eat this pretty pussy."

I've still got her hands pinned with mine and I move them over to one hand so I can reach down and feel how wet she is. "Fuuuuck Fallon," I say to him, "she's dripping for us."

"Show me," he demands. Running my fingers through her folds, I spread her lips to show him and he groans, falling to his stomach to get closer to her. I keep her held open for him as he runs his tongue from her opening to clit, and then back down again. "Baby girl, you taste so fucking good," he groans into her pussy.

Lily cries out when he dives in and eats her like he's starved. "Reach your arms behind my neck and hang on to me." I help her, running my hands up her arms until she's settled, moaning out louder the longer Fallon sucks on her clit. Once she's got a hold on me, I stroke up her skin until I've got one of her tits in each hand.

I pluck and twist her nipples while she shakes in my lap, Fallon building her up to her first orgasm with us. I can't stop from kissing the side of her head, ear, and neck while I watch him bring our girl over the edge.

"There you go… good girl, baby…" I croon when she explodes against his tongue, wrenching my neck forward from the strength of it. It takes everything in me to not pull my cock out and sink into her to feel her pulsing around me.

Fallon pulls his face away and rubs his thumb over her clit so he can watch her as she continues to fall apart. "Fucking beautiful…" He looks at me once her body relaxes against mine. "She tastes amazing Rhett. I don't think I'll ever be able to get enough." He sucks her flavor from his fingers, making me crave a taste as well.

Reaching between her legs, I slide two fingers just inside her, not too deep, to wet my fingers and then bring them to my mouth. Her flavor flows over my tongue and my eyes close as I shift my cock against her ass again. I reach down and run my fingers over her again and groan, "Fuck. You're soaking my hand."

"Hmm," she hums, eyes still closed, relaxing into the after effect of her orgasm.

"Sweetheart, will you let me inside of you?" I ask her as I run my other hand through her hair. Fallon is sitting up, sliding his hands up and down the inside of her legs, squeezing her thighs while I continue to play with her folds lazily.

"Baby, do you want to keep going?" I can hear the desire for her in his voice, but if she's not ready, neither of us will push her tonight. He's massaging her foot now and it looks tiny in his hands.

Lily looks back at me and gives me a shy smile and bites her lip. "I'd like to, but only if you want. We don't ha-" I cut her off with a fast kiss and then press my forehead to hers.

"I definitely want to, baby girl." Her breath fans across my lips and I tilt my head to look at Fallon. "Lift her, would you?"

He scoops her off of my lap, keeping her legs spread open with his arms under her knees. I don't move from my spot, but I quickly pull my boxers off and toss them to the side while Fallon kisses the fuck out of our girl.

"Give her back to me." I hold my arms out and try not to pull her away from him, anxious to sink inside of her. I have to remind myself to take it slow since this will be her first time.

I hear him murmur, "Okay sweet girl, I'm going to put you back down." He leans her back and I wrap my hands around her waist, settling her back where I had her before. Only this time, my cock is wedged between her wet folds.

Closing my eyes, I take a deep breath while he places her legs back over mine. I brush her hair over her shoulder and kiss along her shoulder and then up her neck. She's very subtly rocking against me as I stroke her along with Fallon. I can tell when he finds her clit again because she arches her back into my chest, pushing her tits out and moaning for us.

Reaching under her, I grab my shaft and line myself up, notching into her small opening. Her pussy lips are kissing the head of my cock and I rock my cock into her about an inch or so. "Do you want me to go slow or just get the uncomfortable part over with for you?"

Turning her face toward me, she places her lips on the side of my neck, kissing sweetly and looking up at me. I can see an array of emotions swirling through her eyes, but none of them are hesitancy or doubt. "Just go quick-" she cries out, the sound reverberating through my body when I punch my hips up, impaling her.

I hold her tight to me with my arms wrapped across her chest. Fallon continues to rub her clit gently, keeping her in some state of pleasure while she relaxes against the intrusion and pain from me tearing through her innocence.

Fuck. Me.

She's so incredibly tight that I wasn't prepared for it. Squeezing her to me even tighter, I use my hold on her to keep myself from thrusting into her again before she's ready.

Panting into her shoulder, I breathe heavily as she whimpers, eyes squeezed shut. Thank God Fallon is here to help her through this while I collect myself. The surge of emotions I'm feeling while lodged inside of her is shattering every expectation I had of how this would go. My legs are shaking while I hold myself in her, fully seated.

Fallon brushes a strand of hair from her face and tucks it behind her ear. "Baby, take a couple of big breaths for me." He's still rubbing her because I can feel her clenching around me as the waves of pleasure battle with the rawness of my thickness forced into her body. "You took him so good, sweet girl. Just keep breathing until it starts to feel better. He won't move until you're ready, right Rhett?"

"Right," I hiss. "Baby girl, you feel so fucking amazing. Tell us when you're ready to move and we'll both help you. You're doing so good for us..." I bite my cheek to keep the gruffness of my voice controlled and look at Fallon. He needs to help her because honest to God, I don't know how I'm going to be able to hold back for much longer.

Sucking in a breath, her voice wavers when she opens her watery eyes to look up at me. "I think I just need a... a minute. That was m-more than I had expected."

Kissing her lips, I try to distract myself from the feeling of her drenched pussy wrapped around me. Focusing on her lips, I run my tongue along her bottom one and my cock twitches when I swallow her groan. "That's the spot, baby girl. Focus on my fingers and try shifting your hips a little and see if it feels better." Fallon directs her, still working her pussy with his fingers. He leans forward and tongues her nipple while I twist and pull at the other one.

I grunt when she circles her hips and slides off of my cock me halfway before seating herself back down. "Fuck... rock your hips again," I tell her. She does and this time when she does, I press up a little harder into her and smile at the moan of pleasure that reverberates from deep in her chest.

Fallon grins back at me and gives me a slight head nod. "She's ready."

# Chapter 10

## *Lily*

I'm being hit with so many sensations at once that my head feels like it's spinning out of control. Between Fallon rubbing my clit, Rhett's thickness pulsing inside of me, and the pinch of pain that is starting to fade mixed with a heavily rooted pleasure, I'm spinning.

With my heart racing, it starts to pound harder when Fallon tells Rhett I'm ready. I don't know if I'm prepared for what's coming next, but I've come this far and I very much want to see this through. Aside from all the sensations coursing through my body, the emotions rocketing through me for these two feels almost crushing.

I gasp when I feel Rhett's hands grip my hips and pull me back a little further up his chest, pulling himself out of me about halfway. Positioning me this way, he's able to move more easily and he drags his cock out only to plunge back inside of me.

The feel of him moving within me feels odd and invasive, but Fallon's fingers circling on my bundle of nerves has me wanting to tilt my hips toward his hand for more pressure.

"Jesus Christ, Lily... you look incredible stretched over his cock." Fallon's looking down where Rhett's steadily slipping himself in and out of me. He grips one of my knees and Rhett grabs the other. They both move my legs up toward my upper body, spreading them even wider than I was before and opening me as wide as my body will allow. The pull in my hips is a good kind of stretch, like when you arch your body in the morning after waking up.

"Baby girl, are you ready for me to move faster?" Rhett grits out against the side of my head.

"Yes, God... please," I moan. With my permission, he releases whatever restraint he had holding himself back because there's no build up to prepare me for the way he immediately begins to pound his cock inside of me. Our bodies are slapping together and the wetness that's leaking from me makes it sound obscene.

I can't stop myself from grabbing on to their arms to hang on and ground myself from the explosion of pleasure that's coursing through my body. This angle has Rhett hitting a spot inside of me that makes my entire lower stomach clench, readying itself for something.

Rhett is sucking on the side of my neck, nipping the skin, and Fallon is speeding up his movements over my clit. I feel like I'm being attacked from so many different areas and I cry from the intensity.

"Fuck yes, Lily," Fallon growls and then he leans over us to slam his lips over mine, fucking my tongue the same way Rhett is fucking my pussy. His fingers slide over my lips and clit more quickly and I can feel myself getting close to another orgasm. Ending our kiss, he's panting over me when he tells Rhett what he's seeing. "Man, our girl is about to come all over your cock and my hand. Christ she's gorgeous…"

Rhett only groans into me and picks up his pace, roaring as he slams into me over and over. With Fallon's hard pinch to my clit, I come undone and scream out their names, clamping down on Rhett's cock so hard that he grunts to keep moving inside of me.

The feel of his cock pounding into me while my pussy flutters and clamps down on him is intense. The constant friction and pressure forces my orgasm to lengthen and won't release its hold on me, and I can feel him driving into a spot that makes me lost control and forces a scream from deep in my throat.

"I'm going to fucking cum," he tells me and then after three of more thrusts, he stills, and I can feel the swelling and pulsing of his cock like a firehose emptying into me. The sounds of pleasure coming from him are rough, his voice gravely from the strain of his muscles, "oh God, your pussy is milking me baby girl."

Fallon runs a hand over my chest. "Your skin is flushed from here to your cheeks." He's still petting me, soothing my muscles from the strength of my orgasm. "My cock is dripping for you

Lily..." His words make me want to reach for him, but I feel so connected to Rhett right now.

I internally panic a little, not knowing what I should do with two of them here. I don't want to make Fallon feel left out, but Rhett is still buried inside of me, panting into my hair as he comes down from his own orgasm. Fallon must see something on my face because he gives me a gentle smile and cups my cheek. "You're fine right there, sweet girl... we've got all night."

Rhett chuckles under me and then groans when I clench around him again. "You've destroyed me, Lily... give me just another minute to enjoy the feel of you around me and then I'll let him take you from me. How are you feeling?"

"Good... *really* good. It wasn't what I expected," I tell them, and then giggle at how breathless I sound.

"What didn't you expect?" he asks, humor lacing his voice.

I tilt my head back to look at him again and my heart jumps at the look he's giving me as he stares back down at me. "It was, umm... a lot more than I thought it would be. Intense... does that make sense?"

"It does," Fallon says.

"Is it always like this? Because I feel like my body just went through a marathon." Reaching up to put a hand over my heart, I try to will it to slow down. "My heart feels like it's going to explode."

"No baby girl, it's not always like that," Rhett says while running a hand over my head and through my hair. "That was nothing like I've ever felt before." Then he kisses my temple and whispers into my ear, "Why don't you go to Fallon? I think he's about to steal you from me anyways."

Fallon's eyes flash with hunger and he doesn't wait for me to listen to Rhett. He grabs me under my arms, pulls me from Rhett's chest, and settles me into his lap. My legs are wrapped around his waist and we're sitting face to face.

I can feel Rhett's cum leaking from me and my eyes widen when I realize that he's going to feel it too. Moving to lift from his lap, he holds me in place, so I try to explain the problem, embarrassed about it, "Fallon, I, umm... I'm going to get..." I don't know how to say it so I whisper, "I'm leaking..."

I'm surprised when I feel him pulse under me, his cock pinned between us and moisture coating my stomach from him. "I don't care baby. I'm about to get you messier." He flashes his teeth at me and then swoops in to kiss me again. Wrapping my arms around his neck, I kiss him back, my body already heating back up for him.

"Lay back for me," he says between kisses, then leans me onto my back with a hand between my breasts.

Rhett stretches out next to me to roam his hands over my nipples, stomach, and then down to stroke my folds, still dripping from his cum. "Still so fucking wet for us." Moving his hand from my lower lips, he slides his wet fingers down my thigh and then grabs behind my leg to open me back up to them.

Fallon looks at me down there, dipping a finger inside me and then back out only to circle around my clit. "Rhett, you're pouring out of her." I blush under his gaze and he chuckles. "It's a *good* thing. It'll make slipping inside you easier."

He demonstrates what he means by pushing three fingers inside of me and the stretch at his invasion makes me gasp and cry out. Rhett is playing with my nipples when he asks, "Does it hurt baby girl? You can tell us if you're too sore."

Shaking my head, no, I smile at Fallon and try to talk through the moans as he continues to slide his fingers in and out of me at a lazy pace. "I'm not too sore… well, I *am* sore, but it's a good sore. I want to… with you…"

"Thank God. I don't think I'm going to last long, not after eating you and then watching Rhett fuck you." Fallon comes down on top of me, Rhett pulling my leg open even wider for him and he settles his cock against my opening. Kissing me, he moves his lips across my cheek and then presses his cheek against mine to speak closer to my ear. "Plus, seeing your blood on Rhett's cock and knowing he and I are the only men to have ever known how you feel… The need to add my cum inside you is visceral."

My breath catches as he slams inside of me the moment he's done speaking. He feels just as thick as Rhett and I feel stretched to the max again, swollen inside from the two orgasms they gave me. Fallon curls his body over mine and begins his powerful rut into my body. He drives me up the bed with each thrust, kissing me the entire time with the same aggressiveness.

I feel Rhett's hand come to the top of my head. "Fallon, be careful. She's about to hit her head," he says then grips my hair in my fist when I turn my head to look at him. I only have a moment to take him in, noting his flared nostrils and fiery eyes as Fallon growls and pulls back from me.

He sits back on his heals, never pulling from my body, and drags me back down the bed by the waist. He's got my hips lifted off the bed and he keeps his pace quick and steady. "Rhett..." he sucks in a breath, then looks at his brother, "make her come for me. I need to come soon..."

Rhett laughs under his breath at Fallon, and I close my eyes when I feel Rhett's fingers move between us. He starts to play with my clit, and has me racing toward another orgasm, which I didn't think was possible. "Oh God..." I moan out. "I... I'm going to come again..."

"*Yes*," Fallon shouts. "Come for me princess..." His body slams into me harder and Rhett is working my clit when he leans over and takes one of my nipples into his mouth.

The dual sensations trigger me, my entire body stiffening and arching up until only my shoulders are on the bed. Tears leak out as I cry and shake through my orgasm.

Fallon growls out, furiously slamming into me with one final thrust and then he grinds his body against me, Rhett's hand still rubbing me. "*FUCK!*" he shouts, "fuck fuck fuck..." his body is contracting and pulsing into me, his heat spreading inside me, while I twist with the pleasure, almost painful, from how sensitive I am now.

"Fallon..." I gasp. Looking at Rhett then, I blink the tears away and touch his face and croak out, "...R-Rhett..." My hand falls to the bed and I'm freaking spent.

"Sweet, beautiful girl..." Rhett croons and kisses me softly on my lips. Fallon gently pulls himself from me and then falls next to me, sweaty and breathing heavily.

"Fuck Lily..." I can feel him studying me but I don't have the energy to open my eyes or turn my head. I can only focus on breathing and trying to ground myself back to reality. Sighing, he drops his hand to my hair and slides it over to the side of my face, cupping my cheek and turning my head to face him. "Baby, you okay? I'm sorry if I was too rough."

Peaking my eyes open, I try to give him a soft smile. I manage to lift my arm up and stroke my fingers across his face, brow, the bridge of his nose. I run out of energy and let my hand fall. "Imgood..." I mumble.

If they say anything else, I don't hear it. I'm sucked into an exhausted, much needed, restorative sleep. I do feel both of their warm bodies pressed into me and I smile to myself at the feeling of finally being wanted.

## Chapter 11

### *Fallon*

Waking up next to this girl for the past week has been life changing. Rhett's room being the largest, we've all found ourselves in here every night since last weekend when we made Lily ours. He already had a king-sized bed in here, but with both of our heights, and our girl squeezed in between us, we decided to go ahead and order a larger mattress. Not that I mind her curling into us, but more often than not, we wake with Rhett and I right next to each other and Lily spread over the top of us.

It's also no hardship having her already on top. Lately, it's been almost a competition between the two of us to see who wakes first and slides her over the top of us to bury ourselves inside of her first. We've also discovered that this doll is not a morning person, so waking her with sex has been key to putting a smile on her face before she's even opened her eyes.

This Saturday morning, I've won at waking up first. Her leg is tossed over mine and she's facing my brother, her hair spread across my chest. Burying my nose in it, I enjoy the scent of her for a moment before sliding my arm under her body and pulling her body on top of mine.

Her legs settle around my waist and I can feel that she's still wet from the both of us fucking her last night. With all of this being new to her, each night she ends up exhausted. Usually, she passes out before we can get her into the shower.

The bonus for that though is being able to slide my aching cock inside of her without too much work. Wrapping my arms around her, I slide her down my body slowly and press up to seat myself inside of her.

Her low, sleepy moan has Rhett's eyes popping open and him reaching for her instinctually. Chuckling, I whisper, "got her first you fucker…" And then I laugh I little louder when he growls and rubs his hand across his face to wake himself up.

"Damn man, I'm fuckin-" His phone ringing interrupts him and he quickly reaches over to silence it, not wanting to make Lily fully wake up. "It's ma… I'll be right back." He slips out of bed and heads into the bathroom while I move under her, slowly fucking her awake.

She moans again and rubs her face into my chest and then grips my arms with her hands when I grind into her, forcing her clit to rub against my body. "Fallon…" she moans.

"Morning baby," my voice is soft, gritty from just waking up myself. Then I groan when she rocks herself against me a little harder.

"Mornin-" she mumbles, still keeping her eyes closed and her face buried against my chest. It doesn't stop her from rolling her hips to take me deeper.

Gripping her hips, I move more firmly now that she's waking up. We move together, just enjoying the feel of each other's bodies when Rhett comes back into the room. "They want us to come spend the day with them since we skipped last weekend...fuck you look hot moving like that baby..."

He tosses his phone on the side table and climbs back on the bed behind her. I widen my legs to give him room. She shudders against me when he runs his hand down the length of her back.

We haven't both gotten in to her at the same time yet, but we're working her up to it. Moving in closer to her from behind, I slip my cock out so he can take my place. Reaching forward, he grips her hair and groans, "Christ Lily, your pussy is strangling my cock."

She laughs into me and I know that she's squeezed down on him harder when he hisses and pauses a moment before pulling out and slamming back in. She cries out when he pulls himself out to let me back in.

We alternate between fucking her until she's pushing back against us and sitting up now. "I'm already close guys..." she tells us, so I reach down and play with her clit to push her over.

Rhett takes his turn again and she explodes on him while he pounds into her, getting himself close to coming. "*Fuck!*" he yells out and wrenches himself free from her, stroking his cock while I slam back inside of her to feel the end of her orgasm. I drive in over and over and release inside of her at the same time that Rhett comes on her ass.

"...I want to go back to sleep." She drops back onto my chest and relaxes her body over mine with me still buried inside of her. Then she jerks her body upright, forcing herself further onto my overly sensitive cock, when Rhett smacks her ass. Whipping her head back to look at him, she scowls, "What was *that* for?"

"You don't get to go back to sleep. Get your perfect, sexy ass into the shower. Dad and ma want us over for the day." He's grinning as he hops off the bed and heads in before her.

She looks nervous, chewing on her lip, at the unexpected plans for the day. Sitting up, I run my hands through her hair and then cup her face. "Baby girl, they want to see you. They miss you."

"Are you sure? I don't want them to feel like they have to keep taking care of me when their job is done." Furrowing my brows, I hate to see her question how people feel about her.

"Listen to me, sweet girl," I kiss her lips until she relaxes and softens against me. "You are not a job. You never were and they both adore you. Even if you weren't with us, they would always want you as part of the family."

She still looks unsure and Rhett cuts in, having heard what we were talking about, "Lily... you're ours, which makes you our family and *their* family. You have your own place regardless, but you have to know you will always belong."

Her eyes start to water and I pull her against me, hugging her tightly. Into her hair, I keep giving her our truths. "This... you and me and Rhett? This is not something everyone gets to experience. You've wrapped yourself around us and we wouldn't survive if you pulled back away. You've become crucial to our survival."

Lily sniffs into my neck and squeezes me back. "Are you sure? Because if you guys aren't sure yet, I need to know. I'm already *really* attached."

Rhett pulls her out of my arms and into his lap, sitting down next to me on the bed. "Positive, sweet girl. You have to know that I love you."

Her eyes widen at him, then over at me when I say, "I love you too, baby. I've never felt like this about anyone or wanted anyone as badly as I do you. You're going to be stuck with the both of us, hovering and taking up all your time." I laugh and Rhett chuckles with me.

"*All* the time," he adds. Brushing her hair back again from her face, he kisses her. "Do you understand or did we freak you out with all of this mushy love talk?"

She giggles through her tears and then shakes her head, "No, I love you guys too. I didn't want to say anything in case you guys weren't looking for anything serious. But I do... a lot." Her lip trembles when she adds quietly, "It also means everything to me, being asked to be a part of a family... *your* family. It's, umm... it's been a really long time since I h-had one..."

My heart breaks for her when I watch a tear slip down her cheek. Groaning, Rhett pulls her into him and I lean over, wrapping an arm around her and press a kiss at her temple. "We didn't need to ask, sweetheart... you already were."

She nods her head and soaks everything in, and I meet Rhett's eyes over her head. He smiles at me, both of us acknowledging without words that this was a pretty huge step forward for the three of us. We give her a few minutes before Rhett says, "Come on... let's get showered and on the road. I don't know about you, but I'd much rather have ma's breakfast than something we throw together."

He pats her thigh and I get up, helping to lift her off his lap. Throwing her over my shoulder, she squeals when I smack her ass and walk her into the bathroom, already steamed with how long the shower's been running.

With all of us squeezed into Rhett's shower, we get our girl washed up and I can't help but think about all of the things we have to look forward to with her.

Now we get to take her home and let mom and dad know that they're gaining a daughter, hopefully 'officially' in the near future. She's in for the shock of her life now that she's going to let us all love on her the way she deserves.

Getting her into the truck, I can tell that Rhett, along with me, is feeling content and at peace with our baby girl settled in between us. Then we both laugh when she turns red at the sound of her stomach growling.

"Shut up…" she huffs out.

Wrapping an arm around her shoulder, I pull her into me and give her a quick kiss and then Rhett does the same.

"Hurry up brother," he says. "We need to feed our girl."

# Bonus Epilogue

## *Lily*

*Fuck, I'm so freaking nervous!*

Holding the test in my hands, I walk into the house after visiting with Cindy. I told her that I had a feeling I could be pregnant, so she insisted I come over there to do the test. She ran out to buy it for me so we could make sure to keep it a surprise from my guys until I knew for certain.

I ended up taking two of them *just* in case and the results were the same.

God bless her, she sent Jeff over to the shop to keep Rhett and Fallon distracted without letting on that something big could be happening.

I've been dating and living with them for three years now and I still can't believe that they're mine. That their *family* is mine. Cindy has told me a few times that I can call her and Jeff 'mom and dad.' I'd rather call them grandma and grandpa.

"Lily?" Rhett calls out to me.

"I'm here!" I yell at him, finding my way through the house to the living room where Rhett and Fallon are hanging out in the living room.

Rhett has his feet kicked up on the ottoman, a beer in hand, and Fallon is squatting down in front of the TV, looking through the movies.

"Hey baby girl," he says, walking to me and giving me a quick kiss on the lips. "Where'd you go off to?"

"Cindy and I had something to do," I tell him. I'm so freaking nervous right now that the tests in my hand are sliding between my fingers.

"Whatcha have there?" Rhett asks, nodding his head at my hands.

Biting my lip, I look up at Fallon with a nervous smile. "Yeah... so ummm... I have to... Fallon, would you sit down a minute?"

I watch as both of their smiles slip from their faces and are replaced with concern.

Rhett cocks his head at me, "Everything okay, sweetheart?"

Clearing my throat, I twist the tests in my hand while I wait for Fallon to sit down. He's still standing next to me so I nudge him with my shoulders. "Fallon?"

"You're making me nervous baby girl," he says, but he sits next to Rhett anyway. "What's going on?"

I take a deep breath and move to stand in front of both of them. "So... I uhh... I went over to Cindy's this morning," I say, fiddling with the plastic sticks, unable to meet their eyes.

"...And?" Rhett asks, leaning forward, resting his elbows on his knees.

My face is heating. God, this is so hard! *"And...* I thought, well, I had suspected that there... that maybe-" I cough and take another big breath. My lip is getting sore from gnawing at it so much and my nerves start to overwhelm me. Add in the hormones and my eyes begin to water.

"Lily," Fallon says, drawing my attention to him. "Whatever it is, we'll figure it out sweet girl."

Nodding my head that I hear him, I try again. "S-So... okay, just... *here.*" I shove both of the tests out in front of me for each of them to take one.

Fallon takes his to look at it, and Rhett keeps his eyes locked on me while he grabs his. "What's going-"

"Holy shit." That was Fallon.

Rhett jerks his head to look at Fallon and whatever he sees on his face has him panicking and then looking down at what I gave them.

They're both just sitting there, not saying anything and unmoving. Their heads are down so I can't read whatever they're thinking, and the longer they stay silent, the more panicked I get.

I can't wait any longer. The need to know how they feel about this overtakes any fear I have, so I drop to my knees in front of them and place a hand on each of their thighs.

"Guys?" my voice wobbles.

Looking up into their faces, they both look at me when they hear my voice and I freeze when I see the looks of awe and shock, their eyes glassy, and emotion filling both of their faces.

"We're pregnant?" Fallon whispers to me.

I whisper back, "We're pregnant."

"Fuck *YES!*" Rhett yells out, laughter mixing into the clogged emotions in his voice. "Holy shit babe! YOU'RE PREGNANT!"

"You're really pregnant?" Fallon asks, croaking out his question again.

I can't get any sound out past my vocal cords so I simply nod my head yes.

Fallon's body falls forward, and he drops his test on the floor to grab me under the arms and pull him up into his body, crushing me to him. "*FUCK!* God damnit Lily... I just... *We're PREGNANT!*" He's laughing now and I relax into his body.

My body is wrenched sideways by Rhett when he pulls me from Fallon's arms and into his own, crashing his lips down on mine. I barely have a chance to catch my breath before he drives his tongue into my mouth, kissing me hard, all of his emotions pouring into it.

Fallon takes me away from Rhett again, only to take over kissing the shit out of me. I can taste salt on his lips, and I pull away to see that tears in his eyes have overflowed. My breath falters, never having seen Fallon cry before. Cupping his cheek, I press my forehead to his.

"Are you happy?"

He tilts his head and places a gentle kiss on my forehead, whispering, "So *SO* fucking happy, baby… God…" He pulls me into his chest, tucking my head into the crook of his neck.

Rhett stands up like, vibrating with energy. "I gotta call ma and dad! Holy shit, Lily!" He grips his hair, laughing at the ceiling. "I can't even…" Turning and pointing at my stomach, he chuckles. *"You've got our baby in there!"*

Taking the few steps back over to us, he lifts me out of Fallon's lap, and I wrap my legs around his waist and my arms around his neck. Bouncing me higher to get my face level with his, his eyes bounce over my face, taking me in. "I love you so God damn much. *Thank you*, baby girl! Thank you thank you thank you." He kisses me each time he thanks me, and my heart feels like it's going to explode.

"Well, it's not like I did much of the work." I laugh and he snorts.

"Maybe not to begin with, but you're about to do most of the heavy lifting… *literally*." His grin is eating up his entire face and then he's kissing me again, walking me to our bedroom. Pulling his lips away briefly, he calls over his shoulder, "Get your shit together and get in here with us, Fall. This little momma needs to be worshipped!"

Looking over Rhett's shoulder, I see Fallon hanging his head between his knees, seemingly overwhelmed. "Fallon?" I call out to him.

He meets my eyes and gives me the biggest smile he can, his eyes crinkling in the corners. "I'm so good, love. So *so* fucking happy." Standing up, I see him follow us, eyes still locked on me, and I can't tear my gaze away. My heart feels like it's going to burst at the realization that this is something that they are thrilled with.

We make it to the bedroom and Rhett drops me on the mattress. He wastes no time and rips my clothes from my body.

A phone rings from the living room and I hear Fallon change directions to answer it. It's a short conversation, only saying, "Yeah, she told us... Fuck yes... Sorry for swearing... I'll call you back later."

By the time Fallon joins us, Rhett is naked as well and I watch Fallon get undressed as Rhett spreads my legs and settles between them. I don't even have a chance to register what he's doing before I feel him bury his tongue inside me, making good on his promise to worship me.

Fallon settles next to me to take my lips and run his hands over my chest, my nipples already incredibly sensitive as Rhett drives me toward my first orgasm faster than I was prepared for.

Sucking on my clit, he drives two fingers inside of me and I scream into Fallon's mouth, breaking apart for them and digging my nails into Fallon's arms. Holy *shit*. That was like one minute, this whole thing so much more intense knowing that we've created something special between the three of us.

"Move over Rhett, I need to fuck our girl. I can't wait." Fallon says, shoving Rhett away from my pussy and crawling on top of me. Lining his cock up to my entrance, he holds himself there when he grips the sides of my face and forces me to look up at him. "You are *everything* to me. To *us*. I love you so fucking much, Lily."

Driving himself inside of me, he holds himself there, whispering, "...*everything*, baby girl."

Rhett runs his hand down my side and then grabs my leg under my knee and pulls it out to the side, spreading me wider for his brother. Fallon grinds himself further inside of me. It's like he can't get close enough and is afraid to pull away.

Fallon doesn't move, he simply circles his hips, digging his cock into me, and holds me tight to his body. Taking my mouth, his tongue wraps around mine and he mimics what his cock wants to do, but can't because the closeness is a necessity.

"Flip over with her Fallon, I need inside… we need her between us." Rhett tells him while getting up from the bed to grab something out of the side table.

Fallon pulls away from my mouth and gives me a wolfish smile before flipping us, spreading my legs over his waist and forcing me to settle him more deeply inside of me. He wraps his arms around my back, pulling me to his chest which causes my back to arch.

Running his hands along the length of my back, he slides them down to my ass and spreads me when we feel the dip of the bed as Rhett crawls behind me.

Fallon's fingers dig into me, holding me open as far as he can. "Fucking *beautiful* sight baby girl," Rhett growls. I feel him run a finger along my spine, until he reaches my second entrance, and circles his finger around it.

We've done this a few times and the excitement kicks my heartbeat up knowing that I'm going to feel both of them inside of me at the same time. Fallon thrusts up into me harder once, giving me that delicious friction as Rhett drizzles lube on my asshole, spreading it around. He dips one finger inside to begin opening me up to him and I groan when shivers course throughout my body.

"Fuck yes, sweet girl... let me in... there's my good girl," Rhett growls as he slides a second finger inside of me, stretching my muscles. "God damn you're so fucking tight when he's got you stuffed like that."

"If she's ready, hurry up man. I need to move." Kissing me again, Fallon nips my lip and grins. "You're squeezing me so fucking hard."

Breathing heavily, I lick my lips, "I'm good... ready, I mean."

"Thank God," I hear Rhett mutter and then slide his fingers out of me. I hear the snick of the cap and assume he's putting more on his cock before I feel the head of him press up against my tight ring of muscles. "Take a deep breath in for me baby girl."

Obeying him, I do and then gasp when I feel the pressure of him pushing forward, past my ring of muscles and Fallon's fingers digging into my ass, still holding me open for his brother.

I squeeze my eyes shut at the burn when the head of Rhett's cock finally pops past my muscles and then breathe out a sigh of relief as he slowly slides the rest of the way in.

Full. Stuffed. They aren't small men and when we do this, it always takes my breath away at how incredibly stretched open I feel.

"Fuck yes…" Rhett groans. "You feel so fucking good baby girl… so God damn perfect for us."

"Beautiful," Fallon adds, releasing my ass and running a hand through my hair.

I'm still breathing heavily and then my breath catches when his fingers grip my hair, pulling the roots at the scalp. "Fallon…" I groan at the pinch of pain. Trying to turn my head, I look at Rhett over my shoulder even though Fallon doesn't release my hair. "Rhett. Please…"

He winks at me before pulling back halfway and then slamming back inside of me. Apparently, it's going to be rough this time and I scream out at the force of his thrust.

"Scream for us, baby girl…" Fallon grits out through his teeth before the two of them begin to fuck me mercilessly.

Rhett's gripping my hips and has pulled me up from Fallon slightly, allowing him to slam his cock up into me while Rhett alternates strokes behind. When one of them slides out, the other goes in, their rhythm in perfect sync.

Both of them are groaning, filling me over and over as their combined efforts send me into a state of bliss where I can only plant my hands and brace myself.

We don't say anything for a long while as they fuck their cocks into me, just enjoying the feeling of being together. I can feel their sweat coating my skin, their bodies sliding over mine and cocks expanding and getting harder the closer they get to the end.

"Jesus Christ, beautiful girl, you're too fucking tight. I can't hold back much longer," Fallon says through clenched teeth.

I can feel my second orgasm rising inside of me from all the nerves they're stimulating and then Rhett does something to send me over the edge. Wrapping one of his arms around my waist, he reaches between Fallon and I to slide two fingers on either side of my clit, pinching it hard which sends me spiraling toward the finish line.

"God, the sounds you make are fucking incredible, baby girl," Rhett groans, leaning over my back and talking into my ear. "I can feel your pussy tightening on my cock. You're getting close, are you?"

Nodding my head, I mumble, "…Yes… God, so… so close."

"We want to feel you cum all over us," Fallon growls and the two of them pick up their pace, our bodies slapping together obscenely.

Rhett runs his other hand up my body and grips my throat, pulling me up and arching my back and I scream out my orgasm as they pound into me, the angle change hitting new spots. Stars explode across my vision as I come undone and help drive my body back onto their cocks.

Fuck. Me.

Black spots dance across my vision as my body continues to convulse around them and they both bark out a yell when their cocks swell impossibly larger and then explode inside of me.

A few more thrusts from both of them have them planted deep inside me, holding still as they both fill me, unloading inside both my ass and pussy.

We're all breathing heavily when Rhett releases my throat and rubs his hand up the side of my face to the top of my head. Forcing my head to turn to him, his heavy breath fans across my skin and Fallon begins to stroke my nipples in front of him.

"That... *fuck* baby girl... if you weren't pregnant before, you are now," Rhett says, still catching his breath and then placing a gentle kiss on my lips and slipping his tongue in my mouth for just a moment.

Chuckling, Fallon, still inside of me, leans up to kiss my neck and then behind my ear. "Thank God we already got the deed done, brother."

I bite my lip and look between the two of them. "You guys really are happy?"

"*So* fucking happy," Fallon assures me. "We love you more than we ever thought possible."

"I can't wait to knock you up again, baby girl," Rhett jokes.

I bark out a laugh, "I love you guys too, but let's just deal with this one first. Yeah?"

Rhett gives me a sly smirk and Fallon's lip tilts up on one side before he says, "We'll see."

THE END

(BE GONE!)

## A Note from the Author

A HUGE thank you to my husband for giving me the time at home to write. Between both of us working full time and raising three children, it can be difficult to try to do a second thing almost full time as well. (Plenty of late nights). He's been incredibly supportive, *even though* this type of genre is not his cup of tea. He hasn't read anything yet (I'll make him at some point), but he's the one that helped me with the synopsis I used when posting each new book.

Another MASSIVELY HUGE thank you to my dear friend Faith C. :) Not only has she provided me with hours of hilarious text conversations, but she's been motivating and encouraging with all of this. Faith is also the one to thank for editing my stories! Turns out, I'm TERRIBLE with commas and I really like to write "in to" instead of "into". Also really, and actually, and pretty… ***shrugs*** I've got no excuse except that I'm stuck in my old ways. Thanks to her, you shouldn't see too many of my typing quirks.

Last, thank you to my friend Jessica F. She's been reading each chapter as I write them, with errors and incomplete sentences and all. She's been my "does this work?" and "does it flow alright?" reader.

Jessica is the one to make sure I'm not missing any major storyline flaw or have any continuity issues.

To Mike who will let me describe my plot lines and plot holes to him. Thank you for all of the brainstorming sessions and being a good enough guy friend that you'll put up with the romance chatter. It's much appreciated!!

Beth, (Mike's wife!) – thank you for helping me with my online presence. I know we've just begun but you're an awesome person with a fountain of knowledge that I can't wait to utilize!!

To all of you, thanks for believing in me. I'm really proud of myself, and you've all played a gigantic part in that.

To my children who will never read this – Mom doesn't appreciate you all going to school and telling your friends that I write porn… IT'S NOT FUCKING PORN YOU LITTLE ASSHOLES!!!!! (But it kinda is and you're welcome for being the cool mom.)

Oh… and to my cats. Thanks for walking on my keyboaa;sfljkew;lrd.

## About S. E. Green

S.E. Green is a Navy Veteran, having served for 9 years. She lives in the middle of Wisconsin with her husband, three loving children, and her mom. Wanting to do something entirely different from the work she did while she served, she joined up with her mom, where they work together to sell products in the incredibly interesting and fascinating world of insurance. (insert sarcasm here – but seriously, I really do find insurance fascinating… it's embarrassing)

S. E. Green is a passionate reader, some would say (her family) that she's bordering on obsessive. She found that when she was craving certain types of books or scenes, they were difficult to find, OR she's already read them over and over. She decided that she wanted to write exactly what she likes to read. With the groveling and the white knight and the innocent and the stalkers and the antiheroes and the alpha males and… each little novella hits one of those buttons for her.

## S. E. Green

She's just a mom with a computer and an imagination.

# THE COMPLETE INNOCENCE BOXSET

S. E. Green

THE COMPLETE INNOCENCE BOXSET

# BOOKS BY S. E. GREEN

**THE DISSONANCE SERIES (novels)**
ATONE
LAUGH (coming soon)

**THE INNOCENCE SERIES (novellas)**
NORA
FAITH
EDEN
LILY
THE COMPLETE INNOCENCE SERIES
BONUS EPILOGUES (ebook only)

S. E. Green

# THE COMPLETE INNOCENCE BOXSET

Thank you for Reading!

Printed in Great Britain
by Amazon